LOST IN THE QUAGMIRE

LOST IN THE QUAGMIRE

THE QUEST FOR THE GRAIL

JAY RUUD

Encircle Publications, LLC
Farmington, Maine U.S.A.

DEDICATION

For Stacey Margaret Jones
who is my Guinevere and Rosemounde in one

"And spake I not too truly, O my knights?
Was I too dark a prophet when I said
To those who went upon the Holy Quest,
That most of them would follow wandering fires,
Lost in the quagmire?"

—Alfred, Lord Tennyson, *Idylls of the King*

ACKNOWLEDGEMENTS

The story of the Grail probably originates in the murky pre-history of ancient Celtic myth and legend, but it appears in mainstream European literature for the first time in the late twelfth-century romance by the major French poet Chrétien de Troyes called *Perceval*, or *Le Conte del Graal* ("The Story of the Grail"). Chrétien's version got a complete reworking in the early thirteenth-century *Queste del Saint Graal* ("Quest of the Holy Grail"), a part of the huge French prose compendium known as the Lancelot-Grail Cycle. This prose version introduced Sir Galahad as the son of Lancelot and the premiere Grail knight, but retained Perceval and added Sir Bors in secondary roles.

This "French book" was the chief source for Thomas Malory's somewhat streamlined version of the story included in his late fifteenth-century *Morte Darthur*, the most influential version of Arthurian legend in English. My own version of the story is essentially a further streamlining of Malory's, with a few bits of Chrétien and the Queste tossed in, and an occasional nod to later retellings, like Tennyson's in the *Idylls of the King*, and T.H. White's in *The Once and Future King*. The mystery involving the conspiracy behind the deaths of so many knights on the quest, though, appears nowhere else but here.

The character of Merlin is also in part from Malory, though originally the character of Merlin was introduced in Geoffrey of Monmouth's twelfth-century Latin chronicle *The History of the Kings of Britain*, which first depicts Merlin as a wonder-worker but, more importantly for my purposes, a soothsayer who utters inscrutable prophecies from a kind of trance. There is also no denying that my comic treatment of Merlin owes something to T.H. White's characterization of the mage.

Gildas is the name of a sixth-century monk who wrote a book called *De Excidio et Conquestu Britanniae* ("On the Ruin and Conquest of Britain"), which gives us the first descriptions of Arthurian-era battles in written European history. Gildas's fellow monk at the (fictional) Saint Dunstan's Abbey, Nennius, was historically a Welsh monk whose *Historia Brittonum* is the first text to refer to Arthur by name as the British leader in their battles against the Saxons. I should note, however, that the historical Nennius lived in the ninth century and was not a contemporary of the sixth-century historical Gildas.

As usual, I need to say a few things about canonical hours, by which time is referred to in the novel. Before the development of accurate clocks, medieval people often thought of the day as broken up into the established times for divine office as set by monastic communities. There were eight of these hours or offices, and the bells of churches, monasteries, and convents rang out to call their members to sing the holy offices at those times. Assuming a day in spring or fall, with approximately equal twelve-hour periods of day and night, the office of prime would occur around sunrise, about six A.M. according to modern notions of time. The next office, terce, would be sung around nine A.M., sext would be around noon, none at about three P.M., vespers at six P.M., compline about nine P.M., matins at midnight and lauds around three A.M. These are the approximate times for events in the novel.

I want to reiterate my caveat that the novels in this series are not intended to be "historical" in the sense of presenting an accurate picture of the "real" King Arthur (whatever that may mean) in the sixth century, as so many modern writers intend to do. Instead, they are intended to conjure the imagined world of the early Arthurian romances, a somewhat glamorized twelfth to thirteenth century—and to further make connections with contemporary lives, with the implication that these are people not unlike ourselves. So expect the occasional anachronism.

Once again, the chess match depicted here in chapter eight is actually drawn from the compilation of games on the "Best Chess Games of All Time" web site http://www.chessgames.com/perl/ chesscollection?cid=1001601

CHAPTER ONE

THE PURE KNIGHT

"You're not going to believe this," Sir Ywain's squire Thomas called to me from the stable door, as I put Sir Gareth's brawny destrier into his favorite stall and made sure he had plenty of oats. "But there's a great block of red marble stone floating in the river outside the gate, and a rich sword stuck in it just waiting for somebody to draw it out!"

"Pull the other one," I scoffed, setting aside Sir Gareth's ornate saddle and closing the gate to the stall. I wasn't much interested in any new "marvels" nowadays, or in much of anything at all for that matter. These days, I went through my duties as squire by rote, with little enthusiasm and still less sense of purpose. If something did not raise me out of this black hole soon, I was not sure what my next step should be. But I nodded to the slouching form of Taber, the chief stable hand, on my way out, and he stared back with cold, indifferent eyes as was his wont.

"It's true, Gildas, you numbskull…"

"As if I didn't have better things to do than listen to your….Hello, what's all this then?"

Through the open drawbridge I could see that, at the river that flowed below the gate on the north side of the castle, a large crowd had gathered. Among them were some of the mightiest nobles in the land, judging by their colorful dress. It was too far off to make out the details of faces or to see what wonder had brought them all there, but I thought I could make out the figures of the king, Guinevere, my lord Gareth and his brother Sir Gawain, and Lancelot du Lac, more imposing than any of the others.

"What could they all be doing down there?" I muttered aloud, half to myself.

But Thomas, as recipient of the other half of the mutter, responded with more than a little impatience, "I just told you, Gildas the Witless. Am I talking to myself here?"

I wasn't really listening. I had begun trotting over the drawbridge and down the slope to the river to see for myself what all the hubbub was about, all the time with Thomas's voice in my ear as he scurried behind me, "I'm telling you, it's a sword in a stone floating on the river…"

As I approached more nearly to the crowd I could hear a dozen voices striving to be heard, and at least three dozen nobles and ladies gathered on the riverbank. There, bobbing up and down on the slow moving current but not carried forward itself, floated a reddish stone, pierced through its top by the blade of a sword—a stone large enough for a man to stand on, for, in fact, Sir Gawain was standing there now. His long red locks wafted on the brisk May breeze that breathed over the water, and he wore only a green tunic and dark brown hose as he balanced somewhat precariously on the bobbing stone. That he had waded into the water to climb upon the floating rock was clear from his wet hose, for the water had come up well over his leather boots. Holding the bejeweled pommel of the sword for balance, Gawain was reading aloud from a strange inscription in gold letters engraved on that pommel:

"'Let no man pull me from the stone,' it says, Sire," he was shouting back to the king on shore, "'unless he be the purest knight in the world, for only he shall wield me!' What do you think of that?"

King Arthur himself was clad only in a dark purple tunic with elongated sleeves reaching to his knees, knees that were covered by royal blue hose. Nor did he wear a crown, and by that I knew that he must have left the castle in haste, struck no doubt by the novelty of the floating stone and not bothering even to grab an outer cloak or any of his royal accoutrements.

I reached the periphery of the crowd and, with Thomas breathing down my neck, sidled up next to Colgrevaunce, Sir Brandiles's squire and my old friend, and soon to be Sir Colgrevaunce, for he was due to be knighted the following day at the annual Pentecost observance in the great cathedral of Caerleon. Colgrevaunce looked down at me—he stood some four inches taller than I, though his skinny frame was often slouched so that there were few who marked his height—and whispered, "Well, the king always insists that he witness some marvel before any great feast day. This is one he won't soon forget. How do you float a boulder, I wonder?" He turned his dark, guileless eyes toward Sir Gawain, balanced on the rocking stone and waiting to hear Arthur's assessment of the sword's curious inscription.

Knitting his brow in deep thought, King Arthur glanced to his right hand where stood the bulwark of his kingdom. "Sir Lancelot," he began. "There is no question you are the greatest knight in Camelot—the most accomplished chevalier in all the world, I daresay. This adventure can be meant for no one but you. Step onto the stone and draw the sword. Claim your rich prize. It will be a fit prelude to our Pentecost ceremony to have the premier representative of the Round Table so recognized before the annual renewal of vows for all the knights."

Sir Lancelot hung his head, his square, rocklike jaw clenched. When he shook his wavy brown locks, his dark brows lowered and his face took on an expression almost of pain. "Sire, do not ask this of me," he said firmly. "The words on that sword say nothing of prowess, or your assessment would hold true. But they speak of purity, and that," he raised his eyes to the sky from which they took their color, "that I have never pretended. Let someone else claim the sword, for it is certainly not for me." With that he lowered his eyes again so that his Roman nose pointed directly to the ground, and he risked a furtive glance at the queen, who stood on Arthur's other side. Guinevere gave every indication of ignoring him completely, keeping her face a stoic blank and gazing off somewhere in the distance. But I noticed her shoulders begin to rise and fall quickly, as her breathing became shallower and more rapid. The king did not seem to notice.

Neither, for that matter, did Colgrevaunce, but that was no surprise. He was often oblivious. "If Lancelot will not seize the sword, it's likely to float on by without any takers," Colgrevaunce whispered to me. "Who is likely to rush in where even Lancelot is not bold enough to go?"

"Shh," I urged. "What's the king saying?"

Arthur scowled and looked down, his mouth in a tense line. "Whoever placed this stone in the river did so to challenge our order of knighthood. If we allow it to float on without assaying the sword, if we refuse the challenge, it will be said that there is no purity or valor in Arthur's court. I will not have that said." After a moment's thought, he called out to Gawain, precariously balanced on the heaving stone. "Nephew! As prince of the royal house you are the face of our court. In you are embodied our courtesy and our puissance. We beseech you, pull the sword from the stone yourself. Deal with this challenge to our honor."

Sir Gawain, still clinging to the sword for balance as he floated some twenty feet from the riverbank, looked doubtful as, for a moment, his green eyes met Arthur's and saw in them the dogged determination that *someone*, by God, was going to give that sword a yank. "Oh, here we go!" Colgrevaunce whispered in my ear as Sir Gawain nodded silently. He looked down and gripped the hilt tightly. "All right," he consented reluctantly, as if addressing the sword itself. "I'll give it a go. I only hope that it doesn't seem like vainglory, for well I know I'm not the purest, or the best, of the knights."

"You are the most courteous, though," the queen called generously from the shore. "Perhaps in the milieu of the court, that may count as purity!" And with that she gave a sidelong glance to the king, the corner of her mouth turning up in a half-smile. For his part, the king half-returned the smile, and I saw his left hand reach down and capture hers in a brief and rare display of affection.

Sir Gawain gave the sword a tentative tug. It did not move but remained fixed in the floating stone. Planting his feet more firmly on the unsteady surface of the red marble, Gawain give the sword a second pull that had all the bulk of his considerable muscle behind it. The sword did not stir.

Now Gawain, whose face (from exertion or embarrassment) had turned as red as his blowing hair, let go of the sword rubbed his hands together and with a determined countenance clutched the sword for one last attempt. He bent forward and gave a tremendous jerk, but his hands could not keep their grip on the pommel. For an instant he teetered precariously on the edge of the floating stone, then, spinning his arms about like windmills, plunged backward into the water.

Colgrevaunce burst out with a sudden loud guffaw, but Thomas instantly put a hand on his arm and whispered "Ssst!" as several among the crowd turned disapproving eyes in his direction. Admittedly, I was suppressing a chortle or two myself, and I think everyone there would have admitted that if it wasn't Sir Gawain himself, heir apparent to Arthur's throne, now standing up in the waist-deep water, his scarlet locks now hanging in his face like the fur of some drowned rat, they would have found it funny.

Sir Gawain looked at the king, bewildered. He looked at Lancelot and then at Guinevere, then searched all the faces in the crowd. He gazed down at his soaked clothing, then back up again, and suddenly burst out into loud, uncontrollable laughter. Relieved, the rest of the folk on shore finally hooted as well, and there were several minutes of raucous mirth until someone, it may have been Gawain himself, took note of a small group of men walking along the river toward the courtiers on the shore. Then all eyes turned to the newcomers.

"Here now, what's this then?" Thomas muttered, his broad flat face twisted perplexedly as he watched the five figures approach unhurriedly along the riverbank. But I had no cause to wonder. I recognized them at once.

Four of the figures, two in front and two behind, wore the white habits and black scapulars of Cistercian monks, like those I had seen the previous year in the abbey at Beaulieu. Like those monks, these four seemed to have taken a vow of silence, for they made no sound other than their light footsteps as they came toward us. When they had come close enough I realized with a jolt that these were in fact monks from that same abbey, for the fifth figure, who walked in their midst, gazed ahead with innocent sky-blue eyes that were an unmistakable copy of those I had just been looking at. The aquiline nose, the mass of wavy brown hair, and the robust jaw made it clear that we could be looking at no one other than Sir Lancelot's offspring: Galahad, as I had seen him earlier at the abbey, but now dressed in chain mail covered with a white surplice on which he bore that figure he seemed to have adopted as his coat of arms: a blood red cross. An empty sheath hung from a loose belt around his waist.

I hazarded a quick glance in the queen's direction as the small party approached. What I saw, before she quickly disguised her feelings, was the unadulterated loathing of a woman for the embodiment of her lover's infidelity. After that flash, her eyes narrowed, her face stony, she once again stared directly ahead at nothing.

Now the monastic party had reached the courtiers, who parted like the Red Sea to allow the monks and their charge to approach and stop before the king. The oldest of the Cistercians and their apparent leader was a stern looking monk with gray tonsure and deep-set eyes, and a reddish scar that stretched from his cheekbone down across his lips and into his chin—a reminder perhaps of a former life as a soldier. This venerable figure made a deferential bow to the king, saying "Your Majesty, I am Brother Nascien, prior of the Cistercian monastery at Beaulieu on your southern coast. I bring you greetings from Abbot Hugh, who sends you by me this young squire—who is, we believe, ready for knighthood."

Sir Gawain, who by now had waded back and had climbed onto the riverbank, snorted briefly at the monk's assertion. "You do, do you?" he interrupted. "He's a likely enough looking lad, I'll give him that. But what do you monks know about it? I would say it's more properly our job at the Table Round to make those kinds of decisions, don't you think? Besides," he added, with a courteous bow in our direction as he noticed Thomas, Colgrevaunce and me standing on the periphery of the crowd. "There is only one vacancy in the order as of today: with King Bagdemagus yielding his place because of his age, young Colgrevaunce there will be joining the table tomorrow at the annual Pentecost festival. He has earned his position after many years' service and training. This boy seems very young—let him stay here and train with us, and after a time he can earn his spurs."

And Colgrevaunce, emboldened if somewhat surprised by Sir Gawain's praise, stretched his narrow frame to his full height of nearly an ell and three-quarters, shook his oily brown locks out of his eyes, and added in a voice that cracked only a little, "Yes. Sir Brandiles will be in need of a squire as of tomorrow. Let him take that assignment. I'm sure he'll learn quickly…"

I looked down and shook my head. I had a feeling this was not going to end well for Colgrevaunce.

Before Prior Nascien could speak again, Galahad himself spoke out. He spoke with a calm authority I had never heard before from a sixteen-year-old, and he said only this: "The time is now."

There was a moment of silence while several members of the court, and Brother Nascien himself, let their jaws hang open. But the prior recovered quickly, and addressed himself first to Sir Gawain. "My lord," he began, "as to that, I served for fifteen years in the personal guard of King Uther, his majesty the king's father, before joining the Cistercian order. I bear a permanent mark of that hard service on my face," he indicated his jagged scar. "Several others of our abbey have seen action as knights, some in my lord Arthur's wars in Ireland and in Gaul." He indicated the three monks that had accompanied him, all of whom were nodding in agreement, most notably a tall broad-shouldered monk with a curly yellow tonsure and square jaw, who looked ready to don armor at any moment. "We are all agreed: this young marvel is as accomplished as any swordsman or jouster now living, and is the greatest man of arms at his age that any of us has ever seen. He is not only ready for knighthood, he is ready to be the premiere knight of the king's table.

"But as for you my lord Gawain," Brother Nascien continued, recognizing the prince surely by his reputation and his red hair, "as a penance for your presumption in touching the sword intended for only the purest of all knights, you shall suffer a stroke from that sword from which your recovery will be not at all certain."

Sir Gawain raised his eyebrows, opened wide his green eyes, and shrugged dramatically, as if to say "Well, I can't win, can I?"

Gazing intently upon the young man's face, the king gradually made the connection that the rest of the court had already seen. His visage collapsed in surprised recognition and he looked to his right toward the pillar of his kingdom. "For the love of God," he cried. "This boy is the son of Lancelot himself!"

The great knight bowed his head in assent. "He is truly mine, my liege. His name is Galahad. Got upon Elaine, the daughter of the maimed King Pelles of Corbenic Castle. At the insistence of his mother and grandfather, he has been raised in a monastery, and there learned spiritual discipline as well as martial arts. I have not seen him for several years, but I flatter myself he does resemble me."

The scene was strange to me. A father and son, separated for years and now brought together with no warning…why were they not embracing? If my own father, the Cornish armor-maker, should suddenly appear in Camelot, we would be hugging one another close and planning a quick trip to the pub to drink our fortunes together. This aloof restraint seemed unnatural, aberrant. But who was I to judge?

"The son of Lancelot, heir of King Ban of Benwick, yes," Prior Nascien proclaimed. "And on his mother's side nine generations removed from Joseph of Arimathea! He has come to fulfill his destiny."

"Pull the other one!" It was Sir Kay, King Arthur's boorish seneschal, who sneered incredulously at the monk's pronouncement.

Arthur himself did not scoff. Why should he? The possibility of a second Lancelot in his court could not but pique his interest in the young man's credentials. But the claims of the monk seemed absurd. Certainly old legends told of Joseph of Arimathea's immigrating to Britain after the crucifixion of Christ, but even if such legends were true, that he should have a progeny here and that such a descent was traceable to this bold young man seemed fantastic at best, pure fraud at worst. But Arthur had a notion of how to deal with this situation: a plan that, as it turned out, played directly into the monk's hand.

"We have here," he began, addressing Galahad, "a great marvel: a sword in a stone that, according to an inscription on the hilt, is intended only for the purest of knights. Good knights have failed or declined the challenge of pulling out the sword. If you want to be a member of the order of the Table Round, my will is that you yourself attempt to remove the sword."

Without surprise or emotion, Galahad looked at the stone and, answering the king as he began to wade into the water, announced,

"This adventure is for me, not for them. It was for this reason I wore the empty scabbard."

Galahad waded into the river until, nearly waist-deep, he stood next to the floating stone. Then, without discomfort or undue exertion, he climbed upon the rock as he might have climbed the castle steps. Without haste or apparent concern, he stood up, balanced himself, and with his right hand reached down and drew the sword from the red marble with no more effort than he might have spent drawing a blade from a sheath. After holding the glittering steel at arm's length to examine it, Galahad slid the sword into the empty scabbard at his belt.

"This was the sword of Sir Balin," Brother Nascien proclaimed. "With it he slew his own brother, and with it he dealt the dolorous stroke that wounded King Pelles, a wound from which the king suffers to this day. It was a sword Sir Galahad was destined to have."

The king stared at Nascien with mild surprise. "Balin? How well I remember that impetuous young man. How odd that he should be somehow connected with this affair. But it certainly does appear that young Galahad here is a knight of destiny. I think that we must make him a knight of the Table, and the sooner the better! And you, lad," he called to Galahad, still standing on the miraculously floating rock. "You have won yourself a sword. Let's hope sometime soon you may get yourself a shield as well, eh?"

At that there was some polite laughter among the courtiers. The king was not particularly witty, but he so seldom chose to make a joke that it was only common courtesy to encourage him in the matter. But in the midst of that amusement, Sir Kay spoke up once more. "A moment, your Grace," he whined. The king's foster-brother, puffed up with his own inflated opinion of his value in Arthur's court, took a deep breath, his prominent nose in the air, and threw out his shallow chest, in the process of which he was also obliged to throw out his considerable belly. Then, his yellow teeth protruding from between his thick lips, he continued: "This was mere subterfuge, can no one else see that? These monks arranged for this floating stone, no doubt buoyed up by some ingenious trick known only to their secret order. They knew it would be here at this time, they placed Balin's sword within the stone, they tutored their young champion there on how to release it from the boulder's clutches. We have all been duped here, your Majesty!"

And with those words there was a great hubbub, as for once Sir Kay seemed to be right on target. "It's true, ain't it?" Colgrevaunce said to me. "What else could it be but a trick? These monks came deliberately to disturb our Pentecost ceremonies. Am I going to be made knight or what?"

It seemed to me a significant stretch to assume that Cistercians from Logres' southern coast should come this far and go through all this trouble for the sole purpose of preventing my friend from his induction. But of course that was the chief thing, perhaps the only thing, on Colgrevaunce's mind. He had been aiming at this goal for years, and particularly since his marriage to the commoner Bess of Caerleon he had bent his force to achieve those skills that would force the court to recognize his worthiness, and so raise both himself and his spouse from the class they had been born to. So eager was he to begin his vigil in preparation for tomorrow's ceremony that, I noticed now for the first time, he was already dressed in his habergeon, which had been a gift from Sir Brandiles for the induction.

"Colgrevaunce," I soothed him. "I admit that this whole rigmarole this morning appears to have been staged, but that doesn't necessarily mean Galahad is some kind of fake, or that the monks' purpose is to ruin your induction…"

Meanwhile Sir Lancelot's face had turned an unhealthy shade of crimson, and his voice quivered with the effort to remain courteous as he answered Kay: "Sir Kay, Galahad is my son, there is no doubting that. That he is even now a better knight than many in this fellowship, yourself included, I believe without question. And anyone who maintains he did not pull the sword from the stone through his own unaided power, that man I will meet in the lists and let God determine the right."

That shut Kay up and it quieted the rest of the crowd as well, for all were quite familiar with the fact that in any trial by combat, God always favored the side with the stronger sword arm, and none was stronger than Lancelot's.

"There is another way," a woman's voice was raised, as smooth and comforting as oil on troubled waters. It was a voice I did not recognize, but I knew it must belong to some deeply respected lady, for all were quiet, and even the king was attentive. I stood on my tiptoes, craning my neck to locate the source of the musical speech, and saw only the back of a raven-hued head, on a body clothed in a long black gown.

Then the king answered her: "And what would that be, sister?"

So that was it. I trembled with some excitement. Though I had heard stories, I had never seen her in the flesh: Morgan le Fay, Arthur's half-sister, rumored to be an enchantress, had not visited Camelot in the four years I had been in attendance on the queen and then on Sir Gareth. But at the great feast of Pentecost, Arthur's allies from across his empire were expected to make their way to Camelot if they could. Morgan had been a significant part of the court when her brother first took the throne, and prior to his marriage to Guinevere had been the first lady of Logres. It was on that long experience that she now drew.

"The Siege Perilous," Morgan replied. "Bring the boy to the table. If he has a special destiny, he should have no fear. To the table, and let him test his valor and his purpose in the seat of peril."

"To the great hall, then," Arthur ordered. "Bring the boy there." Brother Nascien nodded. Arthur strode purposefully up the incline toward the open gates of the castle. Nascien and the broad-shouldered monk flanked Galahad as they, followed by the other two monks, fell in line after the king. Lancelot and Guinevere were close behind, with Sir Gawain and my own master Sir Gareth following, escorting their aunt Morgan. We turned to make our way with the rest of the courtiers to the great hall of the castle, beneath which stood the Hall of the Order, which housed the Round Table itself.

"Siege what now?" Thomas whispered to Colgrevaunce and me as we followed the procession.

I shrugged and Colgrevaunce looked blank, but a voice behind us, punctuated by some huffing and puffing, volunteered an answer: "Siege…Perilous…whew. Slow down a bit, can't you youngsters?"

I looked over my shoulder and was surprised to see King Bagdemagus of Gorre with his squire, his son Meliagaunt, following closely behind us, though it was clear that the king, a man now well into his seventies and somewhat round of shape, was having a difficult time making his way up the slope toward the castle. The old king wore a royal blue tunic over sable hose and fine, dark leather boots. As his position demanded, he also wore a purple cloak edged with ermine and fastened at the shoulder. But he was breathing hard as he climbed, and sweat was streaming down his round ruddy face and into his full white beard. His son, who seemed aloof to everything, gave us no greeting, but did place his hand on his father's back to give him minimal assistance as he struggled toward the castle.

"Sorry, my lord," I said as we waited for the pair to catch up. "I didn't realize there was anyone behind us. You were saying? About this 'Siege Perilous'?"

The king stopped to catch his breath before moving slowly onward. "I'm the oldest man at Arthur's court," he began, and I could see I was not going to get a direct or abridged answer to my question. "That is, as long as your friend, the old necromancer Merlin, is holed up in his cave. Been an ally of Arthur since he was the boy king, and one of the original members of the Round Table. Ah, those were the days, let me tell you. Cador of Cornwall. Hoel of Britany. Sir Kay and Sir Bedivere when they were in their prime. King Pelinore. Tristram. Lamorak. Plenty more who are no longer with us. Time for me to go too, you know. Colgrevaunce, my lad, you are getting my place at the table—see that you don't disgrace it!"

"Yes sir," Colgrevaunce responded. "I mean, no sir. I mean, I will fulfill my knightly duties to the best of my abilities, sir."

Hoping to get the old king back on track, I prompted him. "And the Siege Perilous? Is that something that goes back to the beginning?"

"Siege Perilous?" the old man responded, as if I had brought the subject up out of nowhere. "Merlin's doing, that was. The table, you know, it was a wedding gift from Queen Guinevere's father, King Leodogrance of Cameliard." He paused for a moment, breathed, and seemed to be searching his memory. "He was a character, that one. Imagine a dining table for 150. Who else would have such a thing? They actually had to build the foundation of the great hall of Camelot around the table, did you know that? And then built the hall itself as a separate room above it. Could never have got it in otherwise. I think it was Leodogrance's little joke. He resented giving his only daughter to this upstart king, I think. Didn't think the boy would last. But since Arthur had rescued him from a siege by…who was it now? I forget. Anyway…"

"Siege Perilous?" I prompted.

"That!" Bagdemagus went on. "The table actually had room for 152. One space taken by the king, of course. There are 150 places for Arthur's retainers, the order of the Knights of the Round Table. There can never be more than that number, and Arthur makes certain each year that there are never any fewer. And that's why you are taking my place tomorrow, young Colgrevaunce; I want you to be sure you don't…"

"What about that 152nd seat?" I asked, doing my best to keep the king on task as we had now made it to the drawbridge and prepared to cross the moat.

"That 152nd seat is what's called the Siege Perilous." Bagdemagus paused again, getting his breath, but it seemed he had no plan to say more. Colgrevaunce, Thomas and I looked at each other with some frustration. Meliagaunt just looked ahead, bored.

"So, and, *why* is it called the Siege Perilous then, sir?" Thomas tried.

"Siege Perilous?" Bagdemagus said as he resumed his walk. "That was Merlin's doing."

"But what did Merlin *do*, then?" I cried out, almost losing my courtesy.

"Fixed it so that nobody could sit in it," the king finally revealed. "No, it was to remain empty, at least until the Destined One arrived."

"Destined One?" Colgrevaunce perked up. "Merlin knew of this?"

"The one destined to do marvelous deeds. The pure knight. Merlin had seen it in one of his visions. He fixed the Siege Perilous so that only the Destined One could use the seat. Anyone bold enough to sit in it who didn't happen to be the pure knight would suffer. Look, I remember in the early days a knight name of Sir Brumand. He was a big name around here until Lancelot arrived, and he hated Lancelot for eclipsing his reputation. To show everyone he was the greatest knight, he decided to do something Lancelot was sensible enough not to do—he sat in the Siege Perilous, despite all the warnings around it."

"So what happened to him, then?" Thomas asked.

"He sat in the seat and caught on fire. Burned him to ashes. And that's the truth." King Bagdemagus stopped once more for breath. By now we were in the lower bailey, and near the great hall. Almost everyone else had made their way into the building, and I looked at Thomas and Colgrevaunce.

"They're going to put Galahad into that Siege Perilous!" I cried to them, and the three of us broke into a run, up the steps and into the great hall, leaving King Bagdemagus to stare after us bewildered.

"Siege Perilous?" he was saying.

We burst into the great hall, with its wooden-arched ceiling and its colorful tapestried walls, and then turned down the stairs into the huge room that formed the foundation of the hall. Lighted by the rows of windows high up near the room's ceiling, just above ground level, I peered through the crowd to the one seat at the table that had always remained unoccupied, directly opposite the king's own place. Pressing closer I watched as the king, Sir Gawain and Queen Guinevere on one side, and a confident Lancelot and Brother Nascien on the other, pressed the young Galahad either to be seated in the chair, or to give up his suit to be made knight. The lad had a faraway—I might say now in retrospect even an otherworldly—look in his eyes as he settled without trepidation into the seat. The room collectively held its breath to see what would happen.

What happened was this: At the moment the young man sat, the tall chair back began to quiver, and golden letters appeared above his head, spelling out the name—"Galahad."

And he did *not* burst into flames.

CHAPTER TWO

THE QUEEN'S CHAMBER

"**I**f he thinks he's going to have his bastard hanging around the castle, well then he'd better think again, that's all I've got to say!"

I was pretty certain that was *not* all she was going to have to say. The infuriated queen had summoned me to her inner chamber and sent her ladies-in-waiting out "for some air"—which was her euphemism for "get out of here, I've got something private to talk about with this person and I don't want you loose-tongued little flibbertigibbets here while I'm doing it." Outside the curtain, in her outer chamber, Master Holly, supervisor of her majesty's household, dozed at his desk, though even if he were awake he was getting to be deaf as a post anyway, and wasn't likely to hear much, nor understand for that matter. Guinevere had been going on now for a good quarter of an hour, and showed no sign of slowing down. She paced up and down her chamber waving her arms within the long hanging sleeves of her red satin gown, and the tongue of her leather belt, which hung nearly to the floor, danced and bounced to her movements like a living thing.

"If we're going to have every low-born by-blow of every knight at the table lurking around Camelot, well, soon it won't be safe for any respectable lady to walk the inner bailey after dark…"

In fairness I felt I needed to point out that Galahad could hardly be called low-born, being the grandson of kings on both sides. But that was not something the queen appreciated being reminded of.

"I don't care if his granddaddy's the pope and his grandma is the Virgin Mary, his bastardy makes him villainous. And he doesn't belong here! And now because he's sat in that stupid chair and managed not to go up in flames the king will have him knighted, and tomorrow with poor Colgrevaunce. There will now be 151 knights of the Round Table? Why does this failed abortion get special treatment because his father is Oh! The Great Lancelot!" Her voice oozed irony at the end, and for a moment I was tempted to point out that it wasn't his parentage but his seatage that had won him this "special treatment," but I thought better of it. No sense whacking the bees' nest when the queen was already in a state.

"What does he expect me to do about it? How am I supposed to act? Am I expected to ignore this…this product of his illicit affairs and welcome his son…his *son*…with open arms the way I do every other new knight, as if it means no more than…than Colgrevaunce? While he sits by, the proud father, doting on his fine son's great deeds of valor? I can hear him now: 'Chip off the old block, eh boys?' God, it makes me disgusted just to think about it."

I bit my tongue and held back the words that would have reminded her that the only *serious* illicit affair Lancelot had ever had was with her. And far from being the doting father, Lancelot had seemed ill at ease, embarrassed, and clueless about how to act when his only son appeared suddenly on the scene at Camelot. But instead I sympathized with the queen with my eyes, and said only "Hmmph!" in response to her tirade. For I knew one thing about Queen Guinevere that had held true from my days as her page until this moment: once she had vented her spleen, she would get down to the thing that was truly bothering her. And I had a feeling that that was precisely what was about to happen.

"Ah Gildas, Gildas," she said, now pausing and shaking her ungovernable blonde hair, which she wore uncovered and unbraided, like a young virgin—a style which, as queen, she was entitled to adopt. "How does it make me look? The spurned lover whom he forsook for the younger Elaine of Corbenic? The barren harpy who could not give him a child, so that he was forced to chase after the golden womb of the fair Elaine? The impotent woman who must suffer public ridicule as her husband welcomes her lover's child, sired on another, better woman?"

"The paragon of beauty and faithfulness, to her husband as lord and her beloved as lover, who forgives like the Virgin Mother and stands with unassailable dignity that cannot be mocked," I finally said. But it was a mistake. I had misjudged my role, which at this point was to be audience, not contributor. I had mistaken monologue for conversation.

She turned on me, rearing her head back like a snake preparing to strike. "Is that supposed to be funny? Are you mocking me, you young puppy? What do you know about love? What do you know about loving someone whom law and custom and religion forbid you to love, and suffering every day the effects of that hopeless passion? What do you know about anything real people have to deal with, when you're nothing but a lowly squire and not likely to amount to much more than that anytime soon, either!"

She had struck, but failed to land a serious blow. For one thing, I knew that she was wrapped up in her own anguish, and was not thinking clearly about what she was saying. And secondly, I was far more self-aware than she was, and knew my own worth and my own heart, neither of which she had come close to touching with her outburst.

"As to that," I answered her, in slow, measured tones, "I am eighteen years of age—two years older than this child of Lancelot's who is about to become a knight of the Round Table. I am old enough to be a man, and old enough to have known love, as you, my lady, know better than anyone at this court. A love I too am forbidden to satisfy. As for my position as squire to Sir Gareth, I no longer care whether I am ever made knight, having now no reason to be so. Whether I stay here or go back to my father's house in Cornwall, or join the Cistercians at Beaulieu to live out my days in silent poverty, chastity, and obedience, is all one to me now. And it seems now that the only worthwhile purpose my life still holds is to be a sympathetic ear to my queen."

Against all expectation, my words seemed to have struck through the queen's egotism and made her step back to see me as another human soul after all. "Oh Gildas, oh my poor lad, I had forgotten who I was speaking to. Of course you understand. You of all people know my pain. But consider—look at my position," she continued in a more subdued, less savage but more pained voice. "I am Arthur's dress-up doll, paraded out to sit beside him on the dais on grand occasions like tomorrow's induction, but never consulted on matters of state—like a pet, or a child to be seen and not heard. And why?"

"Because you're not a man?" I volunteered the obvious answer.

She raised her eyebrows and stared down at me bemused. "Of course, that is the official line," she acknowledged. "Women are never brought into counsel with the king's cloud of advisors. But unofficially, in private moments, you know perfectly well that a wife's counsels are more important than any other. If the husband trusts and values his wife. Or some other woman he may be close to. Look at the early years of Arthur's reign, when his sister Morgan held sway in Camelot. By her counsel were many decisions made. And she did everything she could to undermine *me* when I arrived in Camelot, that's for sure. But I am childless, my dear Gildas. I have miscarried in my most important duty to the kingdom: I have failed to produce an heir. And so the king must depend upon his nephew Gawain as heir apparent, rather than a child of his own flesh. Unless he were to acknowledge and legitimize his own bastard, that smarmy weasel who passes as his youngest nephew, that repulsive boy Sir Mordred."

My gorge rose at mention of that name. My archrival and archenemy. My nemesis. If he only knew he were.

"Can't you see that having this Galahad in the court, this casual memento of my own lover's one-night-stand, does nothing but underscore my own failings as a wife and as a queen?"

"In your own mind, perhaps, my lady," I answered her truthfully. "But you speak as if your relationship with Sir Lancelot is common knowledge in the court. How can the rest of the court see this as an insult to you when they do not know anything about why you should feel insulted?"

"Oh, they suspect," she answered softly, her eyes rolling to the side and her face getting a far-away expression. "But for the most part you may be right." At that she shrugged her shoulders and sat on one of the small chairs in the chamber. She looked at me with steady blue eyes and pursed her coral lips, and spoke now in her normal voice, so that I understood at last that she had finally, having passed through bouts of histrionics, rage, and self-pity, reached the point of sincerity, so that I recognized that what she said next was what was truly behind her torment.

"Ah, Gildas," she sighed. "You know you're the only person I can stand. Forgive me all of it…I know you will. But listen: can't you see that this Galahad, whenever I see him, can only remind me of Lancelot's unfaithfulness? That he is a symbol crying aloud to me that at least for that time, Lancelot preferred the arms of another woman over mine. In all these many years, I can honestly say that I have *never* been unfaithful to him…"

"But my lady, the king…" I interjected with a bit of skepticism.

"Ha!" She very nearly spat. "The king! He has not entered my bedchamber for years. Certainly not since he knew me to be barren."

"Well…" I ventured. "Perhaps he has not felt welcome there…"

That observation was greeted with a silence that hung in the air for an uncomfortably long time. When she picked up the thread of her narration, it was with a far more subdued voice. "For whatever reason," she began, and let another pause fill the air before she continued, "he has chosen not to require of me any payment of the marriage debt for many years. I have been true to Lancelot. But he has been unfaithful to me. Galahad's existence pounds into my brain the emptiness of these many years of devotion. You're a fool, Guinevere," he says to me. "You're a fool! You're a fool!"

"But my lady, you know that Sir Lancelot has accounted for that mistake by the story he gave out concerning that night in Corbenic. He was roused from his sleep and told that you, my queen, were in a private chamber in the castle and that you were demanding his attendance on you. When he entered the chamber it was dark as pitch, but he found a lady eagerly waiting for him in the curtained bed. They spoke not a word for fear of their secret love being known— that is, in Lancelot's mind, his secret love of you, my queen—but consummated the love there in that room, before he slipped back to return to his own chamber. He was as surprised as you to learn later that it was Elaine in the bed, and that the tryst had been arranged by her father because of the prophecy that she would give birth to the knight of destiny, sired upon her by the knight of greatest prowess on earth. My lord Lancelot was never false to you in intent, but was true to you even in his infidelity."

"Hmmph," Guinevere scoffed. "Pull the other one. Any man who has ever been with a woman will know immediately, without the aid of sight or voice, whether the woman he is with is his beloved or another. Don't blush, Gildas, I know you do not yet know these things for yourself, but whoever made up that ridiculous story knows nothing about love. And so I hope it wasn't Lancelot who made it up. He had to have known, before they had gone very far, that I was not the woman in that bed. Why…if you'd seen her you'd know, she's a diminutive woman, a dwarf compared with me."

"Well…but…but even so…" I stammered, thrown somewhat by this frankness and my own gullibility, "I believe there is a point at which no man is likely to stop in the pursuit of, er, of Venus' gifts even if urged to do so. I still maintain that at least at first, Lancelot had no intention of betraying you…and perhaps then was not able to stop himself from so doing," I finished, lamely I admit.

"Yes," Guinevere responded. "All men are animals, you are certainly correct about that. Excepting you, of course," she said, shouting over my protests. "You, my dear Gildas, are an angel."

Her spleen now spent, the queen had settled down into her more habitual state of mind, the one in which she met difficulties with a bold smile and a healthy dose of irony. "Believe me, Gildas, I shall find a way to make Sir Galahad's life at court miserable—either for him or for his father, or for both." Her left eyebrow was now raised with mischievous portent and with a thin-lipped smile she asked, "And now, Gildas, are you ready for a surprise? For I did not call you here merely to discuss my paramour's bastards with you."

"No, Lady?"

"Oh no. The invitation was sent well before that regrettable incident at the river. There is something else. You know that at our annual Pentecost ceremony, the king invites all those who owe him allegiance to attend the festivities?"

"That is well known, Madam."

"Well," the queen now rose and stepped to the wooden door that separated her private closet from the rest of her suite. As she opened it, she purred, "Well here is someone who has dropped by and would like a private conversation with you."

I peered with some curiosity into the room. There, seated primly on the queen's own bed, looking up at me with large, innocent brown eyes and a teasing smirk on her face, was my lady Rosemounde.

***

She was dressed in an expensive-looking dark blue gown, highlighted with gold filigree, and covered by a long embroidered surcote. Those brilliant dark eyes seemed slightly red and puffy, as though she had recently wept, though there had been an obvious attempt to gloss over the redness with some concealing powder or other. Her abundant waves of dark brown hair were hidden, as was proper for a married woman, under a linen headdress with a barbier around her chin. She looked quite proper but it was definitely awkward to stand before her there in the queen's private bedroom while she sat on the bed and the queen silently closed the door to give us our privacy. Nor did I have any way of knowing how much of Guinevere's ranting she had overheard while waiting here in this closet, though after some thought I decided that hardly mattered: as the closest and most trusted of the queen's ladies-in-waiting, Rosemounde must, in the past, have been privy to the queen's private thoughts at least as much as I was. But silence hung in the air between us until I realized that she was not going to begin the conversation. She must have been waiting to see what my attitude was going to be. But I did not know how to begin. What does one say to the love of his life after she has married someone else in his absence and disappeared from his world? Caution, I urged on myself. There are unseen pitfalls here.

"My lady of Orkney," I began, and saw her noticeable wince, as if her married title were the lash of a whip. Well, if it had stung her, so much the better. Did she not at least deserve that much? "Permit me to congratulate you on your marriage. Though I realize it has been several months, you may recall that I was absent from Camelot when your nuptials took place, and so was unable to take part in the festivities."

Her dark eyes burned like fiery coals into my own, and her lips pouted in a mixture of disappointment and puzzlement, as if she could not tell how best to respond to my distant yet polite manner. As a result she said nothing. And again we remained in awkward silence. As I tried to think of what to say next, I raised my eyes to the tapestry on the back wall of the chamber, behind the queen's bed and so directly above Rosemounde's head: It depicted the militant Jewess Judith, holding her bloodied sword in one hand and the severed head of the Assyrian general Holofernes in the other. Unconsciously my hand reached tentatively toward my neck and I swallowed hard. I went on:

"I trust you are adjusting well to married life, my lady. Though I understand the weather can be somewhat harsher as far north as the Orkneys." After another moment without any response from the lady, I added somewhat lamely, "Camelot does feel your absence, however, I daresay."

At that Rosemounde finally threw her head back in frustration. "Seriously, Gildas?" she cried. "You're going to talk to me about the weather?" She rose from the bed and stepped toward me, her index finger aimed directly at my nose. "And drop this phony distant courtesy you're affecting. They've taught you well here at court, haven't they? Taught you to disguise your real feelings. Taught you to sling darts under the veneer of polite and courteous behavior. Well stifle it because it's not going to work with me, understand? As for this marriage, God knows, Gildas, we've had this conversation before. You, armor-maker's son from Cornwall. Me, daughter of Duke Hoel of Brittany. The world is not constructed to serve our desires. Do you think my father was going to pass up an opportunity to be joined by marriage to the family of the greatest king in Christendom? What was I to do about it?"

"You might have protested," I shot back, surprised at myself for having the boldness to do so. "By canon law a woman cannot be compelled to marry against her will. You might have refused to agree to the wedding. You might have stood up to your father, Duke though he is."

"Do you think I didn't?" She was shouting now, and the tears that she had covered up when I had first entered the closet sprang forth now as she wept through her anger. "You don't know the kind of pressure that can be put upon the daughter of a noble house. My father's first daughter had been raped and murdered by a monster," I cringed at the memory of that story. "His second daughter had just been widowed by the murder of her husband, and so that left me as the only daughter through whom the 'great alliance' could be made. When the opportunity to be married to the king's own nephew presented itself, my father could not lose the opportunity. Believe me when I tell you I pleaded with him to allow me to marry for love. But he told me that was for scullery maids and tavern sluts. I had a duty to my family and to my country. He has no legitimate heir to the Breton lands. I must produce one, one that would be a scion of the king's own house, and would solidify Brittany as a favored ally protected beneath the wing of the imperial eagle. To that I could only counter with the son of a Cornish artisan. You were not even a knight."

"No, I was not." She had me there. But I had always hoped that what I lacked by birth I might make up for through hard work, training, and preferment—with the help of the queen and my master Sir Gareth—and become a knight of the Table Round, whose nobility was beyond question. "But I might have been. I was well on my way. You might recall that I had to interrupt my training in order to sail to Brittany to clear your sister's name and prove her innocent in the deaths of Tristram and La Belle Isolde. And in my absence, you were matched, betrothed, wed and married. And gone."

"Gildas," she grabbed the front of my tunic and shook me. "When I refused to marry Sir Mordred, my father threatened to disinherit me. Said he would legitimize my siblings, marry the widow to Mordred and make Kaherdin heir to the duchy. Do you know what that would have meant?"

"Yes!" I snapped. "It would have left you free to make your own decisions. It would have left you free to marry me."

She shook her head slowly and began pounding ineffectually on my chest with her small, white fists. "No. It would have meant the convent, and a celibate life. I would have been lost to you forever."

Taken aback by that comment, my brow furrowed in confusion, and I responded to that the only way I could. "Are you not that now?"

Rosemounde sighed, and sat back on the bed with her face buried in her hands. When she raised her dark eyes to me there were tears streaming from them down an innocent, blank face. Why did I feel there was an unspoken plea here? Then, slowly, the edge of Rosemounde's mouth twisted upward slightly in her characteristic smirk.

I backed suddenly away, thinking I had come upon one of those pitfalls. "No, no, my lady," I stammered. "I have seen more closely than I care to the suffering and distress that can be caused by these relationships of 'courtly love.' The constant anxiety of our former mistress is incentive enough for me to avoid that kind of liaison. It has always seemed to me more of a strain on love than a boon to it."

Rosemounde's smirk became broader, and she burst out, beneath her tears, into a schoolgirl giggle. "Oh Gildas," she blurted out. "Don't flatter yourself. Much as I do love you, you are not Lancelot, after all. No," she went on, "I mean only that I have the opportunity now, this way, to visit Camelot on occasion, and reconnect with those I have been close to here. Orkney is indeed far away, but at least I am not consigned to a convent for the rest of my days, locked away from male company. Locked away from you."

I could feel the blood reddening my face and, shamed that I may have misinterpreted or discomfited her, tried now to move on to less stressful small talk. "And Sir Mordred is willing to give you the freedom to pursue these regular trips back here to Camelot? I see that he has brought you along with him to the court for Pentecost. Very few of the king's vassals bring their wives on the journey. You must have pleaded with him convincingly to get him to bring you this time, and so soon after the wedding."

I could sense palpably the shiver that went through her at the mention of Mordred's name. And the frown that clouded her face made it clear to me that she was not yet ready for small talk. She only said quietly, "As if any pleading from me would be of any concern to him at all. No, his brothers, Gareth and Gaheris, who are at court for most of the year by themselves, were bringing their wives, Lyonesse and Lynnette, to Camelot for the induction ceremony, and they asked Mordred to bring me down to keep those ladies company. And Mordred, though he would never do anything just to please his brothers, thought it was a good opportunity to use me as a spy in his brothers' households, to make sure they weren't keeping anything from him. I swear to you Gildas, my husband believes that all people are as devious as he is."

I snorted. "Fine husband your father chose for you, my tender flower."

The tears were starting to well up in her eyes again. "Oh Gildas, if you only knew the whole of it." But she shook it off and asked me seriously: "But Gildas. I have heard that you have given up on your goal of becoming a knight of the Table. Sir Gareth has let it be known that you are considering returning to Cornwall."

"Perhaps," I shrugged. "Speaking of your convent, I have even thought about a vocation, perhaps in a monastery or a friary."

"But Gildas, why quit now? After all the work you've put in, why throw it all away when you are so close to knighthood? Colgrevaunce is to join the order tomorrow. Surely you cannot be far behind."

I waved her question away with a kind of annoyance. "My lady, there was one reason and one reason only that I sought the status of a knight of the order: I wanted to be worthy of you. That is no longer possible. I have no reason any more to care about knighthood. It no longer promises to give meaning to my life."

"And being a monk...or an apprentice armorer...these will give your life more meaning?" She was up on her feet again. "Look, I'm not the only woman in Logres. You are eighteen years old. You can love again. You will love again. Leave me to my Orkney life and get on with yours—become a knight. Marry a beautiful young lady and make her happy, as I know you can."

"What?" I teased her. "Am I to choose from 'scullery maids and tavern sluts'? My lady," I cooed to her. "Do you really think that having had a taste of heavenly bliss, I can ever be satisfied with mundane shadows? There is no moving on for me. Not in this life."

She drew close and pounded again on my chest with her harmless fists. "Gildas, I'll say this only one more time. I need you to become a knight. I need you to be the greatest knight you can be. I laughed and said you were not Lancelot. But that is who I need you to be."

"But why my lady?" I asked, dumbfounded.

"Because," she said, turning her back to me, her voice turning hard. "The time may be coming when I am going to need you." And with that she dropped her embroidered surcote to the floor, reached back with her hands and tore the seam of her blue gown down the back, slipping it down to her elbows.

There, in crimson streaks across her back, was a vivid pattern of bruises and welts, some probably several weeks old, some freshly scored within the past few days. I stared for a moment and gasped, before the meaning of those wounds came home to me.

With an inarticulate cry of pure animal pain I sprang for the queen's fireplace, above which she always had a burnished sword hanging. I threw down the scabbard and lifted the sword as if in full charge. "Where is he?" I demanded. "Let me at him. I'll bring these blows to bear upon his own hide tenfold before I cut off his ugly, arrogant head!"

"No," Rosemounde answered in a calming voice. "This is not the time or place..."

"Time and place be damned, I'll disembowel him in the cathedral during high Mass! I don't care, this villain shall not live another day!"

"But he shall, he shall," Rosemounde insisted. Gently she took my head in her arms and held it to her breast, shushing me in soothing tones. "Don't you see, my love? This is why you must be made a knight of the table. Mordred is a knight. He has skills at arms that are beyond yours. If you challenge him now you will almost certainly lose. And to attack him outright you run the risk of enmity with his brothers, with Sir Gawain and Sir Agravain, even perhaps Sir Gareth. And if with them, then with the king himself. Mordred is twisted. More evil than anyone suspects. I can continue to suffer what I have been suffering. But the time is coming when Sir Mordred will show himself what he is to the world. And that is when I will have to get away from him. And that is when I will need you, my love. When I send for you, you must be ready. You must be a knight of the Round Table with the prowess of a Lancelot. Do you see, my love? Do you see now?"

I saw. She was right of course. I was not ready. Not yet. But I vowed then that I would be. And when I was, Sir Mordred had better look to himself. Because I was coming for him.

CHAPTER THREE

THE GRAIL, OR
SOMETHING LIKE IT

Galahad stood aloof, his shining eyes focused over our heads or somewhere beyond us, on something the rest of us mortals could only imagine. He made no sign that he acknowledged anyone else in the cathedral—not the king, not his father who sponsored his knighting, and certainly not Colgrevaunce, who stood next to him at the altar and, though towering over him by a good three inches, might just as well not have been there at all, so fixated was the entire congregation on the actions of the pure knight.

The cathedral of Caerleon was packed tightly with well-dressed bodies—every knight of the Table was present, most with accompanying squires and some with pages as well, some of whom were forced to gather around the open doors of the church for lack of room in the actual nave. The rest of the court (clerks, servants, members of the palace guard) as well as most of the city of Caerleon were also present. Close to the choir and seated on small wooden chairs were the women of the court: There sat the queen, arrayed in an elaborate gown of purple samite with gold filigree, her golden hair combed upward to help support the heavy crown of state she wore for this high occasion. On her left side sat four of her ladies-in-waiting, in gowns that nearly rivaled the queen's, and all wearing either a simple toque or barbette on their heads. To the left of them was the king's sister, still garbed all in sable, with her raven hair cascading down her back, as if in deliberate contempt of Saint Paul's directive to keep her head covered in church. On the queen's right was my lady Rosemounde, dressed today in a simple long-sleeved gown of green satin and wearing a modest linen oval veil upon her head. My heart had sunk down into my bowels when I saw her, and my rage had boiled again as I searched the cathedral, in vain, for the brute who had married her. The sisters Lynette and Lyonesse sat together on Rosemounde's right, wearing long embroidered cloaks and elaborate cone-shaped hennins on their heads. Dressed far more simply in a white gown and black smock, her head covered by a gray veil, sat Colgrevaunce's bride, the formidable Bess of Caerleon, looking a bit out of place among that daunting band of noble women, but as certain as any of the others that she belonged here. There were a few other women of the court in attendance, but beyond two rows of chairs for the ladies, all others in attendance stood on the stone floor of the cathedral. I stood perhaps a third of the way back in the crowd, waiting with Thomas and with the lad Lovell, Sir Gawain's younger son and squire, straining to hear and see the ceremony.

Notably absent, I remember thinking, was Galahad's own mother, the princess Elaine, and her father King Pelles, maimed king of Corbenic Castle. Had they been made aware that Galahad would be inducted this day into the Fellowship of the Round Table? They would have been invited, certainly, since King Pelles was vassal to King Arthur. I remembered having seen him, with his daughter, the very first Whitsunday I had been in Camelot. A man looking older than his years, he had to be carried in on an open litter by two attendees, since he was unable to rise and walk by his own strength. His daughter had sat with him in the church and at the banquet following on that occasion—I remembered her as petite blonde woman, but one who wore a veil at all times, as if she scorned to reveal her features to the *hoi polloi* of Camelot. She was renowned as a beauty, who might have been married to any number of suitors: skilled in music, in embroidery, but also in more rigorous pursuits, like hawking and hunting—she was said to be a proficient archer. But she would never marry. Pelles had seen to that with his bed trick that had matched her with Sir Lancelot.

Since her appearance was such a rarity, I wondered if anyone at Camelot had ever seen her true features—anyone but Lancelot, that is, and that only the morning *after* their notorious tryst. And I remembered her avoiding any contact with either the queen or with Sir Lancelot, though at the time I would not have guessed why that should be. In any case, the Maimed King and his daughter had not attended our annual service again, Pelles using his handicap as an excuse to beg off King Arthur's invitation. Still, one might have expected Pelles to make the effort to attend his grandson's induction, or at least to send Galahad's mother. But perhaps, I reasoned, the monks of Beaulieu Abbey had given Pelles and Elaine no more warning than they had given us of Galahad's immanent knighthood, and so I pushed mother and grandfather to the back of my mind to focus more closely on the ceremony.

By now I had gotten used to the induction held on Whitsunday every year. It always began the same way: The knights to be received into the order, in this case Galahad and Colgrevaunce, knelt in wait at the altar, where they had kept their vigil since matins the previous night, some twelve hours earlier. Then when the cathedral bells tolled the hour of sext, led by William of Glastonbury, the Archbishop of Caerleon, the king along with Sir Lancelot and Sir Brandiles, sponsors of the inductees, processed into the cathedral down the long central aisle. The king's chaplain, Father Ambrose, followed by a dozen canons of the cathedral, brought up the rear of the procession in order to assist the archbishop in conducting Mass prior to the induction ceremony.

And so the Mass was sung. My eyes glazed over as, in bookish Latin, the Archbishop intoned the service, allowing Galahad and Colgrevaunce each to partake of the body of Christ—Galahad eagerly and confidently, Colgrevaunce with awe and trepidation.

The two inductees now stood as the Mass concluded, and seamlessly the Archbishop continued into the induction ceremony. He called the king to the center, and Arthur stepped up, his back to the altar so that he faced the two inductees, and bid them to come forward. They did so, then knelt again in an attitude of prayer. Now Lancelot, whose blue tunic was augmented by an ermine edged sable cloak, and Brandiles, in a scarlet tunic and fancifully embroidered green cloak, stepped forward as well, their colorful garments adding to the pageantry of the occasion. Each held a pair of golden spurs, and as the inductees knelt at the altar, their sponsors fastened the spurs to their black leather boots.

Now the king reached behind the altar and lifted up two swords: one a newly forged sword to be presented to Colgrevaunce, the other (as I recognized by the jeweled pommel) the sword of Sir Balin that Galahad had yesterday pulled from the floating stone. King Arthur held them high as the Archbishop moved again to the center, made the sign of the cross over them, and called out the customary prayer for the blessing of the swords in English, so that the whole congregation could hear and understand:

"Father of justice and of mercy, grant, we pray, your blessing on these swords, which thy humble servants, Galahad and Colgrevaunce, wish to gird about them. May they use these swords with prowess and with prudence in the defense of thy Holy Church, and of all widows and orphans and any others who may be in need, and may they always be faithful in striking with these swords only in the cause of the right. In the name of the Father, and of the Son, and of the Holy Ghost. Amen."

And as the congregation echoed that "amen," Sir Lancelot and Sir Brandiles stepped toward the two inductees, embraced them, and placed a kiss of peace on their respective cheeks, as a sign of welcome into the brotherhood of the noble order of the Knights of the Round Table.

Now Arthur prepared to deliver the colée. Setting aside for the moment Colgrevaunce's newly forged blade, he raised the jewel-studded sword from the stone high above his head, and brought the flat of it down with full force on Galahad's right soldier. The pure knight did not flinch for an instant, but took the blow with the same indifferent aloofness he had displayed throughout the ceremony. The colée was intended to be something the knight would remember always, that would put him in mind of the liege lord who had made him knight, and of his obligations to duty and to chivalry. Galahad did not seem so moved. But then he did not give the impression that he would ever forget his duties, either.

The king handed the sword of Sir Balin to Sir Lancelot as he picked up Colgrevaunce's bright new weapon. Colgrevaunce steeled himself for the colée, but even so, when the blade came down upon his shoulder he winced and, indeed, very nearly collapsed. Sir Brandiles had to steady him as he seemed somewhat dazed, then took the sword from King Arthur and, as Lancelot was doing with Galahad, began to fasten the sword around Colgrevaunce's waist.

Now Arthur's voice boomed with the words that would end the knighting ceremony itself, ensuring that all that throng crowded into the cathedral could hear his proclamation: "As rightful King of Logres and as Emperor of Ireland, Brittany, Normandy, and Gaul, and as head of the noble order of chivalry, I hereby accept you into the order known throughout the world as the Knights of the Round Table. Rise, Sir Galahad and Sir Colgrevaunce, Knights of the Table Round."

The cathedral burst into loud cheers and applause as, beaming, Colgrevaunce turned to face the congregation. Spotting his Bess in the seat close to the choir, he waved to her and threw her a kiss and, looking around until he spotted our little group of squires out among the crowd, waved to us as well, drawing his sword and brandishing it a bit to show off. It was at that point rather than any other that I felt a twinge of jealousy. I had always been more accomplished than Colgrevaunce in the martial skills. Only in the past year, since he'd married Bess, did he really begin to make significant progress in his training, while I, at least in the past months, had grown lackadaisical, having lost direction and drive in my quest to achieve knighthood. But now, Rosemounde's plea still ringing in my ears, I would devote every fiber of my being to the pursuit of excellence. By the next Pentecost, I swore, I would be standing where Sir Colgrevaunce was standing now.

In stark contrast to Sir Colgrevaunce's triumphant joy, Sir Galahad showed no particular emotion at all as he turned to face the congregation. Even as Lancelot tried in vain to cheer him and congratulate him, Galahad ignored his father, or perhaps was so much in his own world that he did not notice the great knight's presence. The only sign that he was pleased was an almost nonexistent smile of satisfied contentment that flickered on his otherwise stony face—and, though I could not see it from where I was, I was assured later by Lancelot himself, there were tears welling up in Galahad's eyes.

Finally it was necessary to conclude the ceremony with the annual renewal of the oath. The Archbishop stepped forward again to take center stage from the king, and called for all the knights of the Round Table to stand if they were not already doing so. He then recited, "Just as in the days of the Apostles, the Holy Spirit descended upon them at Pentecost and sent them forth to build the Church, so in our own time the Knights of the Table Round, heirs of those first Apostles, are sent forth each Pentecost to defend and preserve that same Church. Empowered by the Holy Spirit, this fellowship renews its commitment to that righteous ideal every year in the reciting of the great oath. Today Sir Galahad and Sir Colgrevaunce will repeat the oath with us, pledging themselves to the order as all the rest of you did on the day you became knights."

Each of the 151 knights of the Table raised his right hand to repeat the vow I had heard so often that I could recite it myself—which I did, silently anticipating what I felt was my certain knighthood the following year:

"We swear always to follow the commands of our king: never to do outrage or murder; always to flee treason; never to be cruel, but in all circumstances to grant mercy to him who pleads for mercy, or forfeit our own worship and the lordship of our lord King Arthur for evermore; and we swear always to give succor to ladies, damsels, and gentlewomen, on pain of death. And we further swear never to go to battle in a wrongful cause no matter what law may try to compel us to do so, and no matter what the worldly reward. All of this we swear, both old and young, the Knights of the Table Round."

***

All of Camelot had gathered for the feast of Pentecost, which because of the great crowd packed into the castle was being served in two venues: the great hall, where banquets typically were housed, and the Hall of the Order, the great foundational space where the Round Table itself stood, a space that was used only once a year, for the annual Whitsunday ceremony after the renewing of the vows. Yet despite the underused status of the hall—or perhaps because of it, to emphasize its extraordinary significance—the space was lavishly decorated, the walls hung with enormous brightly-woven Flemish tapestries that covered all four walls of the Hall of the Order. These depicted scenes of great martial prowess, to inspire the knights of the Order to go and do likewise. On the north wall, behind the king's seat at the table, was portrayed Aeneas and his Trojan refugees, overcoming the native Latin forces and establishing what would become the new Roman nation: The scene pictured the stern and stoic Aeneas, lifting his bloodied sword high over the dead body of the hapless Turnus, with the victorious Trojans, the vanquished Rutulians, and the hard-won Lavinia looking on. Next, on the east wall, the tapestry showed Aeneas's great-grandson Brutus, represented in full war-cry in battle with the giants who inhabited Albion, and upon whose defeat he was able to rename Albion "Britain" after himself, founding his capitol at New Troy on the banks of the Thames.

On the south wall, behind the Siege Perilous, was hung a depiction of Belinus and Brennius, sons of the British King Dunvallo, sacking the city of Rome: The tapestry rendered the two brothers clasping hands, their own differences forgotten, with a burning Rome in ruins behind them and the brothers readying to go their separate ways— Brennius to remain in Italy to rule the Roman kingdom and his brother to return and establish a dynasty in Britain itself. Finally, on the west wall, the tapestry displayed the Roman emperor Constantine, British born, leading an assault on Milvian Bridge while gazing into the sky at the image of the cross, the words *In hoc signo vinces* ("In this sign you will conquer") woven into the textile around the cross. It occurred to me for the first time that these scenes were not simply intended as inspiration for the knights, but as a political statement as well, for who here could question the justice of Arthur's conquest of Rome as his birthright, descended as he was directly from these figures on the walls.

Despite its being in part sunk into the earth, the Hall of the Order was well lit by rows of high windows that let in floods of sunshine during daylight hours. In the corners of the hall, between tapestries, elaborate gilt-copper wall sconces hung, holding wax candles. There were also silver candelabra spaced along the circumference of the Round Table, so that the candlelight might complement the natural sunlight on cloudy days or during meetings of the order that extended into the hours of dusk.

With the other table squires, I joined the knights of the order waiting to dine at the Round Table. The stone floor of the hall had been strewn with sweet smelling rushes for the occasion, and table settings of pure silver knives, spoons, and bowls for wine were at each of the 152 places at the table. Table squires, one for each knight, stood behind their lords' seats, while a score of serving lads and pages stood within the circumference of the table, where they would hold various dishes to be served, still warm, to the hungry knights. For the architect of Camelot had created an ingenious system for the great table: from the kitchen, which lay in the lower bailey along the wall west of the great hall, a tunnel ran directly under the Room of the Order and emerged in precisely the middle of the table itself. Thus food could be brought straight from the kitchen into the hall and served to the knights seated around the table from inside, avoiding the need to pass a dish down to a knight seated fifty or sixty seats away, and ensuring that the food stayed warm. It was widely rumored that Merlin himself had given the architect the idea for that innovation. And it was well known that another covered passageway led up the stairs from the kitchen directly to the great hall on the second floor, which insured that the guests at that banquet enjoyed well-warmed dishes of their own. The number of servants involved in this noisy commotion exceeded the total number in Camelot, and so pages and even some of the victualers from the city of Caerleon were pressed into service on Pentecost. Sir Kay, the king's seneschal and thus the warden of his household (including, perhaps most importantly, his kitchen) bustled about, watching all the servers and stepping out occasionally to check on the traffic into the room upstairs. Huffing and puffing, he came back into the Hall of the Order, mopping the sweat on his face with the puffy maroon sleeve of his satin tunic. His eyes bulged and when his lips parted he announced in a powerful voice (which had in it no small hint of well-deserved pride in pulling off yet another Pentecost feast), "Gentlemen! The first course is on its way! Please be seated and prepare to fall to!"

Kay's announcement was followed by some good-natured grumbling as dozens of knights tried to find their assigned seats. It reduced the chaos somewhat if every knight had a siege assigned only to him. It also reduced the sometimes acrimonious competition over social status, determined by how close one sat to the king and on which hand. Today King Arthur sat on one side of the table, with Sir Galahad in the Siege Perilous directly across from him, and seventy-five knights between them on each arc of the table. On Arthur's right hand sat Sir Gawain, and next to him Arthur's next eldest nephew, Sir Ywain. On the king's left sat Lancelot, and down from him his kinsman Sir Bors, followed by Sir Ector and Sir Lionel, Lancelot's other close kin.

Sir Gareth's siege was several seats further down from Sir Lionel, where my master sat between Sir Perceval of Gales on his left, and his good friend, the Moorish knight Sir Palomides, on his right. Sir Colgrevaunce, I noticed, was on the other side of the table, several seats down to the left of Sir Galahad, with Sir Brandiles on his left and the vile Sir Ironside, the Red Knight of the Red Lands, on his right. My eyes quickly scanned the scores of faces and finally lighted upon that of the beastly Mordred, seated several positions down from Colgrevaunce, toward the king's position and that of his other brother, Gawain. I breathed a heavy sigh, but there was relief in it, for had he been close to my master I would have found it very difficult to keep my hands from throttling him by his scrawny neck.

As table squire to my master Sir Gareth, my first task was to help him wash his hands. The table was provided with silver hand basins or gamellions and ewers or pitchers of water at intervals of every five knights or so. I reached in, lifted the ewer and poured water over Sir Gareth's hands into the gemellion, then handed him a small towel to dry them with. Next, from a silver flagon that had also been placed near his siege at the table, I poured him a cup of fine claret. As I performed these duties, I was able to catch snippets of the conversation going on between Gareth and his table companions. The topic on everyone's lips seemed to be the surprising arrival of Sir Galahad the previous day, and the marvels that attended upon that appearance.

"Why must everyone question these wonders?" Sir Perceval, one of the newest and youngest of the knights, was asking. "Why can't we just accept them? These are miracles intended for us, to show us the way to deeper spiritual things."

"Or they are simply the artifices of talented hucksters, as Sir Kay suggested. What do we know about this Brother Nascien, anyway?"

"Ah, my lord Gareth, it may be so," Sir Palomides chimed in. "But the Siege Perilous, what of that? It was not created by this Brother Nascien, but many years ago by Merlin himself, and so is no trickery. And the lad met that challenge, did he not?"

"Yes, yes," Sir Gareth conceded. "I do admit that feat is harder to ignore."

"Then it is as I have said," Sir Perceval interjected. "A true marvel! A portent of the Divine at work in the world!"

"Well…" Sir Gareth's skepticism trailed off as the banquet's first course arrived.

"For what we are about to receive, may the Lord make us truly grateful!" Sir Kay's abrupt and perfunctory grace had the sound of a military order rather than a prayer, and it was greeted with scores of hardy "Amens" as the knights prepared to devour the feast.

Pairs of servers emerged from the tunnel out of the kitchen, each pair holding a wide silver tray on which an entire quarter of a stag was carried. One of these trays was set down near Sir Gareth's place at the table, intended for a score of knights in that vicinity. I stepped forward with Sir Gareth's plate, and using the great knife that had been brought in on the tray, carved a healthy portion of venison from the roasted meat and placed it before Sir Gareth at the table.

"Good God Gildas," Sir Gareth cried. "How many courses are there? Keep giving me portions like this and I may explode!"

"Only about four or five more," I told him.

"Well, keep it up and I'll make you eat it."

"Promises, promises…" I said, stepping back into my respectful squire's pose behind his chair.

***

It was just as I said this that, quite abruptly, all the many voices in that hall ceased, and amid the silence I could feel, rather than see, that something quite extraordinary (and it seemed to me not altogether pleasant) was about to occur. The room had grown dark, all those high windows suddenly provided no light as the sky outside turned black as night, and even the candles around the hall were suddenly snuffed out. There was a burst of lightning that flashed an eerie pulsating pattern of dim light on the faces of the astounded knights who sat around the table. A crash of thunder ensued, followed abruptly by an intensely bright sunbeam that stabbed through the clouds and into the hall, splitting the darkness with a shaft that shot from the window to the very center of the Round Table. Now the faces of the assembled knights, reflecting the intense brilliance of that sunbeam, appeared to me to take on a fairness that they could not display in the mundane light of day. Sir Palomides' smile was all the more winning, Sir Gareth's wind-blown blond hair all the more striking, Sir Perceval's earnest eyes all the more charming.

And then, within the dazzling beam itself, it seemed to me I could make out a kind of ghostly shape. I blinked my eyes, assuming it was a trick my vision was playing on me, the result of the sudden burst of light after the profound darkness that had preceded it. But I could make nothing out in that intense light—perhaps it was a shadow cast by something passing outside the window; perhaps it was just a spiral of dust, or of steam rising from the roasted venison.

I became aware that somewhere on my right hand, one of the knights was rising from his siege, and somehow I did not need to be told that it was the Siege Perilous. Sir Galahad, in a calm authoritative voice, was proclaiming to all the assembled order: "It is the Grail. The Holy Grail from which Our Lord drank the wine, his own Holy Blood, at the Last Supper. Brought to the land of Logres by his disciple Joseph of Arimathea. It is the quintessence of all holy relics. It is still somewhere here in Logres, even now."

Sir Galahad's words lingered in the air, just as the shadow of steam lingered in that intense sunbeam, for long moments as the astounded knights, seemingly struck dumb by the vision and the revelation, continued to stare open-mouthed at the ray of light. Then, as abruptly as it had appeared, the sunbeam vanished as the dark clouds outside dissipated, and the hall was filled with natural light just as before, and servants scurried to relight the sconces and the chandelier.

But the vision appeared to have left some peripheral effect, for the hall seemed filled now with most pleasant aromas, of spices and savory dishes, and one by one the knights began to consume with relish the course that had been laid before them as if each was enjoying the cuisine he loved best in all the world.

It was no surprise that the impetuous Sir Gawain was first of all the knights to break the spell of silence. What surprised me was just what he said. "My lords," he shouted, leaping to his feet and demanding the attention of the entire room. I could see in his eyes an excited glint that betrayed a kind of fire that had been kindled within him. "We have been granted here a marvelous vision—one that marks this fellowship as the most glorious in all the earth, God's own blessed warriors. There must be a purpose in His revelation to us of this glorious relic. And I for one will see His will done! I hereby vow today, before God and this company, that I shall not rest two nights in the same place, nor shall my sword leave my side, until I have found this holy relic, and brought it here to Caerleon's cathedral to the blessing of all Logres and our king's great empire!"

And that was the spark that ignited a conflagration around that table. The king, a look of pure dismay in his eyes, stared up at Gawain shaking his head. It was as if Sir Gawain had opened a door the king had wished to keep closed; but now it was opened, there was no going back. My master Gareth, looking somewhat bewildered himself, muttered, "What on earth is my brother talking about? I saw nothing in that beam but some shapeless shadow."

Sir Palomides was equally baffled. "Nor did I," he agreed. "Probably the shadow of some bird flying by the window outside. What kind of vow is this, to search for a phantom of the imagination?"

But Sir Perceval was of a different mind altogether. "How can you say you didn't see it?" he demanded. "It was clear as the day, definite as the hand in front of my face! A jeweled cup, as golden as the luminous sunbeam itself!" And with that Perceval stood, joining his voice to Gawain's and announcing, "I, too, swear to make this my quest! I will seek the Grail forever, if need be, even if it costs my life!"

Now others began to rise as well, joining themselves to Gawain's vow. Sir Ywain was among the first, and Sir Gaheris, then Sir Kay, not to be outdone, along with Sir Bleoberis and Sir Mador. When Lancelot himself stood up, overwhelmed, it seemed, by the pressure of his comrades, and reluctant to gainsay anything proposed by his son—who had yet to acknowledge him—then all of his party followed suit: Sir Ector, Sir Lionel, and last, his lips pursed thoughtfully and his eyes wide open, the faithful and stolid Sir Bors. There was no stopping them now. Almost to a man, and all proclaiming loudly their pious intent, nearly the entire Table rose and pledged to follow the quest of the Grail. Sir Gareth was one of the last to swear, and did so, I felt, somewhat reluctantly. Last of all was Sir Dinadan, the sarcastic, jesting knight who had been my companion in the investigation of the deaths of Tristram and Isolde. True to form, Dinadan's oath was a bit twisted: "All right," he began, "if you're all going, then I'm going too! I don't know what *you* saw, but I know *I'll* never see it sitting around here. So I'm going on the quest too, if only to laugh at those of you who fail! But just to be clear: it's a cup we're looking for, right? Hundred and fifty knights? Scouring the forest? Looking for a bloody cup. That's high-minded chivalry for you."

In the end I saw only three knights who had kept their seats and declined to take on the sacred quest: Sir Palomides and his brother Sir Safer, the Moorish knights; and across the table, his dark countenance smoldering with ill will, the contemptible Sir Mordred.

Two other figures remained seated, facing each other directly across the Round Table. King Arthur, his head now in his hands, seemed resigned to the madness that Gawain had unleashed, that had gathered strength like an avalanche that he could see plunging down upon his kingdom. On the other side of the table Sir Galahad, oblivious to the pandemonium around him that his own voice had perpetrated and his lips barely bent in a thin smile, his eyes focused somewhere beyond the hall itself, had not joined the other knights in their vow. To him it was redundant. He had always aimed to hunt for the Grail. It was his destiny. Or so he had been told from the time he suckled at his mother's breast. Now, here in Camelot, the time had finally come.

CHAPTER FOUR

THE TALE OF SIR GARETH

"Well, this was certainly a great idea. Let's just ride forth without a clue as to where we're going or how to find whatever it is we're looking for, which we're not even sure exists and didn't actually see in the first place," I grumbled, riding through the deep forest of Logres in the rain behind Sir Gareth, whose spirits seemed just about as dampened as my own after two days of riding through an apparently perpetual downpour that seemed to have started the moment we left Camelot with more than a hundred other knights—all in search of a centuries-old cup that may or may not have ever actually been in this country—if, indeed, it ever existed at all. After the first day, all the knights had gone their own way, either alone or in small groups, to take what adventure God was going to give them. I admit there was a bit of a thrill to it in the beginning: For someone eager to learn chivalry and advance to knighthood, what could be better than a real live quest, even if my job was basically to lug Sir Gareth's armor and weapons on a large horse trailing his own great destrier?

"Keep your chin up, oh faithful squire of mine," Sir Gareth joked as his dancing blue eyes looked back at me, his leather hood protecting his fair hair from the steady rain. "I'm just as certain as you that this quest is a wild goose chase, but what did you expect me to do? After my own chin-wagging brother went ahead and started this thing, there wasn't any way out for me if I wanted to keep my worship."

"You have another brother who didn't come," I ventured, burning at the thought of Mordred, sitting indifferent at the table while everyone else was jumping up to take the vow.

Gareth spat and turned to look ahead again. "That one. He has no worship to lose. And there is a reason he stayed behind to spend more time in Camelot, rather than return again to the north. With all the other knights gone, I think the little conniver is trying to insinuate his way into the good graces of my uncle the king. And he'll have his Rosemounde in the queen's chamber the whole time, spying on her. Don't be surprised if he convinces the king to trust him and to displace Gawain and name himself as heir to the throne."

This was most certainly news to me. Quickly I kicked my horse out of its slow amble to trot up next to Sir Gareth where I could converse with him more easily. "What? What makes you think that? Could the king be that gullible?"

"The king is wise," Gareth said, "but also vulnerable. He is only as strong as his retainers. And remember, Mordred is King Arthur's son, though unacknowledged. A son can have a powerful influence on a father—look at Lancelot. Do you think he would be foolish enough to have undertaken this quest had it not been his own son who initiated it? With Sir Gawain and Sir Lancelot both gone on the quest for who knows how long, Mordred will be the king's sole knightly supporter in the castle. No wonder Arthur looked so broken when we all left."

"As did the queen," I recalled, though I was well aware that her chief sorrow was the lengthy absence of Lancelot. I smiled briefly at the thought that her threat to make things at court miserable for Galahad was never able to take shape, since he had left as abruptly as he had come. And thinking of Gareth's words I smiled more broadly at the thought of my lady Rosemounde spending her time back in the queen's apartments among her ladies. She would be protected there, insulated from the foul temper of that beast of a husband. But then I frowned again, for if what Sir Gareth said was true, then all of Logres stood in danger of falling into the clutches of the beast.

"And so, knowing all of this, you still opted to come on the quest."

"My worship, Gildas, my worship."

"What about Sir Palomides?" I persisted. "He is as worshipful a knight as you, and yet would not come on this quest."

Gareth rolled his eyes at me. "You know that Sir Palomides and Sir Safer are Moorish knights…"

"But both have been baptized," I countered. "They have forsaken Mohammed for Christ—Palomides years ago, out of love for La Belle Isolde, long before she died. And Safer quite recently. As Christian knights, would they not forfeit their worship by refusing to seek the holiest of Christian relics?"

Sir Gareth sighed. "I spoke with Sir Palomides about that," he told me. "More than anything else, it is the red cross on Galahad's surplice. When he first saw that, Palomides told me, he cringed. His memory of the crusade, of the great slaughter of his people and of the Jews in Jerusalem at the hands of the crusading knights, all bearing that same Red Cross on their shields, haunts him to this day. He cannot be a part of a military adventure whose symbol is that blood-red emblem. So it is not cowardice, nor loss of worship, that lies behind Sir Palomides' decision to forego the quest. Or his brother Sir Safer's."

"He will stay at Camelot, then?"

"No," Gareth said, with some disappointment in his voice. "If he were there, his presence might mitigate Sir Mordred's influence. No, he and Safer have decided to seek the Grail, but to do it in their own way. Instead of mounting and seeking the Grail as a part of an armed force, they have decided to lay down their swords and pick up their walking staffs, and go on foot as pilgrims through the forest, seeking the Grail by peaceful pilgrimage, and not through force of arms."

Though my jaw dropped at that revelation, I had to admit, it made a lot more sense than sending an army to find a holy relic. "Well," was all I could say. "Good luck to them!"

"Amen to that," Sir Gareth agreed. Then, after a moment's thought, he returned to his earlier comment. "Those brothers of mine, though. Such a study in contrasts."

"How do you mean?" I asked, for though I had no difficulty seeing his point once he had made it, I must admit that I had not even been keeping Gawain and Mordred in the same place in my brain, much less considering them as brothers.

"Well, you know, Mordred—dark, secretive, conniving, aloof, devious. Gawain—open, gregarious, impulsive, and prone to speak and act without thinking. Something my dear half-brother Mordred would never do."

"Well, we saw Gawain's impetuous streak twice, I suppose, this past week."

Sir Gareth's brow knit briefly. "His bounding up to swear that crazy oath was certainly one example. What else were you thinking of?"

"Why, when he waded onto the floating stone to try to pull out the sword. He did it upon the king's request, of course, but Lancelot certainly had no difficulty excusing himself from that challenge. If the warning on that weapon can be believed, Sir Gawain has set himself up to be struck down by Sir Balin's sword."

"That's always been his way," Gareth shrugged. "So quick to act. So quick to do his liege lord's bidding! And that is not a bad thing."

"Not a bad thing surely, but certainly an unhealthy thing."

"That is no joke, Gildas my lad. It's like the time he challenged the Green Knight."

"Green knight?" I asked.

"Did I never tell you about my brother Gawain and the Green Knight?" Sir Gareth laughed, a twinkle coming into his eye. "Well that is certainly an oversight. Let me strain your credulity a little bit and give you the story straight away."

And he cleared his throat. I settled back in the saddle, knowing that once Sir Gareth had got it into his head that a story was necessary, there was no stopping him. And why would I want to? A good tale would pass the time and make me forget how uncomfortable I really was, drenched and stuck on this horse in the middle of the forest.

"So," Gareth began, drawing out the long "o" while he considered just how to begin his tale. "This happened a long time ago, when Gawain was still quite young, and Arthur and the Round Table were in the springtime of their lives as well. So, long before Gawain married Dame Ragnell, mother of the young Lovell and our friend Sir Florent. Back then, as you may have heard, my brother was known as a ladies' man. Had a different lady in every court in Logres. Why, there's a great story of when the king of South Wales caught Gawain in bed with his daughter…but that's another story altogether.

"Now the time I'm talking about was just after Queen Guinevere came to Camelot, and she was with the king hosting a big Christmas banquet, with the young Gawain up there on the dais with her and the queen, and all the other knights and ladies of the court having a great time eating venison and roasted swan and candied fruits and guzzling all the wassail they could stomach, when with no warning at all the doors of the great hall are flung open and in rides a massive fellow all dressed in dark green armor, riding a great destrier and the horse is dressed all in green barding as well, and in his hand he's carrying a fearsome battle-axe of the sort called a guisarme, mounted on a pole even longer than he was. So he trots that horse up and down the tables in the hall, all the time making these sarcastic comments about how Arthur's famous court doesn't look all that impressive to him, and how the knights all look so very puny, and on and on. And Arthur says well, if he thinks that, maybe we can fix him up with a knight of the Round Table to joust with and maybe we'll just see how that turns out.

"Now I wasn't there, you know, so I didn't see this next part myself, but this is how they tell it. The knight dismounts and takes off his green helmet, and what do you think? His hair, his beard, his skin, even his eyes, they're all green as well, just about the same shade as the armor itself."

"Well now you're just having me on. I thought this was a real story about sir Gawain," I dismissed him. But Gareth raised his right hand and swore it was true—or at least, he had been assured it was true by those who had been there, including Sir Gawain himself.

"Now the knight, who's been using his battle-axe as a walking stick while strutting around the hall, says no, he's not going to joust with any of Arthur's knights. No, he says, what he has in mind is more of a Christmas game. Let's strike a bargain, he says. Anybody in the court who's got the nerve to stand toe to toe with him, he says, can take his axe and chop off his head right then and there.

"So now all the knights are looking at each other, like they're thinking 'what kind of fool is this knight, offering to have his neck severed? It's either some trick or else he's just plain crazy.' And they start to shuffle their feet. But after he's let that sink in, the Green Knight adds the real gist of his challenge: 'Yes, he can cut off my head, just so long as he gives me the chance, one year from today, to return the same blow, providing I'm still alive to do it.'

"Well the whole group is pretty sure by then that this is a first-class looney in their midst, or else that it's all some trick and somehow the Green Knight knows he's going to survive the blow and will come back to decapitate them at the winter festivities next year. Merry Christmas, here's your head, sort of thing. And nobody makes the slightest move to take him up on his offer. The Green Knight sneers at them, and says, 'Where's the vaunted courage of Arthur's knights? Where's the superior chivalry of the Round Table? I guess that's all talk, then, eh?'

"And meanwhile Arthur's fuming. He stands up and steps down from the dais, grabs the axe out of the knight's grip, and starts weaving it around, you know, to get the feel of it. 'I'll show you where the courage of Arthur's kingdom is, Sir!' He declares. 'Bend your head down and bare your neck to take the blow. If it's beheading you want, then I will oblige you myself!'

"And of course the knights are all breathless, distraught to see their king and lord risking his own neck, but unwilling to step up and deal the blow themselves. And I'm talking about all the great knights. Don't think Lancelot wasn't there—he was, though pretty young, but he wasn't about to do something as unchivalrous as cut off the head of an unarmed man, nor risk his own life for nothing without being able to defend himself if it turned out he was in that pickle next year. Meanwhile Guinevere's got her face in her hands, afraid to look. But who do you suppose *did* step in and save the king?"

"Pretty sure, considering how the story began, that you're going to tell me it was Gawain."

"Got it in one, Gildas my lad," Gareth teased. "Gawain, his courtesy so exaggerated he seemed to be having a laugh at the Green Knight, pipes up and says 'Stop, Uncle, your life is too valuable. I may be the least of all your knights, but if you would grant me the privilege of taking this challenge in your place, I would descend from the dais and take the axe in my own hands.' So naturally Arthur is relieved to hand the weird chore off to somebody else, and the Green Knight seems pretty pleased that it's Gawain himself who's to be the butt of his joke, or whatever it is. He bends over, pushes his long green hair from around his long green neck, and says, 'Strike true, Sir Gawain. But remember: you must bend the same way and take the blow from me in the same way in a year's time.' And Gawain says, 'I understand the bargain. Now keep still and let me aim this right.' And he measures the distance with his eye while the Green Knight stands immobile, bent at the waist and silent. Then with a quick movement, Gawain lifts up the axe and brings it down in a quick, deadly arc, straight down and through the knight's neck, and with such force that it strikes the stone floor of the hall and gives a startling clang. Well there's no shortage of blood spewing from the knight's fallen body, and the head starts rolling around under the feet of all the court ladies, and Guinevere is so shaken up that she stands up screaming, trying to get away from the rolling head. But then she notices two green hands reaching down to the floor and picking up the severed head. The knight's body has sprung back to life, and he's risen up and retrieved his head. He grasps the head by its long green hair, and then holds the gory thing out at arm's length, right in the queen's face, and the grisly eyes open and stare straight at her, and she's so terrified she very nearly faints.

"But the head keeps talking. It summons the horse, which trots on up to the headless body, and the Green Knight gets into his saddle, still holding his head out at arm's length, toward Sir Gawain, and the head says 'Remember our bargain! Seek me on New Year's Eve at the Green Chapel!' And then off he rides, as quickly as he had arrived. Gawain and Arthur look at each other, and the queen looks at them both, and after a minute they all just burst out laughing, because the whole thing is so absurd."

"Well, I won't argue with you about the absurd part," I concurred. "Who was it told you this story? And, more important, why did they think you were going to believe it?"

"Scoff if you will young Gildas," Gareth went on, "but I'll have you know that I didn't just hear the story from Sir Gawain, but the details were confirmed by the king himself and by my aunt Morgan."

"Morgan le Fay?" I blurted, alarmed. "What did she have to do with anything?"

"You may actually find out," Gareth replied, "if you stop interrupting me and let me finish the story. So listen: most of the year goes by and Gawain has put the whole incident out of his head, until it gets to be around All Saints' Day and the weather starts turning colder, and that puts him in mind of his promise. Some of his fellows—Gaheris and Ywain for sure, but never the king—try to tell him that it was all a big joke and that there's no reason for him to go looking for trouble by trying to find this Green Chapel or whatever it is. But Gawain won't be talked out of it: he's convinced his honor, his worship, depends on fulfilling his word to the Green Knight, even though the whole contest was a trick to begin with.

"So Gawain sets off on his great destrier, Gringolet, that he rode in those days. He searched for weeks, from one end of Logres to the other, asking everybody he met if they'd ever heard of a place called the Green Chapel, or a Green Knight who frequented the place. It got to be Christmas Eve, and still Gawain was clueless, and on top of that he was in a great wilderness in foul weather—not unlike ourselves at the moment, by the way—and had nowhere to take shelter for the night or to hear Mass on the high holiday on the morrow. The way Gawain tells it, he prayed to the Virgin Mother, and suddenly out of nowhere a castle appeared, with welcoming fires within, and he made his way to that refuge as fast as Gringolet's legs could carry him.

"It turns out that the host of that place was a jolly lord name of Bertilak, who's got this stunning and succulent young wench of a wife—blonde hair, blue eyes and buxom. And the wife has this constant companion who's an old crone, about as pleasant to look on as your great uncle's blistered behind. But the three of them and all their household welcome Gawain like he's the prodigal son come home again, and they fete him and feed him for a few days until Gawain, feeling like maybe he's gotten too comfortable, tells the lord 'I'm due to fight a battle in three days, on New Year's Eve, at a place called the Green Chapel. I don't know if I can find it by then but my honor demands that I try.' And jolly old Bertilak gives a belly-laugh and says that chapel is just down the road, not ten minutes from there. Says he'll have one of his squires show Gawain the way on the morning of New Year's, but in the three intervening days he says he wants Gawain to stay and rest up from his travels right there at his castle.

"But now Bertilak proposes a Christmas game for Gawain. An exchange of winnings. 'I'll be off hunting every day,' he tells Gawain, 'and you'll be here in the castle. If you agree, I say we trade whatever it is we win during the day when I get back home in the evening.' Well I'm not sure what he expected Gawain to win there knocking around the grounds of his castle, but Gawain wasn't about to offend his host, who'd been so hospitable to him, so he's says 'Sure, let's do it.'

"Well the next morning Gawain finds out pretty fast what it is he might win in that castle. The hot young lady of the house comes into his bedchamber to wake him up, sits down on his bed, and starts giving him these hints that, being all alone in the castle and all, there's not much she could do if he decided to have his way with her. Now Gawain, of course, has the ethical problem that it's not often seen as courteous behavior to bed your host's wife in thanks for his hospitality, plus the very practical problem of the pledge he's made Bertilak to share anything he got in the castle with him. Besides that, of course, his gentility requires him to be courteous to women at all times, no matter what their behavior. So with some very quick thinking, Gawain sidesteps her advances, mumbles something about his being unworthy of so beautiful a lady as she is, and after taking a kiss that she pretty much forces on him, he manages to get up and avoid her the rest of the day. When Bertilak returns home, he brings a deer carcass with him, and gives it to Gawain, who has the cook whip up venison for dinner. And he gives the host a kiss on the cheek, refusing to tell Bertilak where he got it because he says that wasn't part of the bargain.

"Next day in comes the lady to Gawain's bed again, this time offering pretty bluntly to make the beast with two backs with him. Gawain has a tougher time. He can't just tell her get out, he doesn't want her—because that would be discourteous and besides, he *does* want her. But he's got Bertilak and his promise to consider too, and so he's got a razor's edge of courtesy to walk. But he puts her off by pretending that she's just joking to test his courtesy, and is able to get away with just two kisses, which he finds it easy enough to exchange for the host's wild boar that night, which he has the chef cook up as a nice pork roast for dinner.

"Which leads to day three: he knows the lady is coming in, and so he's up waiting for her when she arrives. He gives her her kisses right away to get it over with, and then he tells her that he can't think of love, can't think of anything, because he has to face the Green Knight the following day and is certain to die, since, unlike the knight, he can't restore his head when it's been cut off. Then the lady springs the real shocker on him. 'I've got this green sash,' she says, 'that will protect the wearer from harm if he wears it into a potentially dangerous situation.' And what's more, she says she wants to give it to him to keep as a token of her love, which he has pretty much spurned.

"Well, talk about a *deus ex machina,* if this wasn't exactly what Gawain needed at just the right time! What a coincidence, he's thinking. And so that night, when Bertilak returns with just the pelt of a red fox, Gawain gives him three kisses and says he's all paid up, but never mentions the sash. Turns out that his life is more important to him than his promise in that silly game.

"But he wakes up the next morning feeling fairly confident. If the belt can protect him from the axe blow, then he's pretty sure he can hold his own in a fair fight against the Green Knight, if it comes to that. He goes to Bertilak's chapel priest to make confession, and he heads off with a squire from the castle as a guide. As you might expect, the winds are howling and the snow is swirling around and it's bitter cold as they ride the three miles to the Green Chapel. But before they get there the squire gives Gawain one last chance to back out: 'Nobody will know but me, and I'll keep my mouth shut,' he says. 'Just keep riding, say you never found the chapel. Nobody will know, and you'll be ahead by…a head.'

I groaned. "Okay," Gareth admitted. "I made that line up. But that was the gist of it. Anyway, Gawain says no, his honor depends upon his making this meeting and taking the Green Knight's blow. So the squire points out the Green Chapel—which it turns out is just a small mound where, I suppose, they held pagan rites back in the days of the ancient Britons—and he turns tail and heads back for the castle, to get out of the blizzard that's building.

"Gawain gets to the hill and starts looking around, but can't find anybody until he hears an odd whirring sound, and realizes it's the Green Knight working a whetstone and grinding the edge of his axe to razor sharpness. 'So you made it,' the knight says to him. 'The smart money was betting the other way…' or words to that effect," Gareth ended, seeing the look of incredulity on my face.

"'Bend down and get the hair off your neck, so I have a clear shot, just like I did for you,' the knight tells Gawain, who bends down and exposes his nape, but as he's doing so he asserts, 'But remember, one stroke is all you are allowed. After that my pledge is paid.' The Green Knight laughs at him and says, 'You really think I will need more than one?'

"So with that the knight lifts up the axe and starts swinging it down. Gawain's got his faith in the green sash, but all he really has to go on is the lady's word, and that axe coming down at him is a pretty solid case against that insubstantial word. So he closes his eyes and flinches, and the knight swerves and misses his neck on purpose. 'No flinching!' he tells Gawain. 'Did I flinch when you swung this thing at *my* head? What is Arthur's court made up of, a bunch of flinchers?'

"Gawain gets all red in the face—you know how he does that…" I nodded. "And then he blusters, 'Well, I can't reattach my head, so it's a little more of an issue for me. You didn't flinch because you knew it wasn't going to kill you. You had an unfair advantage. But swing that thing again, I won't flinch.' So without another word, the Green Knight raises the axe on high one more time, and down it comes. But again the axe swerves at the last minute. 'Just making sure you weren't going to flinch this time,' the knight said, and Gawain, now furious, spat out 'Stop playing around! Make your axe stroke and torment me no longer. I've braved two of your strokes already. I won't stand still for another if you don't take it now!' And so the grim-faced knight set his jaw, lifted the axe, and brought it down decisively."

Gareth paused. After a moment of waiting for him to continue, I shouted exasperatedly, "Well what happened? Gawain is still here, so I'm pretty sure he didn't die. How did he keep his head?"

"Oh, *now* you believe the story?" Gareth teased, the corner of his mouth curving upwards. "No, Gawain didn't die. The axe missed the nape, and just barely creased the side of his neck. When he saw a drop of blood from that wound spilling in the snow at his feet, he sprang away, drew his sword and warned the knight, 'All right, I've kept my word. Try to swing any more weapons at me and you'll have to go through my sword!' But to his surprise the Green Knight wasn't threatening any more. He was leaning on his axe, relaxed, and laughing loudly. The knight was shaking his head and saying, 'Gawain, you are the best of knights. You've pretty much proved that you're the paragon of courtesy. Who else would have kept his word and met me here? Who else would have searched so hard for the Green Chapel, and stood still for three swings of the axe at your head? Sorry about that little nick at the end—that was for the green sash.'"

"What?" I cried out "What did he know about the green sash? That doesn't make sense."

"Oh, it made perfect sense. Turns out that Bertilak was actually the Green Knight. The lady Bertilak was doing everything under her husband's direction. Everything. Gawain thought that the beheading game was the test. And it was, of course, but he didn't realize that the gift exchange was a test too. Bertilak was totally impressed when Gawain resisted his wife's temptations, so the two strokes when he missed Gawain's neck were the strokes for those two days. The last day, when Gawain took the sash, he broke his word, and that's why with the third axe stroke, Bertilak nicked Gawain's neck. But just a little bit, he said, because it really wasn't much of a slip, and Gawain had only done it to save his life, which anyone would do. Or that's how Bertilak saw it, anyway. Gawain looked at it another way. He cursed himself for cowardice, and paid no attention to what Bertilak was saying. For him he either had to be perfect in his courtesy, or he was a complete fake. The whole thing was like taking his idea of who and what he was and turning it upside down. It devastated him. He's never been the same since.

"And do you know what the strangest part of the whole thing was? It was our dear aunt Morgan who was behind the whole plot. Remember the old crone that was Lady Bertilak's companion? That was her—that was bloody Aunt Morgan in disguise."

"Morgan? But why would she do all that? Why would she want to destroy her own nephew?"

"Well, that's not all that surprising. She hasn't had the smoothest relationship with her brother the king, so why should we expect her to get along with the rest of her family? But the fact is, she couldn't have predicted it would be Gawain that accepted the Green Knight's challenge. I think she really expected, and hoped, it would be Arthur himself. Because her main goal was to get at Guinevere, who she's always hated. It scared the life out of the queen when the Green Knight stretched his severed head out to her, and Morgan hoped Arthur would be in the position of having to stand for the beheading stroke. She wouldn't have gone all the way to the point of really cutting off his head. At least she says she wouldn't—just as she didn't with Gawain. But the stress of waiting for that blow would have driven Guinevere crazy for the whole year. When it turned out to be Gawain, Morgan decided she would see how far she could push him. You know, test the whole idea of Arthur's chivalry, see whether anything so idealistic is even really possible. Gawain impressed her."

"A lot more than he impressed himself, apparently."

"Yes. Gawain declined Bertilak's offer to come back to the castle—he wouldn't face those women again. The sash, of course, was nothing more than a green sash, it had no magic powers. But Gawain decided he'd keep wearing it as a symbol of his failure."

"Well there's a healthy reaction."

"Yes, well, he got back to Camelot and told the whole court the story, and told them he was going to keep wearing that sash, and they all laughed. He thought they were laughing at him for his failure, but they were laughing at how seriously he took his one little slip. But for courtesy's sake, the knights all vowed to wear green sashes of their own. It became a kind of symbol of the order. And they all wore them. For years." Gareth grew thoughtful. "Gawain stopped wearing his sash the day he, Agravain, and Mordred killed Sir Lamorak. That was the day that he knew some failures of courtesy really are soul killing. None of the other knights wore those sashes anymore either. Not after Lamorak."

And we let the silence fill the air again. But some things were bothering me. "But why would Lord Bertilak let his wife do that? And why would she consent to it? And what about the beheading thing? Why would Bertilak take Morgan's word that he was going to be all right with his head separated from his shoulders? It doesn't make sense to me. Why were they in it with her?"

"There had to be a reason," Gareth told me. "It may be that she had found the wife for him in the first place, on the condition that they would do this for her. Or, and this is more likely, she may have been threatening them. Probably threatening the woman with disfigurement. Maybe death—that would get him to agree to the beheading game, even if he wasn't sure he was going to live through it. If he really loved the woman, that is."

"So the real victims in the story may be Bertilak and his wife, then," I said thoughtfully. "And Morgan is a powerful enchantress then, eh? She can cast a spell that allows Bertilak to lose his head and stick it back on? Not to mention turning him all green? And she can disguise herself so that even her own nephew doesn't recognize her?"

"She's a powerful sorceress," Gareth agreed. "A lot of it is certainly tricks, but I don't think anybody has ever explained how she did the head rolling trick. But you don't want to get on her bad side, that's for sure."

"I suppose it's like Merlin," I suggested. "A lot of what he does is sleight of hand, or it's some kind of advanced engineering feat, like moving the Giants' Ring from Ireland. But every so often he'll do something really astounding."

"The difference is this," Gareth cautioned. "Morgan le Fay is a malevolent force. Never underestimate her. Family or no family, she is very dangerous."

"The other thing the story tells me is what motivates Gawain," I said. "What has always motivated him. He does what Arthur wants— he likes being the heir apparent. Furthermore, he wants desperately to be the best knight in the world. And he's not. And he knows he's not."

"And that's my brother, all right."

At that point I realized the rain had stopped. The sun was actually making a determined effort to peak out from behind some clouds, I pushed the hood back from my head and shook some of the water out of my hair and hood. Then I heard Gareth exclaim, "By God, look at this!" When I lifted my head I could see that there was a white abbey directly ahead of us. We would have a roof over our heads tonight. And walking out the door of the abbey, Sir Ywain himself came strolling. When he saw us, he laughed. "Well, what do ya know?" he said. "Here's two more!"

CHAPTER FIVE

MIRACLES

The White Abbey was a new Cistercian Monastery called Saint Sebastian's, so new that neither I nor Sir Gareth had heard of it before. Isolated out here in the wilds of the forest, these monks were not eager to have visitors, but they were friendly enough to those of us who stumbled upon their sanctuary. One of the younger monks who acted as stable boy took our horses into the barn to brush and feed them, while Sir Ywain put his arm around Gareth's shoulder and walked in through the front gate and into the cloister of the abbey, while I followed respectfully behind.

Ywain had not yet removed the chain mail he had been wearing on his two-day ride from Camelot, but he did make a nod to fashion with the dark blue hooded cloak that he wore over the armor. He wore his hair and beard long and frizzy so that his dark mane framed his face in a way reminiscent of his famous mate. The Knight of the Lion fixed us with his dark brown eyes and confided quietly, "They've put us all here in the refectory, just off the cloister," he gestured the way into the dining hall. "They don't know what else to do with us, but it will be comfortable enough to sleep here—no worse than sleeping on a pallet in the great hall at Camelot. And they *are* feeding us. Or at least they say they will soon."

When we stepped through the door, we were surprised at how small the space was. There were only two tables, each of which could seat up to eight monks. The space was not large enough to accommodate many more, and it seemed clear that the monks wanted to remain a small community, and grow no larger than the number that could fit around these tables. It was less of a surprise to find Sir Galahad sitting rather stiffly at one of the solid wooden tables, but the true shock was seeing who was sitting across from him—King Bagdemagus and his son Meliagaunt.

Galahad nodded to us politely as we entered, and even spoke up, saying "Welcome, my friends, to this house of God," as if he were the abbot himself. Which for him was downright chatty.

After nodding to Galahad, I sat next to King Bagdemagus, saying, "Your Highness, what are you doing here? You had retired from the Round Table—you were going back to your kingdom to live out your days there."

"What, and miss this?" The king responded. "Look, I was a knight of the Round Table for twenty-eight years. I've borne arms for nearly fifty. In all that time, do you think I've ever had the opportunity to be a part of anything like this? Bloody hell, man, it's the greatest quest ever conceived of in the history of chivalry. And I'm on it. By God I'm on it now with my son, and we're going to do something really worthwhile."

"Really worthwhile?" I asked. "What do you call your life as a knight of the Round Table? You freed Logres from Roman dominance. You established Arthur as emperor of the known world, and helped him protect his people in peace and justice. What is this quest going to do? Find an old relic and bring it to a church? If you even find it! It's like a needle in a haystack. How is this so worthwhile?"

"Worthwhile? What's worthwhile?" The king was getting a little confused. "Oh, the thing. The Grail. But it's the true blood, you see. The real blood of Christ that was held in that cup. This world, it doesn't last. It passes soon as flowers fair, you know, as they say. So you know, those battles won for Arthur, those kingdoms of this world that he's now king of, they're going to pass away. His kingdom is going to pass away. Nobody knows that better than me. How much longer am I going to be in this world of shadows? Not long, not long. But this quest, it's about the things that don't pass away."

"What?" I asked exasperated. "What doesn't pass away? That cup? It's just a thing. That church you're going to put it in? That's going to crumble too, eventually. How is finding this Grail going to build up your honor in heaven, more than your protecting damsels and orphans and the defenseless as a knight of the Table? Who are you helping with this quest?"

"God," Bagdemagus answered matter-of-factly.

"God doesn't need your help!" I asserted. "But people do! Those widows, those orphans, those helpless victims of injustice. That's what knights were created to do. That's the oath you all take."

"Myself, then," the king proposed. "I'm helping my immortal soul. Now let me be, I'm going to eat." For just at that moment, three of the white-clad monks had brought in bowls of pottage—an oat stew mixed with peas and beans, presumably from the abbey's own garden. It was somewhat ascetic fare, particularly compared with the meals at Arthur's court, but it was a welcome sight after two days in the saddle. Still, as the six of us fell to our supper, I shook my head in silent puzzlement over the appeal of this strange quest.

I caught Meliagaunt's eye, and though his face remained impassive, he shook his head as well, and told me in a low, gravelly voice, "When he gets something in his head, he sticks with it. There's no reasoning with him. Believe me, I've tried."

We continued to dine in silence, the monks having left us alone, until the silence was broken from an unexpected source. "It is true that God does not need us," Sir Galahad was saying, so quietly and calmly that for a moment I didn't even realize he was speaking. "But He wants us. He wants us to glorify Him, to show all the world His glory. To perform this quest is to work for the greater glory of God." He had replaced his wonted distant stare with a concentrated gaze into my face. His piercing eyes looked straight into my soul, it seemed, as he softly made his case.

"But why?" Sir Gareth asked, not completely buying into Galahad's frame. "Why does this glorification of God need to be performed by knights in arms? Does jousting really advance the glory of God? Look at Sir Palomides and Sir Safer. They were among those very few knights of the table who did not stand and vow to go on this quest."

Sir Galahad clearly did not know what point Gareth was trying to make. He looked puzzled—the first real expression I had seen on his face. "They are moors, are they not? Heretics?"

Gareth snorted, unable to hide his irritation. With a bit more control, he explained, "Sir Safer and Palomides were born in Moorish lands, that is true, and were among the Saracen army at Jerusalem when it was stormed by Sir Godfrey and his army. But they have been many years in Christian lands. Sir Palomides was baptized almost upon his arrival in Logres when he fell in love with La Belle Isolde, knowing she would not give her love to a Muhammadan. And Sir Safer followed him to the baptismal font quite recently, having seen the seriousness with which Sir Palomides took his faith."

"Then why did they not take the vow," Meliagaunt wanted to know, looking at his father, who was now sound asleep sitting up on his bench. "It seems to have been a madness that extended even to those who were not sitting around the table itself."

"Frankly," Sir Gareth confided, "it was Galahad's coat of arms there."

"The red cross?" Galahad asked, looking down at the surcoat he still wore over his armor, even here at rest, on which the cross was emblazoned, *gules*. "They *must* be pagans, if the sign of our Lord offends them."

Gareth shook his head vigorously. "Not so," he insisted. "It has naught to do with that. The red cross was the banner of the crusading army. I told you that Palomides and Safer were at Jerusalem. They saw their friends and comrades, as well as thousands of Jews within the city, gathered for safety within their temple, put to the sword, even though they were unarmed. Sir Safer and Sir Palomides could not bring themselves to go questing, even for the most sacred of all relics, if it was under the banner of the crusaders. They felt that their honor demanded they forego that quest."

"A Christian army would not have done those things," Sir Galahad responded.

"They were there!" Sir Gareth asserted. "Were you?"

"I was not yet born," Galahad answered, misunderstanding the rhetorical nature of the question. "Nevertheless, it could not have happened."

"You're saying they are lying?" Gareth wanted to know.

"I would not impugn their honor with such a statement," Galahad replied. "But their assertion can have no truth in it, however that must be explained."

Wow, I said to myself. Was it faith, stubbornness, or self-righteousness that made Galahad what he was? But Gareth, unfazed, continued. "My point is that Sir Palomides and Sir Safer have decided, rather than pursue the Grail on a quest in arms, seeking to do battle in order to uncover the Grail's whereabouts, to seek it instead as pilgrims. They have laid aside their arms, taken up pilgrim's staffs, and set forth on foot to perform what in their old religion they called a *hajj*."

"Commendable," Sir Galahad admitted. "A pilgrimage to a holy site—or to visit a holy relic—shows proper reverence for our Lord. Still, I maintain that it does not glorify Him in the way our quest shall."

"I won't argue with you," Gareth conceded. "I'll just leave it, as I must, to God Himself to decide what most pleases Him."

"I'm sure he's already decided," Sir Galahad finished, without a trace of irony.

"Well," Sir Ywain contributed, "we have a chance to test these opinions right here at this monastery, and as soon as tomorrow."

"Why, what do you mean?" Gareth asked him.

"When I first arrived, the monks told me that there was a shield housed within this monastery that seems to be cursed. They say that no man has ever borne the shield who was not severely wounded or killed within three days."

Sir Gareth looked puzzled. "Well, I've got two questions, then. In the first place, why would they keep this unlucky shield here in the abbey; and second, what does this have to do with what we were talking about?"

"It is relevant," Sir Galahad answered for Ywain. "For do you not see? Such a shield is intended as a sign: only a knight whose quest is favored by God would be able to bear such a shield. Clearly that is why none has yet been able to bear it in health—those who bore it before did not have our quest or purpose. The monks here no doubt have worked this out themselves, for why else would they keep an item with such a disastrous history around?"

"Yes," Ywain agreed. "That is essentially what the monks intimated to me when they told me of it."

"Well, that's one way of looking at it I suppose," Gareth responded. 'But isn't it just as likely—and frankly, I would consider it a lot *more* likely—that the men who bore this particular shield were not particularly good knights, and that they were outmanned by their opponents, and that anyone who comes along who is in fact a knight of some ability would not have the same bad luck? Which is to say that luck has nothing to do with it at all, and I suspect neither does God. A good knight will use a shield well. An unskilled one will be beaten."

"You may believe what you will," Galahad replied lightly. "But I consider this first adventure to be significant in this quest for the glory of God."

"Then this adventure shall be mine!" exclaimed King Bagdemagus, who had woken up at just the right time. "I shall take that shield and I shall wield it for the glory of God! This I swear!"

"But Father," Meliagaunt cautioned him. "If there is anything to what is being said about the history of this shield, it could be dangerous, especially for a man of your age…"

"My age?" Bagdemagus bellowed, his round cheeks glowing red with ire and his white beard shaking. He worked his flabby jaw as if he were chewing on the matter and snapped, "I'm still a better knight than half the young upstarts I see around me. And my purpose is purer. I came on this quest—the last one of my life—to do something, not to sit and watch others accomplish great feats. If I can bear the shield and glorify God in that way, then I will do so! If not, well, one of you young twerps can try it after me. But I'm going to try it first. Now I need to get some sleep, especially if I'm going to be put to the test in the morning with this shield business." And the king rose up and claimed one of the tables, where he had Meliagaunt begin setting out a bedroll for him, while he started pulling off his traveling clothes. Gareth and I certainly were ready to follow suit, and I assumed I would sleep on one of the benches while my master took one of the tables. As we prepared to bed down, Gareth muttered, "Could somebody please explain to me, how on earth Bagdemagus bearing a shield without getting himself killed glorifies God in any way? It's madness, Gildas, Madness."

Since Gareth had spoken *sotto voce*, so that only I could hear him, I responded in the same manner. "At his age, I think that even being able to lift a shield may be a testament to divine miracles." Gareth snickered quietly and turned over, pulling a blanket around him. I did the same, rolling the other way—and falling right off the narrow bench, bumping my nose sharply on the stone floor. "Ouch!" I complained. Then whispered to Sir Gareth, "That may well have been God's punishment for my flippancy. I'm going to shut up now and go to sleep.' And with that I rolled over again, and, exhausted from those two days of solid riding through the rain, fell asleep wrapped in a blanket on the floor of the refectory.

***

The bells of the abbey were tolling prime when the monks came to the refectory to wake us. They were about to sing the morning Mass and they would need the dining hall for their breakfast afterwards. I got up and stretched, and found that sleeping on a stone floor can give you some really stiff joints in the morning. But I pulled on my clothes, rolled up my blanket, and stuffed it in a pocket of my cloak. We filed out of the building and headed for the small church off the cloister, in order to hear Mass. After all, if we were on a quest for the holiest of relics, we ought to act as if we were faithful devotees of the church. Actually it was Galahad, of course, who led the way without a word, and the rest of us, silently understanding his intent, followed him into the sanctuary.

There was something moving about hearing the Mass sung in that modest church by that small contingent of monks. There wasn't a huge sound from that choir, only a small and sincere one, and the voices were not world-class tenors or basses, but only the honest expressions of faith by everyday men who had given up everything else in their lives to devote them to God. And I could understand a little more of what Sir Galahad was feeling, though like Sir Gareth, I saw the monks' manner of praising God more genuine and earnest than what could be seen as the knights' more self-aggrandizing approach. I couldn't help thinking that this quest reminded me, in a strange way, of Sir Gawain's pact with the Green Knight. It had to do with shadowy, questionable notions of honor and glory. In the long run, if no one was being served, then what was the point of honor? That it may make you feel good for having done something that benefited no one in the world, not even yourself? Shouldn't real honor and glory come in what we do for others? That was what the Pentecost oath was all about. That was the oath that these monks took too, wasn't it? Not for the first time since losing my Rosemounde to her beast of a husband, I thought about chucking the whole chivalry thing and joining the monks for a life of denial and self-sacrifice. After losing Rosemounde, I had nothing else that I cared about discarding anyway. But then she had told me…begged me…to pursue knighthood for her sake. Much as I might be drawn to the cloistered life, I could not deny my lady Rosemounde anything. Even if she would never be mine.

At the end of the Mass, King Bagdemagus rose quickly and, huffing with the exertion of kneeling and rising again so quickly, he waddled over to the abbot and inclined his head respectfully.

"My lord Abbot," he began. "Uh…brother…?"

"Lawrence," responded the thin-faced monk with the beaklike nose and piercing hazel eyes. He did not smile. His cheekbones protruded like outcroppings of rock on the face of a cliff.

"Well Brother Lawrence," Bagdemagus continued still breathing hard, "we've been given to understand that you have in this abbey a shield, one that seems to have a kind of fate attached to it, whereby anyone wearing the shield is killed or maimed within three days. It seems to us, therefore," and with that he looked around, as if he were speaking for the entire fellowship of the Round Table, "that the shield is destined for a great knight who comes with noble purpose. Since we have all taken upon ourselves the glorious and sacred quest of the Holy Grail, we believe that this shield may well be destined for one of us. And so, Brother Lawrence, I present myself as a candidate to possess the shield. In other words, dash it, I'm proposing to bear the shield. Is it you I should be addressing?" The king ended on a bit of a note of uncertainty, since the abbot had neither spoken nor moved his eyes from Bagdemagus's own.

Finally Brother Lawrence answered. "What you say is true. The shield is here. How are we to know, though, that you are the knight destined to bear it?"

It was Galahad who answered. "Just let him carry the shield. If he is not the destined knight, you will know within three days. He will be either dead or sorely wounded." King Bagdemagus looked around at Galahad, his eyes popping out of his face. He had not really thought about it in those terms, and now seemed even less confident. But he was a knight of the Round Table, by God, and he shook off any doubts and carried on.

"The shield is here," Brother Lawrence gestured to the altar. He stepped to the front of the church and, reaching behind the altar, pulled out a triangular jousting-style shield of the sort intended for a knight on horseback. It was made of sturdy wood covered with a layer of leather and then topped with a thin layer of bronze. It was painted white and, much to our surprise, bore the symbol of a red cross. "Yes," the abbot held the shield out to look at it one last time before handing it over to King Bagdemagus. "We believe it must originally have been some crusader's shield. But I yield it to you, sir," he now held it out toward the king. "I pray you prove to be its destined bearer. For if you are not, I fear you will not fare well with it."

By this time I was more certain than ever that King Bagdemagus was making a huge mistake, and would have told him so, had not Sir Ywain anticipated me.

"Ah, King, can't you see for yourself this is foolishness?" he growled, shaking his shaggy mane. "If there's anything to this notion that there is a destiny around this shield, can't you see that the red cross makes it clear this shield was intended for young Galahad here? It's like they knew he was coming. And look, you know he has no shield. Wasn't this meant for him?"

I had forgotten that Galahad, after drawing his sword from the stone, was still shieldless, as King Arthur had noted at the time. And I began to wonder to myself. This all seemed like too much of a coincidence. Still, King Bagdemagus would not budge.

"What you say may be true," he conceded. "But I have made a vow and will carry it out. By your leave, sir," he nodded to Sir Galahad, "I will take this adventure. If I fail, I leave it to you to complete this challenge."

And with that, Bagdemagus took the strap of the shield, the *guige*, and slung it over his shoulder and left the church, calling out loudly for Meliagaunt to saddle his horse. The squire, looking down with some concern, stepped briskly after him.

I looked at Sir Gareth, who raised his eyebrows and glanced at Sir Ywain, who shrugged. I said, "Well, if I were King Bagdemagus, I would have had breakfast first." Gareth and Ywain chuckled, and Galahad said, "Proper nourishment is important." But then he added, "But of course, man does not live on bread alone. If he is nourished by the spirit of God in his quest, King Bagdemagus will have strength enough."

I was pretty sure that at Bagdemagus's age, he was not going to have strength enough for this adventure no matter how many gods were propping him up. But I wasn't going to argue with the pure knight. Most immediately I was in need of some food, and said so, so the four of us stepped into the cloister to make our way back to the refectory, where the monks were already breaking their fast with a small meal of rye bread and cheese. The tables being full, we stood quietly along the back wall, waiting to sit when we could to partake of whatever fare they may be able to share with us.

As the monks ate in silence, one of the brothers, I believe it was the prior, stood at a lectern in the front of the room and read aloud from a Latin book of saints' lives. The monks did not like to waste time in idleness when they could be learning something, and today's lesson concerned the good Saint Ephrem, whose feast day this was. Now of course at the time I had never heard of Saint Ephrem, but as far as I could make out, with the scattering of Latin I understood at the time, Ephrem was a teacher and a deacon in the church who affected madness to avoid being made a priest. How that qualified him for sainthood I wasn't quite sure, but apparently Ephrem lived in a cave above the city of Edessa in Syria and did a lot of writing, especially defending the orthodox church against the many heresies of his day—which was, as near as I could figure, some three-quarters of a millennium earlier. It was all a bit hazy to me until the very end of the lesson, when the prior talked about the many songs Ephrem had written. I remembered the music of the Mass I had just heard, and understood why someone who could bring that kind of pure cerebral beauty into the worship of the creator of all harmonies should be celebrated with a saint's day in the church calendar. The prior ended by quoting lines from Saint Ephrem's *Testament*:

> Lay me not with sweet spices,
> For this honor avails me not,
> Nor yet use incense and perfumes,
> For the honor befits me not.
>
> • • •
>
> Give ye your incense to God,
> And over me send up hymns.
> Instead of perfumes and spices…

For me, the whole lesson seemed to underscore the reactions I had been having since this quest began. The true saints, people like Ephrem, were not seeking honor and glory—they needed no incense at their burial. If they honored God it was through the lessons they taught and the songs they wrote, things that were passed on to others, rather than those that gained worship for themselves.

The lesson over, the dozen monks did not linger, for they all had work to get to, whether in the gardens or in the scriptorium, and one by one they cleared away their dishes and passed out of the refectory. A portion of a loaf of dark bread and a wedge of yellow cheese remained on one of the tables, and the prior nodded to us and gestured to the table, as if to say we were welcome to what was left.

We needed no second invitation, and pulled up the benches quickly to share the bread and cheese. "It's too bad," Ywain began, breaking the silence that the presence of the monks had seemed to impose on the room. "Galahad, too bad the king claimed that shield, and you the only knight to set out from Camelot without one."

"It's no great matter," Galahad replied, chewing and swallowing carefully, and reaching up as one of the monks brought in a tray bearing four cups of ale for our breakfast. Taking a large swallow, he continued, "If I am not destined to have this shield, God will provide another." By now I was getting used to that way of his, and so was less annoyed than I had been at first.

"Will you wait here at the abbey, then, for Bagdemagus?" Sir Gareth asked Galahad. "If he fails, the shield will indeed be yours after all."

"I shall wait for three days," Galahad said with finality. "No longer. If King Bagdemagus fails, he will do so within that time. If he does not, I cannot wait any longer to continue this quest. I feel there is a kind of urgency about it: I have felt since the beginning that the Grail has a destiny of its own that gives us only a small window to achieve it before it is taken from this land."

"What," Gareth said, puzzled. "You mean someone is coming from foreign lands to steal it from Logres?"

Galahad shrugged. "I know no more than what I have said." And with that he was silent again, and went on eating.

"Well I won't be staying," Ywain said with certainty. "I told Thomas to ride quickly to Lady Alundine's castle, and tell her I would be home straightaway. I want to spend a day with my wife before I go prancing around after this relic anymore. And I want to pick up my lion to bring along with me."

Gareth grinned. "Well, if anybody is coming to steal our Grail, your lion will give them second thoughts!"

"The Lion of Judah," Galahad said quietly.

At that moment our peace was shattered when Meliagaunt burst abruptly into the room. He was panting and bent over to relieve the strain of apparently having run from the courtyard. It had been less than an hour since he had left with King Bagdemagus, so we were all somewhat bewildered to see him back. But we didn't have any time to think about it.

"Come quickly, please!" the young squire pleaded. "He's

destroyed—I fear he's dying…"

We bolted through the door and down the cloister, hustling after the racing Meliagaunt. In the courtyard, Bagdemagus was slung over his horse, blood streaming from a substantial wound in his chest. By the time we arrived, the abbot and two other monks were examining him. Meliagaunt and I gently slid him from the horse to lie on his back in the dust, while Meliagaunt began to remove the king's armor as quickly as he was able. We had to sit him up to take off the mail, and when we did, the oldest of the monks, who I assumed must be their infirmarian and herbalist, gave a subdued gasp when he saw the gaping chest wound. Someone had driven a lance well into the king's chest. The wound was high up, and I could hope for that reason that it had missed the old man's heart and lungs—for if it hadn't, he would certainly die.

"We must get him to the infirmary quickly," the old monk ordered, and Ywain stepped forward to take Bagdemagus's arms while I grabbed hold of his legs and we followed the monks to a small building just north of the cloister and church. A visibly shaken Meliagaunt and a comforting Sir Gareth walked behind.

"How on earth did this happen?" Gareth was asking. "You had scarcely left the abbey…"

"So true," Meliagaunt replied with a grim, gravelly laugh. "We had gone barely two miles when we entered a fair valley, and ahead we saw what looked like a hermitage—a small hut where we assumed some holy man must live. But it proved to be far more sinister, for quite suddenly from behind the hut a knight appeared, on a white horse and dressed in pure white armor, and he began to charge us, his lance proffered as if to strike my father from off his horse. I handed the king his own lance and, grasping it in hand he laughed and said, 'Now we'll see some action!' But he really didn't see much. He spurred his horse forward, but his lance broke on the white knight's shield, and that knight's lance broke through my father's mail and knocked him clear off of his horse, so that he ended up unconscious on the ground.

"The white knight grabbed the shield from where my father had dropped it when he was felled, and he handed it to me, all the time lecturing Bagdemagus, as if he could hear anything lying there half-dead."

"Lecturing him? What was he saying?" Sir Ywain asked.

"Oh, about what you'd expect: 'You, knight, have done a foolish thing. That shield was intended only for the one knight without peer in all the world!' And then he looked at me and said, 'Take the shield to Sir Galahad. He will know what to do with it.' And he made to ride off, but I asked him who he was, and he refused to tell me—just said that I had no need to know his name, and that it must remain unknown to all earthly men. And then, like an afterthought, he said, 'And tell your colleagues that in this holy quest of the Grail, they are to bring no women with them, nor are they to engage in any carnal pleasures, for this is a holy quest and must be undertaken in the utmost purity!' And off he rides."

"Hmmph," Ywain scoffed. "Well, all I can say is, the lady Alundine will get all of my attentions tonight, priggish white knight or no priggish white knight."

Sir Gareth broke in with some concern. "But did you recognize this white knight? Who was he? What business does he have setting up rules for this quest?"

Meliagaunt shook his head distractedly. By now we were in the small hall that the monks used as an infirmary, and we laid the unconscious Bagdemagus down on the bed. The old monk—Brother Luke they called him—was busy at some shelves against the wall, where he was grabbing a handful of various herbs and potions, and so Meliagaunt stood at his father's head, stroking his white hair with a tender hand. "No. I don't know. He had his visor down the entire time. He did mention Brother Nascien…said that Nascien had made this rule about keeping pure and keeping away from women and all…" he trailed off, his eyes filling with tears as he hovered over his father, now gripping his limp left hand.

"A rule that I will honor with complete disregard as quickly as I am able," Sir Ywain asserted, and looked around at the rest of us, nodding his head in all seriousness.

CHAPTER SIX

THE TALE OF SIR BALIN

Sir Ywain had left that same day, following almost immediately upon our settling King Bagdemagus into the infirmary. Nor had Sir Galahad waited around much longer but, armed with his newly acquired shield, bid us farewell and rode off, determined to find the Grail. Sir Gareth, however, was in less of a hurry, and thought it might be a good use of our time to keep poor Meliagaunt company, and to wait at Saint Sebastian's at least until we could be fairly certain, one way or another, of whether Bagdemagus would die of his wounds.

It had been three days now, and the king had regained consciousness, though he was in and out of his senses. Brother Luke was now confident that the point of the lance had missed Bagdemagus's heart, and probably his lungs as well. We were hopeful, then, that he would not die directly of the wound, but the greatest danger now was that the wound would fester and the flesh decay, and kill the king after all. The infirmarian had employed a treatment I had never seen. He claimed to have learned it from Moorish physicians in his early years when he was a crusader: he had placed a handful of maggots in the wound and then bandaged it tightly, with cloths wrapped snugly around Bagdemagus's chest. The maggots, he said, would eat away decayed flesh, and prevent festering. If they worked their magic, the king would yet live.

I sat on a stool in the infirmary next to King Bagdemagus's bed, the late afternoon sun streaming in the window. It made the room one of the cheeriest in all Saint Sebastian's abbey, and that was important. Illness and injury were made more tolerable, if only slightly, by the promise of bright sunshine when that was possible. I was spelling Meliagaunt, who for the past two days had seemed a ragged husk of a man as he fretted constantly over his father's condition. I had volunteered to sit with the king for a few hours while the overburdened squire got some badly-needed rest. But the king was in and out of lucidity. The fall and perhaps his injury had rattled his mind, it seemed, so that we were not always sure when he spoke whether he was addressing us, or someone fifty years in the past. As I sat with him he was slurring his speech and talking about things I could not relate to at all. "Don't be so stubborn, you fool," he was mumbling just now.

"Was I being stubborn?" I asked, humoring him as best I could, though I had no idea where his mind was, or when he thought he was speaking, and to whom.

"Just give her the sword," the king went on.

"But it's my sword," I tried. "Who is it you want me to give the sword to?"

"The lady, of course, She's the one who wants it." His voice was less slurred now, but he still was making no sense to me.

"Ah," I said, trying to get him to be more explicit, so that I could better converse with him, and perhaps bring him into a real conversation instead of crying out random pieces of memory. "Which lady was that again?"

"The lady Lily of Avalon, who do you think, dunce!" Bagdemagus responded. His eyes remained half closed, but his irritation made him a bit livelier.

"So who is it that won't give her back the sword, then?" I asked, trying to draw him into a connected narrative and so, I hoped, into coherence.

"Balin. Sir Balin le Savage, the Knight with the Two Swords. One of the greatest knights, but one of the most uncontrollable."

"Sir Balin?" My ears perked up with real interest. "The one whose sword Sir Galahad plucked from the floating stone?"

"Who? Stone? No, Balin had drawn the sword from the lady's

scabbard," Bagdemagus corrected me and I realized I had gone too far. Let's go back and start from the beginning, I thought.

"This Sir Balin," I began. "How did he come to be at Camelot?"

Bagdemagus heaved a sigh and seemed to shut down, but then I realized he had been gathering his wits and focusing on his memories of Balin le Savage. "You know, it's a funny thing. King Pelles had been an ally of King Lot when Arthur defeated the rebel kings. I joined Arthur's side, but Pelles was vanquished with Lot, and was supposed to pay tribute to Arthur." I rolled my eyes, thinking the king had gone off on a completely new tangent, but it turned out he was just making a connection. "Arthur sent Sir Brumand, one of his greatest knights, to King Pelles to try to collect the tribute from him." Bagdemagus stopped to catch his breath. He was gathering strength now and warming to the story.

"Well, on the way back, with Pelles' promise that he would pay the tribute within a month, Sir Brumand ran into two unknown knights, wearing no coats of arms and bearing pure white shields. They were set up on the road a half mile from Camelot and were challenging all comers to jousts. Brumand, of course, could not pass up this kind of contest, and immediately armed himself and took on the knights, one at a time. Both the disguised knights felled Brumand on the first pass. So Brumand was quite impressed—he hadn't been so easily defeated before—and he conversed with the knights in friendly fashion, though they refused to reveal their identities to him. Brumand begged their leave to return to Camelot and to inform King Arthur of these events, and the duo agreed, since this was in fact their whole purpose for parking out there in the first place."

The king gave a few little coughs, then stretched slightly, winced with the pain, and continued his story a little more quietly: "When Arthur heard about the knights and their challenge, he issued orders to all the court that no one was to go out to meet these knights in combat unless they first gained the king's express permission, and having ensured that he wouldn't be disturbed, Arthur armed himself in some old, castoff armor, and took up an unmarked shield. He took an unremarkable destrier from the stable and rode forth, visor down, to meet the pair of knights in this disguise. You must remember that this was nearly a quarter of a century ago, and Arthur was still in his chivalric prime. He wanted to test himself against these upstarts who had felled Sir Brumand." I nodded and the king shifted position again and motioned for a sip of water, a cup of which Brother Luke had left next to the chair in the room. After a few cautious swigs, Bagdemagus went on.

"So when Arthur rode up to the two anonymous knights, they challenged *him* as well. Arthur wouldn't tell them his name either—sauce for the goose is sauce for the gander, eh?—but he asked them why they were doing this, and they told him they were trying to discredit the knights of the Round Table because of some personal grievance one of them had. That's all Arthur needed to hear: He was so angry at these upstarts trying to demean his knights that he took them both on at once, and knocked them both from their horses. That pretty much made a mockery of their campaign to show up Arthur's court."

"So," I said, still waiting for the point. "And one of those knights was Sir Balin?"

"Sir Balin? Of course. And his twin brother Balan. When the king had defeated them, they stood up and took off their helmets, and identified themselves: Balin and Balan of Northumbria. Arthur actually recognized Sir Balin from having seen him at court briefly a few years past. When Arthur took off his own helmet and the brothers saw who it was, they fell to their knees and bowed their heads. Balin, a ruddy knight with long brown hair and intense green eyes, burst out with the defense that, having been exiled from the court by Sir Kay two years before for having struck one of Arthur' servants, he had vowed revenge on all Arthur' knights, for Sir Kay's sake.

"The king was somewhat baffled. 'I must say, that consequence seems just to me, due to your lack of courtesy. To blame all my knights for it seems excessive.'

"At that word Sir Balan piped up. He was more soft-spoken and tactful than his mercurial brother, and tried to smooth the king's ruffled feathers. 'We were really trying to lure Sir Kay out, knowing that he can't resist this kind of challenge. If my brother had been able to unhorse Sir Kay, I think he would have been assuaged.'

"'And why do you need to be assuaged, sir?' The king addressed Balin. 'Your courtesy should be subject to the will of your liege lord that you behave peacefully and compassionately to your fellow knights and to widows, orphans, and the disadvantaged.'

"'My lord,' Balin stammered, 'I have always had difficulty controlling…'

"'From youth he has been subject to fits of melancholy,' Balan broke in. 'I must tell you, my Liege, that as children my brother and I were among those orphans of which you speak. Our father, a wealthy franklin, had been murdered for his land by a very wicked lady called Lily of Avalon. As a member of the noble class, she was immune from prosecution under your father, King Uther, and so we could do nothing about it. Our mother died of grief the following year, and we were left destitute at the age of nine. That was when I first began to notice and deal with the dark moods of my brother.'

"'But how did you become knights?' Arthur wanted to know.

"'King Ban of Benwick,' Balin answered. 'We stowed away on a ship that sailed across the narrow sea when we were eleven, hoping to find a new life in France. King Ban caught us poaching game in his forest one day and took pity on our story, and made us pages. We grew into knights in his court, and then set out for Logres in the hope of joining the Table Round.'

"'And yet now you are trying to *discredit* my Table!' Arthur protested, not without the hint of a wry smile." Bagdemagus stopped, wheezing a bit. He had been going on for some time, and he was clearly now in his perfect senses. Whatever the condition of his chest, his mind seemed to have regained its proper function.

"So Sir Balan explained to the king: 'Sir Balin's melancholy is sometimes dangerous. It was all I could do to keep him from doing violence to himself—as I have often had to prevent in the past. This challenge seemed less dangerous, and I hoped to spend his violence in some healthier direction.'

"King Arthur thought for a moment, bowing his head and weighing the decision before he pronounced it. 'Rise, Sir Balin and Sir Balan,' he began, and as they did so, he went on. 'You have shown yourself to be doughty knights, defeating several of my court with your challenge here. You also have the good will, I understand, of my close ally King Ban. And I have two empty seats currently at the Round Table. I invite you to join my order of knights, and we will swear you in at the Pentecost celebration this summer—with this one caveat: Sir Balin must learn to control his melancholy and his violent tendencies. He must learn the meaning of courtesy as practiced among the Knights of the Round Table. I give you two directives here. First, Balin, you must focus on a knight of the court who seems to be the paragon of chivalry and courtesy, and model your behavior upon him. And I believe that the best possible model you can have is Sir Lancelot, greatest of my knights and son of your benefactor, King Ban of Benwick.'

"'Ah,' Sir Balan remarked. 'We knew him, of course, very briefly from Ban's household, though most of the time we were there he was being fostered elsewhere.'

"'But to model my life on the offspring of that paragon, King Ban, is for me an honor and a privilege. I shall certainly do this, my lord King.' Balin bowed low. 'And what is the second condition, oh my Liege?'

"'This second is only a suggestion,' Arthur began, and actually, I was told later by Balan, seemed to blush as he said it. 'Many of the knights find that devoting their love and service to a lady of the court encourages them to behave as gentlemen in all social exchanges, and to act as chivalrous knights on the field for her sake, not wishing to look bad or weak or boorish in their ladies' eyes. I think this is a healthy and a civilizing practice, and I encourage both you, Balan, and your brother to emulate the other knights and choose a noble lady to admire. From afar, that is. Until you have done such feats of chivalry and behaved with such courtesy that you will deserve her.'"

I let the king stop for breath, and then asked him, "So, did Sir Balin follow the king's advice when he returned to Camelot?"

"Oh yes," King Bagdemagus grunted, shifting a bit in the bed to relieve a little of the discomfort in his chest—and, I should think, the itching as well. I couldn't keep my mind off of the maggots that were under that great swath of bandage. "Sir Balin patterned his every move on those of Sir Lancelot, and learned patience and courtesy in the bargain. He recognized that the Great Knight had no peer, and he dreamed of becoming a second Lancelot in Arthur's court. As for a lady, he chose the one noble woman in court he could never hope to have physically—Arthur's beautiful young queen, Guinevere. She was unattainable and he knew it, which he felt made his love the more pure, and he strove to appear noble in her sight. Furthermore, Sir Brumand's regard for the two brothers blossomed into a warm friendship, and along with Brumand's cousin Sir Nascien, the four of them were as close as the fingers on your right hand, with the thumb being maybe Brumand's faithful squire, Grunamund. At Pentecost Balin and Balan were inducted into the order of the Table. And Balin had no more of his dark moods and so the brothers lived contented and comfortable in Camelot for the next year, with Sir Balin's reputation as one of the great knights continually on the rise."

"Wait now," I said, my ears tingling as the king panted a bit to catch his breath. "Did I hear you say Sir Nascien? This is the same Brother Nascien that brought Sir Galahad to court?"

The king looked bewildered for a moment, but then his face lighted up. "Of course!" he cried. "I knew I had seen that monk somewhere before. Yes—he was obviously a lot younger then. But of course, so was I, what? Heh, heh. Yes. Nascien had been in King Uther's employ. He had pretty much given up arms when Arthur became king, but he lived with his cousin Brumand, who was a knight of the Table, and so was part of that little knot of camaraderie they had with the twins. How odd that he should turn up here now, after all these years. I remember once when I..."

"But Sir Balin, my lord," I steered him back to the topic at hand. He was making sense now, and I didn't want him going off on a tangent again.

"Yes, Sir Balin."

"And the queen? And Lancelot?"

"Oh, that," Bagdemagus sounded chagrined at what he was about to reveal. "Well, so taken was Balin with the queen that he bore a token of hers on his shield, and all the knights knew of his reverence for her. And so fervent was his hero-worship of Lancelot that his other friends, Brumand especially, became somewhat annoyed by it.

But Balin was able to control his depression and his episodes of rage with great facility as long as he maintained his emulation of those models of behavior. That is why it was such a tragedy that one day, having followed Lancelot at a distance to see what he was about, Balin observed the Great Knight and the young queen meeting alone in a grove outside the castle. He thought it was strange until he saw Lancelot take her into his arms and kiss her tender mouth. In one gesture, both pillars of Balin's world crumbled to the earth."

I blanched. I had not thought the queen's affair had been common knowledge, and certainly not for so long a time. Bagdemagus, panting on his bed, shrugged as best he could from his prone position. "I will not say that there was anything to Balin's suspicions. Such things are not for me to speculate about."

"So how did Balin react to that?"

"It threw him into a deep gloom," Bagdemagus answered. "And the rage burned within him like a glowing coal. To make matters worse, this occurred just when his brother Balan was away from Camelot, off on some task the king had assigned him to. It was unfortunate that it was just at that point that the woman came to Camelot."

"What woman was this?" I asked him.

"She said she was an emissary of the Lady of the Lake, but I'm sure that was not true. I suspected at the time, and still do, that the king's sister, Morgan le Fay, had brought her to court, to stir things up to make the new queen uncomfortable. It was no secret that Morgan resented Guinevere and would have had her gone if she could. Well during a feast, I forget which one, this woman came into Arthur's court with a challenge. She wore a floor-length ermine coat of great beauty, and her blonde hair flowed free with only a gold circlet around her brow containing it. When all eyes were on her she unfastened the coat and let it fall to the floor, and the whole court gave a gasp. She wore only a tightly fitting garment of white silk that left little to the imagination of those chaste knights sitting at table in the great hall. Around her waist was a belt and scabbard that held a bejeweled sword."

"The sword in the stone that Galahad drew!" I blurted.

"The same. Well this woman pronounced a challenge to all the court: 'Approach me, knights of the Round Table,' she invited. 'Pull this sword from its scabbard! But I warn you, if you are not the best knight in the world, then the sword will bring you ill luck. Come! Who is brave enough to face my test?' What she expected I don't think anybody realized at the time. I remember watching Morgan le Fay's eyes glow, though, and I put it together later that she wanted Lancelot to draw that sword. It was her way of discomforting the queen, you see—have Lancelot approach that barely clad woman before the whole court. She was conniving that way, you understand. She thought she could sow a good deal of discord between the queen and the Great Knight. But Lancelot would have nothing to do with it. All eyes went to him when she declared that it must be the greatest knight of all who drew the sword. But Lancelot could smell a trap when he found one, and merely looked around the room to see who else might be persuaded to take the bait. Well that's when Balin had had enough. In his bitter mood he muttered something like 'coward!' at Lancelot, and stepped up himself, thinking nothing of approaching the scantily-clad lady. He grasped the sword and pulled it from the scabbard, and admired its newly forged blade and the jewels in its hilt. But the damsel—and Morgan—would have none of it. This was not going as planned. 'Give that back!' says the lady. 'You offered, I've drawn it, it's mine,' says Balin.

"But it was Lancelot they wanted to catch in their web, so Balin was ruining their plot. Sir Brumand tried to calm things—he told Balin, look, you've got a good sword already, what do you need that one for? You want to be the knight with the two swords? And Balin smiled and said yes, that's just how he wanted to be known. And finally the damsel issued a warning: 'That sword will only bring you sorrow,' she said. 'If you keep it, you will only use it to harm the friend you love most in all the world.' But Balin only sneered, saying he'd take his chances.

"Then the worst happened. The damsel, now in a state of fury, turned to the king and said, 'I demand, Sire, that you force this knight to return my sword to me! Otherwise I will let it be known throughout Logres that you did not do justice to the lady Lily of Avalon when she appealed to you before your entire court!'

"Well at the name the melancholy Balin turned choleric. This was she—this was the woman who had stolen his ancestral lands and destroyed his parents, leaving him an orphan and a beggar. And fate had brought her into his hands at this moment in time. So while the king was still clearing his throat, Balin's rage burst forth, and with a single wide sweep of the sword he beheaded the lady then and there. The knights were paralyzed with shock. Guinevere screamed and actually fainted with horror. I saw Morgan smirk—she seemed pleased now at the direction the little charade had taken."

I could feel my mouth hanging open until I finally remembered to use it. "Good Lord! What did Arthur do?"

"Well Lancelot moved first. He had his sword out and was holding Balin at bay appealing to the king to decide the knight's fate. 'She slew my father and stole his land!' Balin snarled, and he was clearly ready to take his own life in his hands by fighting with Lancelot. 'But this violence is prohibited in the presence of the king!' Lancelot shouted back. 'Remember your courtesy, sir! Your courtesy!'

"'*My* courtesy, knight? And what of your own?' was Balin's response, to which Lancelot screwed up his face in puzzlement, since of course he had no idea what Balin was referring to. But he looked to the king, and said, 'My lord, what shall be done with a knight who has committed murder in your royal presence? The old law condemned such felons to death. Is that your will in this case?'

"But Arthur, who was of the opinion that the remedy for the death of one person was never simply the death of another, shook his head. Still, he addressed angry words at Balin: 'Sir Balin, I advised you some months ago that you must curb your dark moods and control your anger. Is this the result of my good advice?'

"And Balin, with no small amount of cheek, answered, 'Your advice, my lord, was in the end not useful to me.' And with that he stuck his second sword into his belt. 'But on my honor—what there is left of it—I aver that this woman deserved death as one of the vilest villains in the kingdom. She stole my father's lands and left him no legal recourse, and drove him and my mother both to death. I defy any knight here to have held his temper under such provocation.'

"'Nevertheless,' the king answered, 'there are legal challenges you could have brought in my court, rather than dish out summary execution without a trial. For this offense, Sir Balin, I banish you from my court. You must leave Camelot and not return on pain of your life, until and unless I send word of a pardon. Now go, and avoid our sight.'

"Not having completely forgotten all courtesy, and grateful that the king had not taken Lancelot's suggestion and had him summarily put to death, Sir Balin inclined his head toward the king and spoke in a confident tone, 'Your Majesty, I take my leave at your command. When you do summon me back, ask for the Knight with the Two Swords. I fully intend to keep this sword,' and with that he held up the steel blade, now splattered with the lady Lily's blood. 'For it has pleased me more than any other weapon I have ever borne.' He touched it to his forehead in a kind of salute, turned his back on the king and strode out of the great hall, sticking the sword once more into his belt. He had soon cleared out his quarters, said his farewells to Sir Brumand and Sir Nascien, and Brumand's squire Grunamund, and collected his destrier from the stables. That was the last we saw of him."

King Bagdemagus stopped and lay back, his eyes closed now. His breathing was sporadic and he winced off and on as spasms of pain stabbed through his body from his chest wound. He seemed finished.

"So that's the end of the story?" I admit to being somewhat frustrated. "What about the curse on the sword? What about the wounding of King Pelles that we heard about? What happened to Balin? Did he see his brother Balan again?"

"I've told you what I knew and witnessed," the king spoke quietly, his eyes still closed. Very deliberately, he spun out the rest of the story. "I heard a number of things about what happened to him later, but I don't know all the details. I know that from Camelot he decided to go to Corbenic Castle to see King Pelles. Despite what that king had promised Sir Brumand, the tribute had never been paid. Turns out Pelles had given up ruling his kingdom and took on a kind of holy life, collecting holy relics and tracing his ancestry back to Joseph of Arimathea. He'd trusted the governance of his kingdom to his younger brother, Sir Garlon the Red, and Garlon had refused to pay the tribute. The last knight that Arthur had sent to collect it, one Sir Berbeus, had not returned to Camelot at all, and Arthur feared the worst.

"So Sir Balin decided he would go to and collect Arthur's tribute from Pelles, or Garlon, or whoever had control of the treasury in that place. Well as I heard it, when he got there, King Pelles welcomed him and bid him come and dine with his court, but during the meal this scoundrel Sir Garlon came close to him and whispered that he'd killed Sir Berbeus and impaled his head on a pike on the battlements of the castle, and planned to do the same with Balin despite what his cuckolded king and whore of a queen could do about it. Well nothing could have stilled Balin's rage after that, and as he had with the lady of Avalon in Arthur's court, so there at Corbenic he drew that new sword of his and, before he could blink, had cut off Sir Garlon's head as well. King Pelles saw the whole thing and grew enraged himself. His brother may have been a bastard, but it was his brother, damn it. Pelles grabbed a spear that was hanging on the wall and advanced toward Balin, who backed out of the room with his bloody sword, and so Pelles called his guard. They all started chasing Balin through the castle. Balin was cornered in a room off the great hall, and the king hurled the spear at him, but missed, and as he followed through Balin swung his sword upwards and caught Pelles in the crotch."

I paled and was nearly overcome with nausea at the thought. "You mean…"

"No more family jewels," Bagdemagus said, quite matter-of-factly. "In the confusion that followed Balin leaped from a window, grabbed a horse, and escaped from the castle. The guard pursued for some hours, but never caught up with Balin. The king never recovered from that wound completely. That was the dolorous stroke that maimed King Pelles to this day.

"But Balin was still in a dark mood as he rode through the wood, meandering back toward Camelot. This Garlon had chided him with an implication that fed his own doubts and besmirched the shattered images of his idols, Lancelot and the queen. He still bore Guinevere's token on his shield, but in a fit of rage tore it off. He wanted nothing on his arms that would connect him with the woman or the court that had disappointed him so deeply. And thus he rode without a token on his shield."

The king paused. He'd been speaking more and more slowly, and though he was now perfectly coherent, I could see how tired he was getting. But the story had been left hanging, and I was eager to know one more thing. "But my lord, you said that Sir Balin never came back to Camelot? Was he ever again reunited with his brother Balan? What became of him?"

"Ah, now *that's* the tragedy…" King Bagdemagus whispered, trailing off. His pause was so long I thought he had gone to sleep, and I felt like pulling my hair in frustration—I didn't have any idea what he meant by "that." Finally, he went on. "Sir Balin wandered aimlessly for weeks. He did not think he could return to Camelot, and was not sure, after what he saw as Lancelot's betrayal, that he would want to even if he could. His armor grew rusty from lack of care, his beard and hair unkempt, and he looked more like a wandering brigand than a knight of the Round Table. He took to calling himself Balin le Savage, for he saw himself as the embodiment of the wild forest, his own dark and tumultuous moods making him as untamed as any beast.

"Finally he came to a remote castle, and was met in the road by a knight in plain white armor, bearing a shield without any sign upon it. The anonymous knight insisted that no man can pass that way: He is the guardian of the castle, he says, and as its protector will not allow traffic within the castle's environs. Well, Balin was not going anywhere particularly, but his fiery personality would not brook any man telling him where he could and couldn't ride. And so the two knights, their visors closed and their shields unmarked, hurled themselves at one another. They fought viciously and without mercy for hours, each injuring the other several times, until both had been wounded mortally and they lay side by side on the turf. Sir Balin, his anger finally quashed, removed his helmet and showed his face, saying, 'Sir Knight, I am done for. You have fought like a demon, and you have slain me. Know that I am Sir Balin le Savage, the Knight with the Two Swords, and one-time member of the fellowship of the Round Table. Please take my sword and have it borne to King Arthur, and tell him how I met my end.'

"When the other knight removed his helmet, it was, of course, Sir Balan. 'Oh brother,' Balan answered. 'Why did you not identify yourself immediately? Someone else will have to bear your sword to the king, for your uncontrolled rage has done for me as well as yourself. I will not live through this day. I killed the guardian of this castle and was forced by their law to take his place, or I would have returned to Camelot long ago, and escaped this fate. A curse was on our house, brother. But it dies with us.' And within a few minutes, they both expired. They had been born together, and they died together, closed in one another's arms like lovers.

"And so they slept. And so" he said, rolling slightly away from me and his voice finally giving out, "so must I."

***

The story had struck a chord with me, even though I realized the king must have embellished it somewhat—how, for example, could he possibly know what Balin and Balan said to each other while they were dying? I stayed in the infirmary for another hour or so, sitting by his bed while King Bagdemagus slept. When Meliagaunt came in to relieve me, he asked if the king had been lucid at all. I told him indeed, the king seemed much improved, and, in fact, if this proved to be more than just a momentary rallying, that Sir Gareth and I would probably be leaving the abbey within the next few days to continue the quest. Meliagaunt nodded, but made one thing perfectly clear: "I and my father are done with this quest. When he is recovered enough, we return to our kingdom and abide there in peace. I want nothing more to do with the Round Table or its quests."

It seemed a rather extreme reaction to me, but I said nothing. Meliagaunt was free to do what seemed best to him, and good luck to him, I thought. My mind was preoccupied anyway with the story Bagdemagus had told of Sir Balin and his doomed life. So many things in the story resonated with the current quest that I needed some time to consider: King Bagdemagus himself had risked his life only for pride's sake, trying to claim a shield that he really did not need, when it was clear that Galahad should have had it. Didn't Balin do something similar? Why should he have kept that cursed sword when he did not need it? What other than vanity would make him want to be the Knight with the Two Swords? As for Galahad, the sword that he had pulled from the stone was the very sword that had been obtained by Balin in a similar manner, through a challenge at the court that no one else would take—not unlike Gawain's participation in the beheading game. And like the Green Knight, the lady Lily had been beheaded at court, much to the horror of the queen. Guinevere's discomfiture in Balin's case had so delighted Morgan le Fay that, it seems, she had designed the whole Green Knight scenario just to disturb the queen once again. King Pelles's claim to be descended from Joseph of Arimathea had caused him to connive to have Galahad born, whose fate, presumably, was supposed to be to attain the Grail—a relic so holy that its miraculous healing powers might help to heal the wound that Balin's cursed sword had caused. And that sword: How would the curse manifest itself on Sir Gawain? Or was the curse ended now that the pure knight had finally obtained it?

My head was spinning with these strands of parallel events as I paced the cloister, and finally I decided to go to see Sir Gareth, and to get his perspective on all of these connections. What did it all mean? Was there a destiny running through all of these events that linked Balin with the Green Knight and the Grail at the same time? I turned the corner into the refectory, where I assumed I would find Sir Gareth. Which I did, but to my surprise he was sitting across the table from his brother, Sir Gaheris, who had apparently just arrived, for he was still in the armor he had been wearing on horseback.

'Sir Gaheris!" I exclaimed, startled, then remembering my courtesy, I inclined my head slightly and said, "My lord, I'm surprised to see you. Are you well?" Gaheris and I had never been close in any way—perhaps it was my revulsion at the knowledge that he had killed his own mother a few years before upon finding her in bed with Sir Lamorak. Beheaded her, in fact. It seemed there was a lot of that going around. Still, he and Gareth were as close as anyone in that Orkney clan, and indeed Gaheris, with his blond hair and clear blue eyes, even looked like an older version of Gareth. Even now, they looked very much alike, but that may have been the expression of gloom and anxiety that clouded both of their faces as I entered the room. I stopped and looked at Gareth, holding my hands out at my sides in a gesture of befuddlement. "What is it my lord? Has something happened?"

"Sir Gaheris has just brought some very disturbing news," Gareth acknowledged. "Regarding Sir Gawain."

A fiery hand seemed to grasp the back of my neck, and I felt that a heavy stone had dropped into my stomach. Was this the prophecy of the sword coming true? What was it? That Gawain would suffer a stroke from the sword that would kill him, or severely wound him? "Has he…has Gawain…been hurt?" I stammered. "Has he been…"

Gareth shook his head somberly. "No," he responded. "No, he hasn't been hurt himself. But it seems that on his quest through the forest of Logres, he had the misfortune to come upon a knight who was attempting to rape a defenseless young damsel. Sir Gawain flew into a rage at the sight and beheaded the knight even as he was pinning the struggling maiden to the grass."

"Hmph," was my only reaction. "A villain was punished in the midst of his villainous deed. I don't see why this is such dire news. Gawain was doing what he should be doing as a knight of the Round Table: He was defending the weak and the powerless."

"Yes," Sir Gareth agreed. "But the knight he killed, it turns out, was actually Sir Ironside. The Red Knight of the Red Lands."

And a knight of the Table Round.

CHAPTER SEVEN

THE TALE OF SIR LIONEL

In a few days we were back in Camelot. Sir Gareth and Sir Gaheris had decided that, for Gawain's sake, they ought to be where they could have the king's ear as news of Gawain's transgression reached the court. If it could even be called a transgression. Certainly knights of the table, as sworn brothers in arms, were prohibited from destroying one another—particularly from slaying a fellow knight who was unarmed, as Sir Ironside most certainly had been, since he was otherwise engaged when Gawain came upon him. But it could be argued—and Gareth and Gaheris were certain to make the argument—that the whole Round Table was being shamed by the outrage Sir Ironside was committing. Certainly the girl herself, if she could be found again, would testify on Gawain's behalf.

On the other hand, this unfortunate slaying may be following too closely upon the ambush and murder of Sir Lamorak, an act Gawain had carried out purely for the sake of revenge on a knight he felt had wronged him and shamed his family by bedding his mother. Did two cases make a pattern?

What neither Gareth nor Gaheris would mention, but must be in the backs of their minds, was the fact that Mordred had remained at Camelot while all the other knights had gone on the quest. We all knew, or suspected, that Mordred was seeking for ways to undermine Arthur's confidence in Gawain as his heir. This was bound to give the little beast ammunition—although Mordred could hardly bring up the murder of Lamorak, since he had taken part in that himself.

87

One day bled into another as we waited and the king refused to grant Gareth and Gaheris an audience. He was contemplating Gawain's situation. The good news was that Mordred had not been in to see the king either. I passed much of the time tilting at the quintain with some of the squires who were still left in Camelot after the exodus of the knights. If Rosemounde wanted me to hone my skills, it was time for me to start honing. I do think that, looking honestly at my jousting prowess, I can look back at that time and say that I had improved substantially, and was as good as any of those squires, and better than most. Sir Ywain's squire Thomas had returned to Camelot when his master had ridden off with his lion as companion after his visit to his wife's castle, and Thomas was an excellent horseman, having trained on Ywain's great black steed Bucephalus, so he had a good deal of advice on precisely how to handle the horse during a joust or, more seriously, in shock combat against a wall of infantry. And when I sparred with sword and shield with Gaheris's squire Hectimere, I could feel the strength of my right arm flowing through my sword and was able to beat Hectimere down with relative ease. So those days of waiting were not wasted.

But something else was happening while we waited. Visitors who stopped at the castle, or citizens of Caerleon who had seen travelers on the road, were hearing curious gossip about misfortunes or misadventures that had happened to knights of the Table in various parts of Logres—a broken arm here, a lost horse there—so that it began to seem that King Bagdemagus's wounding and Sir Ironside's death were not isolated incidents but part of a larger pattern. But it was all rumor and gossip, until the beginning of our second week back at Camelot. That was the day Sir Palomides arrived.

His white garments were covered with dust as he walked across the drawbridge and under the raised portcullis. I was in the lower bailey as he came through the gate slowly, his head bowed. His clothes were those of a pilgrim, and he leaned on his staff as he walked. Behind him he led a mule—whether he had brought the mule with him when he left or purchased it along the way, I did not know, but he clearly needed it because it seemed to carry a large bundle that hung down on both sides of the animal. As I looked closer, it slowly grew apparent to me that this was no bundle. It was a man. And a man whose skin was as dark as Palomides' own. It could only be Sir Safer.

I ran to intercept Sir Palomides as he trudged into the bailey. A few of the other squires followed me but as Sir Palomides saw me approach, his downcast face broke into tears. It was as if he had been holding on until reaching the castle, his home, and seeing me made him feel he did not need to strain to bear his burden any further. He could not stand, but dropped himself into the dust, heaving with sobs. I crouched down facing him, holding out my hand, which he grasped. "Oh Gildas, my friend. See what they have done to my poor brother. Sir Safer is dead, Gildas. He is no more." And the big man's shoulders heaved.

Sir Safer's body, flung over the back of the mule, was pierced through the back with a spear or lance that had been driven straight through his body. I was thunderstruck, my voice paralyzed by shock. What could I say? I could assure him that Sir Safer was in a better place, was where no hunger or pain could ever reach him again. Consolations that always seemed empty to me in those days. For in truth we do not know except through faith what lies beyond this world, and at moments when we lose the one we love, faith is at its weakest. Sir Palomides seemed beyond consoling. It may be that he would remain so for some time. It may be that he would always remain so. And so all I said was, "If I could bear some of your sorrow, my lord, I would do so."

"Unarmed! We were walking unarmed through the forest. My brother greatly desired to see the Grail if it could be found, though he did not believe that it would be found by force of arms, but rather by piety. And so we donned this pilgrims' garb. Had he had his sword and shield…" his voice trailed off.

"Who did this, Palomides?" I asked.

"I don't know his name. And I could not recognize him again if I saw him. It was a knight all in white armor with a perfectly white shield—no coat of arms, no sign of identity. He never raised the visor on his helmet. He rode out of the trees, reined his horse to a stop when he saw us, then shouted out "Pagan Moors!" and proffered his lance. He spurred his horse forward, and I ducked to the left as he came on.

My brother ducked right, but not far enough or quickly enough, and was run completely through by the lance. I called after the butcher, calling him a recreant knight and an unchivalrous cur, but he was long gone and never heard me. I tell you, I was so angered I would have fought him barehanded as I was. But I never had the chance."

"What did you do?"

Palomides shrugged. "What could I do? I carried Sir Safer's body to a hermitage we had passed, borrowed their mule, and have carried him back here for burial. I can think of nothing beyond the next thing I must do. I must arrange for a Mass for him. After that, I do not know. What am I to do, Gildas? I have lost my Isolde, and now I have lost my brother. God can take nothing more from me. Except my life. And that would seem a blessing now."

By now Father Ambrose, the king's chaplain, had arrived. "Oh my sweet heaven!" he cried when he saw Sir Safer's bloodied corpse. He quickly made a sign of the cross over Safer's right cheek, the only part of his face the priest could reach on the body as it hung over both sides of the mule. "Take down the body and bear it to the chapel," he said very quietly to two of the squires who had gathered around the scene. Then looking up at Palomides with apologetic eyes, he added, "We must prepare Sir Safer for burial."

Sir Palomides nodded. Then slowly, he took from the small pack the mule had been carrying a trapezoidal psaltery, of a shape common among the moors. He hung it by a strap around his neck, and began a slow march after Sir Safer's corpse, plucking out a dirge-like melody as he walked. I walked with him, head down, a comforting hand on his heaving shoulder. When I glanced toward him tears were streaming down his face, and he began to sing one of his own compositions, accompanying himself on the harp as he followed his brother to the chapel.

> *The same womb bore us,*
> *The same land reared us.*
> *Our enemies feared us*
> *But the Heavenly Chorus*
> *Now sings at your wake.*
> *Now you've gone, my best ami, and I cannot follow.*

At Jerusalem's gates
We fought the crusaders.
We survived the invaders
And cheated the fates,
Left them in our wake.
Now you've gone, my best ami, and I cannot follow.

Your strength sustained me,
But now you are slain
By a coward villain.
No more let me see;
Let me no longer wake…
You have gone, my best ami, but soon I shall follow.

***

But that was only the beginning.

Two days later was Sir Safer's funeral Mass and internment in the cathedral at Caerleon. It was a small, quiet affair attended only by the king and queen, a few of the squires in residence at Camelot, and a few of the queen's ladies-in-waiting. I was there with Gareth and Gaheris. Sir Mordred did not attend, and apparently would not allow the lady Rosemounde to attend either, much to my chagrin. I had not seen her since I returned from the aborted quest, and could think of no excuse or ruse to visit her without raising the suspicions of her vicious lord.

But three days after that sad affair Sir Gawain's squire, Lovell, arrived alone back at the castle. Naturally Sir Gareth and Sir Gaheris were eager to hear why their nephew had come back without his father, and what had happened with Sir Gawain after the unfortunate encounter with the justly deceased Sir Ironside. But Lovell's news was not good. A kind of madness had come upon Sir Gawain, Lovell believed. After the slaying of the Red Knight, Sir Gawain gloried at having rescued an innocent maiden, but in his heart he grieved so greatly that he had killed one of his brother knights that he could not sleep, rest, or eat. "It shall come back upon me," Gawain had repeated. 'It must come down on my head.' He believed he had violated his chivalric oath. And although Lovell kept assuring him that his oath demanded he save the girl, Gawain was sure that he could have done so without killing Sir Ironside, and therefore believed that he must suffer for the violation of his knightly code.

It was after some days of this, with Gawain mad with despair, hunger, and sleeplessness, and murmuring to himself that he must be chastised, that the Pure Knight appeared.

"It was Sir Galahad," Lovell said. "He rode toward us through the woods on his snow-white stallion. He had a shield that bore the crusader's sign of the red cross and he had the gem-encrusted sword that he had drawn from the stone."

"The sword of Sir Balin," I nodded. "And yes, Sir Gareth and I were with him when he obtained that red-cross shield."

"Well, when father saw him, he nodded his head, and through his tears he said, 'Yes! My castigating lord has arrived!' He leaped up on his destrier and drew his sword, and with visor down galloped toward Sir Galahad. Father bore no shield when he attacked Galahad, and his visor was down, so I do not believe that the Pure Knight knew for a moment who it was that was charging him. He merely drew his own sword and met the challenge head on, parrying Gawain's sword with his shield and sweeping his own blade back with such power that he slashed into Gawain's side and knocked him from his horse, so that he lay on the ground unconscious."

Gareth and Gaheris looked at each other wide-eyed, and Gareth grabbed the front of Lovell's brown tunic. "Good lord, Lovell, what happened then? Where is he? Why did you leave him?"

There was a bit of fear in Lovell's face at his uncle's vehemence, but he was able to stammer, "I left him…with…Sir Galahad, in an abbey…"

"So his wounds are being searched?" Sir Gareth, relieved, let go Lovell's tunic and breathed again.

"At the Abbey of Saint Sebastian's. Galahad knew exactly where it was and, when he helped me make a litter to place father on so that his horse could drag him without great discomfort, he led us straight to the abbey. There the infirmarian took him, Brother…"

"Brother Luke," I finished the sentence. "Yes. We know him, and the abbey you mention."

Lovell seemed unsurprised at the news. "Ah. Well, they took father into a large room with several beds, and King Bagdemagus was in one of them! And his squire Meliagaunt waiting with him. They were rather surprised to see us, but Bagdemagus said, 'Ah, the curse of the sword has taken its vengeance upon Sir Gawain. How I wish I had never touched the shield.' I didn't know what he was talking about…"

"Never mind," Gaheris said. "What happened to Gawain?"

"Well, as I say, we brought him there, and Brother Luke and some of the other monks began working on him. Then Galahad—he's a very strange person, don't you think?"

"Tell me about it," I mumbled.

"Well Galahad says, without any expression at all on his face, 'And so the fate of the sword has worked itself out for Sir Gawain. I hope he will not die. But these monks will care for him as best they can. And I must be away on the quest; I cannot leave it. But you I would advise to ride to Camelot and try to get word to Gawain's brothers. One of them will no doubt want to be here to monitor his progress.' And with that he was off, back on his horse and riding away as quickly as he could. But what he said made sense to me, and since I didn't know where either of you was, nor Agravain either, I came here, because I knew Mordred must still be at the castle. What a stroke of luck to find you here as well!"

"Well," Sir Gaheris said thoughtfully. "We have had no word of Sir Agravain either. But I do think that one of us should remain in Camelot in order to consult with the king, when he deems it time to do so. Gareth, if you will stay here, I will ride with Lovell back to the Abbey."

"And what about Mordred?" Lovell asked.

Gaheris glanced at Gareth from under lowered brows, and said only, "Don't concern yourself about Mordred, Lovell. Your uncle Gareth will see to that. Now we should be off as soon as possible. I know you have just ridden hard for two days. Let Gildas take you to the kitchen to get you some refreshment, and we'll have Hectimere take your horse to the stables and get you a fresh one, and one for me as well. I want to get to Gawain's side as soon as I can."

"Yes, my lord," Lovell responded, dragging himself after me and trying not to look as exhausted as he felt as we walked toward the kitchen.

***

And still that was not all.

King Bagdemagus. Sir Ironside. Sir Safer. Now Sir Gawain. All these were casualties of the quest. It was beginning to look as if this holy quest had something more of the devil about it than otherwise.

Three more days after Sir Gaheris had left with Lovell to succor Gawain, I was breaking my fast with Sir Gareth, sitting near a window in the lesser hall that looked out over the lower bailey, when I noticed another knight riding slowly into the castle, this one on a black destrier and wearing armor to match. His shield, hanging across his back, bore the crest of a griffin rampant sable on a field of gold: the coat of arms of Sir Lionel, Lancelot's cousin and the brother of Sir Bors. I saw a squire run to him to help him with his horse, but the knight shook his head and gestured at the light brown stallion he had been leading into the bailey. And in a moment of startling déjà vu I saw that something was slung over the back of the horse. The squire examined the load, became agitated, and called for help. Three other squires and two stable hands came running, and Sir Gareth and I leaped up ourselves. "Another one!" he muttered, and, rubbing my forehead as we ran, I entreated any god that might be listening that it might be a case like Sir Gawain's, and not one like Sir Safer's.

Sir Gareth and I reached the bailey at a dead run, and as we sped past Sir Lionel I could see by the ghostly pallor of his cheek that there was no hope. Four men were lifting the tall, thin body from off the horse and gingerly setting it down on its back in the dust, while Father Ambrose was approaching once again from the chapel. It appeared that last rites were once more in order. I gently pushed two of the squires aside to get a better look at who it was this time that had been brought back to be buried in Camelot.

And I stopped breathing. The blood rushed from my face and the strength left my limbs. My heart made a cry too deep for utterance as I sank to my knees, my face writhing and my mouth agape. The dead knight was Sir Colgrevaunce.

***

Sir Lionel sat dazed on the steps leading from the bailey into the lesser hall. His helmet was off and his burly head of long black hair was in his hands. Sir Colgrevaunce's body had been borne to the chapel. Sir Gareth, Hectimere, and I stood before the broken knight, pressing him for the story. We did not like what we were hearing.

"Who did this to Colgrevaunce?" I demanded of him.

He raised his dark, pained eyes to mine and answered in a voice barely above a whisper: "I did."

"You?" Sir Gareth cried. He looked at me with eyebrows knotted in confusion. "How did that occur? Was he not wearing his coat of arms? Could you not identify him?"

Lionel shook his head. "It was nothing like that," he answered honestly. "I could see his face clearly when I buried my sword in his chest."

A burning rage flared in my own breast, and I leaped to my feet in righteous anger, shouting, "You say that with such ease? What kind of monster are you, to have killed your brother knight in full awareness, for no reason at all?"

"Oh, there was a reason all right," Lionel said, a self-mocking irony creeping into his voice. "I killed him because he was trying to stop me from killing my brother Bors."

"You were…what?" My disbelief had grown as towering as my ire. Near mad with shock and rage, I looked about desperately for a gage to throw down at Sir Lionel's feet, to challenge him to fight. I could think of nothing else. Finding none, I stepped forward and struck Lionel across the face with the back of my hand. Sir Lionel's eyes blazed an instant, but he did not move, and his expression remained

95

morose rather than combative. But I continued: "I challenge you as a recreant and a destroyer of good knights…"

Sir Gareth put a hand on my shoulder and, with some authority, pulled me back down to sit beside him. "No you don't," he said firmly. "Sir Lionel, if you feel up to it, perhaps you could tell us from the beginning just what happened, so that we can understand what may have led you to slay your brother knight."

Sir Lionel took a deep breath and sighed. "I hardly know where to begin," he said. "It was a series of things, and it just kept building. I suppose it started when the three knights captured me…"

"Three knights? Who were these knights?" Gareth wanted to know.

"I do not know," Lionel admitted. "The one who was apparently their leader wore white armor, and kept his visor closed. I never saw his face. The others were well armed, but I could see their faces. But I didn't recognize them, had never seen them before. I can tell you, though," and with this his voice rose in anger, "I would certainly know them if I saw them again! But the three of them ambushed me, knocked me from my horse and tied my arms behind me. They stripped me to the waist and put me back on my horse, and then drove me off the path I'd been riding and deeper into the woods. As we rode, the two lesser knights found a thorn bush in the wood, and each of them plucked a branch of it, and they began to beat me with those branches as they guided my horse between them.

"Back on the path, though, I saw the great destrier Pegasus, and recognized my brother Sir Bors coming toward the spot I had been intercepted. I had made no sound when those villains were whipping me, but now I cried out, 'Brother! I am here!' I know he saw me. I even saw him begin to arm himself to take those recreants on: He fitted his helmet, brought forward his shield and proffered his lance, all the time those scoundrels kept beating me."

"And so he came to help you? He challenged those knights who were flogging you?" Hectimere prompted him.

"No, he did not," Lionel growled, some of his original anger at his brother still simmering. "Just as he saw me in my predicament, another knight came riding on the path from the other direction, and this knight was dragging a young maiden behind him. She was screaming, her clothes were shredded, and he began to pull her off the road and into the woods. The girl was certainly about to be assaulted—raped and probably beaten, possibly killed. She pleaded with Sir Bors to save her: 'On your honor as a knight and for the sake of the Blessed Virgin Mary, save me, Sir Knight!' She called to him. Her attacker already had his sword out, and when she screamed to Bors he struck her in the mouth with a mailed fist. I saw Bors hesitate. He looked towards me, looked toward the maiden, who was by now disappearing into the forest in the direction opposite the one I was being taken. I saw him lift his eyes to heaven, and gallop after the maiden. I thought at that point that I was seeing my last chance for life ride away on Pegasus."

"But clearly you escaped from your captors," Gareth said. "How were you able to do that?"

Sir Lionel shrugged. "After they saw Sir Bors chase the knight with the maiden, they pulled me off my horse and tied me, naked as I was, to a tree, and stuffed a gag in my mouth so that I couldn't again call for help. By that time, I was bleeding from a thousand wounds on my back and chest, made by the thorns they had beaten me with, and blood was running from every wound, so that I seemed to be watering the ground with my own gore. They told me they were going to leave me there, well off the road and without hope of rescue, to bleed to death or to die of thirst or hunger or exposure, whichever got me first. They would be back, they said, in three days, to slit my throat if I somehow survived that long. And they rode off. But once they had left, I realized that the knots they put in my bonds were ill-tied, and I was able after a few hours, despite my weakened state, to set myself free. After that I struggled to the road, and dragged myself along until after a few miles I came upon a hermitage, with a kindly anchorite who took me in and salved my hurts, fed me, and let me rest." His voice choked up when he mentioned the anchorite, and I could not guess why. I thought perhaps he was so grateful for the kindness that it made him emotional. But I was wrong.

"I had been in the hermitage for two days. My wounds were chiefly shallow cuts and bruises, and so I felt well on my way to recovery. The hermit fed me with medicinal broths of his own making. And on the third day I saddled my horse, Hades, and intended to ride for half an hour with my arms, to test my strength and see whether I was ready yet to continue the quest. I did feel somewhat giddy, and my mind was troubled by disturbing waking visions. But I attributed that to my physical weakness. There were dark clouds that morning, a threat of a storm later on, so I wanted to get my ride in before the rain started. But on that morning, whether by chance or fate, my brother rode up to the hermitage. I was standing in the doorway with my arms crossed, watching him approach. I knew it was him from afar, since I could always recognize the noble Pegasus, and besides, his shield with the sign of the silver ox rampant on a red field is quite recognizable, even if he were riding with his visor down, which he was not. When Bors saw it was me he spurred Pegasus on and galloped to the door, and he leapt from his horse and ran toward me, arms outstretched to embrace me, crying 'Brother! You are safe! Thank heaven, I feared the worst!'

"But I was having none of it. 'You didn't fear it enough to lift a finger to help me, I noticed,' I shot back at him, avoiding his embrace and turning away. 'I am safe, no thanks to you, now why don't you keep on riding, we have no need of you here.'

"And at that Bors falls to his knees and starts pleading. 'Forgive me, brother,' he says. 'You know I was honor bound to protect the maiden, as a part of my oath—and yours.'

"I couldn't believe what I was hearing. 'It was a matter of life and death for me!' I told him. 'You were willing to give me up to death, your own flesh and blood, to fight for a maiden's virtue? And a maiden strange to you at that?' My blood was boiling. Things around me all seemed to take on the color of blood, and I stepped over to my horse, my great black stallion Hades, where my sword and lance were. I mounted him, all the while Bors staying on his knees and saying 'I shall not rise until I am forgiven.'

"'If that's your choice, that's your choice,' I told him. 'Then you'll die on your knees.' And I swung myself into Hades' saddle, drew my sword from the scabbard that hung from the pommel, and rode directly toward Bors. He was not thirty feet way, and the horse rode directly over him, knocking the senses out of him."

My mouth had dropped open in horror. "Savage!" I blurted out.

"Were you mad?"

Sir Lionel's head sank into his hands and his muffled voice spoke, "I cannot say, but I had no more reason at that time than a charging bull. I sprang from my saddle and rushed to where my brother lay. I knocked his helmet off—I remember being struck by his hair. He had always kept his hair cut close, to avoid vanity, he always said. But now, because the quest had preoccupied him, I suppose, he had neglected it and it had grown long, brown, and wavy. And so I grasped him by the hair and raised his unconscious head as far as my knees, bringing back my sword to cut it off."

By now I had heard enough of severed heads to last me the rest of my life. Hectimere broke in with a fearful cry, "You didn't go through with it, though? Did you? We don't have still another body to expect?"

Lionel shook his head. "Not Sir Bors' body, at any rate. But as I was preparing to take my own brother's life, the kind hermit who had salved my hurts and nursed me for two days came rushing from his hermitage and, seeing what I was about, rushed at me to grab my sword arm and prevent me from slaying my own closest kinsman. But—I dread to say it—just as he approached I turned toward him, my sword arm moving in front of me in a practiced movement of defense, and the hermit, unused to such weapons, ran headlong into my naked sword. I tried to pull it out of his path, but he was too fast, and enough of the sword penetrated his chest that it pierced his heart. He was dead almost immediately."

"So you killed the man who had saved you? And that wasn't enough to stop your madness?" Sir Gareth sounded exasperated.

"It was not." Was Lionel's only answer. He folded his huge hands together and leaned his head upon them as if praying. But he went on. "I stared at the hermit in shock for a moment, but it only seemed to increase my rage. In my mind, I blamed Bors for that good man's death as well. I still held my brother by the hair, and now was even more determined to end his life, but that is just when Sir Colgrevaunce rode up.

"'Lionel, what are you doing?' Colgrevaunce cried out. 'That's your own brother, Sir Bors! Are you mad? Put down your sword!'

"'He has done me the greatest wrong I have ever endured,' I shouted back. 'Were he ten times closer than any brother, father, or son, I would have his head in payment!'

"'Not while I live, I swear as a knight of the Round Table!" Colgrevaunce answered. 'I charge you, as you are a true knight, to leave your brother and meet me in single combat. I shall withdraw and give you time to arm yourself.' And with that he backed his horse off to the edge of the clearing in which the hermitage stood, and I sheathed my sword. I stepped into the hermitage, where I had stowed my arms, and as quickly as I was able I clad myself in a hauberk of fine chain mail, with a coif of the same material, and over it fitted on my black conical helmet with the eye slits. To me Colgrevaunce seemed a huge threat—a monster sent by the devil to strike me down. A minute later I was in Hades's saddle, my lance proffered. Sir Colgrevaunce proffered his own lance, and we spurred horses to come at each other. The clearing was not wide, and we could not have been more than forty yards apart when we launched at one another.

"But I was by far the more experienced knight. I struck his shield with much more force than he was able to muster, and so unhorsed him on the first pass. When he stood up he was shaken, but drew his broad sword and took a defensive posture. I alighted from Hades and bore upon him with all my strength and rage, and with the power of my right arm I was beating him down when Sir Bors began to stir. Sir Colgrevaunce noticed this as well, and called out to Bors in a kind of desperation, for he was realizing that my strength was overpowering, and he could not hold me off much longer. 'Sir Bors!' he cried. 'Awake! Can't you see that I'm being beaten for your sake? Your brother will kill me if you do not get up and help me fend him off!'

"But Bors was too woozy. He shook his head, held it in his right hand, and squinted in our direction, uncomprehending. And seeing him awake just maddened me the more. I wanted to make short work of this annoying gnat, this Colgrevaunce, so that I could focus on my real target: my traitorous brother. And so I redoubled my efforts against Colgrevaunce, and soon had him driven to his knees. He was no longer parrying with his sword but only holding out his shield against the furious pounding of my sword arm, and with one final, mighty hammer blow I drove the shield from his hands. He still had some fight left in him, and tried to drive his own sword home, wounding me under my left arm. But that was his last act. My next stroke drove my sword under his rib cage and struck at his life. He was able to call out softly as he died: 'Sir Bors! I die for your sake. Avenge me I pray you—at least I have been able to draw some of this villain's blood.' And that was it. He was dead."

"Murderer," I growled at Lionel. "The king shall hear of this, and he will exact justice, of that I'm sure."

At that he snorted. "The king can condemn me no more stridently than I condemn myself. I look at these acts and cannot believe it was I and not some other character who did these things. For look, I had killed Colgrevaunce. I had killed the hermit, though unwittingly. But I had not had enough of blood, and told my brother, 'Arm yourself, you faithless dog, for I will give you no quarter. Your death is coming!' And I strode toward him with my sword upraised, my shield lifted in case he did fight back. Reluctantly, Bors began to rise and grope for his sword and shield, which he had thrown to the ground when he knelt to me. He rose to face me, his shield raised defensively, and I stepped toward him ready to batter him even harder than I had pounded Sir Colgrevaunce.

"At that precise moment, a bolt of lightning shot down from the sky and struck a tree on the edge of the clearing, splitting it down the middle and leaving a burnt and smoking core of a trunk. It was accompanied by a clap of thunder so loud that both I and Bors put our hands to our ears. There was no way to interpret this other than as a direct sign from God, telling me to leave off trying to harm my brother, for fratricide was a far worse sin than anything Bors might have done to injure me. Bors looked in my face, saying, 'God is displeased, brother. Leave off now.' And so I did. Without more words, Bors and I dug a grave and buried the hermit near his hovel. Then I told Bors that I would take Colgrevaunce's body and return here to Camelot, and he said in that case he would continue the quest, which he had good hope of achieving. He bid me farewell and wished me peace. And I let him go. Alive. And my own rage finally cooled."

He had finished. But there was too much that was unsaid. Sir Gareth probed. "And so it is over now. But what caused this unwonted rage of yours? How could you have lost your reason in that way?"

"I don't understand it," Lionel replied, shaking his long black locks. "It's never happened to me before. I truly think I was mad. Or perhaps under some kind of spell."

Sir Gareth and I looked askance at one another. I knew how I felt about the "under a spell" excuse, and I was pretty sure he felt the same way. There was a responsibility here, and by God I was going to see that it would be brought home to Lionel, one way or another. Sir Gareth's words, though, were neutral and perfectly reasonable. "Well," he told Lionel. "You had better get yourself cleaned up and rested. The king will certainly want to see you about this matter, once you've had a chance to settle down and collect yourself. Perhaps tomorrow or the next day." I found it interesting how Gareth had suddenly become the spokesman for the royal office, though he himself had been unable to get an audience with the king. But I suppose as Arthur's nephew he just naturally assumed the role. At any rate Sir Lionel did not question Gareth's authority, but simply said, "Yes. I must get out of my armor. I must rest. Sleep is what I need. I shall no doubt see the king later." And he ambled off to his quarters—to the closet he shared with his brother Bors in small rooms off the great hall. Hectimere volunteered to take Lionel's horse to the stables, and so left Gareth and me alone.

***

"He was under a spell? Come on!" I ranted once everyone else was out of earshot.

Gareth shrugged. "He was clearly carried away. It seems like a kind of madness was upon him. But a magic spell is absurd."

"Not something the king is going to buy," I agreed. "And Colgrevaunce's soul demands justice. I may have been his best friend. I feel compelled to avenge him if the king will not do justice."

"No, Gildas. Sir Lionel is one of the doughtiest of all the knights of the Table. You are likely to end up like Colgrevaunce yourself if you go against him. No, let the king handle the matter. At least there is one positive in all of this: the king can no longer look at Gawain's case in quite the same way. Compared with Lionel's unprovoked and treacherous murder of Sir Colgrevaunce, Gawain's justified defense of the assaulted maiden on Sir Ironside no longer looks like so grave an offense."

"Well," I cautioned, "killing is killing. But I agree, Sir Lionel's offense is far worse." After a moment's thought, I added, "I wonder who should break this to Bess?"

"I wonder," Sir Gareth said, looking at me with eyebrows raised. "Didn't you just say you were his best friend?"

I closed my eyes and swallowed. But I couldn't think of anyone else who was better equipped to take on the task. Opening my eyes, I said, "I'd better go to her right away. We don't want her to hear this from some idle gossip."

"Do you want me to come with you?" Gareth offered, though he did not sound especially eager to do so.

"I don't think so. She will feel more natural and less constrained if it is just me. And she won't hold back, either her tears or her anger."

"No," Gareth agreed. Then after a few moments' silence, he said very tentatively, "Does it strike you as an odd coincidence that Sir Lionel's capture and flogging would take place at just the time and place that another knight was dragging a maiden off to assault her, and that both of these things should happen at precisely the same time that Sir Bors happened to be riding in that direction?"

"Very odd," I concurred. "If I were reading it in a romance, I would scarcely credit it. But one other thing struck me in Lionel's account: the anonymous white knight on his white horse. Is it not likely the same one that felled King Bagdemagus?"

"And who struck down Sir Safer as well!" Gareth agreed. "These are not random events, Gildas. They are being orchestrated. Someone is using this quest of the Grail for the sinister purpose of destroying as many knights of the Round Table as he can."

"There can be no other rational explanation," I agreed. Though after a moment's thought I had to concede, "Gawain's situation does not fit the pattern, though. It was Sir Galahad who struck him down, with the sword Gawain had tried to remove from the stone. And Sir Ironside was killed by Gawain himself, not by any white knight."

Gareth shrugged. "It may be that those events were truly random. Or it may be that we do not know enough about them yet to see how they fit the pattern. At any rate, there is some dire force at work here, and the king must be informed."

"Then inform him. You're his nephew, he should listen to you. But I think the time has come to call in help of a different kind. I'd say it's time we turned to Merlin."

CHAPTER EIGHT

MERLIN

Later that evening I was sitting in Merlin's cave, exhausted and depressed from the events of the day. I had been to see Bess of Caerleon, Sir Colgrevaunce's young wife. It may have been the most unpleasant task I had ever performed. She certainly had taken it just as badly as I expected her to. Having just been lifted from her dismal life of poverty and subjugation to a bullying father by her unexpected marriage to her hero, a squire in Arthur's court on his way to becoming a knight, she was suddenly cast down again into despair—and, almost certainly, back into poverty, since Colgrevaunce had not yet gained any lands or property, despite his elevated status as knight. Perhaps the king would provide something for her upkeep. At least I had mentioned that possibility. She had, of course, chided me for thinking of the mundane when it was her heart that was torn to shreds, but once that heart was sewn back together, she would wonder where her rent was coming from. Her main concern, of course, had been justice—as it always had been with her. Sir Lionel must be brought to justice, she vowed, or she would hound the king into his own grave.

And so I sat commiserating with Merlin over that particular encounter, and over the other strange events of the past few weeks. He in his turn was sitting with his considerable eyebrows lowered like a thundercloud on his worried face. From my seat, I could hardly avoid staring at the huge tapestry on Merlin's back wall, depicting the Holy Grail itself. I had seen this tapestry every time I had visited Merlin's cave for the past four years and never took much notice of it, but the irony of its being here at this moment struck me as almost perverse. It displayed the Grail, pictured as a golden cup, enshrouded in a sort of mist or cloud and floating in the air above a tall man dressed in bishop's vestments and miter, who looked disturbed, as if the Grail had somehow vanished from his sight. This figure, I assumed, must be Joseph of Arimathea, and behind him on a sloping hillside stood a host of knights in armor, mounted and ready, it seemed, to ride forth and recover the vanished cup. One of these, to my initial shock, was wearing armor of pure white.

"Well, you can hardly expect anything else from the girl," he was saying. "A great shock. A great shock to all of us, you as well, I should think."

"I admit it was a blow. One I never expected, at least in this quest. It seems to me the dangers of this adventure are far outweighing the benefits. Actually, I'm not really sure what the benefits are."

"I'm not a devout spiritualist, as I'm sure you recognize," Merlin answered. "But my mother was a nun…"

"Yes, yes, raped by an incubus," I said, with obligatory accompanying eye roll.

Merlin shrugged. "Such was the story she put out. At any rate, I was raised in a nunnery, at least for part of my childhood, and so I do think I understand a little something of the way the mystical mind works. The benefits of the quest are personal, not social. For someone like Galahad, and perhaps one or two others in the court, it is a chance to refine their relationship with the Almighty, a chance to do great deeds for the glory of God and then to obtain at least temporarily a great relic—the chalice of Jesus of Nazareth's Last Supper, and to see in it, here in this physical world, a glimpse of the power of Christ in glory."

I nodded. "I guess that convent upbringing wasn't completely wasted on you, Old Man. But neither I nor Sir Gareth has been able to understand how the quest—with a hundred and fifty Round Table Knights scouring the countryside—is going to do Arthur's kingdom any good. If there are wrongs to be righted in the meantime, who does Arthur send? The kindly and courageous Sir Mordred? The only one left at court to bend the king's ear every day with his poison tongue?"

"It will not help Logres in the slightest," Merlin agreed. "It might, of course, add to the reputation of Arthur's knights if one or two of them actually achieve this quest. But since the Round Table is already considered the greatest assemblage of knights in the world, I don't see any societal benefits. The absence of the whole order of knighthood certainly puts the court at risk. But more than that, it seems there is some malevolent force at work behind this quest. Someone, perhaps this mysterious white knight or someone he is working for, is bent on destroying as many knights as possible."

"Exactly!" I exclaimed. "Sir Safer dead. Sir Colgrevaunce dead. Sir Ironside dead. Gawain and Bagdemagus severely wounded. Who's next? Someone needs to stop this white knight."

"Well, from what you've told me there are different strands to all of this. Remember that the white knight who laid Gawain low was Sir Galahad."

"Yes," I answered thoughtfully. "Could there be any connection? I mean, from what anyone can see, the only difference between Galahad and the mysterious white knight is Galahad's red-cross shield. Perhaps he simply keeps his shield out of sight when he deals out death to innocent knights like Sir Safer, or when he kidnaps Sir Lionel and has his cronies beat him with branches of thorns…all right, I guess that really doesn't sound like him, does it?"

"No, and you've already told me that Galahad was in the monastery when Bagdemagus was assaulted by the white knight after wearing the shield. So stop playing the Cornish dolt and think harder. Look, this whole Grail story is long and convoluted, and has deep, deep roots. I was there when Sir Balin foolishly grabbed the sword and used it on the lady in court. When he later wounded King Pelles, Pelles became obsessed with finding the Holy Grail because he was convinced it would have miraculous healing powers. He knew the legend that Joseph of Aramathea had brought the Grail to Logres, and he was convinced by court genealogists, no doubt hoping for handsome gifts from the king, that he was descended in a direct line from Joseph. He had no son of his own, only his one daughter Elaine, and so he had to use her to beget a grandson who could find the Grail for him. And Galahad is it."

"So you don't believe in any kind of destiny or fate that is governing the affairs of Galahad as he seeks the Grail?"

Again the shrug. "As I say, I am no spiritualist. But Galahad has been raised, in the castle Corbenic and later in the monastery, to believe this is his destiny, and he is monomaniacal about it. It is all that motivates him—the Grail and his own salvation."

"But didn't you insist on the Siege Perilous standing empty for so long at the Round Table? Your own prophesies had a lot to do with how this all got started, didn't they Old Man?"

Merlin pursed his lips and looked at the floor. "My 'prophesies' as you call them," he said after a few moments, "are not, as you well know, clear pictures of precisely what is going to happen. They come to me in debilitating headaches and are only dim suggestions of what *may* happen. Nor do I believe, despite what others say, that they are sent me from some transcendent authority. They have always seemed to me my mind's own conclusions after much rumination, coming out in enigmatic pictures of possible future events."

"In other words, prophesies," I concluded.

"If you insist," Merlin sighed. "What I foresaw in the case of the Siege Perilous was this: King Pelles was obsessed with finding the great relic. He had bet his kingdom on begetting a worthy knight, and would bring up his grandchild with that monomaniacal vision. There was only one company a lad with that training could be expected to enlist with when his time had come, and that was the Round Table. The Siege Perilous ensured that, when Galahad's time came, there was a place waiting for him at the table, and he did not have to serve for years as a lowly squire before getting his chance to join. No offense."

"None taken. But what about the curse on the seat, that burned Sir Brumand to ashes when he sat in it?"

"Oh, that," Merlin scoffed. "I booby-trapped the chair. There was no magic or prophecy about it. Rigged it so that any kind of weight on the seat caused a flint to spark and set off a load of Greek Fire I had concealed within the siege. I didn't really know it would kill him, though I did regard that as a possibility. That was why I was so careful and specific about the instructions: no one was supposed to sit in the chair until the chosen one came along. Sir Brumand was a fool, full of self-conceit, and trying to show up Lancelot at the time. The warning was the best I could do. And it only needed to happen once."

"I don't doubt it," I mused, scratching my chin. "Who would be crazy enough to chance it again after that? But listen, Merlin, we're talking around the main point here. I know I've usually come to you with specific charges from the king or queen to investigate some particular crime…"

"As the murders of Tristram and Isolde, for instance."

"Exactly," I agreed. "Well this time I don't have any mandate from the sovereign, and no single crime, but a whole string of misfortunes that seem to have originated with this quest, and that Sir Gareth and I find very suspicious. Do you think you can help us with this?"

Merlin half closed his eyes and spread his hands magnanimously. "You know I would do anything for Beaumains," he said, using my master's old nickname from his days working in the castle's kitchen. "And I'm quite accustomed to helping *you* out when you get in over your head as well," he joked, sending me a sly half-smile. "Let's consider this whole mystery logically one question at a time. But as you know, I do my best thinking about one set of problems while reflecting on other puzzles altogether, so…" with that he rose and walked halfway across the room, stopping at a small table. "White or black?"

***

Merlin had a passion for chess second only to his passion for the beautiful Nimue, one of the women attached to the court of the Lady of the Lake. Indeed, he had taken up residence in this cave in a fit of depression when she spurned him the first time, and had of late been more and more isolated from the court since Nimue had married Sir Florent, Gawain's oldest son. And since Nimue never came to the cave to play Merlin at chess any more, he was always very eager to get me to play with him, though I had yet to win a game. I kept thinking he would let me win someday, just to keep me interested. I think he used to let Nimue win once in awhile, to keep her coming

109

back. But so far he hadn't given me that incentive, and I wasn't really sure I wanted him to. Of course I picked white.

"Queen's pawn to queen four," I opened.

"Always the queen's pawn, aren't you Gildas?" Merlin had his little joke. "But that suggests one of the questions we ought to be asking: This fellow in the white armor. He's involved in this whole business up to his eyeballs. He fells King Bagdemagus. He kills Sir Safer outright—and that is an act of pure murder, whatever else is going on, for which this white knight must be brought to justice. He imprisons Sir Lionel and has him beaten. The question is, is he in fact the ring leader of this apparent conspiracy, or is he, like your chess piece, merely a white pawn? King's knight to king's bishop three."

"The pawn of whom, though? Or is that your second question?"

"It is actually the third question. But make your move."

"Oh…uh…queen's bishop's pawn to queen's bishop four," I countered.

"King's knight's pawn to king's knight three," Merlin said, and then continued, "What are these disasters intended to do? Who is chiefly the target of the attacks? What do those involved hope to accomplish, or at least whom do they most wish to cause distress? Are they aimed at destroying the Round Table in general, and in that case are they aimed at King Arthur himself? Or are they intended to harm the clan of Orkney, since Sir Gawain has been especially targeted? Or perhaps is there a special grudge against Sir Lancelot, his two close kinsmen deliberately being put at odds as they were?"

"Well, the attack on Sir Safer seems to have nothing to do with either the clan of Orkney or Lancelot's faction in the court," I reasoned. "Nor does Bagdemagus's defeat. And certainly not Colgrevaunce's death, though I admit that could be seen as a side-effect of an attack on the kinsmen of Sir Lancelot. Still that makes it seem like more of a general attack on the Round Table. But what about Gawain's killing of the Red Knight of the Red Lands? The white knight doesn't seem to have been involved with that encounter. That seems more of a random event. And, uh…king's's knight's pawn to king's knight three."

"We don't know that there was no connection between that event and the white knight," Merlin answered. "Only that we have yet to find any. We need to question Sir Gawain about that further, if he's able to speak to us about it. Queen's bishop's pawn to queen's bishop three."

"King's bishop to king's knight two," I responded. "So we're assuming that whoever is behind these attacks is someone with a general grievance against King Arthur or the Round Table as an institution? Is that what we're saying?"

"Yes. Which of course brings up question number…"

"Three," I humored him. "Who could be masterminding this whole thing? Well you must have some idea. Who are Arthur's biggest enemies?"

"He made many during his early years as king. Members of the Irish royal house, for instance, whom he crushed in battle. Those attached to the Roman imperial court as well, of course, from the time he defeated Lucius. And by the way, queen's pawn to queen four," Merlin answered.

"Pawn takes pawn," I said, jumping at the chance to win a piece, any piece, from him.

"Bishop's pawn takes pawn," Merlin answered. But that was OK. We were still even.

"More recent enemies, then." I persisted. "Ones that are closer, and more likely to be influential here in Logres. For instance, I'm thinking about the king's own sister. Oh, and queen's knight to queen's bishop three."

"Morgan?"

"Morgan le Fay, indeed!" I answered. "I've heard some awful stories of her. Wasn't she the one who really started this whole rigmarole leading to the Grail quest in the first place? Wasn't she the one who sent that woman with the sword to Arthur's court to trap Lancelot, and ended up sucking in Sir Balin instead? At least that's what King Bagdemagus thought. And what about that business with Sir Gawain and the Green Knight? She very nearly got her own nephew killed there, according to Sir Gareth, and he thinks she's very, very dangerous. And she's always hated Guinevere. Isn't she a likely candidate?"

"King's bishop to king's knight two," said Merlin. "The lady Morgan is a powerful sorceress and a woman of complex motives. She has the kind of sweeping mind that can see the whole chessboard and conceive of plays dozens of moves ahead. The kind of mind that could conceive of something this large. And she has the spite to carry it out. I'm not sure she has the patience to have planned it out over twenty years, as you may be suggesting with those examples of yours, which definitely go back at least that far."

"But her targets in the past have included Sir Gawain, and he has been targeted now; and Sir Lancelot, and it is his kinsmen who seem to have been singled out. The people being hurt are people Morgan has had it in for from the beginning. So, king's pawn to king three," I added. "Why does Arthur have her around, anyway?"

Merlin shrugged. "Family. What can you do? Anyway, it may be better having her here than having her off somewhere plotting the king's demise, or, as you say, more likely the queen's. Easier to protect yourself, perhaps, from something within the walls of your own castle, what? And, by the way, castle." Which he did, sliding his rook beside his king and flipping the monarch to the other side.

"King's knight to king two," I responded. "So you're saying that Morgan is a prime suspect in this business then?"

"One element about these strange occurrences does make me think immediately of Morgan," he admitted. "Both Sir Gawain, when he slew Sir Ironside, and Sir Lionel, when he attacked Bors and killed the hermit as well as our friend Colgrevaunce, regretted their dark deeds afterward and spoke as if they had lost control of their rage in a way that they felt was unusual and even frightening. At least I am extrapolating that from what you relate of what Lionel said when he arrived, and what Lovell said of Gawain's actions after the slaying of the Red Knight. Both could easily have been under a similar spell of some kind, and as we have already acknowledged, Morgan is a very powerful enchantress. She could make a knight do almost anything, I would think. Look at the Green Knight! Which reminds me, queen's knight to queen two."

"But I'm also thinking about Mordred," I mused, switching suspects on the old man. "He's awfully suspicious, isn't he? If you think about motive, he hates the king at least as much as Morgan hates Guinevere, and for better reason." The king's unacknowledged son had never been considered Arthur's heir apparent, and barring some disaster, never would replace Gawain in that role. Not to mention the small detail of the fifteen-year-old King Arthur's trying to kill Mordred immediately after his birth. "If these events succeed in thrusting Gawain from the king's favor, and if they help to quash the influence that Lancelot's kinsmen have in the court, then the one with the most to gain out of all of it is Mordred. And castle," which I did, mirroring Merlin's earlier move. I wasn't revealing to Merlin my real reason for wanting to investigate Mordred: I was hoping to find him guilty of deliberately trying to sabotage the Round Table, and laying traps to catch knights on this quest because it could mean, if my prayers held any sway, the execution of the bastard. How I hated him for what he had done to my dearest lady. How I wanted him dead because of it.

"Queen's knight's pawn to queen's knight three," Merlin countered. "Mordred is a dark and sinister presence in Camelot, that is certain. I wonder why the king keeps him around," he said, raising one of his unkempt eyebrows at me.

"Family," I mimicked him. "What can you do? But actually, Mordred is in Camelot because he himself chose to stay there. Of all the knights of the table, he wanted nothing to do with the quest. Why would he do that if not to plot against Sir Gawain while he was away?" In this, of course, I was only mouthing Sir Gareth's pet theory. "And why, if he didn't know the quest was somehow set up for the knights to fail, would he recuse himself and forego whatever glory might be gained in the pursuit of that elusive goal? And queen's knight's pawn to queen's knight three. On top of all that."

"Mordred would benefit from the downfall of Gawain, and of Lancelot's family, there is no doubt. Perhaps the most to gain of anyone. The throne itself. That's motive, my lad. Queen's bishop to queen's rook three."

"Queen's bishop to queen's rook three," I mirrored his move. "So what are you saying? You think Mordred is behind this then?"

"I didn't say that. King's rook to king one."

"Well what then? You think Morgan is pulling all the strings then."

"Make your move."

"All right, queen to queen two. So Morgan then?" I pushed.

"I didn't say that either. King's pawn to king four," Merlin responded.

"Pawn takes pawn," I jumped on the chance to take another of his pieces, but couldn't shake my frustration. "So what are you saying? Who do you think is the culprit here?"

"Queen's knight takes pawn," Merlin evened the score again. "How should I know? You've just brought me this, and all we are doing is thinking of possible suspects. We have no evidence of anybody doing anything."

"All right," I said, resigned. "King's rook to queen one. What's next?"

"Knight to queen six," Merlin continued. "There is another question we have not yet asked."

I started up at that. "What is it?" I couldn't see what we had neglected in what we knew so far. Merlin did not answer. He merely looked at me calmly with those piercing eyes for several moments and then, when I made no response, gestured toward the chessboard. "Oh!" I said. "Uh…queen to queen's bishop two."

"Think, Gildas. What is something that at least two of these events have in common? Knight to king's bishop seven. Taking pawn."

"King takes knight," I said with some excitement. Was I actually winning this game? Or was this a case of Merlin's letting me win, finally? But I considered Merlin's question. "Well, the White Knight is there in several of them."

"Of course, but we've already considered that. Knight to king's knight five," Merlin said. "What else do you see? Other than the fact that you are in check?"

"King to king's knight one," I responded. Then it came to me. "Do you mean the fact that two of these incidents involved an assault on a woman?"

"Indeed, you've hit it!" Merlin cried. "King's bishop to king's bishop three."

"Well, queen to queen two," I mumbled, thinking. "But what can that mean? I don't see what we can make of that."

"No?" Merlin responded. "Nor do I. But I can imagine a number of things. Knight to king's knight seven."

"King takes knight," I said. I almost added, "Of course." Was he getting carried away and not paying attention to the game? But I did want to hear what he thought about the two assaults. And I suppose he was just waiting for me to ask. So I humored him. "All right, what exactly can you imagine?"

"Queen's pawn to queen five," Merlin began. That done, he answered me: "Neither woman involved in these incidents has come to Camelot to report them. Is that not suspicious? In both cases, a knight lost his senses and began killing one of his comrades. What if these were traps, for Sir Gawain and for Sir Bors, or, perhaps, both Sir Bors and Sir Lionel—and, for that matter, both Sir Gawain and Sir Ironside? What if it was all part of an elaborate plan? And what if there were not two women but the same woman in both incidents?"

I spent some time digesting that. I didn't know how to respond, and let it sink in. "King's pawn takes pawn," was all I said.

"Queen's bishop to queen's knight two," Merlin barked. "These events are complex and involve a host of malefactors. The White Knight himself. The scoundrels who captured Sir Lionel and beat him. The brute who was dragging the woman off to be saved by Sir Bors. And perhaps the woman herself, who had previously laid a trap for Sir Gawain? And is one of these the mastermind behind the whole conspiracy? Or must we add one more culprit to the list? God's nostrils, boy, how far does this thing extend? And how many more on this quest will be harmed by it?"

"I don't know. Um…king to king's bishop one. Where do we start with this? How do we investigate what's going on with a hundred and fifty knights wandering all over the forests of Logres?'

"Queen to queen two," Merlin answered. "I don't really know. But one thing is certain: we can't simply stand about waiting for the knights to all return and hear their evidence then. I would love to talk to Sir Bors, to learn more about the woman he rescued, if that is in fact what happened. But who knows when he will be back?"

"So are you saying we need to go out into the forest ourselves and try to track the knights down before other murders occur?" I asked. "Queen to queen's bishop two, by the way."

Merlin shuddered. "Queen to king's knight five," he said, and then added, "And end up like Sir Safer? No thank you. That, I think, needs to be a last resort."

"Bishop to king's rook three," I continued. "So what *should* we do, then?"

"King Bagdemagus has given us all the information he is like to," Merlin began. "And I think that we are unlikely to hear anything new from Sir Palomides. But I think it may prove fruitful to talk a little more to Sir Lionel, given the things we have already talked about. Queen takes bishop. And check, again."

"Oh, king to king's knight one. How do you mean? You want to ask him about what, the woman?" I asked.

"Rook to king eight. Check." Merlin said, though I didn't understand the move at all.

"Rook takes rook," I said quite simply.

"The woman, yes," Merlin finally responded. "Ideally he will be able to describe her in some way. And we need, of course, to talk to Sir Gawain as soon as we can. If he is healthy enough to bear up under the cross-examination. I want to hear his description of the woman, and I want to hear both of them describe to me as specifically as they can the symptoms of the temporary madness they both claim to have been under. I hope Sir Gaheris can bring Gawain here quickly. King's bishop takes knight."

"All right, that makes some sense to me," I granted. "Queen to queen three. But shouldn't we question Morgan and Mordred as well?" I knew how I wanted to question Mordred: on the rack, or with a garrote, or burning coals. My blood boiled again at the thought of my Rosemounde's ravaged back after he had brutalized her.

"We should be very, very careful with them. Under no circumstances would it be a good idea to allow either of them to guess they are being considered as suspects in this conspiracy. If we talk to them at all, it must be very, very carefully. None of your boisterous rushing in with impertinent questions to rouse their suspicions and put them right on their guard."

"Well, what? How are you going to find out anything if all you talk to them about is the weather? How do you propose we approach them? 'Oh, my lord Mordred. People are getting killed out there. How do you feel about that?'"

"Don't worry about it. Just let me deal," Merlin said smirking. Then he added, "I've always wanted to say that. And queen to king's knight seven. Checkmate."

I was quiet a moment and looked at the board with some disbelief. "I thought I was winning!" I cried.

"No. You weren't."

"But I was taking all those pieces…"

"Just a distraction," Merlin told me.

"Come on—if I hadn't made that last move with my queen, you couldn't have done that. You were losing!"

The old man's face was impassive. "Just misleading you, all the way," he repeated. And then, "I wonder. Are we being misled in this quest? What are we missing?"

"I don't know," I said. "But when will we talk to Sir Lionel?"

"Tomorrow," Merlin said. "First thing. Let's sleep now. You want to bed down in the cave?"

"Sure," I said. "I'm too tired to walk back, and too anxious to get started in the morning to have to try to rouse you again."

He looked at me in a kind of mock astonishment. "You're accusing me of malingering or what? God's pinkies Gildas, don't complain about the mote in my eye and ignore the great windmill in your own!" He went around the cave blowing out the candles, while I found a rug I could curl up in close to the smoldering log on the fire. "Let's just see who will be the first one up in the morning, shall we?"

But I was burrowed into a blanket, trying to get to sleep. I was exhausted from the day's events, but when I shut my eyes I saw only one thing: the crimson welts on the back of my beloved Rosemounde, marks I vowed to avenge with every breath I took until finally, seething from tension, I dropped off into a troubled sleep.

CHAPTER NINE

THE TALE OF SIR YWAIN

"**S**hake your bones, boy, we're burning daylight!" At the top of his lungs and from out of nowhere. When I opened my eyes, Merlin's face was so close to mine that he seemed to me to have only one eye, and that unruly tangle of eyebrow was brushing my own forehead. I jerked my head back with a sudden start, only to crack it on the leg of the chair behind my head as I lay on the floor of the old man's cave. "Thought *I* would be the one hard to rouse in the morning did you?" He continued his loud and rather annoying harangue. "I've been up for hours, looking into a few old books, while you've been lying there snoring with your mouth wide open. Ha! Let's get a move on, I want to get to Camelot before Roger is out of breakfast—I'm hungry! Don't know about you!" All of this was said as he pulled on his threadbare robe and cape, kicking my own clothes over to me and making rolling motions with his hands to try to hurry me up.

And so I dragged myself into my simple brown wool tunic and fastened a belt around my waist, ran my fingers through my sleep-tousled hair and called it good. I managed to trudge after Merlin through the woods and toward the castle, carrying my boots in one hand so that I could more easily wade through the ankle-deep stream that bubbled its way past the caves on this cliff face and toward Lady Lake. When I sat down to pull them on, Merlin again waved me forward impatiently. "What is your hurry?" I finally asked him, rising again and trekking along the path he was bustling ahead on. "It's less than a mile to the castle, and we haven't even got a plan of what to

118

do! Gawain won't be there yet, so we only have Lionel to interview, as you pointed out yourself."

"I told you I'm hungry. Sometimes when I'm in my cave, I forget to eat."

"Sometimes when *I'm* in your cave, I can't figure out why you *have* nothing to eat there!" I snapped back at him. It was true. Nimue had been in the habit of bringing supplies when she visited him: bread and cheese, some nuts, and sometimes dried grains or vegetables. Once in a while he had even had a barrel of wine or small beer. But lately, there was nothing. I made a mental note to bring along food whenever I visited the old man in the future. We were coming out of the woods now, on a path through the fields north of Camelot, and Merlin was still moving at a brisk clip, pretty speedy for a man of his age, which I figured at that time must have been about a hundred and thirty. Well, not really, but I was eighteen at the time and he certainly *seemed* that old to me. Besides that, he was chattering at a clip that matched his walking speed, all about how he wanted to see Beaumains—his old nickname for Sir Gareth from the knight's days in Roger's kitchen—to get his take on what was going on in this quest out in the forest of Logres.

All of this made me wonder what was really going on in Merlin's mind. He would not be in this big a hurry simply because he was hungry. "All right, hold on now, old man," I called after him, stopping a moment to rest. "I may be a stupid chess player, but I'm not a complete idiot, you know."

Merlin stopped and turned around, breathing hard and, though he wouldn't admit it, glad of a short break himself. "No," he said, "I don't know that. And what is it you're talking about?"

"Your big rush, Merlin, your hurry-up walk. This isn't just because you're hungry. I know better than that."

Merlin sighed. "All right, all right. I just didn't want to tell you right away because I wasn't sure what kind of reaction I'd get from you. But I've decided we really need to talk to Mordred after all." He saw my wince but kept going, beginning his fast walk toward the castle again. "I have heard that he is out hunting almost every day now, since the knights of the Table have all left Camelot. And a hunting party must take off pretty early in the morning. So I want to catch him before he leaves the castle."

"Well, I certainly consider that brute capable of anything," I told Merlin. "He's definitely someone who could be behind this whole conspiracy, especially if it helps bring down Arthur's government. But last night you said we should proceed cautiously, and not let him know we might be suspicious of him. What changed your mind?"

"Well," Merlin began. "It isn't just that he declined to go on this quest when every other knight pledged to take part. That may simply have been wisdom, a hesitancy to be carried along by the tide of emotion for something he could see was bound to end in disappointment and failure for the vast majority. No, I began to think carefully about what had happened to Sir Gawain. Think about it: Gawain is confronted with a rape. Everyone knows that Gawain is known as the paragon of courtesy; the protection and courteous treatment of women is the chief concern of his knightly deeds. Anyone who knew Gawain would know this, and would know that Gawain would be very likely to avenge that damsel with all his force. But what everyone did not know was the enmity Gawain felt specifically toward the Red Knight of the Red Lands—partly for the sake of his brother Gareth, whom Sir Ironside came close to killing (something many people know), but also because of the fact that the Red Knight had originally challenged Gawain himself out of hatred and jealousy—something only Gareth and perhaps Gawain's other brothers were privy to.

"But the trap seemed also designed to crush Gawain mentally: All at court were familiar with Gawain's obsession with perfection in courtesy. His performance in the case of the Green Knight demonstrated that, and his quest for perfection—to be what Galahad in fact is—would have to lead him to go on this quest. His rashness and desire to please his uncle would of course spur him on to take that sword from the stone, and the perpetrator of these crimes counted on that. But Gawain's anguish over killing an unarmed knight, an anguish brought on and made intolerable by his guilt over the attack on Sir Lamorak, that seems to have been a preconceived outcome of this whole trap, and that is something, like the earlier recognition of the Red Knight's enmity, that only one of Gawain's own brothers was likely to know. And so, dear Gildas," Merlin breathed, as by now we were approaching the drawbridge into the castle's bailey, "that is why I want to talk to Mordred."

It made sense to me. But I couldn't see how Merlin could possibly approach Mordred without revealing our suspicions to him. And I hadn't been completely honest with Merlin about my enmity toward the king's bastard son. I still could not get the sight of my lady Rosemounde's scarred back out of my mind's eye, nor could I expunge my deepest heart's desire to see her tormentor dead.

But I didn't really get time to pursue the matter further, because we were now on the drawbridge and making our way into the castle grounds under the barbican. From the gatehouse above the open portcullis a familiar voice greeted us through one of the arrow slits in the stone facing of the structure. "Oh, it's bloody Gildas. And for a moment I thought somebody important was approaching our gate. Well, back to sleep boys, there's nothing of any substance going on here."

Merlin bristled for a moment, but I looked up at the narrow opening from which had come the voice of Robin Kempe, captain of the king's guard, and shot back a volley of my own. "Yes, go to sleep, boys, so that the Saxon army that's hot on my heels can take the castle completely unawares. Nobody in Camelot will be surprised, since they really don't expect anything else from a company commanded by the addled captain of the king's guard."

"Ah, young Gildas, your witticisms always slay me. Or is it your face that does? I forget. You're right, though, I will probably be laughing so hard when those Saxons approach that I'll be unable to notch an arrow to my bowstring. But I see you've got the old necromancer with you again. Good morning, Lord Merlin. Still keeping company with folks of low character, I see."

"That will change as soon as we get through this gate," the old man muttered, and we walked through and into the upper bailey. Still Robin called to us as we walked under his gatehouse, "Touché, old devil! But seriously, I'm just glad one of you isn't coming in slung over a horse! We've had quite enough of that lately."

"You can say that again, Robin!" I called back. He resisted the obvious comeback, and Merlin began gazing around as soon as we walked into the castle grounds, looking for a hunting party preparing to leave. Peering across the courtyard to the lower bailey, which ran past the great hall and the chambers adjacent to it, Merlin spotted a small party leading horses standing around the single story kitchen that lay below the great hall. "God's jawbone, there they are!" He cried. "Come on, boy! Catch them before they leave!"

We bustled toward the kitchen, and on the way I was able to recognize Hectimere and Baldwin, the squires of Sir Gaheris and Sir Agravain, standing at the door to the kitchen, where they were picking up several "plowman's breakfasts"—fresh baked bread with slices of goat cheese—to sustain the group on their trek through the woods in search of the king's deer. If they had luck, there should be venison for dinner this evening. William of Newcastle, the king's chief forester, sat on a brown palfrey alongside his two apprentices, Tom and Henry, who held William's two bloodhounds as well as the queen's greyhounds, Aeneas and Dido, straining at their leashes and ready to chase down some deer. The queen must have asked William—or perhaps Mordred—to give her hounds this exercise. Mordred himself sat on a black palfrey, alone and behind the rest of the party.

As we approached, Hectimere and Baldwin called out greetings to me, and Dido and Aeneas leapt on me joyfully. I had had a lot of experience exercising the two of them when I had been page to the queen. As I patted their soft heads I felt a pang of guilt about my own borzoi hound, called Guinevere after the queen, whom I had not taken for a romp in the woods in many days, distracted as I was with the quest and the carnage it seemed to be producing. Mentally I vowed to give my girl a good run at my very next opportunity.

Merlin, meanwhile, had accosted Sir Mordred. The king's youngest nephew glared at the old mage with dark, piercing eyes, his raven hair blowing around his shoulders in the morning breeze. His stony face betrayed no emotion at all. It never did.

"A good morning to you, my lord," Merlin greeted the bastard with faux good humor. "A fine day for a hunt, wouldn't you say? I envy you, riding out and getting all that fresh air."

Mordred did not answer. He merely continued to stare. Not a big one for small talk, the bastard.

"I felt I ought to give you my sympathies. You know, for your brother Gawain's sake. I hear he was struck down by the mysterious white knight on this quest. The consequence, apparently, of his pulling the sword from the stone on that day of Pentecost not long past. They tell me he is even in danger of dying from his wounds!"

"Yes, *that* would be a tragedy," Mordred sneered, his voice dripping sarcasm like pus from a lanced boil. "Whatever would we do without our precious Gawain, prince of courtesy?"

"Yes," Merlin continued, undeterred. "Only it begins to look more and more as if what happened to Sir Gawain was in fact a well-orchestrated conspiracy to bring him to ruin, and with him your uncle Arthur as well."

Mordred once more only stared, though I thought his eyes betrayed a spark of real interest when Merlin mentioned a conspiracy. And the rigid face cracked slightly when a corner of the mouth tilted slightly upwards at Merlin's use of the word "uncle."

Oh how I yearned to put my mailed fist through that sneering countenance, and turn his impassive face into a bloody pulp, the way he had bloodied my own angel's flawless back. But I fought back the urge and said only, "You don't seem particularly disturbed by this plot against your brother."

Mordred just snorted. "Please. There's a new plot against my brother every week. I assume they are all concocted by absolute morons, or one would have succeeded by now. Though I suppose at some point someone with an actual brain will be offended by my charming brother, and might come up with a plot that actually works. Of course, that would be a tragedy," he added, looking at me with mock horror.

Merlin pounced. "Someone as clever as you, my lord? Tell me, if you were to set a trap for Sir Gawain, what would it look like?"

Sir Mordred smiled a knowing smile, and shook his finger at the mage. "No you don't, old man. If I did have designs on Sir Gawain do you think I wouldn't have the sense to keep it to myself?"

Merlin shrugged, keeping the conversation as light as possible.

"You mistake me my Lord," he retreated. "But think of this trap laid for Gawain. Whoever set him up to fail knew one thing for certain: that he would be devastated in conscience if he killed a fellow knight of the Table unarmed. There are reasons for that, which only Gawain and his brothers would be aware of."

Mordred only snorted again, and kicked his horse into a trot. "Well," he said, "I see my companion squires have finished securing our midday snack. Much as I'd love to stay and continue our scintillating conversation, my companions await me and I must leave you." And off he trotted.

"Well I'm dashed," Merlin muttered. "If he were pure as the driven snow, he couldn't have come up with any way to look more suspicious. What do you make of it, boy?"

But just as he said this, Mordred paused a moment about a hundred yards from us, and turned back. "Of course, one thing to keep in mind about Gawain," he called back to Merlin. "Gawain confesses everything to his priest." And with that, Mordred left the courtyard and cantered across the drawbridge, following his mates who had all ridden out by this time.

Merlin stood for a moment with his mouth open, watching Mordred disappear. After a moment, he blinked, shook his head, and said, "Let's get something to eat. I'm hungry."

***

We stepped to the door of the kitchen and peered in through the stifling heat, where John Potter, the baker, was still standing. He greeted us with, "Hey, and I suppose you two'd like a couple of plowman's breakfasts yourselves, eh?" From the brick oven to the right of the doorway I caught a whiff of fresh baking bread and my stomach growled with anticipation.

"Absolutely!" I answered him, and added, "With a cup of small beer while you're at it too, if it's not too much trouble." John handed us the bread and cheese and called to one of the kitchen lads to bring us drinks and be quick about it, and within two minutes we were sitting on the grass of the upper bailey, making a picnic of it.

After a bite of bread, I finally broke the silence with Merlin. "All right, you've had time to digest it. And I don't mean the bread. What do you make of Sir Mordred?"

"He's a surly, sarcastic little carbuncle, isn't he?" The old man said thoughtfully. "But to talk that way about his brother when he knew we were trying to uncover a plot laid against him, well, either Mordred is too dimwitted to conceal his guilt, or so certain of his innocence that he doesn't care what he says to us. And I'm afraid it is more likely the latter, because if there's one thing that boy is not, it's dimwitted."

"Well, if there's another thing he's not, it's innocent. But I'm afraid you're right," I found myself agreeing with him despite my own prejudices. "He actually seemed to perk up when you talked about a conspiracy, as if he was interested in learning more about it himself. And what was that comment about a priest all about?"

"I'm not sure what to make of it," Merlin admitted. "If it's true, which it may well be, it's Mordred trying to tell us that there were others who knew of Gawain's murder of Sir Lamorak, including his own confessor. On the other hand, it could be that we're wrong, that Mordred really *is* guilty, and that he's just trying to throw us off the track."

"And so what we know for sure is…" I prompted.

"Absolutely nothing," Merlin said, and took another bite of his bread and cheese.

I gave a half-smile and sat down next to Merlin on the grass of the bailey, enjoying the brief respite to break my fast before the work of the day, which at this point I assumed meant another conversation with Sir Lionel. Moving from Mordred, who had brutalized my beloved Rosemounde, to Lionel, who had murdered my good friend Colgrevaunce, was no picnic. So I might as well enjoy a short one now. But I had just bitten into the bread and cheese when I caught sight of another knight coming through the main gate where Sir Mordred's hunting party had just exited.

I immediately recognized the great black destrier with the white star on his forehead, which seemed to be shuffling into the bailey, his head down, his breath coming hard. He had come a long way, and had carried a heavy load. Bucephalus, named for Alexander's celebrated war horse, resembled the descriptions of that great beast from the Alexander romances. And I knew who would be sitting in his saddle. Like the horse, his head hung down, his brown mane waving in the breeze. He wore the same blue cloak and hood over the same rusty chain mail he had worn when he left the Abbey of Saint Sebastian several days earlier, but Sir Ywain's left arm was in a sling and his mail armor was spattered with blood all down his left side. He rode as if half asleep, but out of the corner of my eye I soon saw Taber approaching from the stables to grab hold of Bucephalus's reins.

"God's moustache!" Merlin swore when he saw Ywain and the shape he was in. "What's happened to your lion friend?" I was up in a second and running toward Bucephalus as Taber helped Ywain down. The old man wasn't far behind me, and I steadied Sir Ywain as he stood shakily on the grass.

"Get a surgeon here, will you?" I called to one of the pages who were now converging on the knight. "He's going to need some help!"

"Oh, for the love of Christmas," Ywain grumbled, "don't bring me one of those crazy bastards. He'll just want to bleed me, and I don't think that's going to be of much help."

With that Ywain went limp in our arms and, with a groan, Merlin flashed me a look of concern and began to strain forward, Ywain's arm held over his shoulder, saying, "Come on, boy, let's drag him to his closet and see if we can lay him down. More mischief from this damned Grail quest it seems."

***

As one of the king's close kinsmen, Ywain had a small closet of his own off the lesser hall, with a bedstead of cords supporting his feather-stuffed mattress. The red curtains that surrounded the bedstead to block the drafts were pulled aside, and after successfully stripping the big knight of his chain mail and calling on his squire Thomas to help wash and bandage the deep wound in his left shoulder, Merlin and I had propped Ywain in the bed on a large feather pillow and, with Thomas, stood by his bedside as he groggily came back into consciousness.

"What?" he said dazedly, glancing about him before recognizing where he was and remembering how he had got there. "Did I pass out? Good Lord, I'm weak. When I recover from this I'll track down that bloody white knight and open his rib cage for him, the priggish villain."

"So it *was* the white knight, then, that did this to you?" I asked.

"Him and his bloody army. He needed a whole brace of beef-witted scoundrels to take on me and my lion together. Oh, my lion…" he broke off mournfully.

"Your lion?" Merlin's ears perked up with some concern. "Where *is* your lion? He was not with you when you arrived here."

"No, not with me at all," Ywain said through gritted teeth. His anger was palpable as he considered his great leonine companion. "When they ambushed me, three of them dropped from the trees with a great net to hold my lion bound and helpless while the white knight himself and two more of his dog-hearted henchmen rode at me with proffered lances."

"All three attacked you?" Thomas asked, concerned.

"Only the white knight drove his lance into my shoulder. The other two were just there to ensure I could not get away. But that white-armored clot-pole took a special glee in piercing me and driving me from my saddle. When I lay in the dust he gloated, announcing something like, 'I told you there must be no fornication by those involved in this quest! It is an abomination to the Lord, and you must not profane this holy adventure! Get you back to Camelot and your pathetic worldly king with his strumpet queen! Tell them only the purest will survive! These are Brother Nascien's canons!'"

"Brother Nascien?" Merlin raised his eyes. "How is it he has taken over this quest? By what right does he pronounce dogma on Arthur's knights? And what has he to do with insulting the king and queen?"

"The white knight used his name in chastising King Bagdemagus, too, I remember. When the king claimed the red-cross shield," I answered. "He seems to be the self-acclaimed master of the quest. It was he that brought Galahad into Camelot. He that trained the young knight up in his purity."

"And it was Galahad who sent us all off on the mad scramble after a ghostly object," Ywain added. "I don't know what I was thinking, but I'll tell you what, I'm well out of it. Someone is going to get killed on this quest if it keeps going this way."

Merlin and I looked at each other, with "Are you going to tell him or should I?" written all over our faces. Finally Merlin cleared his throat and broke the news as gently as he could. "You've been away many days, my lord. News has been trickling in gradually, as have a number of the knights. I'm afraid there is bad news."

Ywain raised his head, then his eyebrow. "Tell," he said, his dark eyes burning.

"First," Merlin briefed him, "Sir Ironside was killed by one of his fellow knights, while attempting to assault a young woman.'"

Ywain looked surprised but not dismayed. He snorted. "Well, Ironside was a brute and a swaggering bully. His death does not diminish my uncle's Table. But who is the unfortunate knight who was forced to slay his brother in arms? He may be having a rough go of it."

"I am afraid it was your kinsman, Sir Gawain."

At that Ywain drew his head back, shocked and chagrinned. "Gawain is it? That's hard. It's not a blow I would wish upon him just now, after…well, it's a bad time for him to try to live with this."

"I'm afraid he has not handled it well," Merlin went on. "Days later, in a kind of frenzy over the affair with the Red Knight, Gawain met Sir Galahad in the forest and charged him. He was severely wounded and even now lies in the infirmary at the Abbey of Saint Sebastian, attended by Lovell and his brother Gaheris."

"Worse and worse," Ywain moaned. "He isn't like to die, is he?"

"We do not know," answered Merlin honestly.

"There is more," I said, not wishing to leave Ywain in the dark about any of it. "A few days ago we heard that Sir Colgrevaunce has been killed as well. And he, too, by a knight of the Round Table: Sir Lionel."

At that point Thomas, who'd been standing by mute throughout the conversation, grew animated as he burst into tears. "Sir Colgrevaunce, Ywain!" he lamented. "Our dear friend! Kind Sir Colgrevaunce, who never betrayed any knight, no, nor slighted any squire. Killed, and while trying to defend Sir Bors against an attack by his own brother!"

"What?" Sir Ywain was positively astounded. "Have we entered a land of mirrors, where nothing is what it seems? Lionel attacking Bors? What next?"

"What's next is the cold-blooded murder of Sir Safer," Merlin answered.

"Sir Safer?" Ywain cried. "Why, he and Palomides weren't even *on* this quest. What could have happened to Safer?"

"The white knight," I told him bluntly. "Almost certainly the same one that attacked you and King Bagdemagus—and Sir Lionel as well, it must be said. His attack on Safer was unprovoked and murderous."

"Well this white knight has got to be stopped!" Ywain cried. "We've lost Ironside, Colgrevaunce, Safer. Gawain, Bagdemagus, and I are incapacitated. And then there's my lion."

"What happened to your lion?" I wanted to know. "You said they had trapped him in a net. What did they do with him after?"

Ywain shrugged. "I don't know. As I lay in the dust after that cowardly white-armed churl flattened me, I saw the rest of his gang riding off, dragging my poor lion along, roaring and flailing his paws helplessly as they pulled him in the nets after their horses. Gradually his roars died away. When I finally felt able to climb onto Bucephalus, I had no idea where to look for him, and thought for my own safety I had better get back to Camelot or to a friendly house as soon as I was able. I can only hope that they did not harm him. He is a noble animal and more faithful than any companion I have ever had. And that even includes my Alundine." His face remained serious, so I do not think that last was intended as a joke.

"Then we can hope for the best rather than fear the worst in the case or your lion," Merlin said diplomatically. "But you are correct. We need to stop this white knight, we need to find out who is behind what seems to be a deliberate attempt to undermine and even destroy Arthur's Round Table through this bizarre quest."

"I don't know if you have any ideas," I told Ywain. "We considered the possibility that Sir Mordred might be in the background of this conspiracy. After all, he did not take part in the quest himself, and he figures to have a great deal to gain by Sir Gawain's disgrace and a weakening of Arthur's power."

"You may say so," Ywain concurred. "But do not make the mistake of forgetting this: Gawain may be the heir apparent as Arthur's oldest nephew. But second in line for the throne is not one of Gawain's brothers, as is often assumed. It is I that have the most to gain if Gawain were to be killed or disinherited, because I am next in line."

"God's eyeteeth!" Merlin exclaimed. "So you are! So how would Mordred overcome that hurdle?"

"He wouldn't," Ywain asserted. "At least, he wouldn't if I still had my lion. No, the only way Mordred can stake a claim to the throne is by having Arthur legitimize him." And with that I realized that Ywain was one of the inner circle that knew of Mordred's true relationship to the king.

"Well, we had already nearly eliminated Mordred as a suspect in this particular case. He may be the slimiest of all brutes, but he does not seem to be behind these quest murders. The only other person we could come up with who has an old grudge against Arthur and might like to see the Table fall is the old enchantress, Morgan le Fay."

"Mother?" Ywain inquired, looking thoughtful.

I felt the blood draining slowly out of my face and began glancing around, searching for a hole I could crawl into. It had never once occurred to me that Morgan was, of course, Ywain's mother, wife of King Uriens of Gorre.

"There is certainly some sibling rivalry there," Ywain admitted. "And for sure, she's played some pretty nasty tricks on Gawain herself." He sighed. "And not too many people know this, but I walked in on her holding a sword over my father's head at one point, after he had allied himself with Arthur against King Lot and his allies. She would have killed him if I hadn't made her promise to let him be. That's why they separated, and she came to live in Arthur's castle, at least until Guinevere came along. But if she was willing to kill Uriens, what wouldn't she be prepared to do to Arthur given the chance? No, she's a dangerous woman, make no mistake. But one thing is pretty certain: Of all the people in the world, I'm her own flesh and blood, and she has always been gentle with me. If she were really behind this white knight's rampage, I'd be the one knight she'd order him not to harm. I think we can agree," he nodded at his bandaged shoulder, "I've been harmed."

Merlin pursed his lips and gave that some thought. "It does seem unlikely that Morgan would be behind your own attack. But I don't know whether we can rule out the white knight's acting on his own, even if someone else is ultimately behind the plot. He does keep mentioning Brother Nascien, for instance, but I have to wonder whether Brother Nascien had all of this in mind when he declared that only the purest should achieve the quest."

"I think we'd better track down this Brother Nascien and question him," Ywain declared.

I looked at him quizzically. "We?"

"Well, sure. What else have I got to do?"

"You've got to lie here and let your wound heal," Merlin told him. "If there's anything you can do to help us, we'll let you know. But it's not going to do us or our investigation any good to have you killing yourself with stress before we find the culprits behind these outrages."

Sir Ywain stuck his lower lip out, looking for all the world like a pouting child. "I guess you're right," he admitted. "But let's do one thing: my mother is an expert healer, conversant as she is in all the arcane arts. Of all the people in Camelot, she may be able to do me the most good in the way of healing. Bring her to me and let her search my wounds. It will not only help me, but we can ask her about these goings on, so you can satisfy yourselves that she has nothing to do with them."

"We can do that," Merlin answered thoughtfully. "But you must be careful during the questioning. Whatever you do, do not let her know we consider her a suspect. Understand?"

"Of course," Ywain answered with a smile. "Then you can focus on a more likely target. Track down this Brother Nascien, I say. Get his story. I'll swear his hands are not clean."

"Not a bad plan," Merlin allowed. "For a knight with the mane of a beast."

Ywain smiled wanly. "When you're out looking for this villain," he murmured, "see if you can track down my lion. Please?"

CHAPTER TEN

MORGAN

I had expected her to be wearing black. I suppose that was just my own preconception of her as an enchantress, or, let's face it, a witch. Anybody who could remove and then restore the head of a man like the Green Knight was a force of black magic to be very wary of. And black as night should be her garments, right?

Well no, actually. Morgan le Fay came into her son's closet attended by her nephew Sir Gareth and wearing a fashionable red bliaut, a gown imported, no doubt, from France. It looked to be made of silk from the east. It was edged at the neckline by gray vair, and was tightly fitted under her bosom, where it was pleated horizontally, then belted by a long girdle tied in front, and completed by ample skirts that floated like great waves around her legs as she walked in the door. Her sleeves, fitted tightly on her upper arms, expanded like the bells of trumpets from the elbows downwards.

As the queen of Gorre (which Morgan definitely was, despite her estrangement from King Uriens, and despite the kingdom having fallen into the hands of Uriens' cousin, King Bagdemagus, upon his death), Morgan, like Queen Guinevere herself, wore her long hair uncovered, and let her extensive locks spread voluminously around her shoulders. Her hair was raven colored, with a few streaks of gray the only thing in her appearance betraying any sense of her real age. For her face seemed smooth as a twenty-year old's, her dark eyes as bright as a young virgin's, her moist lips as luscious in appearance as my lady Rosemounde's. Or at least almost so.

"You can stop worrying, Yewey dear, Mother's here," she said, without a trace of irony, as she flounced in through the door. Sir Gareth, trailing right behind her, carried a small white leather bag that contained, I expected, potions or herbs or whatever it was the lady Morgan planned to use to treat Sir Ywain's dire wounds.

"Funny," Ywain answered her, lying back on his pillow and gazing up toward the ceiling with a sigh. "That's usually when I *begin* to worry."

She raised an eyebrow and drilled her gaze into him, scolding him with her eyes. "Now Yewey," she cajoled. "You know you need me and you know I can help you, so why don't you keep a civil tongue in your head."

"Yes Mother," Ywain muttered through clenched teeth. "Do your magic."

This is a close and loving family, I said to myself. Sir Gareth set the leather bag down on Ywain's bed while Morgan unwrapped Ywain's bandage from his mutilated shoulder. She gasped audibly when she saw the depth of the angry-looking wound, which still bled copiously. "Give me that jar of maggots, nephew!" she ordered Gareth. The knight drew a covered ceramic jar from the bag and, with his upper lip wrinkled in disgust, handed it to Morgan, and then stepped back to stand next to me.

"Yewey?" I queried from her corner of my mouth.

Gareth rolled his eyes. "She's always called him that."

"How does someone get such a wound on a quest for a holy relic?" Morgan asked. Her face was nearly buried in Ywain's shoulder. She sniffed the wound to make sure it was not festering. Then she opened the jar to let the maggots enter and clean the wound, taking a fresh bandage from the white bag and binding Ywain's shoulder again. Having heard no answer to her question, she asked again, her voice rising with impatience. "How did you come by this wound? Tell me!"

"This quest is not the peaceful idyll most of the knights expected," Merlin began, taking charge of the conversation. "Many of our knights have been fighting amongst themselves, even to the point of death."

Morgan looked up from where she was readying the broad cloth bandage to bind the maggots into Ywain's wound with wide eyes and a look of what certainly seemed to be genuine surprise on her face. "It cannot be!" she objected.

"No, no, it's absolutely true," Merlin asserted. "There is, moreover, an anonymous white knight riding about, claiming to enforce the laws of the quest, punishing knights he deems unworthy of the God-given adventure. That is what happened to Sir Ywain."

Morgan scowled, looking down at Ywain's bandaged arm. "So that is what happened? This white knight gave you this wound?"

"That he did," Ywain concurred. "Drove his lance right through my shoulder. Sent me crashing to the earth. And what's worse, his cronies dragged my lion off in a net. I don't know what they've done with him."

"Your lion!" Morgan's brows lowered with concern. "What could they want with him?"

"They can only want one thing," Merlin interjected. "To hurt Ywain. There is no other reason to seize that noble beast."

"But why would this white knight *want* to hurt my Yewie?"

"He warned me ahead of time," Ywain admitted. "Said that a knight on the quest must refrain from contact with ladies—said it was Brother Nascien's decree that only the purest of knights would have any chance to attain the Grail."

Morgan lifted an eyebrow. "Something, knowing you, that I would think was somewhat beyond your personal capabilities."

"Yes mother, I spent a night with my wife before setting out. Apparently I deserved to be skewered for that."

Morgan waved her hand, as if casting aside an obstacle that had the restraining power of a cobweb. "Some of these monks have little left of genuine humanity," she opined in her most scornful voice. "This Brother Nascien must be one of those. Perhaps I should pay him a visit in his cell one night, and see just how strong his convictions are, or whether there is anything left of his manhood."

"Yes," I couldn't help speaking up, rather eagerly, at that. "I'm sure you would hold the religion of these Cistercians in low regard. I have heard rumors that you were an adherent of the old Druid tradition…and that the reason you and Arthur have been enemies since his rise to the crown is that he brought Christianity to the kingdom of Logres."

Morgan scoffed, making a buzzing sound through her lips. "My God, where on earth did you hear that? That's about the silliest thing I've ever heard."

"Uh…but someone said…"

"It's nonsense, boy. The kingdom has been Christianized since the time of the Emperor Constantine. Sure, there have been monks and priests that've railed against me, claiming that I practice black magic, but I'm sure your own mentor there, son of an incubus that he is," her eye glinted at Merlin, "has endured the same kinds of accusations. But that's just superstitious people afraid of any kind of new knowledge. No, boy, no. The reason I've never gotten along well with my little brother is that he only came into being when that bastard father of his raped my mother. And with the help of that old necromancer standing beside you there." Merlin closed his eyes and sighed, with an air of having heard this same speech before. And often.

"The truth of the matter is, Aunt Morgan," Sir Gareth stepped in, wishing to get the discussion back on track before it went any further afield than it already had, "that this mysterious white knight has been the cause of a number of violent attacks on questing knights: he has killed Sir Safer, for example. He's put King Bagdemagus in the infirmary. He's nearly destroyed Sir Lionel—an act which led ultimately to the death of Sir Colgrevaunce. It seems as if someone has designed this whole quest rigmarole to wreak havoc on the knights of the Round Table…"

"So what we want to know, Mother," Ywain broke in, "is whether *you* are the one behind all of this."

There was the sharp sound of Merlin's palm slapping against his forehead. I was pretty sure this was not what he had had in mind when he told Ywain not to let Morgan know we considered her a suspect.

The smile froze on Morgan's face, and fixed itself there like a porcelain mask. But the eyes had ceased smiling, and shone with a piercing kind of light. In a voice of affected casualness underscored by flimsily contained rage, Morgan responded, "I? Someone believes that I might be conspiring to kill Arthur's precious knights? What could possibly cause one to entertain such a ludicrous idea?"

"History, Mother," Ywain replied. "History."

"You must admit," Merlin stepped in, trying what he could to rescue the situation, "that your past relationship with the King has been…shall we say, rocky?"

"That business with Sir Launfal, for instance," I put in, thinking to help the situation. "There might be some lingering ill will there, since it did not turn out well for you—you were exposed for making false accusations…"

"Well, your testing of Gawain was pretty mean-spirited as well, in that affair of the Green Knight," Gareth put in.

"Not to mention your earlier outright attempt to have the king killed in the affair of Sir Accolon and the theft of Excalibur," Merlin concluded.

Morgan's smile had evaporated from her face and in its place her visage glowered and reddened. She raised herself to her full height and lifted her chin so that she could gaze imperiously at us down her aquiline nose. "Am I to understand that this is why I have been brought here? To have all four of you attack me with these slanders? You dare to insinuate your charges against me, a queen? The sister of your Lord Arthur? A mother grieving over the wounds of her only child?"

"Now, Aunt Morgan," Gareth cajoled. "You are here to minister to your wounded child. We are not here to stand as accusers. The question has arisen, due to these acts of unwonted fratricide among the knights, whether someone with a deep-seated grudge against the king is behind these things."

"Yes, nephew," Morgan relaxed slightly, her lips twisting slightly into an ironic smile. "Always the little peacemaker, aren't you? Smooth the waters, that's your motto. Make a stand sometime, why don't you? Ha. You chide me with my wantonness, is that it? Yes, I lusted after Sir Launfal. He was handsome and good and I was young and full of life…"

"And married," Ywain murmured under his breath.

"Oh, shut up, Yewie," she went on. "I did my duty by my lawful husband. I popped *you* out, didn't I, nine months after the wedding? What hypocrites you men are. You think Uriens didn't have his little whores and lemans on the side? Where do you think that little bastard Uwain les Avoutres came from? But it's oh so forgivable when it's one of you who does it—nature of the beast, what? Boys will be boys—but there's hell to pay if a wife wants something other than her domineering old lecher of a spouse. So yes, I loved Launfal. How was I to know that phony mystic water-slut, the Lady of the Lake, already had her claws in him? Well, scorn me and you risk my wrath, that's all there is to it, so sure, I accused him before the court. And no, it was not my finest moment when I was shown up. But the Lady knew she'd made an implacable enemy at that point, I'll tell you that."

"Still you stayed in Camelot," Merlin observed, "rather than retreating to Uriens in Gorre."

"He was a dotard by then and he beat me," Morgan said simply. And a chill ran up my spine as the image of my dearest Lady Rosemounde's back floated before my eyes. Perhaps Morgan was not so much to blame after all.

"I stayed with my loving brother," she bit off the irony with gritted teeth, "and in Camelot found another to love. The young and gallant Sir Brumand. Oh, he was a beautiful boy, and knew just where to tickle me to get his reward."

"Thanks for *that* image, Mother," came Ywain's grumble.

"But that was just about the time that Lancelot came to Camelot. Now Arthur has always been a stickler for respectability, you know. True courtesy requires it, he firmly believes. And my small affair with Sir Brumand rankled him no end—though we were perfectly discrete. No one in Camelot knew anything about it except for Brumand's young squire—a beautiful lad named Grunamund, with curly blond locks and lovely green eyes, who I think fancied me a bit himself. But somehow Arthur got wind of it, and wanted none of it in his court, he told me, and invited me to leave Camelot if I could not restrain my lascivious inclinations, I think was how he put it. Well I wasn't going anywhere. And I wasn't about to restrain *any* of my inclinations, lascivious or otherwise. Especially when I could see plainly what my blind cuckold of a brother could not: that the peerless Sir Lancelot and the untarnished Queen Guinevere were rutting like dogs in heat right under his sanctimonious nose. Oh, how I hated them, and hated the hypocrisy. And Sir Brumand came to hate them too, particularly Sir Lancelot, of whom he was so jealous. Why should Lancelot's reputation so far surpass that of his fellow lecher and adulterer Brumand? Many times Sir Brumand talked of challenging the Great Knight to combat, but I dissuaded him every time. I loved him, but I was not blind. Even I could see that Lancelot, whatever else he was, was in every sense the master of the unsheathed sword."

"So you saved Brumand from Lancelot. But you couldn't save him from himself, could you?" Merlin prompted her.

"Is that a taunt, old man?" Morgan hissed. "No, Sir Brumand saw that Siege Perilous and became obsessed. From defeating Lancelot in the field he set his heart on proving he was the best man, the Chosen of Arthur's knights, by sitting in the seat that you, old necromancer, had reserved for the Destined One. And so he sat in that seat that *you* designed, and *you* burned him to death. Didn't you, old man?" She looked at him with uncompromising, accusing eyes, the jaw jutting forward in defiance.

With a deference that everyone in Camelot always reserved for the king's sister, whether or not she deserved it, Merlin shrugged and answered only, "Thus was the chair designed, my lady. None could have sat in it uninjured at that time."

"And so my Sir Brumand died," she continued. "Through the devices of a cur like you and your kennel master Arthur the Prig, and Arthur's bosom friend Sir Lancelot, though he was more interested in Arthur's wife's bosom, wasn't he?"

"As you say," Merlin cleared his throat, "Sir Brumand died."

"And you would upbraid me then with Sir Accolon? Ah, Accolon of Gaul was a fun-loving young whelp, but not in the same league as my Brumand. But he served his purpose. After Brumand died, the youth Grunamund fled to Gaul to become a knight in his own right, but that meant I had no allies at court. But that has never phased me. I seduced myself an ally in Accolon. I had only one objective: to take revenge on that child of my mother's rape, that haughty prude who looked down on my affair but overlooked his wife's. Yes, I hated you, old devil, and that hypocrite Lancelot as well, but it was Arthur who lorded it over the whole court, it was Arthur who was responsible, so it was Arthur I was going to bring down."

"But what did you do? What did this Accolon do?" I asked, curious despite myself. I had not heard the story before.

"Nearly killed the king with his own sword, as I've heard it," Sir Gareth ventured.

"It's no secret," Morgan shrugged. "Accolon accompanied Arthur when he visited King Uriens in our castle at Gorre. It was no difficult feat seducing Accolon: He was young and hot and lustful as a sparrow. And besides, I had promised to make him king of Logres, and to reign as queen beside him (well, truth to say, it would have been *over* him), if he would fight an unnamed knight for me when I sent him word. For I had a scheme I'd been working on for months before they arrived. It involved a quarrel between a local Lord, Sir Damas, and his younger, disinherited brother Sir Outzlake. The honorable Outzlake had been demanding single combat with Damas, or some knight willing to fight for him, to determine by trial whether the loss of Outzlake's inheritance was lawful or God's will. Damas was a knight of little prowess himself, and would not take part in such a challenge, but instead had formed the habit of waylaying good knights that passed through his lands and locking them in prison where he starved them, offering them release if they would fight his brother in this trial by combat. So I knew that if I could get Arthur and Accolon involved in this, on different sides, I could set up a situation where they would fight each other, and I could arrange to have Accolon win."

"But Arthur was an invincible warrior when he was young. How could you think you'd make him lose?" I interjected.

"It was not he that was so invincible," Morgan corrected me. "It was his bloody sword, that bloody weapon that Bitch of the Lake had given him, along with the scabbard, which rumor said made him invulnerable to the blows of swords."

"Fairy tales for babes," Merlin scoffed. "Such rumors were rampant at the time, because no one could believe one as youthful as the new king could be so skilled and deadly with the sword."

"Although the fact is," Gareth put in, "Excalibur is a remarkably well-forged weapon. I've never seen its equal."

"As it proved," Morgan continued, "a good deal of Arthur's prowess did indeed revolve around the quality of his sword. What I did was lay a trap for him when he was out hunting for a great hart with my reconciled husband Uriens and Accolon. The three of them came to a wide barge on a river, where they were feasted and offered beds for the night. But the barge was manned by my servants, who had mixed with their wine a potion I had concocted from the fruit of poppies, a potion that put them into a sleep that seemed enchanted. My servants moved them while they were unconscious—Arthur to the dungeon of Sir Damas, where he woke to find himself among several other knights who were being starved by that cowardly lord; Accolon to lay beside a well on Outzlake's estate; and Uriens into his own bedroom, next to his loving wife.

"The little wrinkle in all of this was that while they were sleeping, I had told my servants to take Arthur's sword and scabbard from him and gird them around Sir Accolon's waist. Meanwhile I had them replace Arthur's weapon with a replica of my own making, with a blade so dull that it would scarcely cut flesh, let alone armor, and so badly forged that it was almost certain to shatter in the heat of any truly vigorous battle.

"Well, you know the rest, I'm sure. I sent a maiden to the prison to tell Arthur that if he'd fight Damas's battle for him, all of the other knights would be delivered from the prison, and Arthur could punish Damas later when he was back on his throne. Then I sent a dwarf to Accolon, and told him that I commanded him to fight the knight who represented Damas in the upcoming trial, as he had agreed earlier. The dwarf also had to convince Sir Outzlake to let my knight represent him in the trial, but that wasn't difficult. The dwarf told him the request came from King Arthur's own sister, and that I guaranteed him victory. Which I was confident in doing, since Accolon, after all, was fighting with Excalibur itself. Besides, I had my dwarf attend him in the battle, and the dwarf slipped another potion of mine into his drink right before the battle—this one an elixir derived from the *Hyoscyamus niger*, or black henbane plant, imported from southern

Gaul. It stimulated Accolon's aggressive behavior, fomenting in him a kind of rage. When he attacked Arthur, he went at him like a Berserker."

Merlin started at that as if someone had stuck him with a needle. I looked at him quizzically but he lowered his eyes and gave me a slight shake of the head.

Morgan went on: "Of course, in full armor and without their usual accoutrements, neither knight knew who the other one was. The battle lasted for hours, with Accolon chiefly on the attack and Arthur with his superior skill and inferior sword fending off blow after blow. At least this is what the dwarf told me later—I was not present for the battle, stuck as I was with my own husband, though I did not think that it would last long. When both knights were nearing exhaustion, at the climax of the battle, Accolon took one last great swing at the king's head and when Arthur parried the blow that ill-forged sword broke in his hand. He was left holding just the hilt, and though he still had his shield, he could not mount any kind of attack. Accolon could not conceivably lose now."

"But he did. Obviously," Sir Gareth pointed out. "What happened?"

Morgan shut her eyes and I could see her jaw set as she clenched her teeth in a kind of controlled rage. "That meddling Lady of the Lake had somehow learned of my subterfuge and had been watching the battle, hidden among Sir Damas's entourage. When Arthur's sword broke off at the hilt, the interfering wench threw off her mantel and showed herself before the crowd. And she called out: "King Arthur!" Well Arthur's head snapped up, and if Accolon had been ready, he could have ended it right there, with the king's attention pulled away from the battle. But so stunned was he to realize that he was in battle with his king that he let his own guard down, and Arthur, much quicker to recover, swung his shield against Accolon's sword arm and knocked Excalibur clean out of his grip, so that it flew across the field of battle. Accolon let his focus waver," she shook her head in acknowledgement of the inevitable. "The king swung the edge of the shield back and brought it across with all his strength to the side of Accolon's head.

Even with the helmet protecting him, he was knocked senseless. It was all over. And Arthur had recovered Excalibur."

"But you thought he'd been killed, didn't you mother dear? Because that's just the moment I came upon you standing over my father's sleeping form holding an unsheathed sword over his head. Isn't that about right?"

She paused a moment, raised her eyebrows and closed her eyes, shrugging with a kind of defeated acknowledgement, as if someone had caught her cheating at chess. "Ah, Yewie, just like your father. Neither one of you could ever take a joke."

"After that incident, King Uriens banished you from his castle, as I recall, and your brother made it clear you were no longer welcome in Camelot," Merlin summed up. "That could surely be motive enough to try to destroy his court."

"Half-brother," Morgan muttered.

"Well, you know that your escapade with Sir Accolon ended up getting me banished from Camelot as well," Ywain added.

Morgan cleared her throat, looking down. "Now, to be fair, it's not really accurate to say that you were banished because of that incident. It was after I sent that lovely robe as a peace offering and apology to Arthur. A robe intended as a gift to his queen."

"A robe that the Lady of the Lake advised Arthur to have your messenger model for us before giving it to the queen," Merlin continued. "And what happened to your messenger?"

Morgan shrugged. "I was exiled, and so could not have witnessed it. I've heard rumors, of course, but such things are always blown out of proportion."

"Well I was there," Merlin replied. "Your messenger put on the robe, and immediately began writhing in pain. By the time we pulled the robe off her flesh where it burned and clung so tenaciously, she had died in agony. A lovely present *that* would have been for the queen."

Morgan shrugged it off again. "It was such a beautiful robe, though, was it not? Perhaps I used a bit too much purple dye in the material and the messenger had some kind of hypersensitive reaction to it? Who can say?"

"Oh, Mother, I think perhaps you could say," Ywain interrupted. "But it was after that that Arthur exiled me from Camelot. And it was my dearest cousin, Sir Gawain, who stood up for me and risked his own relationship with the king. 'Whoever banishes my cousin germane banishes me as well,' he told Arthur. And we went off together. I'm certain that I was only called back to court, or at least was called back as soon as I was, because of the stand Gawain took in that matter. And so I must ask you, Mother, why you treated Gawain in such a vile manner in the affair of the Green Knight?"

Morgan did not answer the question immediately. She took a moment, her eyes gazing to the side, as if contemplating something a long way off. "Did you know," she asked, "that when Sir Accolon died of his wounds a fortnight after the battle, Arthur had his body delivered to me in Gorre? It's true. He couldn't resist rubbing my nose in my failure, but worse, he cruelly forced me to grieve over the corpse of the second lover I had lost to cruel death in less than a year. While his peerless queen enjoyed her Lancelot with impunity. I wanted revenge on both of them. What woman with an ounce of blood in her veins would not? The robe would have punished her, and would have made him feel just a little bit of what I had felt again and again." Another brief pause, and she shook off her reverie: "But Gawain?" she continued after a pause. "He was collateral damage. I thought it was Arthur who would take up the knight's challenge. Gawain was a fortuitous substitute, though. He was Arthur's heir, wasn't he? He was the paragon of courtesy in the court. If he could fail, then Arthur's court would be exposed as a sham."

"But he didn't fail," Sir Gareth put in. "My brother was up to your challenge, and he demonstrated that courtesy is no sham, whatever else may smack of human weakness."

"No," Morgan snapped a little too quickly. "He didn't fail in courtesy, *that* time." But with that, her face softened, and she seemed to relax and adopt her public face of pleasantry once again. "But these things are long past. You all know that my brother and I have been reconciled for years now, and I am again welcome at his court, as you see me here now. And my Yewie, of course, is one of Arthur's greatest knights. And all is well in our family once again."

"Oh, I daresay," Gareth responded, not without a touch of irony. "We are a loving clan, aren't we?"

Morgan pursed her lips and ignored the insinuation, feigning rapt attention to the bandage she now wrapped about Ywain's shoulder, trapping the maggots under the dressing upon which she had poured out a potion from her bag. "That's *betony*," she said in a low, almost distracted voice. "Bishopswort. It will help with the pain and speed the healing. I will be back to change the dressing tomorrow."

She picked up her bag, her head bent, and made as if to start out of the room. But before taking a step, she pulled herself up to her full height and with her dark eyes flashing once again looked imperiously down her nose at each one of us in the room. "As I have said, my brother and I have had our ups and downs, but we were reconciled years ago. These things you bring up are relics of a bygone age. I am no danger to my lord Arthur or his kingdom. Now, if I have leave of you fine, important men, your humble servant will toddle off to her needlework." And with a hint of a smirk she glided out of the room, her red silk skirts floating like sea foam around her ankles. She did not look back. Sir Gareth, having attended her on her way into the room shrugged his shoulders, flashed us a half grin, and left to attend her on her way out.

Sir Ywain looked up to us from where he reclined on his bed and said, with absolute sincerity, "There, you see? I told you Mother could have had nothing to do with this current mess." And he closed his eyes, leaning his head back and breathing a sigh of relief, as if having just gone through a physical ordeal. Which, given her vigorous searching of his wound, he had.

I flashed Merlin a furtive glance. I was not as sanguine as Ywain about what we had just experienced with Morgan le Fay, and I could see by Merlin's downturned mouth that he was feeling the same. "Well, that may be our cue to leave as well," he told Ywain with forced geniality. "We should go and let you rest. I can see that you probably could use some sleep."

"Yes," Ywain said. "I don't mind admitting it. I'm exhausted. And damn it, I miss my lion."

***

"We needed to get away from Sir Ywain. I fear there are things we should discuss that he may be unhappy about," Merlin told me quietly as we stepped along the passageway to head out into the bailey.

"I know! " I exclaimed. "He thinks that she convinced us she's not a suspect? Wow. If that woman is innocent, I'm a bloody Saracen."

"Such language," Merlin tsked. "Where do you pick up that kind of talk? But I agree. God's elbows, Gildas, what she said about the henbane potion smote me between the eyes, it seemed."

"I noticed that," I admitted. "What was that about?"

"Well don't you see?" He asked, though he was looking at me without focus and his mind seemed to be drifting. "It explains so many of the strange happenings on this quest. Why would Lionel attack his brother? Why was Gawain moved to kill Sir Ironside rather than simply subdue him? Had they drunk that potion? Were they chafed into raw berserk bellicosity by consuming that tonic? And where were they given it? Where indeed did…how did they…" His voice trailed off. He began to stagger a bit, and when he held his hand up to his forehead, I could see that one eye was bulging while the other was squinting. I knew these signs. Merlin was about to have one of his spells. It was inevitable, and I should have expected it. As he crumbled into the grass, he muttered something about the images of his vision: "The Mother of light is the mother of darkness," Merlin croaked as I lifted his head into my arms. "But the widow triumphs." And with that his eyes closed, and I knew he would not be lucid again for hours. Maybe days.

CHAPTER ELEVEN

HIATUS WITH JOUSTING AND DOGS

While Merlin lay in his usual stupor in Sir Gareth's quarters, there was little I could do to further our investigation. I couldn't see what our next move ought to be, and while I doubted at this point whether Merlin did either, at least I knew that he'd be decisive whenever he came out of his spell, and so the next morning I spent with Sir Gareth himself, working on my training for knighthood under his gentle supervision. I found the physical exertion of the training soothing to my mind, which kept surging in different directions—nearly unhinged when I thought about my Rosemounde and her brute of a husband, or craving justice (or revenge) at the thought of Colgrevaunce's unprovoked slaughter. In my training I could shut off my mind, at least for the duration of the session. Although when my lady Rosemounde wed the king's nephew I had lost my sole purpose for wishing to become a knight—my desire to become worthy of my lady's hand—I had gained a new inspiration after witnessing the marks of Mordred's brutality. I wanted to hone my knightly skills to the point where I could challenge that monster, her husband, on the field of battle, and break every bone in his body if I possibly could.

Sir Gareth had brought me to the listing field of the practice area to have a go at some true battle maneuvers. I wore a solid plate-metal helmet that covered my entire face except for an eye slit, wide enough to see out of but narrow enough to make too small a target for even the most skilled jouster. Hanging from a strap over my shoulder and covering the left side of my body was a reinforced wooden shield painted white, reflecting my as yet unheralded knighthood and reminding me of my own less than noble heritage. But I thought of my father as I adjusted the chain mail hauberk I wore, which was adding nearly fifty pounds to my horse's burden and my own. My father's mail was some of the most sought after in Logres. He had been apprenticed to one of the great craftsmen of Gaul, in the city of Chartres, well known for its armorers. There he had learned the intricacies of his profession. I looked down at the tiny interwoven rings, each one originally opened so it could be connected to four others, and as many as a hundred thousand of these rings would go into the manufacture of a well-made hauberk like the one I was now wearing. Months of an armor-maker's time. I hoped that Sir Gareth had paid the craftsman handsomely for the mail coat.

In my right hand I held a twelve-foot long wooden lance, with a crown-shaped metal cap at the end for use in jousting and sparring, rather than the deadly sharp, leaf-shaped point of the battle lance. The wood of the lance broadened out as it receded from the point, forming a flared skirt around the hand-grip that would lodge the lance into my right armpit upon impact and prevent the force of the blow from knocking the lance completely out of my hand. It was made of solid oak, and would take a prodigious blow to shatter, but I knew that in tournament jousting, a shattered spear was desirable, since it indicated that you had hit your opponent solidly, rather than with simply a glancing blow. In true combat, of course, a shattered spear might be a serious disadvantage. You would want a squire to be carrying an extra lance or two.

But all of these accoutrements were nothing compared with my greatest asset of all, the powerful dark brown destrier Achilles whom Gareth had loaned me to ride this morning. Standing around eighteen hands tall, he was the foal of Gareth's own great horse Ajax, bred in Spain and worth every farthing of the 80£ he had paid for him—a full third of his annual income, even as one of the king's great barons. Achilles, as Ajax's own offspring, had cost the king's nephew far less, but was worth at least as much. I sat atop him on a new jousting saddle, with a raised cantle in the rear to prevent me from being pushed from the saddle, and a high pommelto in the front to protect me from lance thrusts below the waist. It was narrower than most riding saddles, and the stirrups hung lower, so that my legs were not widespread and my carriage was more similar to my standing than my riding posture, a position that enabled me to nearly duplicate my stance while fighting on foot, and increase my effectiveness from horseback.

I would need to be particularly effective today, for instead of tilting at the quintain, which had been my occupation day after day for some months now, Sir Gareth deemed me ready to engage in a live joust. And, in absence of a large number of other squires and knights from Camelot due to the madness that was this Grail quest, Gareth had offered himself as my opponent. Oh, it was encouraging, I suppose, to have one of the best jousters of Arthur's court offering to spar with me on the practice field as if he considered me a worthy opponent. Though I knew, of course, that he was deliberately trying to buck up my confidence, which he likely construed to be his duty as my master. And so, of course, I wasn't confident in the slightest, having thought about it too hard and convinced myself I was Sir Gareth's charity case.

Now I sat atop my tall saddle, my lance fewtered—resting in the leather support attached to the right side of my saddle—as I held the long weapon straight up. I looked across at Sir Gareth some fifty yards from me, waiting on Ajax, who was stamping his right foot impatiently. Gareth's own helmet sported a visor, which was now raised as he called to me across the field, "Now don't try to do this at full speed the first time, Gildas! We'll come together at more of a trot, just so you can get the feel of it! When I start Ajax coming at you, you kick Achilles into a slow charge!" And he dropped his visor and leaned toward me.

With some trepidation I leaned forward myself—about a thirty degree angle was optimal in jousting—and lifted the spear to couch it under my right arm, angling it to the left, where I would pass Sir Gareth and endeavor to unhorse him, or to break my spear on his shield trying. My own shield hung from my neck onto my left side, where I held it by the grips that had been riveted into the shield just near its center point, and hung it a little forward so that it rested on Achilles' neck. I told myself to focus on the four rivets in the center of Gareth's shield, as that would provide me with the best target I could find. Gareth's shield, bearing his crest of the silver unicorn rampant on its field of gold, had its four rivets square in the center of the unicorn's torso, and so that's where I would aim my blow. As I looked down at Gareth on Ajax, I noticed that the point of my lance was wobbling, the result of my own trembling—was it fear or anticipation? And then I saw that Ajax had started ambling toward me. I used the pressure of my thighs to urge Achilles forward, and as he began his trot I pushed my feet hard into my stirrups, for it was from them that my thrust would take the main support for its power.

I knew that we were going at a gentle pace, but as the blood thumped in my ears I swear I felt as if Sir Gareth were bearing down on me at full tilt. As we approached, I tensed my shield arm to protect my left side, and thrust with my couched lance. I felt the force of Gareth's lance strike with enormous power on my own shield a split second before I made contact. It was enough to jolt me out of my concentration, and I felt my own thrust glance weakly off the knight's shield, missing the four rivets and sliding ineffectually toward the right.

With a prick of my rowel spurs, I brought Achilles to a halt after following through the encounter. A bit chagrinned, I turned to face my master, who I expected was about to dress me down. I was wrong.

"Well done, Gildas my lad!" Sir Gareth cried. "I gave you a good thumping with the lance, one that would have knocked at least half of the knights of Arthur's Table over the backs of their saddles, for sure! You handled your shield with great skill on that pass. Do you know what you did wrong, though?"

I thought about it for a moment. "My mind," I said. "I was distracted from my own blow by my surprise at the strength of yours, and so I didn't deliver as true a thrust as I might have."

"Absolutely right, Gildas! And they all told me you were a half-wit. But that's only half true! Look, you need all your wits, so don't divide them. Know that the blow is coming and be ready for it, but no matter what happens, focus on hitting those rivets. Your left hand will help prevent you from losing, but your right hand is the only thing that will help you win! So be sure your left hand knows what your right hand is doing, right?" He laughed out loud. "Didn't Our Lord say something like that? Let that be my nod to the Grail Quest. Let's have at it again, shall we?"

I turned Achilles and we ambled back to where we had started the original tilt. Once more I fewtered the lance, flexed my feet in my stirrups, looked down at Gareth, leaned forward and couched my lance.

"This time let's try it at full tilt and see what happens!" Gareth shouted to me as he put down his visor. That sent a wave of heat into my stomach. I took a deep breath and then leapt into action as I saw Ajax start toward me. My thighs squeezed Achilles in the command to charge and I let him have his head as we hurtled toward that living battering ram that was bearing down upon me. I felt a rush of a breeze fly into my helmet and around my ears, felt my muscles tighten of their own accord, held tight my shield and at the same time put all my strength into my right arm. Backed by the force of Achilles' thundering speed surging from the stirrups through my legs and body and into my arm, I saw those four rivets in the unicorn's breast and aimed at them, and with a bang-bang I felt the severe blow to my shield, but also felt my lance driven back with astounding power into my right armpit—then, the surprising release of that pressure. When I looked back to see what had caused that unexpected release, I saw the shards of my oaken spear lying shattered on the field. Gareth, stopping Ajax's course, looked back as well, and laughed as he held up to me his own lance, or what was left of it.

"Now that was some real jousting my lad!" He roared. "Let's pick up a couple of new lances and have at it again!"

We tossed aside the splintered remnants of weapons and rode over to the side of the field near the castle wall, where we had left two spare lances. There Thomas stood, holding another great war horse, watching us. "Well struck, Gildas," he exclaimed, as he held up the two replacement lances for Gareth and me to use. "Best I've seen you do, I'd say."

"Thanks Thomas," I said, reddening. Praise from another squire, when we were all in competition to see who could be knighted soonest, was always welcome, and hard to come by.

"I just left Sir Ywain, sleeping again. Not much to do while he's laid up and the castle is as empty as it is. Thought I'd come down and have a go at the quintain, but I see you're doing the real thing."

"We're having at least one more tilt," Sir Gareth said. "Thanks for the lances—it's a pain to get in and out of the saddle with all this gear. Gildas? To arms!"

We rode to our starting positions one more time. Gareth put down his visor, proffered his lance and couched it beneath his arm, and kneed his horse into a charge. I did the same, tensing my grip on the shield, the lance, and bracing my feet in the stirrups. I leaned forward, squeezed Achilles with my thighs, and shot toward Sir Gareth, worrying less about defending myself than about giving him a great wallop.

The next thing I knew, I was lying on my back in the dust, shaking my head to quiet the ringing in my ears, and Achilles' long face bending down and staring into mine, as if to say, "Are you okay? How many hooves am I holding up?"

In my right hand I still held the stump of my lance, which had shattered again upon impact with Sir Gareth's shield. My left arm felt rather numb, and my shield was lying face down a few yards behind me. I seemed to remember striking a good blow, but must this time have taken my concentration away from my shield arm, long enough for Sir Gareth's blow to knock my shield away, battering my arm and left side and sending me, if I remembered correctly, head first backwards over the cantle of my saddle, leaving me flat on my back in the dust of the field.

Sir Gareth's face finally floated into view, through the eye-slit in my heavy helmet—a helmet which, I realized, must have saved my head from being crushed like a pumpkin by this fall. "Ah, Gildas, you've got to remember to focus on both sides of your horse: the offense and the defense, the right hand and the left. You struck a mighty blow, though—see? You've splintered your lance again! Good show! Now get up—shake off the small hurts, boy! Here!" As I slowly rose to a sitting position, reaching up to remove my helmet, Gareth tossed his own lance to me. It was still whole, and I instinctively caught it in my right hand.

"Why don't you spend the rest of the morning with Thomas here, tilting at the quintain? I think we've had enough live practice for one day. Ajax is tired. And besides," he laughed as he cantered off, "we've run out of lances! Have Achilles brushed and fed when you bring him back to the stable." And off he rode.

***

Merlin was still not stirring by mid-day, so I quickly assented to sit down to an informal dinner with Thomas, Sir Gareth, Sir Palomides, and Sir Gaheris, who had just returned from Gawain's sickbed with the news that, while not completely recovered, Gawain would be brought back to Camelot in a wagon accompanied by his son Lovell within the next two days. Gareth and I welcomed the news, though Gareth lamented the fact that he still had not been summoned into the royal presence to defend his brother's misdeeds. Perhaps Gawain's return would hasten that meeting, he hoped. In the meantime, there was some comfort in the fact that, to our knowledge, Sir Mordred had not visited the king either while we had been waiting. We wondered who had been visiting the king in the meantime, and as a group decided that the one way to find out what may be going through the king's mind during all of this was to have someone talk unofficially with the queen. And all eyes turned toward me.

"Yes, all right," I sputtered. "I'll apply to see her this afternoon. I'll have to…I don't know…find some excuse. Perhaps I can suggest a walk around the grounds with her greyhounds—we used to do that a couple of times a week when I was her page, and she always seemed to enjoy those walks. Besides, my own Guinevere could use a walk as well!" I referred, of course, to my borzoi, the sighthound I had adopted from my friend Captain Jacques on my visit to Brittany last year. I had named her Guinevere because—well, you know, she and the queen had a lot in common, including the belief that she was in charge. But I had another ulterior motive for volunteering to discuss matters with the queen: namely, I had every intention of persuading the queen to bring the lady Rosemounde on this walk, and any time spent with my beloved was precious to me. And so it was agreed: After the meal, I would visit the queen's rooms.

To make matters worse however, we also learned at dinner from Sir Palomides that three more knights had straggled in together that morning, having given up the quest for the Grail and come back in a sullen, defeated mood. Returning were Sir Ozanna le Cure Hardy, Sir Bleoberis, and Sir Breunor le Noire (who was always called "La Cote Male Taile"—the "Ill-Tailored Coat"—a nickname Sir Kay had tagged him with upon his first arrival at court). But they came with a new tale of woe: another knight, Sir Uwain les Avoutres, the natural son of Ywain's father King Uriens, had been killed on the quest— run through the body by a battle lance. The three knights had come upon Sir Uwain in the woods some leagues from Camelot, just as he was breathing his last. He did not know who had killed him—all Uwain had said was that he was struck down by a knight who bore no blazon on his shield. Sir Gareth and I looked at one another. It sounded too much like the other killings involving the White Knight to be a coincidence.

***

And so it was that, sometime around none later that day I exited the queen's inner chamber and, with Her Majesty on my right arm and the lady Rosemounde on my left, walked down the wide staircase leading down into the lower bailey, where the queen's new page stood holding three very excited dogs on leather leashes. The queen wore a long purple gown with an embroidered surcote over it. Her blonde hair blew free in the breeze, with only a circlet of roses and lilies holding it in some semblance of order. Though it was unheard of for married women to go with heads uncovered, a queen was not subject to such mundane conventions, and Guinevere was not about to be bound in any way. Rosemounde, more modestly, and for her, appropriately, wore her brown hair braided and twisted up under a round linen headdress, and wore a barbier around her perfectly formed chin as well. She had a simple blue gown, almost rustic, though her sleeves hung down fashionably, well below her knees when she held her hands folded at her waist, which she did now, clutching a small nosegay, as we reached the bottom of the steps and the dogs began frantically to leap up on us in their joy and excitement.

"You hold Aeneas and Dido," I told young Peter, who seemed particularly befuddled as the greyhounds leaped about, twisting him up in their leashes. "Let me take Guinevere," I meant my dog, of course. "Short-leash them, like this." I wrapped the leash around my left hand so that Guinevere had only about eighteen inches to jump around in. "Take one in each hand and hold them close on either side of you. They'll walk a lot better that way." I meant, of course, better controlled. "And keep back, two or three paces behind us, or they'll keep wanting to jump on the queen. And believe me, you don't want to be the page that lets the dogs get muddy paw-prints on her surcote." I spoke from experience. Peter looked up at me with wide blue eyes and a completely blank expression, and I wondered whether I ever looked so completely clueless when I was his age.

"You were, you know," the queen whispered to me as I fell in beside her with her namesake borzoi at my left heel.

"What's that, my lady?" I asked.

"You were quite as wide eyed and innocent as that one when you first started with me five years ago," the queen answered.

I supposed my surprise registered a bit as I looked up at her, and she gave a quick laugh. "So mindreading is another of your many talents, my Queen." I said. "I suppose if being Arthur's queen doesn't work out, you can always join a group of itinerant mummers as a carnival attraction!"

Sometimes, I know, I presumed too much in my familiarity with the queen, and while Her Majesty laughed that comment off, Rosemounde at my left glowered at me momentarily over my breach of courtesy. For a moment I was happy there was a large dog between us.

"So, Gildas my lad," the queen began as we started our walk through the lower bailey. "You are the one that wanted this little stroll. What exactly did you want to ask me?"

I sputtered a bit at her directness, but remembered to keep up the wall of courtesy. "Your Majesty, what could I possibly want of you other than your own charming company, and that of my lady Rosemounde?" I refused on principle to call her my lady of Orkney.

"Oh stop the act, Gildas, I know you too well," Guinevere scoffed as she slipped her hand into the crook of my right arm. "You have a favor to ask me, and unless I miss my guess your master Sir Gareth has put you up to it. He's hoping you can use your vast influence with me to see whether I can get him in to see the king about Sir Gawain. Is that not it?"

I was surprised at how clearly she could see through me, even though it had been a couple of years since I'd been in her service, and I cleared my throat momentarily to disguise my consternation. I stammered a bit in answering, "My lady is, once again, clairvoyant. I put myself into your hands, my queen. Tell me what return I may make to Sir Gareth."

"Tell him the king doesn't want to see him. Tell him he's not interested in talking with Sir Mordred, either, if that's what Gareth and Gaheris are worrying about." At this mention of her husband, I could feel Lady Rosemounde physically blanch, and once again the fire of anger burned in my belly at the thought of her tender back. Guinevere continued, "It is Sir Gawain himself that the king wishes to see, and will accept no emissaries. When Gawain is recovered enough to come back to Camelot, he will gain immediate audience with the king. And he will have to answer for his unbridled use of force in his encounter with Sir Ironside."

"Some knights have no true honor," Rosemounde pronounced, looking straight ahead, as if the queen and I were not there at all. "They have no courtesy. Brutal force is the only thing that they understand."

We looked at her, not sure whom she was addressing or whether she expected any kind of response. She seemed fragile, perhaps even ethereal. I did not want to let her go unanswered, and said quietly, "You are referring, my lady, to Sir Ironside?"

Rosemounde blinked as the trance-like humor seemed to leave her, and turned her face toward me with a sad little smile. "Of course," she replied. "What else?"

At that point we turned left and began to stroll leisurely past the buildings along the outer wall of the castle, passing the kitchen (toward which my dog sent a plaintive whine or two, pulling her leash and looking longingly at the door) and the great hall on our left, while I pondered what else might be said to further the cause of the Orkney clan, so that I could report back to Sir Gareth that I had done my level best to gain the queen's sympathies. "Of course," I began, "Sir Gawain is not the only knight who has killed another on this quest."

"True," the queen nodded somberly. "There is the sickening affair of Sir Lionel and your dear Sir Colegrevaunce. The king could not put off addressing that. That is why he met privately with Sir Lionel yesterday."

Now I was truly surprised. I had heard nothing about this and I am sure that Merlin, Sir Gareth, and Sir Ywain were as ill-informed as I was. The fact that it had been, as the queen said, a private meeting no doubt had the effect of its being a secret meeting as well. Only the queen seemed to have been aware of it. And Sir Lionel himself, of course.

"Don't look so surprised, Gildas, the king actually does consult me occasionally about matters of state. In this case, he talked to me about whether it was appropriate to show mercy in the case of Sir Lionel. That's what we queens are for, you know," she added almost conspiratorially, glancing over at Lady Rosemounde, who answered her with a smirk. "We're the ones who are supposed to make a big show out of pleading for mercy, so that the king can grant it as a favor to us without looking weak. Mustn't be soft on crime, you know, it loses you the respect of your knights."

I could see that she was veering off the subject into something else entirely, but I really needed to get her back on track. "So you're saying that King Arthur is of a mind to pardon Sir Lionel, then? Even though he killed Colgrevaunce—and apparently some poor hermit as well—without provocation, and only because they were trying to keep him from killing his own brother?"

"Well, if you put it *that* way…"

'What other way is there to put it?" I demanded in frustration, a bit rashly it must be admitted, considering my obligation of courtesy toward the queen, and when I glanced at Rosemounde from the corner of my eye she had one of her eyebrows raised and a fairly judgmental look on her face…her lovely face, that made me hang my head momentarily in shame and embarrassment. But I was breathing hard, surprised myself at the strength of my feelings about Sir Colgrevaunce's death. I hadn't been thinking about it consciously, but was shaking now in anger and exasperation. I did not go so far as to apologize.

We passed the lesser hall and turned to the right, walking under the guard room in the northeast tower of the castle's outer wall, while I waited in silence for the queen to answer my outburst.

"Oh, my Gildas, you *are* a silly goose," the queen finally said, choosing to take the matter lightly. "Sir Lionel is repentant. Deeply, deeply repentant. I saw him as he left the king's chamber. He is a broken man. Surely his remorse should count for something, should it not?"

"If he's repentant, let God forgive him for the sake of his soul. But on this earth, under our earthly laws and under our worldly king, he must be made to pay for his crime. Lionel should be executed." I said it with rancor, surprised, again, at the bitterness in my own voice.

The queen bent her head in acknowledgement of my feelings. She could see that they were too strong for her to dismiss or cajole me out of. She sounded conciliatory when she said, "The state of his soul is between him and his confessor, but I'll grant you that at the very least he is guilty of significantly violating the laws of chivalry…"

"A double murder? Attempted fratricide? Yes, I'd say those items are not exactly on the list of things the knights swear to every Pentecost Sunday."

"As I was saying," the queen continued, narrowing her eyes and glaring at me, miffed at my rude interruption. Immediately I bowed and deferred to her, glancing at Rosemounde on my left and receiving a chilly reception there as well. "The king would have barred Sir Lionel from the Order of the Round Table, and made sure that he was exiled from Logres, but his willingness to take responsibility for what he had done, and his grievous repentance, have convinced the king to keep Lionel on in a kind of limbo until the return of Sir Bors, whose testimony the king will require before deciding what finally to do about Sir Lionel after all."

I was ready to chafe at that information as well, but after a few moments of silence decided it would be to my benefit to say nothing right now. I was aided in this decision by the lady Rosemounde reaching over and lightly touching my arm, a kind of warning as I interpreted it that my carping had gone on long enough and it was time for me to keep my mouth shut for a while. In the silence that followed, we turned westward, moving past another guardhouse that stood on the southeast corner of the outer wall of Camelot, and began moving toward the mighty stone keep, the tallest in Christendom at some ninety feet high. It was huge and invulnerable, with walls three feet thick at its base. The last defense of the castle, it was even now manned by members of the royal archers at each window slit. The mighty fortress made King Arthur's castle all but impervious to attack from without. But as I gazed at it looming above us as we walked, I could not help reflecting that it was not an attack from outside that we needed to fear, but rather this troublesome quest's violence among the Round Table knights themselves that threatened to bring down Arthur's perfect world. And at that moment I decided the queen needed to hear it.

"Your Majesty, I have nothing really concrete or completely worked out to support this, but I fear that Sir Lionel's behavior is only one part of a much larger threat to King Arthur's Table than anything we have yet envisioned."

"Indeed?" The queen's eyes widened and her brows sprang to their highest elevation. "I know that a number of knights have suffered accidents on this quest, but my impression was that the increased number of incidents is simply the result of the fact that all the knights are engaged in this latest quest. You don't see it that way?"

"My lady, I do not," I answered. "Think about it. Two of the premiere knights of the table have committed homicide against their fellow knights. Sir Safer has been murdered by the same white knight, we believe, who earlier struck down King Bagdemagus and later Sir Ywain. That same unknown knight also, we have just learned, seems to have been behind the death of Sir Uwain les Avoutres." Unaware of this latest disaster, the queen blanched visibly when I spoke of it, and when I glanced left I saw the lady Rosemounde gasp and put her nosegay to her face.

"Well someone must stop this White Knight, then!" Queen Guinevere declared. "But how can you be sure there is any connection between him and these killings wrought by Lionel and Gawain?"

"Well, we can't," I admitted. "Though Sir Lionel has said, I believe, that it was a white knight who first captured him. Some malignant force is behind this quest, my lady. This Quest of the Holy Grail was set up deliberately with a goal of decimating the King's great Order of Chivalry, and destroying the Round Table."

"And this malignant force, you believe, may well be my husband. Isn't that true, my darling Gildas?" The lady Rosemounde broke her silence and looked squarely at me. The queen, looking around to make sure she had not been overheard, chastised Rosemounde with a look.

"Shush, you foolish girl," Guinevere spoke *sotto voce*. "Do you want all Camelot to hear you?"

Prompted by the queen's wariness, I looked over my shoulder myself, but saw only poor Peter, now some twenty paces behind us, stopped and tangled among the leashes, with Aeneas and Dido trying to run circles around him. I laughed a bit in spite of myself, and mercifully walked back to him to help him out of his tangled quandary. Of course, I had to bring Guinevere with me, who up to that point had been prancing along at my side perfectly well behaved, but as we approached the other scampering dogs, she began leaping into the air on her outstretched leash like a fighting fish on the end of a line. "Short leashes! Short leashes!" I whispered to him. "Don't give them so much play on their leashes or they'll wrap them around you. Here, watch what I do with the borzoi!" I was able to calm Guinevere down and hold her on about six inches of leash, at which she writhed her head and whined at me, turning the whine into a yowl that made it seem as if I was tormenting her. I scowled down at her and muttered, "Wow! You're as accomplished an actress as your namesake, aren't you Guinevere?" Peter stifled a laugh, but held on to the two greyhounds with authority, and they began to walk more calmly at his side. I turned back and rejoined the ladies, Guinevere the dog on my left hand, Guinevere the queen on my right.

But the dog was not quite settled down. Without warning, when my left hand relaxed a bit, she made an upward lunge planting her paws on Rosemounde's shoulders and licking her full on in the mouth. "Guinevere, you silly bitch!" I cried, at which point the queen, stopping and glaring at me under thundering brows, pronounced icily, "I beg your pardon?"

"I…the…the dog, my lady, I'm talking to my dog, you see…" I babbled. But I could see pretty clearly that the queen was not amused. On the other hand, Rosemounde was. For the first time since her marriage I heard her laugh out loud with real abandon. The queen glanced over at her and, unable to keep her severity in the face of that mirth, allowed herself to smile and shake her head. Meanwhile the other Guinevere looked up at me with innocent eyes and nuzzled her nose into my hand so that I would pet her.

The queen turned and continued the stroll, and Rosemounde and I kept pace with her. "Your Majesty, and my lady Rosemounde, I apologize for the excitement displayed by my dog. Normally she is far better behaved. She seems repentant now, and I am as well." By now we were crossing the middle bailey with the well to our right. Here there was no one else in sight, and I spoke in lower tones, finally addressing Rosemounde's earlier comment, if not the expressed sentiment. "As for your disgrace of a husband, my lady…"

"Watch yourself, Gildas," the queen cautioned. "I may not hear such language concerning the king's family."

"As for the noble Sir Mordred," I corrected myself with undisguised irony. "There is certainly every chance that he is indeed behind this ignominious plot. Who else would stand to gain so much from the breaking of the alliance between Lancelot's kin and Arthur's own? From the disgrace of Sir Gawain and the shaming of Sir Lionel as well? Nothing short of the kingdom of Logres is at stake here."

The queen frowned. "I had not thought things had deteriorated so much," she muttered, "or that so much may be at stake."

"The trouble is," Rosemounde continued thoughtfully, "I have seen or heard nothing. This seems like a vast conspiracy you suggest someone has been weaving, yet my noble husband, as you call him, has to my knowledge been in contact with no one. He has been alone since the knights went out on this quest, and even before that consorted only with his brother Sir Agravain since we have been at Camelot. If he is involved in a conspiracy, I cannot say how he could possibly be in touch with any fellow conspirators. I will not say that Sir Mordred is innocent, but I suspect he is not guilty of this particular crime against the king and the Table."

I admit that I was somewhat disappointed to hear it. Certainly nothing would please me more than to have Mordred involved in a plot against the king that would disgrace him and set him up for charges of treason. But it didn't look like that was going to happen. And I had to admit, it didn't seem likely. "You may well be right, my lady," I replied to Rosemounde. "We did have a chance to speak to him earlier, when Merlin first became interested in these events—at my urging, I'll admit."

Now I could see that they were all ears. My speaking of a conspiracy was mildly amusing for them. Merlin's suspicions were something to be taken seriously. Don't think I didn't notice the difference. "Really?" the queen mused. "And what was the result of that interview?"

"Mordred gave every indication of being a scoundrel. No offense, my lady."

"None taken," both Guinevere and Rosemounde spoke at once, then glanced at one another a bit surprised.

"But I mean to say," I continued, "that if he had been guilty, he would have tried to cover up his bitterness toward the king and Sir Gawain, would have tried to appear innocent. He is either innocent in this matter or the stupidest criminal in history."

"Oh, he's definitely not stupid," Rosemounde concurred.

"All he told us, and I'm not sure what to make of it, is that Gawain told everything to his confessor, and so that's who we should question."

"Hmph," the queen said, and looked thoughtful. I stopped walking, and looked at her closely. "My lady? Is there something amiss?"

"You struck a chord," Guinevere answered. "I'm remembering something that Sir Lionel said when the king interviewed him. No, I was not there, but I got a report that was very nearly word-for-word. Lionel mentioned to the king that when he first arrived at the hermit's cell where he eventually killed Sir Colgrevaunce, he met Sir Gawain himself, who had just left the cell. He'd been there, you see, to confess, he told Lionel. Isn't that strange?"

More than strange, I thought. Uncanny. It was the first real clue we had had, I thought. At any rate it was the first thing I'd heard that linked the two murders—of Ironside and Colgrevaunce—and I could think of nothing else. No, not though the lady Rosemounde was speaking in my ear.

"What? Oh sorry my lady, my mind was elsewhere, thinking of something the queen said."

"I was saying, isn't that your friend Master Robin bowing to you up there?"

We were passing the barbican now, turning to the north and walking by the main castle gate. Robin Kempe was standing in the gate above the portcullis and bowed to the queen, raising his eyebrows as he saw me walking with the lady Rosemounde and winking at me unobtrusively. I rolled my eyes at him and waved him off, but could hear a bit of raucous laughter as we passed into the upper bailey and bore down on the great hall again, to which the queen's rooms were attached.

"Well if you ask me," the queen spoke after a few moments' silence, "the king's sister, that sorceress, has something to do with this. She's always wanted Arthur off his throne. She's tried before to set up her own lovers in place of the king. All because of Arthur's father, Uther, and the supposed rape of her mother. After all this time. I mean, get over it!"

"Your Grace, that is much easier to say than to do," Rosemounde corrected her mistress, with more authority than I'd seen in her ever before where the queen was concerned. "Who knows? Perhaps the queen Ygrayne raised her daughters amid a constant litany of her humiliation, willing them all the time to exact some sort of revenge, even if it must be on her own son."

Surprised at Rosemounde's show of independence, the queen shrugged, and added, "Perhaps it was so, my dear. In any case, Morgan's failures in the past have kept her quiet of late. I've been under the impression that they have inspired her to give up. I hope I am right."

"So that you rest assured we are looking into every possibility," I told the queen, "let me tell you that we have, indeed, talked with Morgan le Fay."

"And?"

"And, Your Majesty," I told her. "We had much the same experience as with Sir Mordred. She made no attempt to excuse herself or prove her innocence."

"Well," the queen concluded. "Perhaps they are in cahoots together? Maybe you and your necromancer master ought to look into that possibility, eh?"

"Certainly, Your Majesty," I humored her. "We'll certainly keep it in mind. And now good day, Your Majesty. Good day, my lady," again, I could not call Rosemounde by her official name, so I left it at "Lady." We stood before the stairway leading to the queen's apartments, and Peter was taking the four-legged Guinevere's leash to return her to the kennels, with Aeneas and Dido. "We will get to the bottom of this," I called after the ladies as they climbed to their rooms. And at that point, I was feeling more confident than I had in weeks. The hermitage. Both Lionel and Gawain had stopped at the hermitage. It had to be important, didn't it? And even if it wasn't, at least we finally had something to try to run down. I couldn't wait to talk to Merlin about it.

I was feeling pretty good. And not just because of the lead the queen had given us. The lady Rosemounde of god-awful Orkney— she had called me "darling." And had meant it.

CHAPTER TWELVE
THE TALE OF SIR GAWAIN

A wobbly Sir Gawain stood before King Arthur two days later in the king's throne room, steadied by his brother Sir Gaheris at his right hand and Lovell, his son and squire, on his left. Gaheris had brought him in by horse litter the day before, when it was finally thought he might be moved from the abbey's infirmary without grave danger to his life, though with his wounds it had still been a dreadfully uncomfortable journey. The king, who had put off Gareth and Gaheris's suit for weeks, ordered Gawain into his presence immediately upon his nephew's return to Camelot. Arthur could wait no longer to hear, from his nephew's own lips, how he could possibly defend himself for the slaying—some would say the murder—of his Round Table brother, Sir Ironside, the Red Knight of the Red Lands.

Merlin, Sir Gareth, and I stood in a line behind Gawain and his supporters, demonstrating our own sponsorship of Sir Gawain's cause. But aside from the six of us and the king himself, the throne room was empty, for the king wanted to keep these things as close as possible. And besides, so many knights were away on this quest that there were few indeed to make up the court.

Certainly Merlin and I, at least, had strong suspicions about these strange occurrences that accompanied the eerily dangerous Grail quest, though we were not yet able to put our finger on a cause of those events. But Merlin, once he had finally risen weakly from his stupor, had been intrigued by the fact that Gawain and Lionel had both visited the hermitage where Colgrevaunce was killed. He felt certain that something else happened there, and was eager to examine the place, though because of Gawain's arrival we could not set off immediately. Besides, it was better to hear what Gawain himself had to say about the place, and, if necessary, to ask Sir Lionel about it as well. But for now, we were here to support Gawain in his interview before the king.

"Well, Nephew," the king began, dispensing with the formality he would have used had this interview been open to members of the court. "You've certainly put your foot in it this time. What do you have to say for yourself?" His voice rose an octave with this last, as he spread out his hands in frustration. "Killing a knight of the Round Table? One of your sworn brethren? How do I excuse this to your fellow knights?"

"My liege," Gawain began, his voice low from both weakness and humility. "I scarcely know how to plead my own case. I was alone in the forest, having just come from confession at the hermit's cell nearby, when I heard the pleading cries of a woman in need. I rode to the spot under a linden tree where a fair-haired woman lay, her shift torn to shreds and Sir Ironside, himself in a state of undress, pinning her hands and growling at her angrily, saying 'Now you refuse me, you tart? No one shames the Red Knight of the Red Lands this way.' But the woman kept screaming, and catching sight of me rasped in a low voice, 'Good knight? I beg you save me from this brigand.' At that point I remember feeling giddy—with shock, fear, agitation, I know not what. Everything before my eyes appeared tinged with red. In my mind Sir Ironside appeared to be some kind of demon, threatening my life as well as the lady's. I drew my sword."

"Were you or were you not aware of who it was you were preparing to attack?" The king probed, his eyes closed in anticipation of Gawain's answer.

"I could see, your grace, that it was Sir Ironside. But that did not stay my hand."

"And you proceeded to decapitate him, there and then, without a second thought. And he unarmed," the king continued.

"He was not armed because he was raping the girl!" Sir Gareth burst in impulsively. "What was he supposed to do, give him time to arm himself and have a joust, and the girl lying there naked?"

"Don't be impertinent!" Arthur snapped, his dark eyes glaring in Gareth's direction. My master let out an exasperated breath and bowed his head slightly in deference to his sovereign, who turned back to Gawain and pressed further: "You were armed and on horseback, and your sword was drawn. You could not have subdued an undefended Sir Ironside without killing him?"

"Your Grace," Sir Gawain replied, "I was carried away by rage. I cannot explain it. I have not felt such rage before."

"A child's excuse!" The king stood up, fighting back his own rage at his heir presumptive. "Am I to tell your fellow knights that I am sparing you the consequences of your murderous act because you just couldn't control yourself?"

"It was Sir Ironside," Gareth burst in again. "He was a known villain and a lecher, and the other knights will celebrate his loss, and cheer my brother for saving that maiden from her appalling fate!"

"And are we then to declare open season on any knights you don't happen to like?" Arthur retorted. "Here, these knights are unpopular this season, have a go at them. No one will punish you because there is no law in Arthur's kingdom. Is that what you want, you loose-tongued son of Orkney? No, I told you not to be impertinent, and I won't tell you again. Open your mouth again at these proceedings and I'll put you in chains, nephew or no nephew!"

"My lord, I meant it not as an excuse but merely as an explanation of my actions, which I still do not understand myself," Gawain admitted, his head bowed, while Gareth fumed in silence and bit his lower lip.

"And now," Arthur ranted, pacing back and forth on his dais, "I have the case of Sir Lionel and the hapless Sir Colgrevaunce to judge as well, and what will it look like if I spare you but punish him? This business of knight killing knight—it all goes back to the cowardly slaying of Sir Lamorak, and rumor has it that I have the Orkney clan to thank for that as well! So you tell me: what am I to do?"

Gawain, head still hung low, reddened until his face matched the color of his long locks, and he stammered, "My lord, whoever it was that was responsible for the ambush and death of the late lamented Sir Lamorak," and at this I noticed Sir Gareth gritting his teeth, and Sir Gaheris, at Gawain's side, beginning to fidget. Sir Gawain was walking a very thin line, and I suspected that his own profound sense of courtesy would have compelled him to confess to that crime to the king, but his sense of family loyalty would not allow him to betray his brothers with the same breath. "Whoever it was, I say, may have been compelled by similar reasons to mine in slaying Sir Ironside. But Lamorak at least was armed and horsed. I cannot say the same for the Red Knight. I feel no sorrow at his death, nor do I believe he would have been spared in a court of law for this crime, but my dispatching of him anticipated his execution in a manner that defied Your Grace's law. I stand ready to receive whatever punishment my liege lord deems appropriate to the situation." And with that, Sir Gawain fell to his knees—not, as far as I could tell, in supplication to the king, but merely from exhaustion after standing before Arthur so long in his weakened condition.

The king pursed his lips and began to pace again, considering how Gawain had dodged the question of Sir Lamorak's murder, and weighing his confession against what he had already decided to do with Sir Lionel. In the meantime Sir Gaheris, more courteously than his younger brother, made his own appeal to the king: "My lord, if I may…Sir Gawain has shown a great deal of remorse for this act already. We know that, troubled in conscience, he deliberately sought out Sir Galahad so that the prophecy he would be sorely wounded by the Pure Knight's sword might be fulfilled. The wounds you see upon him now are his penance for his sin."

"Yes, yes, duly noted," answered the king. "But sin is not my province. I must deal with law. And in that realm, the key factor here is the damsel. If she will testify before the court, it will give me some justification in mitigating your sentence. Come now, where is the girl? Can she testify?"

Gawain was slightly taken aback. "Well, first, your Grace, I must say that while she may indeed have been a maiden, she was no girl. She was rather small, but a full-grown woman, of, perhaps, thirty-five years. Fair haired and comely, but certainly not in the first blush of youth. What happened to her, though, I cannot say. In my brief struggle with Sir Ironside before I slew him she slipped away. I do not know what became of her. But I would certainly know her again if I saw her: golden hair, the palest of gray eyes, a pert nose and dimpled chin. But where she disappeared, I am at a loss to say."

The king scowled. "Then we have nothing to prove your innocence. Or rather I should say the mitigating circumstances behind your actions." He sighed again, this time with resignation. "Very well, here is what I shall do: In the case of Sir Lionel I have suspended judgment pending the return of Sir Bors to Camelot. I'll make a similar proclamation regarding these charges against you. We will send members of our guard to comb the countryside and search for this woman. Until she can be located and brought before the court to testify, we shall place your judgment, as well, in abeyance. That is all I can do for now." And with that the king stepped down from his dais and began to walk purposefully toward the rear door of the throne room.

From his knees Sir Gawain called after him, "Your Majesty is most merciful…"

"Don't count on it," Arthur snapped back, and slipped out the door, to be accompanied by two members of his palace guard up to his private rooms.

Gawain slumped forward when the king left, exhausted from trying to hold himself erect in his emaciated state. Sir Gaheris and Lovell lifted him up and supported him, half-carrying him out of the throne room, while Gareth and I followed behind walking in silence to Gawain's private solar further along the corridor of the palace. As Lovell and Gaheris laid him gingerly down on his cot, Sir Gawain gave a tight-lipped moan, and I wasn't sure whether it was from the pain from his wounds or the travail of his soul over his uncle's berating.

I had a feeling of déjà vu again there in Gawain's closet, remembering standing at the bedside of Sir Ywain just a few days earlier. I even blurted out, "Perhaps we can get the lady Morgan to search Sir Gawain's wounds? Her ministrations seem to have had a good effect on Sir Ywain…"

Merlin glared at me with undisguised astonishment, and Gareth looked at me as if I'd just told them I was the Pope. Sir Gawain, however, found the comment surprisingly amusing, and even laughed—somewhat cautiously for fear of bursting open a wound. "No, young Gildas," he began weakly. "My dear aunt Morgan, bless her black little heart, is more likely to help me toward an early grave than to help make me whole again. No, I'll take my chances with the king's infirmarian. I think I may be better served there."

I felt my face grow red and I shrugged a bit, but Merlin stepped in and covered my embarrassment with his own urgent prying. "My lord Gawain," he began. "I have been incapacitated for the past day or so and as a result I'm not aware of how much you've been told about the bizarre and ruinous incidents happening on this Grail quest…"

"Gareth and Gaheris have filled me in somewhat," Gawain said, still breathing hard but trying to sit up, concerned about what he had heard. "Sir Ywain attacked? And Colgrevaunce killed by Sir Lionel? These are troubling developments."

"And King Bagdemagus, of course, with whom you shared a sickroom at the abbey," Sir Gaheris put in.

"But there is more yet," Merlin added. "Sir Uwain les Avoutres is the most recent casualty—cut down by the same knight in white armor responsible for many of these other outrages. And worst of all Sir Safer, unarmed and murdered without provocation."

Gawain's countenance fell. He had not yet heard of Sir Uwain and Sir Safer's loss. Almost as an afterthought, I added, "And of course, the poor hermit, slain by Sir Lionel when he tried to prevent him slaying his own brother."

At that Gawain's head snapped up, and his expression changed from sorrow to disbelief. "The hermit? You're talking about Brother Bertrand? He whose cell Sir Lionel approached to have his wounds looked to—just after I had confessed? You're saying he killed my confessor?"

"Indeed, my lord, he certainly did so—I am sorry to see it move you so. I hadn't realized that this hermit was your confessor…"

"For many years," Gawain murmured as he hung his head. Then, glancing up at our puzzled expressions, he explained. "Oh,

I did occasionally use the palace chaplain, Father Ambrose. That hermitage, as I guess you know, is two days' ride from Camelot, so I could only visit Brother Bertrand when I was on some quest or some business for the king. But I had a special relationship with the hermit."

We all continued to look at him curiously. Even Gareth, his closest brother, and Lovell, his own son and squire, seemed at a loss. Seeing that his explanations were raising more questions than they were answering, Sir Gawain took a deep breath and spoke again. "Brother Bertrand and I had a…a kind of special bond. Many years ago, he was chaplain at the castle of a noble knight named Lord Bertilak, whose castle I was visiting over Christmastide one year." At that I looked over at Sir Gareth, who cocked his head at me and shrugged. Gawain went on, "I made a confession to him that Christmastide, and it was…well, I guess I would have to say it was a bad confession. I failed to confess…something that I had taken and kept for myself treacherously…"

"No, brother…" Gaheris interrupted.

"Yes! I do not fool myself. I had kept this…this token and hidden it, but kept the act hidden as well, even from the one I was confessing to, and I suppose I must say that the reason I was making the confession was because I had a battle to fight that day and feared I would not live until evening. But do you see, even under those circumstances, when I thought I would be facing God that very day, I could not face Him with a clean conscience, because I withheld that sin from Brother Bertrand. And I remember him asking me sternly, as if he knew there was more, whether I had anything else that I wished to confess. And I said no—because the truth is, I did not wish to confess it at all! And that was the sin…a sin that endangered my soul."

"Well, even if all of that were true, why…and how…would you find him again, and in that hermitage?" Gaheris wanted to know.

"It was pure serendipity," Gawain shrugged. "A few years had passed, and I'd been sent by the king as an emissary to King Pelles at Corbenic if I remember—something having to do with a tribute they were expected to pay the king, I think, but that doesn't matter—and I happened upon the good brother on the path. Well he recognized me at once, and after a moment I remembered him as well. He took me to his hermitage and there we talked about my earlier adventure at Lord Bertilak's, and the Green Chapel. I remember telling him how very right he had been when he urged me to make a full confession, and how I had suffered because of it. And he offered to hear my confession then and there. He absolved me of my sin in holding back the green girdle…the token I had kept from him, from God, before. And I have to tell you, it was as if a huge weight was lifted off my shoulders. From that day on, I have used Brother Bertrand as my personal confessor at least once a year, when I have had the chance. And you tell me now that Sir Lionel has killed him? I must take time to consider this. It may be that honor will compel me to challenge Lionel in the lists."

"It seems an odd coincidence, my lord," Merlin began, insinuating his way into the conversation with what I could see was about to become an interrogation. "His showing up like that, just as you were making your way through the wilderness on official business of the crown. In my experience, such coincidences are extremely rare."

"That, I suppose, is why they are called coincidences," Sir Gawain replied, the corners of his mouth turning up at his own small witticism.

"Yes, I daresay, I daresay…" Merlin responded, his mind engaged in some subtle calculations behind his outward veneer of the doddering old man. "But can you tell us any more, my lord, about your last meeting with him? It was, I believe you said, right before your encounter with Sir Ironside."

"Moments before," Sir Gawain agreed. I had not ridden more than a furlong—two at the most—when those screams alerted me to the danger."

"And you rode to find the rape occurring," Gaheris prompted.

"And the woman—you will know her if you see her again?" Sir Gareth wanted to be assured. "Even though you are not likely to see her again in the same state…"

"Of nakedness?" Gawain scoffed. "Not likely. But no—her eyes were what struck me at the time—gray as glass, and looking at me with an expression not of fear or pleading, but triumph. I remember thinking at the time that my appearance, at which she immediately stopped her outcry, must have emboldened her with the knowledge that she would be avenged on her attacker."

"Yes, well, there may be other explanations for that…" Merlin said under his breath, but then aloud, "But I was speaking of your time with the poor hermit himself. Had anything unusual happened with your confession, or in your time with Brother Bertrand? Or was it simply a typical confession?"

"Oh, nothing about my time with Brother Bertrand was ever what you would call a conventional confession," Gawain shrugged again. "We were old acquaintances, and he always asked me for news of the court when I saw him. So we chatted about this and that…"

"Specifically what would the 'this and that' consist of in this case?" Merlin pressed.

"What are you implying, old man?" Gawain looked up with some annoyance mixed with suspicion. "Are you trying to make some point about my murdered confessor?"

"Just curious," Merlin replied. "About what reason someone might have had to get rid of the hermit."

"Well apparently Sir Lionel had a compelling reason: He wanted to kill his brother!" Gawain insisted. "You're way off track here, and ignoring the obvious."

"Sometimes things are obvious, my lord, because they are what someone wants us to see," Merlin answered courteously. "I assume you talked with Brother Bertrand about court affairs? About the quest that the knights, including yourself, had sworn themselves to?'

"Of course."

"And of Sir Galahad's arrival at Camelot? The sword in the stone? The Siege Perilous?"

"Yes, that too. My confession I will keep to myself, but we did talk about those things informally over a cup of wine."

"Wine?" Merlin raised his substantial eyebrows as he glanced down at Gawain's face. "Your hermit was not particularly ascetic, then? Surviving on cold water and acorns, that sort of thing?"

Gawain waved the old man off. "Now, don't start implying that Brother Bertrand was some sort of hedonist or epicure or some such thing. Remember, he was an ordained priest. He had a small altar in his cell and glorified God by celebrating a brief informal Mass every morning. So yes, he has wine, and on the rare occasions that he has visitors, he can offer them a cup of unconsecrated wine. As he did me. Rather wretched stuff it was, though, I remember now..."

"The wine had gone bad?"

Gawain shrugged again. "Maybe it had started to. Had kind of a moldy or bitter taste to it. But what are we talking about wine for? Brother Bertrand is dead, killed by bloody Lionel and the king not likely to do anything about it."

"As he is letting *you* get away with killing the Red Knight, it seems," Sir Gareth reminded him. "Let's not walk too far down that path, my brother, if you don't want to be condemned out of your own mouth."

Sir Gawain looked testy, but nodded in acquiescence. He had wrapped his arms around his chest by now and his eyelids were drooping heavily, and we all realized that he must be exhausted by the ordeal of his journey and his interview with the king, and now even with talking among ourselves. Gareth was the first to suggest that we leave. With a nod, Merlin took his leave and I followed behind him, heeding my master's suggestion. Sir Gareth, I assumed, would stay with Sir Gawain after everyone else had left, to insure his comforts were taken care of before retiring himself.

***

Merlin walked across the bailey with his head down, concentrating, and I walked beside him, pretty much befuddled. What the purpose of all this talk about Brother Bertrand and his Mass wine had been was beyond me. It seemed like random conversation to me, and I was waiting for Merlin to clue me in to what he had been doing. After two solid minutes of silence, I was still waiting.

"All right," I finally cried. "Tell me! What's so important about Gawain's confessions? About the hermit's wine? Were you just chatting with Gawain about whatever came up?"

"God's bunions, boy, how are we going to find out anything if we don't probe? Everywhere we turn there are traps and pitfalls for Arthur's knights on this quest, so every detail could be important."

"Or not," I countered. "Seems to me what we need to find out is who and where the white knight is, and who is behind his murderous rampage, if it's not he himself."

"And *why* he is on this rampage, you forgot to say," Merlin corrected me.

"The *why* is for later. The *who* and *where* are for now, so that he can be stopped," I argued. "Is Gawain's confessor the white knight? I think not. Seems like he wasn't much of a hand in a battle, since Lionel dispatched him pretty quickly. Besides, he's killed Sir Uwain, at least, since Lionel killed the hermit. I'm sorry for him, but why do we need to know whether he had let his wine go bad?"

"Dolt of a Cornishman, haven't you learned by this time that sometimes the obscure details are the only ones that matter? Think about this a moment. This Brother Bertrand—he suddenly appears on a trail Sir Gawain is following? He suddenly decides he'd rather be a hermit than have the cozy life of a chaplain in a nobleman's castle? He spends his time just waiting for Sir Gawain to come by once a year so that he can hear his confessions? What's that all about?"

"Coincidence?" I echoed Gawain.

"In my experience, coincidence is generally engineered by somebody who's trying to get away with something and trying to appear innocuous. Bertrand was working for someone. Someone powerful who was dying to spy on Sir Gawain and keep track of his every move."

"Someone like Morgan le Fay," I proposed, suddenly seeing the method in Merlin's madness.

"Someone like Morgan le Fay, precisely. What makes you bring her into it?"

"Lord Bertilak. If I remember Gareth's story of the Green Knight right, Morgan was the one that put Bertilak up to the whole test of Sir Gawain. She was even there in disguise at the fellow's court. If she had her tentacles around Lord Bertilak, how much easier would it have been for her to squeeze Brother Bertrand too, and get him to work as her spy?"

"You are definitely on the right track there, my lad," Merlin nodded. Now he quickened his step, and I realized he was walking purposefully toward the stables. "But there is more. Remember that Morgan is conversant in the medical arts—"

"Hard to forget after watching her bandage Sir Ywain's wounds, maggots and all," I gagged.

"Indeed. But her chief claim to fame is her potions. Remember that Sir Lionel told us the hermit had fed him healing potions? This feeds right in to what I was saying the other night, before my…my unfortunately timed spell. The henbane potion she spoke of using on the knights in her episode with Excalibur. It's precisely what could have maddened Lionel, and Gawain too, to the point of attacking their fellow knights. Sir Lionel said he'd been fed potions. Gawain had wine that tasted like it had gone bad—almost certainly, I'm telling you wine treated with the henbane leaves. Both knights fed these drugs by Brother Bertrand. And Brother Bertrand, we suspect, the tool of Morgan le Fay, mistress of potions. There is no question!"

I pondered that. It certainly made sense as Merlin portrayed it, and the lady Morgan certainly seemed a likely candidate to be behind these strange occurrences, judging from her past record, but it didn't all add up to me. "But Merlin," I ventured. "The White Knight attacked and nearly killed Sir Ywain. Haven't we already ruled Morgan out as a suspect in this?"

The old man nodded, pursing his lips. "That is true. But we have been assuming all along that these events are all connected. But consider: Sir Gawain was wounded by Sir Galahad himself. King Bagdemagus, Sir Safer, and Sir Ywain were struck down by the anonymous White Knight. But Sir Ironside and Sir Colgrevaunce were killed by Gawain and Lionel, their brother knights. Are these separate catastrophes or somehow all related?"

"It would be another unlikely coincidence if they were not related, part of a conspiracy to destroy the Table."

"I agree, boy, but it may also be that there is a mastermind behind all of this that does not let the right hand know what the left hand is doing. Could Morgan be behind the murderous rampages of Lionel and Gawain, and not be aware of the exploits of the White Knight?"

"But wait," I interrupted. "Sir Lionel says that the White Knight kept him bound and ordered his beating. And Lionel drank the hermit's wine and suddenly wanted to kill his brother. What do you make of that connection?" Merlin scratched his head. "That, my dear Gildas, may in fact be just a coincidence."

By now we had reached the stables, and Merlin roused Taber, the chief stable master, who looked at us with rheumy, blinking eyes as he yawned and scratched his chest through his unkempt brown tunic. "We need two horses for a four-day ride," he told Taber, "on the king's business!" And while Taber went to fetch and saddle the mounts, Merlin turned again to me, continuing the conversation. "I'm not saying that Morgan is necessarily directly involved in this conspiracy, either. It may be that whoever *is* behind it made use of her knowledge of herbs. And so she certainly must know more than she is saying, at the very least. But I believe to get to the bottom of all this, we need to get away from Camelot and see for ourselves the scene of these crimes—I want to visit this Brother Bertrand's hermitage, if we can find it. The answers to more than one question may be waiting there."

"The hermitage? But that's somewhere near Saint Sebastian's Abbey, as far as I can tell, and that's two days ride from here."

"Precisely why I have asked Taber for the loan of two horses for four days. Mathematics, my dear Gildas, you should learn some sometime. You *are* coming with me, I assume?"

I let out an exasperated sigh. "I think sometimes you forget that I am Sir Gareth's squire, not yours, and I can't be riding off for four days without even a by-your-leave."

Merlin conceded with a slight tilt of his head to the left. "Well go to him, you Cornish lunkhead, and get his leave, will you? Meantime I'll stop by the kitchen and get some bread and beer and a few other edible things to see us on our way. But put a bit of hustle in it, will you? We're burning daylight here."

I ran off to find Gareth. He may have still been in Sir Gawain's closet, or he may have made his way to his own quarters by now. In any case, I expected him to give me leave—he was not likely to be going anywhere or needing me for anything important while Gawain lay in limbo. Still, I couldn't help but wonder what he saw in a squire who spent most of his time chasing after a mad old necromancer, and the rest of his time sulking about a woman married to another man. But that wasn't likely to change soon.

CHAPTER THIRTEEN

A PASTORAL IDYLL

"Well, I'm surprised you didn't bring along a nice romance and some of the queen's embroidery while you were about it, you Cornish blockhead," Merlin was enjoying himself berating me as we kept an ambling pace in the direction of Saint Sebastian's Abbey, along that same path that I had ridden not long before in Sir Gareth's company. But at least it wasn't raining this time. It had taken us a quarter hour longer than Merlin had planned to get started on our journey because I had made a few extra stops. After getting Gareth's leave to be away for a few nights, I had stopped to pick up my sword and shield. Though I didn't feel the need to ride all that way in the discomfort of armor, I was wary enough after the many casualties suffered by Arthur's knights in the course of this quest not to leave the castle without some kind of protection. At the last minute I had also grabbed a crossbow, which I kept in easy reach hanging from my saddle, the sword in its scabbard on my belt, and the shield carried behind me over my shoulder. If I was going to encounter any White Knights, it was not going to be unarmed.

And, of course, I had also picked up Guinevere—the four-legged one—from the kennel, and she was cavorting about alongside the horses, prancing with the pride of her royal namesake, her head jerking at every movement. I pitied the rabbit that came within chasing distance of her this morning. The borzoi needed a good run, and her nose, ears, and eyes were sharp enough to detect any possible threat to us long before we would have been aware of it ourselves.

More than anything else, I had Sir Safer's fate in mind: No one was going to take us unawares.

"I've brought the necessities, Old Man," I answered Merlin. "I've traveled with you before, and I don't think your conjurer's tricks are going to be much protection against an armed knight like this white armored chap who seems to attack without warning and aims to kill."

"I've survived this long without the likes of you protecting me. If you put all our faith in your sword and let your wits go dormant, you'll be lucky to live to be half my age."

"Well, by my estimation your current age is about a hundred and eighty, so half of that won't be bad at all," I needled him.

"God's sideburns, Gildas, am I going to have to get down from this horse and box your incorrigible ears for you? With age is earned respect, and if I'm as old as you say, I'd better see some of that respect from you, or I'll chop you up and feed you to that undisciplined dog of yours!"

"Guinevere's not undisciplined, she's independent," I answered him. "She's a dog with a mind of her own."

"Well, so she has a mind. That's more than her master has," Merlin jibed.

And so we continued a pleasant day. We spent little time discussing the case itself—what more was there to say until we had a few more clues? And so between the exchange of such pleasantries as these, and a few songs and old tales, we rode on, often in silence. In those silences, I contemplated the thick woods, mainly oak, hazel and birch trees, with some pines interspersed, with nests of swallows, finches, larks, and woodpeckers singing or squawking among their branches. Most of these flew away at the sight of Guinevere bounding through the trees, but as twilight began to approach, a great bustard ran across the path and caught Guinevere's eye. She shot after the bird like the dart of a crossbow, and within minutes came proudly strutting back to us, the dead bird in her mouth.

"Ha!" Merlin exclaimed. "I believe your very intelligent dog has just declared it suppertime! It's time we stopped and camped for the night. You make a fire, if you can manage such a task, and I'll clean this bird. We'll divide it three ways, for Guinevere certainly deserves her share!"

And so the pastoral idyll of that day came to an end. After supping we spread our blankets on the dry ground, over a bed of dried pine needles, and slept out in the open under the early summer stars. Guinevere slept next to me on her side, her whole body pressed tight against my own, as happy a dog as I had ever seen. I should have dropped immediately off to sleep, after a long day of riding in the sun and the fresh air, but I could not. For all that day, despite the fine weather and the singing birds, my mind had been elsewhere. It had been with my lady Rosemounde, agonizing over her brutal marriage, all the while twisting my stomach into knots, boring a hole in the back of my neck. The welts on her back rose to my inward eye to block out even the most beautiful of finches or birch trees. By the time I finally dropped off into fitful slumber, I had determined to share my burden with the old man the following day. Merlin was, after all, the greatest sage in the kingdom. What good was that if it couldn't help me figure out how to help my lady? Tomorrow, then, I murmured through my veil of sleep. Merlin would know what to do.

***

It was approaching the longest day of the year, and so we awoke the next morning before prime. After a quick breakfast of bread and cheese that Merlin had brought along from Roger the cook, we were saddled and riding through the morning dew on what promised to be a day as pleasant as the last, and we were placing friendly bets as to whether or not Guinevere would snag us a rabbit for supper that evening—winner got to be White in the next game of chess in Merlin's cave. And as we began to take up our wonted pace again, I fumbled for a way to broach the subject of Rosemounde's abuse. I decided to come indirectly at the subject, and begin with some general conversation—in part because I truly did not understand the phenomenon, and hoped Merlin might shed some light on husbands' abuse of wives. I struck upon what I thought a brilliant segue into the topic, using our current investigation as a lead-in.

"Merlin," I opened, "this Morgan le Fay is a frightening woman, with these enchantments and potions. Is there no law that can restrain her?"

"Well, the king is the law and we are his investigators here, Gildas. Certainly if she has caused these raging moods that have ended in deaths, she ought to be culpable."

"Is she not subject, though, to Arthur as her brother as well as king? And before that, to her husband Uriens?" I persisted.

"Well, you saw how well that worked. She would have killed her husband had Sir Ywain not been by to prevent that act. But Uriens had not the heart, or perhaps had not the will, to punish her for that action, as the law certainly gave him the right to do. Besides, he died not long after that, and Bagdemagus became king, and Morgan a widow—which gave her a good deal more freedom under the law, as well as by custom. As for Arthur, he is not one to impose the male prerogative if there is any alternative. Even, as you know yourself, with his own wife."

"And yet many husbands do," I prompted the old man.

"They do," Merlin agreed, "as the law and the church give them that right. *Nulla est mulieris potestas, sed in omnibus uiro domino subsit.* That is canon law."

I rolled my eyes "You know I don't understand Latin, you old windbag. What does that mean?"

"I'm not responsible for your lack of culture," he said with a sniff. "If you don't know Latin it's time you learned."

"Well save the lecture for later and just tell me what that means!"

"'The woman has no power,'" he translated, "'but in everything she is subject to the control of her husband.' That is the Church's position."

"But that seems awfully, I don't know…arbitrary or even… dogmatic, doesn't it?"

Merlin looked at me askance from under his lush eyebrows. "We're talking about the Church, you Cornish nincompoop. Dogma is their middle name. Look, even so great a scholar as Saint Augustine himself said that a woman, in her marriage contract, was essentially pledging herself to be her husband's slave for life."

"Slave? Oh come on, that's going too far, isn't it? I mean, what could possibly justify that kind of thing?"

"Well," Merlin said, drawing things out to torment me in his own annoying way, "if you read Latin, you could have perused all the arguments. Women, it has been claimed since antiquity, are inferior to men. The philosophers said that this was because men were naturally more rational than women: Women, you know, are supposed to be cold in their humors, so that what they consume flows to the nether parts of their body, making their hips larger…"

"What!" I scoffed.

"And men, being warmer in their humors, have bigger chests and, of course, heads, since their sustenance goes to those regions. Hence men are by nature more cognitive. The Church adds its own justification: Man was made by God directly from the elements, and so was made in God's own image. Woman, made from man's rib, was an imperfect likeness of God, and therefore less godly, more passionate, less rational…"

"This is absurd, you old charlatan!" I exclaimed, having had enough of these specious assertions.

Merlin frowned and raised his hands in surrender. "*I'm* not the one who claims these things. I'm merely answering your own foolish questions. What have you to argue against the combined weight of centuries of theology and philosophy?"

"How about my own experience?" I asserted. "I suppose I've met a few women who were dull or tractable—or yes, broad in the hips!" I threw the description back at him like a taunt. "But how does one explain Morgan le Fay herself? She's clearly a lot smarter than her husband was—and, it certainly seems, a good deal smarter than her son or her nephews—except maybe for Gareth. And at least as smart as the king himself. And then there's Guinevere—and I don't mean the dog this time. The queen can certainly out-argue me any time. And what about the Lady of the Lake? She only seems to keep men around as bodyguards but rules her own kingdom apart from, and at least as effectively, as the king's or any man's. Nor do I see any lack of rationality in my lady Rosemounde. She can show me where I've gone wrong in my thinking without breaking a sweat." I paused a moment, and then added, "Probably not an image she'd appreciate much…"

"All of whom, I suppose, your average theologian would identify as viragos, unnatural women who must be brought into the proper relationship with the men responsible for them," Merlin shook his head. "These monks and friars who write these treatises, you know, Gildas, are pledged to celibacy. They don't have your experiences with real-life women. They don't have *any* experiences with real-life women. They just know that they can't have one of their own, and so they simply repeat what they see as the rational authority of writers who have gone before them. Celibate male writers who have gone before. And so the charade continues *ad infinitum*. Uh, that means to perpetuity, for those imbeciles in the audience who do not speak Latin."

"But there you've touched on the very core of the problem," I answered him. "The women must be 'brought into line' you say. And how is that done? Men are bigger, stronger…"

"Those warm humors…" Merlin agreed, with an ironic half-smile.

"And so they use brute force to make their women toe the line. How is beating your wife in keeping with the higher rationality of men? Pure force is not reason…how can the Church or the law accept that as something appropriate?" By now I was shaking, since we were approaching the topic that truly concerned me most.

Merlin shook his head in a kind of resignation. "That practice is a kind of bastard effect borne of two unrealistic, untenable, but virtually unquestioned conditions. The first of these is the universally accepted assumption that the subjection of women to men is natural and divinely sanctioned. The other is the legal and ecclesiastical principle that marriage must be indissoluble because blessed by God. So anything the wife does that displeases the husband can make her subject to physical 'correction,' and she is trapped in the situation for life because what God has joined together no man—or woman—is allowed to put asunder."

"But surely," I pressed the point, "the law can't condone physically harming your wife…"

Merlin raised his eyebrows and shrugged his shoulders. "There are levels of condoning, I suppose. Augustine talks about his own mother being beaten by his father, and talks about other women in the town where he was raised showing their bruises in public. He doesn't seem to discourage the practice. The emperor Justinian's law code did provide a fine for men who treated their wives too roughly, but it also forbade wives to leave husbands who mistreated them. And since Justinian, that's been the law for church and state."

"But it's not right!" I protested weakly.

Another shrug. "The Church says it is. Canon law says men ought to punish their wives' disobedient behavior publicly—like with iron muzzles and spikes pressing down the tongue. She's not likely to answer him back after that, you can imagine. In Gaul they've got a law that gives every man the right to beat his wife as long as he doesn't beat her to death."

"Oh fine. And what happens if he goes too far? Another fine?"

"Perhaps," Merlin answered. "But it would be hard to enforce. Look, the laws do not favor wives in any situation. I've heard of a Flemish law that allows a husband to beat his wife, slash her with a knife, and bathe his feet in her blood, as long as he doesn't kill her and can nurse her back to health afterwards. There's another law in parts of Arthur's kingdom that allows a man to beat his wife until she is nearly senseless, but restricts him from beating her until her senseless body farts, because that would be a sign that she had lost all control and may be dying."

"*Enough!*" I cried, the image of what her beast of a husband could do to my lady without suffering any legal consequence was causing my gorge to rise and I was beginning to tremble with anger, fear, and disgust. That Merlin could be so cavalier about these matters was irksome as well, and I exploded, "Can nothing be done? Why does your creature Arthur, the good and pious king, not do something about these laws?"

Merlin pursed his lips and considered. "I suspect it is not for lack of will. I think no one has brought these things to his attention thus far. But wait, that's probably not the true reason. Even Arthur can only go so far. He is a man ahead of his time, with progressive ideas that no one before him would have tried. Consider the case of the rape of Bess of Caerleon a few years ago. You remember that Arthur pronounced death to the perpetrator, even though he knew it to be a member of his own Round Table. Under previous kings, and in other kingdoms, a rapist would be fined and imprisoned. If the victim were a noble woman, her family may demand more savage punishments, even castration. But a lower-class woman? In most cases, Bess's rape would have been a misdemeanor. The knight would have paid a fine, and that would have been the end of it. Arthur chose to act in a way that protected women no matter what their class. But in this kind of case? He would be taking on the entire Church establishment by discouraging wife-beating—and the prejudices of his own knights and vassals as well. There is only so far ahead of your time you can be as a ruler. Nobody is this far ahead."

"It sounds as if you are, Old Man, though you speak largely in jest," I admitted.

"Ah, but remember, I am the child of the devil, and a practitioner of the black arts as well. What I say is not going to influence society. Only when men start to believe what their experience tells them and not what some authority tells them will we get a change. Only when there are more Gildases in the world to listen to me is *that* going to happen."

"But Merlin, can you tell me why in the world a man would do such a thing to his wife? I mean, if you want to talk about what the Church says, man and wife are one flesh, aren't they? So a man who hurts his wife hurts himself? And doesn't Saint Paul say somewhere that husbands should love their wives as Christ loved the Church, and sacrificed himself for her? Where is the love in this kind of beating? Where is the sacrifice?"

"There is no sense to it. There is certainly no love or sacrifice in it. Just power and domination. It's a kind of sickness, I think." Merlin scowled and looked thoughtful. I don't think he expected that question. "It may be that he has no control over his anger, and becomes jealous or resentful of his wife's actions. Or perhaps his own father abused his mother, and so he thinks that is the way a man relates to his wife. Or it may be that someone brutalized the man when he was a child, so he makes someone else suffer as he has suffered.

Or it may be," his voice rose as if he was thinking of something new, "that he is a man whose concept of himself is low, who feels he has no real worship, and who can only make himself feel he is a true man by making someone else feel weak. And what better weakness to exploit than that of your wife—whom the Church has already told you is your slave, whom you have every right to brutalize according to civil and canon law, and who cannot bring charges against you because she is subject to your every whim? Such men may beat their wives and feel no remorse at all."

"And is such a sickness of the mind curable?" I wanted to know.

Merlin looked down, his brows lowered like thunderclouds. "Some kinds of madness may be assuaged by tenderness and calm—I have seen it happen. This kind…I cannot say. It seems it would be very difficult. The man would have to go back and relive his whole life. He would have to undo all the things that twisted him in his youth. And he would have to be willing to change. If beating his wife is the only thing that makes him feel like he has any worth, why would he want to change it?"

I realized at that point that I had been riding with my fists tightly clenched, and in fact my jaw hurt too from grinding my teeth at Merlin's explanations. Tired of holding it in, I let out a huge sigh of frustration and hopelessness, and blurted out, "He's beating Rosemounde. That beast Mordred, he's beating her. I want to kill him."

The old man's own jaw dropped and he raised his gray head to look at me. He seemed, strange to say, at a loss for words, something quite nearly unheard of for him. "Oh my dear boy," he began, in tenderer tones than I have ever heard from that voice of practiced irony. "I had no idea. And here I am making jokes and flippant remarks about the topic of wife abuse in general, while all the time you are very personally concerned with a very specific case of the crime. Can you forgive a foolish old man?"

The attitude was so unwonted on the part of the old necromancer, and my own emotions so raw from having finally released what had been tormenting me for weeks, that eighteen though I was and quite nearly ready to become a knight, I could not suppress the tears that welled in my eyes. And now that the floodgates had been opened, I burst out with feelings long suppressed. "I want him dead!" I screamed. "I want to gut him like the pig he is!"

"My boy," Merlin shook his head. "Whatever else he is, Mordred is a skilled knight, who has killed before, and not necessarily in a fair fight."

"You refer to the murder of Sir Lamorak?" I responded. "A coward's act. Would he dare face a man in fair combat? My master says…"

"Your master is his brother," Merlin reminded me. "There may be some…difficulty about that. Besides, Mordred is cunning and not to be trusted, but no coward. I have seen him in the lists as, I'm sure, you have yourself. He is a knight of the Round Table, and his skills and experience are superior to yours. The time may come for you to challenge him but it is not here yet. You must wait and hone your skills."

"And while I wait, the monster flogs her every night."

"Surely she is safe in Camelot," Merlin insisted. "She sleeps in the queen's rooms—he cannot get at her here."

"Until he decides to leave, and go back to Orkney, where he can beat upon her willy-nilly with the blessing of Church and state. What about the king?" I proposed, hitting upon a new idea. "Can he not go against law and custom in what is for him a family matter? Can he not simply tell his bastard to cease and desist, or risk, I don't know, imprisonment? Exile?"

"Imprisonment and exile are not the punishments one metes out in a family matter, my boy. And think of the position you then put Rosemounde in. Once he knows the secret of his cruelty has been revealed throughout the court, who is he going to blame, eh? It would have to be her fault, it can't be his, and he would punish her all the more savagely, now certain he must chastise her more ferociously to prevent her betraying him again. You asked me what kind of a man could do such a thing as this Mordred has done. Mordred is precisely the kind of man I described to you. Think of it—abandoned as a baby after his own father tried to have him killed. Never aware of or accepted by his father and so a man with no feeling of self-worth.

A man whose only demonstration of power is in the domination of those weaker than himself, a domination that makes him feel the power, the manhood that the rest of his life denies him. That's your Mordred. It needs no physician to tell us the sickness of his mind."

"Then you are counseling me to do nothing," I murmured, defeated.

"I'm counseling you to bide your time. The queen knows of this?"

"Of course."

"And the queen has chosen not to reveal the secret to Arthur. She is a cunning woman and knows what she is about. She can protect your Rosemounde better than anyone else right now, trust me," Merlin advised, looking at me not unkindly. "She will keep the girl by her side as long as she is able to do so, and postpone any thought of Mordred's returning with her to Orkney, at least for now. He cannot leave in the midst of this Grail quest, in any case, for doing so leaves his king with too few knights protecting the castle. Take heart, Gildas, something will be done to ensure her safety. The queen will not let this be."

The queen. The queen had let me down before—she was far from infallible. Still, what Merlin said gave me some shaky comfort at last. But I did not tell him about Rosemounde's plea to me: become a knight, she had told me. Train well. Earn membership in the Round Table. And then kill the bastard. That must remain my life's goal.

***

The rest of that day was quieter, and mostly uneventful. Guinevere did in fact chase a rabbit and bring it back to us sometime around none, so I won the bet. Not that it really mattered, since Merlin always let me be white, there being no chance of my ever beating him. Once again, I gathered some dry wood for a fire and Merlin prepared the rabbit for dinner. Guinevere and I particularly enjoyed our roasted meat. But we ate fast and mounted up again, determined to reach the Abbey of Saint Sebastian before nightfall. And, given the long daylight hours of that early summer day, we managed to do so, not long before the sun went down. I had been expecting to see King Bagdemagus and his son Meliagaunt in the abbey's infirmary, but Brother Luke, the old infirmarian, recognized me and let us know that Bagdemagus and his son had departed not two days earlier, the king still wobbly but certain to live, and had headed for home in their kingdom of Gorre. And of course the rest of the monks weren't saying much, what with their vows of silence and all. Brother Lawrence, the abbot, bade us welcome and allowed us, again, to sleep in the refectory. We rose before breakfast and, passing on the abbot's invitation to hear his monks singing prime, we ambled off to find Brother Bertrand's cell, munching for sustenance on our own store of bread and cheese as we rode.

The hovel, as Sir Gawain had told us, was about half an hour's gentle ride farther along the same path we had taken past Saint Sebastian's Abbey. Nestled into the birch trees on the right on the east side of the path, it was nearly invisible, camouflaged by the trunks and branches. We dismounted, and tied our horses to the nearby trees.

The cell itself was oval shaped, built of branches of timber wedged and tied together and resting on a rough stone foundation. It was perhaps twelve feet by ten, and its roof was made of turf. Turf and leaves served, as well, to stop up the spaces between the thick branches forming the walls in order to keep out the drafts of winter. The one small entrance to the cell was open to the elements, and faced the southwest in order to let in as much light as possible. There was a small garden before the cell in which a few vegetables grew, no doubt to augment the hermit's meager table. There were also rows of herbs. Guinevere trotted up and down the rows of garden plants, sniffing at each and occasionally giving out a snort or sneeze, depending on just what she thought of the herbs' scents.

"Well, it seems our Brother Bertrand was an herbalist of sorts, doesn't it?" Merlin noted, examining the groups of plants carefully.

"Maybe it's just seasoning for his supper," I suggested, glancing around myself. "Your herb knowledge has got to be better than mine. Anything here look like henbane to you?"

"From what I've read in herbalist lore," Merlin said slowly, looking carefully down the row at the southern edge of the garden, "the *Hyoscyamus niger* plant grows tall, some three feet high, and has yellow leaves with veins—in fact, like those at the end of this row!"

Guinevere was just into several of these plants, and began snorting violently when she sniffed them. "Better keep your dog away from them—those flowers are going to be poison to her, as to us."

I ran toward Guinevere, who, thinking I wanted to play, bounded off to the other side of the cell, her tail wagging frantically. Merlin stepped closer to examine the yellow-flowered plants. "Leaves shaped like eggs with sharp points and covered with sticky hair—yes, this is definitely black henbane. Well, not exactly a brilliant job of detection, eh? He was growing it right out here in the open."

"Yes," I said. "Apparently the dog could have solved this case without our help!"

"Solved?" Merlin jerked his head up to peer down his nose at me, as he did when he wanted to make it clear that I should feel wrong. "Who says this case is solved?"

"Well, the hermit clearly was producing the herbs that poisoned Gawain's and Lionel's minds. And it's Morgan's recipe, isn't it? And look," I was suddenly struck by my memory of Merlin's pronouncement earlier, when he had gone into his trance. "The words of your vision, remember? 'The mother of light is the mother of darkness,' you said, and then 'The widow triumphs.' Morgan is a mother, isn't she? And Ywain is certainly a bright light in Camelot, but she's also a mother of darkness, right? And a widow, as you said, now that Uriens is dead? She triumphs because her potions serve her purpose right? Doesn't it make sense? Obviously she's behind it and Brother Bertrand was her accomplice. So we go back and bring her before the king."

"God's eyeteeth Gildas, you Cornish imbecile, you've never based so many mistaken conclusions on so many false assumptions in your whole life. You know you can't rely on those cryptic visions of mine—they never make sense until the truth is known. Certainly it appears that the hermit was raising henbane in his garden. I'll grant that he probably did give it to Sir Gawain and Sir Lionel, for they described effects likely to have come from the plant. But the only connection with Morgan le Fay is that she used a similar drug once before. It is certainly possible that there is a trail from Morgan to Bertrand, but Morgan has no monopoly on herb-lore. And if she were responsible for these murders, why on earth would she tell us about using the plant earlier on Sir Accolon? And the real question here is, what, if anything, does the White Knight have to do with the poisonings? Are they separate phenomena, or two prongs of the same attacker? Who is ultimately behind this? No, dear Gildas, this case is far from solved." He looked about for a moment, and I heard Guinevere scratching at something, playing out of sight behind the hovel. "Let's take a look inside," Merlin proposed.

He strode through the door, tilting his head curiously before ducking it to fit through the doorway, and I followed cautiously behind him. The hermit was apparently a poisoner, so who knew what else might be there in the cell? But as my eyes adjusted to the low light in the hovel, I could make out the very simple furnishings of the ascetic's life: a small wooden table fixed in the earthen floor, a wooden bench large enough for two to sit at, and a crucifix hanging from the rough patched-together wall above the table, and on the table was a single candle and a loaf of bread. In the corner was a small wine barrel. A crude shelf had been fastened to the wall opposite the crucifix. Five vellum manuscripts lay on the shelf, along with a number of dried herbs laid out in bunches side by side. Merlin was standing at the shelf, looking through the herbs. Meanwhile I looked out of the one small window in the cell that opened toward the back, and watched Guinevere sniffing and digging away at something in the earth. "Oh, Guinevere stop that," I scolded half-heartedly. "You're going to get your paws all muddy and get them on my clean hosen."

"Yes," Merlin murmured, half to himself, and I looked back toward him. "Here's the dried *Hyoscyamus niger* right here that he must have put into the wine, and into Lionel's broth. He was drugging them for sure. But why? And who's behind it?"

Suddenly through the window came a pathetic howl that made me jump. Outside I could see Guinevere crouched over the hole she had been digging, lifting up her head and yowling over something she had done or found. I made for the door, ducking my way out and muttering, "What's she crying about now?"

"Your dog is very histrionic," Merlin observed as he followed me out the door. "What did she do, get a thorn in her paw?"

"Probably something like that," I admitted, circling to the rear of the cell, where I stopped so abruptly that Merlin actually ran into me.

Guinevere had been digging, to our horror, at a shallow, hastily dug grave. She had uncovered the face of the deceased, and looking down, we could recognize the white ecclesiastical Cistercian robes clothing the body, and the tonsured skull that made it clear he had been a monk. The face was not much decayed, and a jagged red scar was still visible from his right cheekbone across his lips.

"My God!" I cried. "Brother Nascien!"

CHAPTER FOURTEEN

THE FISHER KING

I shouted at Guinevere to get away, and she danced off, giving the shallow grave a wide berth as she rolled in the grass and gamboled in the hermit's garden. The body had been in the ground long enough to begin to decompose, but only slightly. Brother Nascien could not have been more than two or three days dead. As far as I could tell without searching the body more carefully, he had received but one wound—a sword thrust straight to the heart.

"We cannot leave the body here," Merlin thought out loud. "His fellow Cistercians will be looking for him, wondering why he hasn't returned. And he needs a proper burial. This…this was his assailants' shoving him into the ground to hide the evidence so they could make good their escape."

"Who is this 'they,'" I wanted to know. "And what was he doing here anyway? How is Brother Nascien mixed up with what went on at this hermitage? Did he know something about Sir Gawain's confession here? About Sir Lionel's drugging and his attack on Bors, and Colgrevaunce?"

"Whatever he knew of those things has died with him. But finding him here gives me a strong certainty that he was far from innocent in these affairs."

"He's the one that seemed to be sketching out a shape for the quest. The one who supposedly ordered that no knight was to go near a woman and all that, the order that sent Sir Ywain to the infirmary."

"Yes, but of course," Merlin said thoughtfully, "no one ever heard

194

him say such things himself. It was always the disguised White Knight who made those kinds of proclamations, wasn't it?"

"Unless he was the White Knight himself. You know he was a trained knight in the service of King Uther, or at least that is what he told us. He could easily have been the knight."

Merlin shrugged. "Possibly. I admit I had that suspicion myself. You say he was in King Uther's service. I don't remember him, but then I did not serve Uther long. If he was still around at the beginning of Arthur's reign, he was not a member of the court."

"No, but King Bagdemagus said that he was close friend to Sir Balin. Nobody seems to know much more about him, except that he gave up arms to join the Cistercians. Maybe that was after Balin died." I said this, of course, because his taking those vows had made a big impression on me. It was something I had thought about myself.

"But this murder of Brother Nascien sheds a new light on things," Merlin went on. "The fact that he is out here rather than back in his monastery is certainly suspicious enough for a supposedly cloistered religious. But that he is out here and is also dead suggests he was clearly not alone. And that whoever his companion was quarreled with him so that poor Nascien ended up slain."

"Do we know that?" I asked. "Could he not have been ambushed by strangers? Or some enemy lying in wait?"

"He was a trained knight, as you reminded me yourself. God's hangnails Gildas, he was a skilled fighter. There would be more signs of the struggle upon him if he had been ambushed—he would have fought hard if he was fighting for his life. Yet there is but a single wound, as far as can be seen. I think Brother Nascien was in conversation with someone well-known to him."

"Well I can't see him being here for any good reason, not in the middle of this disastrous quest. Instead of being at Beaulieu, tucked away in his monastery, he's here, visiting, I suppose, his old friend the hermit, Brother Bertrand. But Bertrand is dead, too. Both of them must have been involved in this conspiracy to bring down Sir Gawain and Sir Lionel. So who was the third? Morgan le Fay? Could she have pulled off this murder?"

Merlin shrugged again. "It would be her style, I suppose, to attack

Nascien when his guard was down. And if, as we conjectured, Brother Bertrand was her agent, then perhaps Brother Nascien was as well. But the White Knight still puzzles me. We know that the White Knight was somehow associated with this hermitage—remember that it was here that King Bagdemagus first encountered him. Well where is the armor? It is not here. It is clearly not on Nascien's body. If Nascien was the White Knight, then it may have been that his mysterious companion did not appreciate what was being done, killed Nascien and took his armor afterwards. But it is also possible that it was the White Knight who killed Brother Nascien, after falling out with him over something."

I stood in silence, letting all of that sink in. "Then this was a well-planned conspiracy from the beginning, involving at least three conspirators—four if Morgan is in on it—and planned around this quest of the Holy Grail. Does this mean that Galahad is one of their number as well?"

Merlin's considerable eyebrows shot up and he scoffed. "That lad is as sincere as the rising sun. There is no guile in him. He believes wholeheartedly in this quest."

"But he was raised in that monastery, brought up by Brother Nascien and his fellows."

"Who have without doubt made use of the boy's goodness and prowess to work their scheme," Merlin asserted. "But what is that scheme? What truly is the goal here, and what is the motive? Every knight seems to be a target. If this conspiracy has been so long in planning—something that grew in the fifteen years that Galahad has been at that monastery—then why does the goal seem so haphazard? I see no rhyme nor reason in it, only indiscriminate blood after blood."

"Well, I guess we'll continue to ponder it then," I said, ready to get away from the shadows that were lengthening around that hermitage. "For now, I think we need to decide what to do about this body, don't you think?"

"The monks at Saint Sebastian's are his fellow Cistercians, and they are close by," Merlin said. "We can carry the body to them over your horse. It's not far for you to walk." I grimaced. Nice of

Merlin to volunteer my horse rather than his own. "I expect they were familiar with Brother Nascien. The fact that they are here and so close might explain why he was able to visit this area away from his own house for such a length of time. They will certainly give him a proper burial, and can send word to their sister house on the southern coast to inquire whether Brother Nascien's body ought to be shipped back there, or whether they are content that it stay here. Come on, boy, let's get him out of that hole and over your horse's back. No one said this job would be pleasant."

No, I thought grumpily as I stooped down to grab the corpse under the arms and lift it out of the ground, pleasant is not a word I would have expected to be using, even when the queen and the lady Rosemounde urged me to get to the bottom of these strange events. Ah, I said to myself, turning my face in disgust from the heavy lump of dead flesh I was in the midst of lifting. The things I do for love.

***

The stony-faced Abbot Lawrence sat across from us at the table in the rectory of the Abbey of Saint Sebastian, his beaklike nose wrinkled as if in disdain, as if he could still smell the decomposing body of Brother Nascien we had delivered into his care less than an hour before. Or perhaps it was simply his personal revulsion at the thought that Guinevere was curled up at my feet under the table as we talked. The monks had been hospitable enough, putting wooden cups with cold water from their well before us on the table to relieve us after a dry trip in. I was particularly thirsty because, of course, I had had to walk here from the hermitage. Brother Lawrence's eyes were half-veiled as he looked down at his own cup and murmured, "It's a terrible thing, a terrible thing, my lords. One of our brothers murdered and left to rot—who is safe in this thoroughfare of woe?"

"Oh, no one is, to be sure," Merlin commiserated with artificial piety. "The only safety is in the Lord, certainly, and then only when we've passed out of the pilgrimage of our lives into the everlasting fortress of God's mercy, isn't that so Gildas my boy?"

I looked at him as if he had sprouted three heads all of a sudden, but he scowled at me and made an almost imperceptible gesture toward Brother Lawrence, so I assumed he wanted me to play along.

"Oh yes," I agreed loudly. "No doubt about it. Brigands around every corner and sin running rampant through the court. I tell you, there've been many times lately that I've thought about taking vows myself, forsaking the world altogether and devoting myself to prayer."

In fact, of course, that last bit was true, particularly since I had lost my darling Rosemounde to the foul hands of Arthur's bastard. Abbot Lawrence raised his head at this, his hazel eyes piercing me with his powerful stare, his thin face slowly moving back and forth as he responded, "No, young Gildas of Cornwall. The convent is not a place you go to retreat from the world. It is a place you go to be closer to God, to focus your attention on His love. We do not have walls to shut the world out. We have walls to reinforce the love within our community. But where there are human beings, there is sin."

I saw Merlin's eyes twinkle, as if this was precisely the opening he'd been waiting for. "As to that, my lord Abbot, perhaps that is why the hermit, Brother…Bertrand was it? Perhaps that was why he chose to live alone, rather than in the community of other monks?"

Brother Lawrence shrugged, and he brought his hands up to rub his protruding cheekbones in a gesture of frustration. "Perhaps. Perhaps Brother Bertrand could not abide the sin he saw even in his fellows at the monastery. These anchorites try to remove all those things that might distract them from full communion with God. But my lords, how can full communion take place in our physical world? The cloister was not enough for Brother Bertrand. I cannot say why. He was established in his hermitage long before our monastery was built here."

"Indeed?" Merlin perked up. "How long before? Do you know his history?"

"Do you know why Brother Nascien would have been visiting him?" I added, thinking this to be the more pertinent question. "Or looking for him? I mean, why would we find his body there of all places?"

"Oh, Brother Nascien's presence at the hermitage comes as no surprise. Twice before he has visited our house—his own Beaulieu

Abbey in Hampshire is our mother house, you see. Several of the brothers here left that convent more than a year ago to found this one. I was brought in as abbot—I had been prior at another house in Brittany. Brother Nascien felt it was his duty to check on us every so often, and he and his companion would visit with greetings from the old abbey."

"Companion?" Merlin's ears perked up.

"Why yes, brother, um, Grunamund has always accompanied Prior Nascien on his journeys here," Brother Lawrence replied.

That struck a chord with me. "Big fellow with broad shoulders? Blond tonsure?" I pressed. Merlin raised his brows and looked at me with some astonishment.

"Yes, that would be him," Lawrence raised his own eyebrows in surprise that I would be familiar with the fellow, but I couldn't help recalling that stalwart, military looking monk I'd seen with Brother Nascien at Camelot. I nodded to Merlin. "He was with that group when they brought Galahad to Camelot."

"And where is this Brother Grunamund now?" asked Merlin. "Surely he must be made aware of Brother Nascien's fate, and perhaps it is he, on behalf of Beaulieu Abbey, who should determine what is to be done with Nascien's remains."

"As to that," Brother Lawrence lowered his eyes, "I think I must take charge. Our brother must be given a proper burial in hallowed ground and it should be done soon. He has waited long enough for that common courtesy. We shall bury him here—in fact, his will be the first grave in our new churchyard. The abbey has not been in existence long enough for any of the brothers of this house to have passed to glory, but it will be fitting to have a loved and respected member of our mother house interred in the first grave at Saint Sebastian's. Brother Grunamund will no doubt approve once he returns."

"Returns from where?" I asked, repeating Merlin's earlier question. The mysterious absence of this Brother Grunamund just at this time, when his fellow was found murdered, put him in a suspicious light as far as I was concerned.

"When Brother Nascien and Grunamund came to visit us, they

generally would visit with Brother Bertrand at the hermitage, and would also pay a visit to Corbenic Castle, which as you know is about two leagues north from here. Brother Bertrand, to answer my lord Merlin's question from before he was rudely interrupted" (with that Brother Lawrence gave me a meaningful stare, and I felt myself blushing) "they knew from old days when he first entered the abbey at Beaulieu. As for Corbenic, I believe Nascien and Grunamund and their brothers held the King's grandson in their keeping at the abbey, where they housed and schooled him at the king's direction. They always made a stop here in Saint Sebastian while on their way to make their report to the king. When the two of them arrived here, oh, a week ago or so?—after spending the night they left in two different directions: Brother Nascien to visit Brother Bertrand and Brother Grunamund to Corbenic to report to the Maimed King."

"A week ago? God's whiskers...excuse me Lord Abbot, but—God's whiskers! Brother Bertrand was killed weeks ago by Sir Lionel!" Merlin lowered his brows in puzzlement. "You mean to say Brother Nascien did not know this?"

Abbot Lawrence closed his eyes as if to shut out a painful memory; I wasn't sure whose pain he was shutting out. Maybe it was just the enormity of death after death that seemed to be piling up. But he answered, "We at the abbey had heard something about the hermit being cut down by a sword. I did not, until now, know the name of the one whose sword had done the cutting. But yes, we warned Nascien, and he seemed quite disturbed by the news. It was at that point that he told Brother Grunamund to go on to Corbenic while he visited the hermitage. He said he wanted to look the place over, to see whether Brother Bertrand had left anything that might prove of value—spiritual value, I'm sure he meant," again he glared at me, as if my face had suggested something else. Which I admit it may well have. "I mean, for the brothers at the old abbey. Or perhaps something Bertrand may have written down that might shed some light on these matters." I wasn't sure what matters he was referring to, except perhaps Bertrand's own murder. But we already had all the light we needed shed on that—by Sir Lionel's uncompromising confession. Or was Nascien's own murder one of "these matters"? If so, Brother Bertrand couldn't shed any light on that, unless he was clairvoyant.

"But my lord, pardon the interruption," I felt the need to say this, even though nobody else at the time seemed about to speak. "But do you have any way of knowing how long Brother Bertrand was at Beaulieu Abbey? I mean, he had been a secular priest prior to that, right? At Sir Bertilak's castle? Do you know whether he ever was visited by Morgan le Fay?"

Now it was Brother Lawrence's turn to stare at *me* as if I, too, had sprouted that third head. Merlin's eyes gazed up to the heavens and he crossed his arms as if to say I was on my own with this one. Brother Lawrence stuttered a bit, not really understanding the question, as far as I could tell. But eventually he said, "I'm afraid I am not privy to that information. Now, I think we may be done here. Once again, you have our thanks for bringing our poor brother here to take his eternal rest. I hope you will excuse me and I wish you Godspeed as you continue your…whatever it is you're doing." The nose on his thin face wrinkled once again into that look of revulsion as he rose and as Guinevere rose from under the table at the same time, pushing her paws far out in front of her and pushing her tail end high in the air in the abbot's direction.

"Thank you my lord," Merlin nodded politely. "You've been a great help to us. We'll see ourselves out." I looked askance at Merlin, having found little of value myself in the abbot's somewhat rambling comments. But as we turned to leave, Abbot Lawrence turned back to us.

"Gildas of Cornwall," he called as I looked back at him. "If you truly are serious about having a vocation," and at this his eyes searched mine with piercing sincerity, "you must remember that attachments to material things—glory, riches, fame, desires (for the love of women, or for revenge on men)—these will draw your soul away from the true love of God. Only when you can say you have transcended these things will you be comfortable in a cloister." He looked down thoughtfully, then looked up at me again: "Many who do take the vows have not realized this. And it is for them a struggle. Go in peace."

***

Guinevere frolicked around the hooves of our horses as we moved at a leisurely walking gait north of the abbey. In a playful mood, the borzoi began to run figure-eight circles around the two horses, returning to them in the center before swinging into a large circle first on one side and then on the other. The horses were a bit skittish at this playful behavior, but they were too old and well-trained to break out and try to chase the dog, who was moving too fast for them to catch up with anyway, unless it were on a straightaway at full gallop. But I wasn't paying much attention to the dog's antics. I was focusing instead on what Brother Lawrence had said to me. How did he know? Certainly my soul was focused purely on my lady Rosemounde—her and the vengeance I longed to take on the vile Sir Mordred. And even if I could not have Rosemounde for my own, the abbot was right—I could never spend my life under the Cistercian rule in my present state, obsessed as I was with love and revenge. If there was a time for me to withdraw from the world, it was not yet. It was not near. It may never be.

I realized after mulling this over for some time that Merlin had not spoken a word since we had left the monastery. Unsure of what this portended, I prodded him a bit. "So what did you mean, Merlin, about the abbot being a big help to us? If you got anything of any use out of what Brother Lawrence was saying, I say you were hearing something that I wasn't hearing, that's for sure."

"If I heard something you weren't hearing, you lump of Cornish slag, it's because all you were listening for was something to pin on Morgan le Fay. She's a red herring, boy, look at the facts and not what you want to get out of them."

It wasn't a gentle rebuke, but I got the point, and I had to admit he was right. We had learned nothing about Morgan at that interview, but what had we learned instead? "I confess to being a blockhead. At least today. Leaving Morgan out of it, what do we know that we didn't know before?"

The old man shook his head as he watched Guinevere continue to wear herself out running in circles. "Sometimes you remind me of your dog—obsessed with running around in the same path and paying no attention to where the path is taking us. Look: Is it not clear to you that this entire conspiracy to destroy Arthur and his knights was hatched between these two monks, probably with the aid, willing or unwilling, of the hermit, and perhaps with the knowledge of King Pelles himself? The death of the hermit was not planned—that took them by surprise, and I'd be willing to bet that Brother Nascien was about to pull out of the plan, perhaps even reveal it to the king, as things had begun to unravel on him. Almost certainly it was this Brother Grunamund that killed him. And it probably goes without saying that this Grunamund must be the mysterious White Knight as well."

After a few moments I realized that my mouth was hanging open, and with a bit of doubt creeping into my voice I began, "And so…"

"And so it's got nothing to do with Morgan le Fay. Or at least she is not the direct cause of this conspiracy. Perhaps the hermit owed something of his knowledge of herbs to her, but that may be the extent of it."

"Well than let's get back to the king, and let him know that we've solved this, and get this Grunamund to trial—let's end this disastrous quest as quickly as it began…"

Merlin shook his head. "We can't."

"Why not?" I asked with some frustration.

"Because I haven't any actual evidence at all against Grunamund. And I've got no idea what the motive for all of this is, or what the ultimate goal of the conspiracy is. Besides all of that, there may be others involved—as I said, we don't know what King Pelles' part in this whole rigmarole is either. We don't know who is still in danger—every knight on this quest is a potential target."

"So…" I asked, realizing that I had merely been blindly following along behind Merlin as he rode north. "Where are we going now?"

"To Corbenic, of course. If this Grunamund is still there, perhaps we can get something from him. If he's not, we need to talk to King Pelles anyway. Come on, let's move a little faster." And with that he broke into a trot. My horse trotted after his, and Guinevere, finally tired out, gave a kind of low moan as she followed along, when all she wanted to do now was lie down and rest.

We were in a country now where there were few trees, and where what were once apparently fertile fields lay fallow and overgrown. It was as if the villagers had given up and gone elsewhere, leaving this area infertile and wild. At one point we rode past a deserted monastery, its roof crumbled away and fallen into ruin, with weeds growing through what was left of the once rich patterned floor, and leaves burying the once sacred corners of what was left of the chapel.

We rode a few furlongs farther north until we came to the bank of a fairly wide river, and looking downstream we saw a small boat anchored in the middle of the stream, with two men aboard, one of whom was fishing off the stern of the boat with a baited line. Guinevere had noticed them too, and sent one of her very rare barks in their direction. That got the men's attention, and the fisherman shaded his eyes as he looked toward us.

"My lords!" Merlin shouted to the boat. "Tell me, is there a place to ford the water, or a bridge across it somewhere close by?"

The older man who was seated and fishing looked up to us and waved. Even from that distance I could see that it was King Pelles himself. "You can't ford the stream anywhere near here," he called back. "The water is too deep and the undercurrent too treacherous for horses. But if I am not mistaken, is that not my lord Merlin? You are welcome to Corbenic my lords. Please, you must be my guests tonight. Ride to the top of that hill," King Pelles pointed off to our right, where a rocky treeless tor rose unwelcomingly along the edge of a small valley. "You'll see Corbenic from there. Ride to the gate and tell them I'm on my way."

Merlin bowed slightly, calling, "Thank you Sire, that is just what we would have wished." We turned our horses and they carefully scaled the craggy tor, with Guinevere taking the lead, leaping gracefully from one rock to the next higher one until, having reached the top, we could see that it was just as the king had said: All about us the land around that tor was wild and infertile, but the solid castle of Corbenic lay below us in the valley. A square keep of dark stone towered over the rest of the construction. It was flanked by two turrets and we could make out a low hall before the keep, with long narrow galleries inside the walls of that sturdy fortification. The small stream that had shaped this valley had been diverted to form a moat around the castle before it forged on to join the larger river on the other side of the tor, and as we descended the hill we followed the prancing Guinevere, making straight for the gate, which had already lowered its drawbridge. Four squires met us as we rode across, and Merlin told the tall, muscular brown-haired one who seemed to be their leader that King Pelles had sent us to the castle and invited us for the night. The squire nodded, murmuring something unintelligible but vaguely welcoming, and two of the other lads took our horses to the stable, while the third put a leash on Guinevere and led her to the kennels where she would be fed and bedded down.

As for Merlin and me, the muscular squire, a grown lad about my own age, with short brown hair and freckles across an upturned nose, ushered us into one of the galleries, and we were seated in that colonnaded, closed-in area out of the warm sun and given a cup of wine each to await the king's return. The squire assured us that King Pelles would have us brought into his presence as soon as he returned from his boat, which I imagined could not be long, since he had seemed eager to entertain us when he called from the river.

But we weren't left to wait long, for the same squire returned and ushered us into the great hall, a huge square room, with a high ceiling lined with magnificently wrought oak panels. In the center of the hall was a massive brass chimney supported by four marble pillars around a large fireplace, where even though we were now in late June, a fire of dry logs burned to take the chill off the cold stone of that room. King Pelles reclined, leaning on his right elbow, on a blue cushioned day bed that stood before the fire. He wore a black satin cap with a purple peak over his gray hair, and was dressed in a long robe of the same fabric and coloring. Our freckled, muscled guide took up a position behind the king, who beckoned us forward with his free hand.

"My friends, I do hope you will forgive me for not rising to greet you," he began as we approached the bed and inclined our heads according to custom. "I mean you no offense, but as you must know I can only rise and move around with great difficulty. Please know you are welcome here, and that we want you to feel at ease."

"Think nothing of it, your Grace," Merlin responded with the same civility. "We understand perfectly." Meanwhile I was looking around for a place to sit, but the only seat in the entire great hall was the king's own bed. Clearly he wasn't all that concerned with our feeling at ease.

Perhaps the Maimed King had noticed my eyes, for no sooner had Merlin spoken than Pelles looked over his shoulder to his young squire and said, "Golagros, have two chairs brought in for our guests, and let some refreshments be brought as well. The lord Merlin will carry news back to Camelot that the king of Corbenic has forgotten his courtesy if we are not more careful."

"As my lord wishes," the efficient Golagros murmured, and stepped out of the hall through a door opposite the one we had come in.

"Your Grace," Merlin began when the attendant had left the room. "Let me preface what I say by telling you that we were not simply passing by Corbenic by chance…"

"No, I thought it unlikely," King Pelles' countenance drooped, and the corners of his mouth turned down into his white beard. "What, then, has brought you to me? And all the way from Camelot itself, it would seem?"

"I and my young companion Gildas," Merlin began, "have ridden this way, looking into the mysterious deaths of some of the knights of the Round Table. In doing so we uncovered another dead body—that of Brother Nascien of Beaulieu Abbey. We understand that he was well-known to you."

The king glanced at me briefly out of the corner of his eye when Merlin introduced me—my impression was that he was unused to paying much attention to underlings, and that immediately upon seeing us he had sized me up as Merlin's attendant, and not as someone of much consequence. He continued to address his comments only to the old Necromancer. "That is unwelcome news indeed," he said with apparently heartfelt dismay. "Yes, Brother Nascien was a frequent visitor to Corbenic. His murder distresses me more than I can say."

"Murder?" Merlin echoed with a bland expression. "I didn't think I had said anything about murder…"

"Oh, you didn't have to," King Pelles waved the comment off. "Why would you have come here to investigate the poor monk's death if there wasn't foul play involved? But what is it you think we at Corbenic can help you with?"

"We want to talk with Brother Grunamund," I blurted out. "He's still here, isn't he? We didn't see him along the road."

King Pelles gave no indication that he had even heard my question. Perhaps I had not expressed it in a courteous manner, I thought, and was about to have another go when Merlin spoke up: "The Abbot Lawrence at Saint Sebastian's Abbey told us that Brother Nascien had traveled here in the company of another monk, a Brother Grunamund, with whom he apparently was in the habit of journeying…"

"Habit?" the king interrupted. "I see that my lord Merlin still enjoys his little puns, what? I'm sure Brother Nascien was always in a 'habit' while traveling." The king's half smile was slightly disconcerting. Surely this humor was out of place at such a moment, and argued a lack of seriousness, or a lack of legitimate concern, on the king's part.

But Merlin, undeterred, pressed on. "In any case, your Grace, we were led to believe this Brother Grunamund had come to visit you some three or four days ago, breaking from his companion at that time while Brother Nascien made his way to the hermit's anchorage near Saint Sebastian and there found his death. It seemed our duty, my lord, to find this Grunamund and to tell him what we knew of his comrade's death, so that he might relay this news to their home abbey at Beaulieu."

King Pelles scowled a bit at that and then answered dismissively, "Well, lord Merlin, I'm afraid you've labored in vain in that case. It's true that Brother Grunamund typically accompanied Prior Nascien when he visited us but Corbenic has seen neither of them for…I don't know, perhaps a year? What would you say, Golagros, is that about right?" He was looking past us now, toward where the young squire had reentered the hall, followed by a parade of servants, each carrying something different.

"What my lord says is true, to my recollection," Golagros said on cue. "As I recall, it was perhaps a year ago that those two monks visited here. Shall we have the table set up now, my liege?" As he said this, several of the servants carrying the various accoutrements filed behind him: First came a youth carrying a long white lance, the tip of which seemed to be reddened by blood. But the youth did not stop in the hall; he continued instead through a door to our right and into another chamber. Two other squires followed him, carrying solid gold candelabra, inlaid with enamel, each of which held ten brightly lit candles. Between the two squires a maiden walked, carrying a large golden cup, set within by rubies, emeralds, and other precious stones. Like the lance, the cup was carried into the next chamber. This trio was followed by another maiden, this one carrying a carving platter made of purest silver. Like those before her, this maiden crossed to the opposite chamber.

Finally, bringing up the rear, came an additional dozen or so servants. One of these carried in a basin of warm water for us to wash our hands. Two other servants carried in two ebony trestles, and four others brought in a broad ivory board to lay across the trestles. A young page held a white tablecloth, which he spread over the ivory table. A servant carrying a tray set trenchers before the three of us, along with a plate of sliced venison. A second server placed knives before us, and delicate silver cups, into which a third poured a fine claret to complement our meal.

"Such is the simple fare I must serve you," King Pelles pronounced with false modesty. "Alas, had I word of your coming, we could have provided you with more appropriate cuisine from the kitchens of Corbenic."

"Not at all, not at all," Merlin responded. "It looks wonderful." I couldn't tell whether Merlin had marked at all the strange pageant that had preceded the meal. I was burning to know what on earth was happening—who it was that was supposed to be served by that cup and platter. But having already received clear indications from King Pelles that he expected me to be seen and not heard, I kept my question to myself.

"If Brother Grunamund is not here at Corbenic," Merlin continued, "we will have to seek him elsewhere. Perhaps he has made his way back to Saint Sebastian, or is even back in Beaulieu by now. We will seek him in those places when we leave your hospitality." After a short pause, in which I stuffed a slab of venison in my mouth and looked to the door at the right side of the hall where those others had disappeared, Merlin added: "But since we have come this way, and have the opportunity to talk over your generous feast, I hope we can gain something of value from our visit here. Perhaps we can learn a little bit more about Brother Nascien and Brother Grunamund. Please correct me if I am mistaken, but my understanding is that Brother Nascien joined the monastery at Beaulieu after some years of service as a knight in King Uther's retinue."

Obviously this was something we knew already, but Merlin was fishing no less obviously than the king himself had been doing moments before we had encountered him.

"That is correct," King Pelles agreed, though it seemed clear to me that he knew he wasn't telling us anything we didn't already know.

"And Brother Grunamund was also a knight before joining the Cistercians, I believe. That was about the same time as Sir Nascien?" Merlin continued, probing slightly.

King Pelles took the bait, but did not run with it. "He was in knightly service, I believe. I cannot say whether he was ever officially initiated into knighthood, I know that he was squire for several years to a knight of the Round Table in King Arthur's early days…a certain Sir Brumand, if you remember him? I'm sure he was at Camelot while you were involved in the boy king's affairs."

Sir Brumand, yes! That was the connection. I knew that I had heard Grunamund's name before. King Bagdemagus had mentioned him as Brumand's faithful squire when he was talking of Sir Nascien's history—Nascien and Brumand had been close companions, along with Brumand's squire and…who was it? Yes, it seemed so strange to think of in this setting here in Corbenic, but I remembered now quite clearly, and knowing that Pelles would not respond to me if I raised the question, I murmured close to Merlin's ear the name that seemed crucial in this context:

"Balin," I whispered.

Merlin gave a nearly imperceptible start, then continued smoothly:

"My lord, forgive my asking, but it seems strange for me to contemplate: Nascien and Grunamund were close companions of the impetuous Sir Balin and his brother. And it is well known that Balin was the knight whose dolorous stroke wounded you so severely that you are still unable to stand or even sit comfortably. My own curiosity compels me to ask: Why, under these circumstances, would you have entrusted your grandson, the incomparable Sir Galahad, to the care of these men who had, prior to their tonsures, been bosom friends with your greatest enemy? To forgive is, of course, our Christian duty, but having your bitterest foes raise your own flesh and blood for fifteen years is an unfathomable act to me."

Pelles made a dismissive gesture. "Water under the bridge. Or over the dam. Wherever it is water goes, what? I can't hold Grunamund's youthful acquaintances against him, even ones as vile as this Balin." His face contorted ever so slightly at that last name, and it came out in a throaty rasp. "Nascien and Grunamund were willing—no, even eager—to foster the young Galahad, and I wanted him brought up with a monastic education, given his noble ancestry. You do know that the boy is descended from Joseph of Arimathea himself, on my side of the family, do you not?"

"We…have heard it said," Merlin answered diplomatically. "And your daughter, the fair Elaine? Did she want the boy fostered at Beaulieu as well?"

"Most certainly," the king replied. "But here she is, why don't you ask her yourself?" I looked around and noted that two doors had opened at about the same time. The door to our right had opened once again and the maiden carrying the golden cup came out, flanked once more by the two servants bearing the candelabra. At the same time, the door behind us had opened as well, and into the hall floated a petite but beautiful woman with long, blonde hair, flowing freely about her shoulders, wearing a gown of pure white samite and slippers of a material that shone like cloth of gold. Once again, the mysterious cup passed by us without anyone acknowledging it, except for the lady Elaine, who was forced to sidestep the oncoming trio, who seemed oblivious to anything in their path.

Merlin and I rose out of courtesy as Elaine approached us.

We inclined our heads as she sat on the bed next to her reclining father, who told her, "My dear, I'm sure that you recognize King Arthur's chief counsellor, the lord Merlin," Elaine nodded at the old necromancer, "and his servant." Pelles made a vague gesture in my direction and the lady Elaine made just as vague a nod, though I muttered futilely under my breath, still nodding my head politely, "Companion. Not servant."

The attendant squires, all but the ever-present Golagros and the squire who stood ready to refill our wine glasses, began to clear away the dishes and scurry with them out the back door through which Elaine had entered, and Merlin took that opportunity to continue the conversation for the lady's benefit: "My lady Elaine, we were just discussing your son's fostering at Beaulieu Abbey. I was asking his Grace whether you were as supportive of that plan as he was."

"Absolutely," she spoke, and the timbre of her voice surprised me. I had expected a high, very feminine tone from a woman of her frame, build and appearance. But it was very low and sultry, and as I gazed at her more closely, I could see that, while still striking, her gray eyes reflected the wisdom of age: She was no longer young—though that, of course, could be said of the queen herself—and there were crows' feet around the corners of her eyes, a glimpse of gray in her blonde hair. To me her low voice seemed appropriate, somehow, for a mature woman of her stature.

"On his father's side my son carries the blood of the world's most perfect fighting machine, the incomparable Sir Lancelot," she continued, and her eyes glanced to her left. "Paragon of secular power. From *my* side he is the descendant of Joseph, priest of the Grail— who brought the holy relic to Logres and charged his descendants to be the Keepers of the Grail. Paragon, I daresay, of spiritual authority. From those two lineages has emerged Sir Galahad: destined to unite spiritual and secular power in universal harmony. Destined to merge the Christian commonwealth with the Heavenly Jerusalem. The Cistercians were the ideal mentors for my boy's spiritual education. And there were former knights there—Sir Nascien and Sir Grunamund—capable of training the lad, of nurturing his natural skills in chivalry, to mold him into the perfect Knight of Christ."

"'Whole armor of God' and all that sort of thing, what?" King Pelles looked at us. "So we figured Galahad would *prophet* by the experience, you see?" He emitted another one of those inappropriate giggles at his own play on words and Merlin looked at me again and raised his eyes to heaven, as if to say we were dealing with a major loon here.

At that point, the back door opened again and out came the candelabra and the golden cup, carried again into the side room to our right, and no one in the hall reacted in any way. It was as if we had all made a tacit agreement to ignore the cup and its appearance. I made up my mind at that point to wait until after the meal to approach one of the squires privately, perhaps this Golagros if he was available, since he appeared the most knowledgeable, and try to wring from him the story of this back-and-forth pageant of the cup. Talk to him man to man. There had to be something behind it, and it didn't look like Pelles or Elaine was planning to explain the charade any time soon.

The other squires had followed the cupbearer back in, and while the cup and candelabra disappeared into the side room, the squires set the table with baskets of delicious fruits—dates and figs, pomegranates with cloves and nutmeg, and delicious confections for our dessert course. Despite the incredibly odd company and the inexplicable goings on at Corbenic castle, I couldn't suppress a smile at the banquet we were supplied, and I held up my glass for more spiced wine.

Meanwhile Merlin continued his questioning of the pair, trying to avoid giving it the appearance of an interrogation. "Your Grace, this Grunamund. Can you tell us anything more about him? I know that he was of military bearing, that he had been squire to a knight of the Round Table. Do you know whether he had any particular grudge against, say, Sir Nascien or against his abbey? Or, I hate to say it, toward Sir Galahad?"

"Why?" Elaine interjected. She seemed far quicker than her father. "You suspect Grunamund had something to do with Brother Nascien's death? Why should he?"

"That is precisely what I am asking you," Merlin responded. "Sir

Nascien is brutally murdered, and suddenly Grunamund is nowhere to be found. Does it not look suspicious to you?"

"Not necessarily," Elaine quibbled. "If we don't know where Grunamund is, he may be lying dead himself somewhere in these woods, killed perhaps by one of Arthur's own reckless knights who have filled these woods in their fruitless quest. Why don't they leave it alone? The quest is for my Galahad alone. No one else is worthy."

The lady Elaine's dismissal of Merlin's question and her odd change of direction back to her son's great mission was apparently enough to convince Merlin that, try as he might, he would get nothing more—or at least nothing coherent—from these two, and so he simply responded with a noncommittal "Hmmph!" and continued to eat dessert. We all sat in silence for an awkward time, with only the sound of chewing to interrupt the silent dark shadows that were creeping in from the corners of the hall. Soon daylight was gone, and the only light was the red glow of that enormous fire, which made the dishes on the plate appear to be filled with blood. I found I had no more appetite, and at about that moment King Pelles sat up and, as if there had been no lull in the conversation at all, declared, "Friends, the time has come to retire for the evening. Please do not be offended that I must leave you to sleep in my own chambers—I need the comfort, and the lady Elaine, of course, needs her privacy." Elaine rose and walked back out of the door she had entered without a single word. She glanced back over her shoulder, her dimpled chin jutting out toward Merlin and me before exiting, and in that moment her eyes reflected the fiery blaze like a devil's gazing into hell. Despite what was by now an almost suffocating heat put off by that fire, I shivered uncontrollably.

***

We awoke the next morning in the Great Hall, where we had spent the night in fine white linen sheets brought to us by that army of squires after they had carried Pelles, bed and all, into his chamber. Daylight was streaming in the high windows of the large room, and it had cooled off considerably after the fire burnt down to embers sometime around midnight. But as we sat up and looked about we saw no one. We rose, Merlin donning his robe, which had been folded neatly at the side of his pallet, and I pulling on my tunic and fastening my sword belt around my waist and picking up my crossbow, both of which had been similarly placed alongside me (my shield I had left hanging on my horse the evening before). But there was no one in sight, and we heard no sound in the hall. We exited that chamber and descended the stone staircase that led down into the castle's bailey, and still we saw no one—not a single servant, squire, or cook making breakfast, not a single guard in the battlements. It was eerie. Clearly my plan of discussing with my fellow squire Golagros the odd procession of lance and cup and silver platter was not about to materialize. "Weird," was all I could think of to say, and Merlin answered, "Yes, and intentionally so."

We heard a subdued yowl from across the bailey and saw where someone had put a leash on Guinevere and tethered her to one of the pillars of the pavilion along the castle's west wall near the gate. There were our horses as well, who it seemed, had been fed and watered and cared for well through the night. My shield hung, as I had left it, on my horse's neck. I noticed, too, that the drawbridge was once again down, and the gate wide open to let us through.

"Well!" I commented, hearing my voice echo in the emptiness of that deserted castle. "Looks like they can't wait for us to leave, and don't let the gate hit us on the way out!"

"Corbenic has always had the reputation of being an enchanted castle," Merlin mused as he swung himself up into the saddle. I followed suit and took the leash off the dog so that she could run free after the horses.

"Is that what this is, then?" I asked as we spurred our horses into a trot, eager to leave Corbenic in the dust. "Enchantment?"

"We are meant to think so," Merlin answered. Clambering over the drawbridge, we turned south to head back toward Camelot by way of Saint Sebastian's Abbey. "It's simply King Pelles's way of playing with our minds. He wants us to think that the castle has, I don't know, some sort of magical significance."

"Do you think perhaps it does?" I asked him, only half joking.

"I mean, what on earth was all of that business last night with the gold cup going back and forth three times, like some kind of ritual procession?"

"That?" the old man answered, breaking into a smile. "That was a curious gambit in a chess match the king was challenging me with."

"A gambit?"

"Precisely. He wanted with all his heart for me to ask what that was all about—to try to find out who was being served by the gold cup. I didn't know why he wanted it so badly, but I knew it couldn't be for our own good, and so I didn't give him the satisfaction. Of course, the funny thing was that you were the one more likely to jump in and ask the question, but the king had already made it abundantly clear that he thought you were beneath his notice and discouraged you from opening your mouth. God's dimples Gildas, he defeated himself with his own arrogance."

Merlin laughed loud and long at that. I had to admit he was absolutely right: I would have asked immediately about that gambit. And I still wanted to know what was going on. Maybe it was some kind of a trap as Merlin insisted. But as I told Merlin, "Still, I'd have given just about anything to know what was going on in that castle. That was the strangest pair I've ever seen."

"More than strange," Merlin said thoughtfully. "There's a wildness there bordering on madness, I would say. But they were also making a great game out of hiding the truth from us. I'm certain there is much they were not telling about how they reconciled with their former enemies—the friends, after all, of the knight who crippled Pelles in the first place—and allowed them to raise Galahad, apparently the great hope of their entire bloodline. And clearly they were lying about Brother Grunamund having been there."

"And how can you be sure of that?"

"My boy," Merlin shook his head in disbelief. "You heard Elaine herself ask me whether I suspected Grunamund in Nascien's death. She was not present when we told her father of that murder. Where could she have heard of it, if not from Brother Grunamund? I don't know whether their connection to this whole conspiracy is accidental, or tangential, or central. But it's something we'll have to determine before this case is through."

I nodded, and then wondered what we were going to find when we got back to Camelot.

CHAPTER FIFTEEN

IN THE THRONE ROOM

As it happened, we returned to Camelot almost on the heels of Sir Ector de Maris, brother of Sir Lancelot du Lac. Sir Ector had given up the quest, and as Merlin and I quickly learned from Sir Gareth, in the week or so we had been gone, at least a dozen other knights had trickled in, most of them with broken arms, wounded legs, or bloodied pates. The old timers Sir Tor and Sir Lucan the Butler had returned, swearing never again to be so foolish as to seek the Grail. Sir Dinas of Cornwall (formerly King Mark's seneschal), Sir Edward of Caernarvon, and Sir Priamus, whom Sir Tristram had nicknamed "the Noble Knight," all decided that their nobility was not sufficient to achieve the Grail, and had come home licking their wounds. Others returned with strange stories: Sir Gumret le Petite reported that he had seen Sir Grummor Grummorson drowned in a river during a thunderstorm. Sir Harry le Fise Lake brought the news that Sir Gliglois had reportedly engaged in battle with a knight armored all in white, and that Gliglois had not been seen again and was presumed dead. Merlin and I looked meaningfully at one another, and the old man asked Gareth if he had any notion exactly when that attack on Sir Gliglois had taken place, but Gareth could not say. It was a hard pill to swallow, however, if that death had occurred recently: It would mean that Brother Nascien was not the White Knight after all, and that we must continue to search for Brother Grunamund. Or even, perhaps, another.

But Ector was the most recently returned of all the knights and, as Lancelot's brother, the highest ranking, being the second son of King Ban of Benwick. We learned immediately upon our own return that the king had commanded an audience that would include Sir Ector as well as Merlin and me, fresh from our own small quest. With the deaths of now six Knights of the Round Table, and the serious wounding of three others, Arthur was waxing impatient for an end to this disastrous quest, or the elimination of this mysterious and deadly White Knight, or, preferably, both. He wanted the newest information he could gather, and he wanted the best minds in the kingdom there to help him sift through the evidence. So it was that, within two hours of our arrival back in Camelot, Merlin and I found ourselves in King Arthur's throne room, along with Sir Ector and my lady Queen Guinevere. Sir Gareth was present as well, representing, I suppose, Sir Gawain's interests, since the king's oldest nephew still lay indisposed in the castle's infirmary. Sir Lionel was present as well, perhaps because of his kinship with Sir Ector, or perhaps because of his own violent experience in the quest. And to my utter astonishment, the king had also invited his sister. Morgan was there perhaps to represent the interests of Sir Ywain, who also lay wounded. Or perhaps she was there so that Arthur could gauge her reactions to the events surrounding this quest, to determine whether she might have some part in them. Or maybe I was just confusing my own motives with the king's. In any case, for whatever reason, Morgan was present, seated to the left of the king's throne on its raised dais on the north side of the room, in a soft chair brought in for the occasion. Queen Guinevere sat on his right, and the five men present stood before the throne, with Ector in the prominent position directly before Arthur.

The king, not dressed for a state occasion, wore only a small gold circlet on his head to stand for his crown. His tunic was a royal blue and he wore dark gray hosen, and that was all. No robes of state, no pompous heavy crowns, only a hard-working monarch trying to determine why his closest retainers were being whittled away one by one. Sir Ector, ill at ease in his unaccustomed role as center of attention, went down on one knee before the king. Standing with Merlin to Ector's left, I couldn't help but notice how his posture duplicated that of King Lot, Gawain's father, in the tapestry hanging on the east wall of the throne room, depicting Lot kneeling in fealty to his conqueror in Arthur's first war.

"My liege," Sir Ector began. "I acknowledge my inability to achieve this quest of the Grail on which I foolishly embarked with my fellow knights."

"That is no shame," the king told him. "Most of the knights are returning to us, having come to understand their human limitations. I think I warned you all of this when you embarked." I knew the king was not generally one to say "I told you so," but, understandably, he couldn't resist the temptation on this occasion.

"But your Grace," Ector continued. "I return having been warned very concretely that the quest was not for me and that I should give it up."

King Arthur's gray eyes looked fiery for an instant—a flash of interest or anger? He bade the knight, "Continue then, Sir Ector. What could have possibly happened to make you so certain that the time had come for you to abandon the quest? And rise, sir, rise, you needn't kneel there through your whole story."

Sir Ector returned to his feet and let out a sigh. I couldn't tell if it was from exertion or if he was dreading making his explanation. But he plunged ahead: "Two nights ago, my lord, I visited the Castle Corbenic."

Well that hit me like a slap across my face. I looked at Merlin and he stared back at me, his considerable eyebrows raised in surprise and perhaps a little disbelief. Two nights ago? We were ourselves being entertained by the Maimed King at the very hour Ector was claiming to have been there. Was he lying? Or were we oblivious to events outside of the great hall in which we had dined?

"I was not allowed to enter the castle," Ector continued. "What happened was this: I came upon the castle while seeking shelter for the night. On the south side of Corbenic there is a chapel that branches off the great hall. Its upper window can be seen from across the moat on that side of the castle, for the wall drops down there as the bailey slopes down to the south. I stood up in my stirrups around sunset that day, calling out to be allowed in to say my prayers at that chapel—since I was on a holy quest, I thought such gestures were important when I had the chance to do so. But a voice came shouting from the window, saying 'Who are you? What country do you come from?' It was a woman's voice, I swear. She had an unusually low voice for a woman, but it was definitely a woman."

"That sounds as if it must have been the princess, the lady Elaine," Merlin interjected. "We met her ourselves—and on the same day you say you were at the castle. But we were not aware of that exchange."

"Well, it didn't last very long," Ector continued. "I told her I was from King Arthur's realm of Logres, and that I was Sir Ector de Maris, brother to my lord Sir Lancelot. But that did not seem to impress her. Because all she said about it was that I could not enter because—and I mean she told me this word for word—because the Holy Grail was in that chapel at that same moment, and neither I nor any of my peers were worthy to enter while the Grail was there."

Not a shadow of a sound disturbed the shocked silence that pervaded that chamber at Sir Ector's revelation. Finally, after at least a minute of our looking around at one another, the king spoke. But all he said was, "What was that?"

Ector's square jaw, reminiscent of his more famous brother's, jutted forth and his blue eyes peered sincerely into the king's face. "The Grail," Ector repeated. "It was there, they said. And more than that, the voice told me that my brother Sir Lancelot was there as well: 'Your brother is within,' the voice cried. 'But you must depart, for neither you nor any of your fellow knights on this quest will achieve the Grail, for you have left the service of the Lord.'"

Sir Gareth scoffed. "Now that sounds like our old friend Brother Nascien again. This Elaine must have spent some time with him, don't you think? The two may be in cahoots—with that White Knight as well."

"It may be so. It sounds the same," Sir Lionel concurred. "But you're missing the import of what Ector is saying: that the Grail is found, and that my kinsman Sir Lancelot has achieved it! This quest is over, and our lord Lancelot has once again proven to be the world's greatest knight!"

"Why so he has!" the queen cried out. "The great quest is

accomplished! Glory to Lancelot…and to God," she added quickly, her spontaneity embarrassing her for a moment, quite uncharacteristically, I thought, and I gave her a tiny half smile that she answered with a warning glare.

"You're right, Lionel," Ector answered thoughtfully. "I am stunned myself. I came here sulking in melancholy because of what the voice at the castle told me about my own unworthiness, but not until this moment have I realized that this quest is over, and has glorified our family by raising Lancelot to, well, to near sainthood, couldn't it be said?"

"As Saint Helena recovered the True Cross, so Saint Lancelot has found the vessel of the True Blood of Christ," Sir Gareth put in, carried along by the moment.

Even the king was caught up. "This quest can now be called finished, and Lancelot will receive the praise due him when he returns. Such an achievement says a great deal about the virtue of chivalry in this court: courtesy begets virtue in the commonwealth, and the glories of God through his most sacred relic, the Grail, are due to the society that has achieved the height of virtue. This quest has sanctified the Order of the Round Table."

Now everyone in the room seemed to be talking at once. I looked around, a little bit annoyed. Hadn't Guinevere, and Gareth, and the king too, been skeptical of this quest from the beginning? Hadn't we all pretty much agreed it was a waste of time and effort, and one that proved to be disastrous for the Table, with six knights dead and three others still nursing their wounds? I looked at Merlin, whose brows were lowered and, as he glanced down at me, reflected the same impatience that I felt.

"My lords!" the old necromancer shouted above the din. "My lords, and ladies," he nodded to the queen and to Morgan. "I hate to burst anyone's bubble, but do you not find this celebration a bit premature? We have yet to hear from Lancelot himself, but have only hearsay—a voice told Sir Ector that Lancelot was present. Besides, and more importantly, what has become of Sir Galahad? We've heard nothing of the Pure Knight, whose sole purpose in life seems to have been to achieve this quest. I do not mean to denigrate the accomplishments of

Sir Lancelot. By no means! But I only caution you all not to celebrate prematurely." At that there were some heads hanging, some lips pursing, some shoulders shrugging, as the lords and ladies present drew back from their initial excitement.

"Besides," I added, emboldened by Merlin's voiced caution and bringing the company back to the real reason for the audience we were currently attending. "We haven't yet examined the evidence we've collected, suggesting a conspiracy to harm the Round Table through this quest, not to honor it."

At that the assembled courtiers changed their collective mood noticeably. Some were surprised by the charge. Others, particularly Gareth and Guinevere, looked expectant, hoping the case would soon be solved. They were going to be disappointed.

"What you don't know is, first, that Brother Nascien is dead," Merlin led with the most sensational point. "Murdered with a sword straight to his heart. He died while visiting the cell of the hermit Brother Bertrand, killed by Sir Lionel."

Lionel hung his head. "We did discover, however," Merlin continued, "in the cell of Brother Bertrand, that he was growing a particular herb that, when fed to a knight mixed with, say, a broth or cup of wine, was likely to cause a kind of uncontrollable rage in their hearts…"

Sir Gareth at that word sprang forward excitedly. "The kind of rage felt by Sir Gawain, when he attacked Sir Ironside! Or," he added generously, "that may have spurred Sir Lionel on against Sir Bors, so that in his wildness he ended the life of the hermit—justly destroyed through his own machinations—as well as that of the luckless Sir Colgrevaunce." Sir Lionel closed his eyes, a look of relief crossing his face, and bowed his head toward Gareth in gratitude. And at that point I knew that if I could excuse Sir Gawain because of the ill effects of that potion, then I must also forgive Sir Lionel for the slaying of the good Colgrevaunce. Though I doubted it would ever be so with Bess, poor Colgrevaunce's widow.

"Black henbane, yes," Morgan le Fay mused. "That would have done it. I've used that herb—for medicinal purposes only, you understand—on several occasions in the past." Suddenly all eyes were on her, some, including my own, more suspicious than others. Morgan, sensing she'd become the center of attention, raised her eyes and glared, taking the whole room in. "*In the past*, I said. But as some of you know, this Brother Bertrand was, in his youth, the sole priest in the chapel at the castle of Lord Bertilak, famously known to this court as the Green Knight. For a time I resided in that castle myself, through the generosity and courtesy of Lord and Lady Bertilak."

"At a time when she was not welcome at home because King Uriens objected to her persistent attempts to kill him," Merlin murmured sotto voce into my ear.

"That was where he became close to my nephew Gawain," Morgan continued. "But he had a good deal of time on his hands there in the castle, what with the rather small congregation, and he was never much for reading his Augustine or his Gregory. He spent a lot of time in the company of Lady Bertilak and myself. Especially with Lady Bertilak. He knew, of course, that I dabbled a bit in herb lore," at that I saw the king himself roll his eyes. "And he was fascinated by it. I taught him a good deal, including the properties of a number of plants, herbs and potions. I do remember his being especially interested in black henbane. I'm not surprised that he used it. So you can wipe the suspicion off your faces," her glare focused on me especially. "This Brother Bertrand had the knowledge and means to have prepared this assault on your precious knights all by himself, my dear brother, and my dear old charlatan, despite your innuendos."

Merlin put on his best show of courtesy, bowing his head toward Morgan and soothingly promising that he was completely convinced that Morgan was innocent, "in this particular case," he added, so quietly that I may have been the only one to hear him. "But what can his motive have been?" Merlin continued. "And what was his connection with Brother Nascien, found dead at his cell, and with Nascien's companion Brother Grunamund, whom we have yet to find but who was apparently with Nascien up until the time he turned off the road to Corbenic."

Morgan had started a bit at the mention of Grunamund's name, and now she became somewhat more animated, as if she was figuring something out that had not occurred to her before. "Wait. You say that Nascien and Grunamund were together? And that they were somehow in league with Brother Bertrand? This Grunamund—large fellow, blond, big muscles?"

"That's him," I volunteered.

"Sure, this all makes sense now," she said, her dark eyes smoldering. She tossed her long raven-colored hair as she tied the pieces together: "Grunamund was squire to the beautiful Sir Brumand—the knight so vilely slain when he sat in Merlin's infamous Siege Perilous. Upon Sir Brumand's untimely death, Grunamund fled to Gaul and was made knight. I had not heard that he ever returned to Logres, but apparently he did so—and became a monk in the same house that Sir Nascien had joined, and in which the young priest Bertrand took his vows when he decided to leave Bertilak's employ and subject himself to the cloister. Nascien, of course, was Sir Brumand's cousin and best friend…"

"But why would Brother Bertrand join with them?" I asked. "He had no such connection with the court or with this Sir Brumand, did he?"

Morgan shrugged. "Perhaps it had something to do with why he left the abbey at Beaulieu. Perhaps Nascien knew something that convinced Brumand to help them. But let there be no doubt, their motive was revenge. For there is no question that Nascien and Grunamund would hold a serious grudge against you, my lord king," she addressed her brother with a hint of irony. "Your resident wonder-working son of an incubus had murdered the good Sir Brumand with his exploding chair. They may well have plotted this entire scheme to avenge the death of that good knight."

"Is it indeed King Arthur these heroes of yours would target, Morgan, or is it perhaps Sir Lancelot?" Merlin goaded her. "As I recall, Sir Brumand had a particular envy of Lancelot."

Morgan shook with intensity—I could not be sure whether it was the intensity of excitement or of hatred. "Lancelot eclipsed Sir Brumand at court, it is true. And Brumand sought to accomplish the Siege Perilous to regain his rightful place in the king's favor. Perhaps Nascien and Grunamund seek to punish Lancelot as well."

"Then it may be that Lancelot's sojourn in the Castle Corbenic is not the great triumph we think, but some kind of punishment?" Sir Ector suggested.

"Let us pray not," the queen put in. "But what is the connection between Corbenic and these conspirators?"

"We do know that Brother Nascien and Brother Grunamund visited Corbenic fairly regularly, apparently to report on the progress of Galahad, whom they were fostering for King Pelles and for the lady Elaine." Merlin contributed. "The lady Elaine told us in vague terms what she had in mind for Galahad—some kind of imperial role that united the state and the church…"

"It gave me the creeps," I gave my own probably unwelcome assessment, as Merlin grumbled, "Not the most helpful observation, boy."

"But it did," I persisted. "That smooth low voice, coming out of that petite body…talking crazy about Galahad's destiny…"

It was Sir Lionel's turn to start. "Her…low voice you say? Petite body? Hold on now—what does this Elaine look like? Blonde?"

"Long blonde hair," I nodded. "Slight stature. Gray eyes, dimpled chin."

"But no maiden?" Lionel persisted.

"Hardly, as the mother of Galahad. She looks fairly young from a distance, though a close look would show her age more."

"My liege," Lionel turned now to King Arthur, as the one in charge of this freewheeling discussion. "I could be mistaken but I do not think so. Recall, my lord, that I was chiefly enraged at my brother because he had left me to my fate among the knights who were beating me because he felt compelled to rescue a maiden who was about to be ravished by a wicked knight. Now, I did not get a close look at this maiden—she was being swept along another path that forked from the one I was being forced along. But I saw enough to realize that she had long blonde hair and a petite body—that small frame was no doubt what persuaded me to think she must be a maiden. But I did not get a close look at her face, though I did hear her voice, and as you describe it now, I remember distinctly how low her voice was— strange, I thought, in one so small. Could it…can it be, my lord, that the maiden in question was this same Lady Elaine?"

Sir Gareth stepped forward at that, his voice rising to a crescendo: "My lord, remember Gawain's words as well. Did he not say that the woman he rescued from Sir Ironside was a woman in her thirties, with blonde hair and dimpled chin? And he mentioned a low, raspy voice he called it, as well!"

Now I recalled something that Merlin had said at the very beginning of our investigation, during our initial chess game: What if it were the same woman, he had suggested? And what if both situations were traps? Now it appeared he had been right. Besides—I remembered his prophecy again: Elaine was the mother of light, of the Pure Knight Sir Galahad. She must also be the mother of darkness, involved in all these murders. "It was the same woman," I spoke aloud what everyone was thinking. "And it was Elaine."

What direction the conference would have taken after that I'm not sure, but we had answered a lot of questions. We were about to have quite a few more raised for us, for at that point Lovell, Sir Gawain's squire, gingerly entered the room, and the king beckoned him forth, knowing he would not have interrupted such a high-level discussion unless it was vitally important. "Master Lovell," Arthur addressed him kindly. "What is it? Is there some new development we must know of?"

With a nervous bow toward the king, Lovell answered. "My lord," he began, his voice weighty with importance. "Sir Lancelot has come back."

CHAPTER SIXTEEN
THE TALE OF SIR LANCELOT

It was after none the following day before we had our chance to speak with Lancelot. The king had insisted on seeing him right away, and in private, so I had little notion of how that interview went. Arthur did not share his counsel with us, but he did give Merlin leave to question the Great Knight at his leisure. "See if his story makes any sense to you," the king had told the mage. But there was no keeping Guinevere from her lover's side, and she had caught me that morning breaking my fast at the kitchen, and pushed me for information about where and when we were meeting Lancelot. Nor could I keep my master from attending the interview: Sir Gareth's friendship with Lancelot went deeper than even his devotion to his brother Gawain, and his interest in this business of the Grail involved both of them now, so he would not be put off. Least of all by me, his own lowly squire.

Merlin was cranky about the others attending, but knew he could hardly put off the queen, and he was willing to have Beaumains with us once again. "But no more!" he warned me, and then, recognizing how heightened was the court's curiosity about Lancelot's quest, he made the unprecedented decision to interview Sir Lancelot in the privacy of his own cave. "It'll keep out prying eyes and ears, and Lancelot can feel free to tell us whatever he feels is necessary."

Of course, neither Gareth nor the queen had ever been to Merlin's cave. And so I had to give them both directions in strictest confidence, and told them I would await them on the other side of the cold running brook, since finding the specific cave in that honeycombed rock was no easy task.

And so as I stood on the bank of the stream just after none, expecting their arrival momentarily, I was nevertheless surprised to see not two but three gentle mounts emerge from the woods to trot across the narrow stream. Sir Gareth led the way, not atop one of his two great destriers but riding instead a gentle grey palfrey borrowed from the castle's stables. He wore a simple short red tunic over dark blue hosen, so that he sat quite comfortably in the saddle. The queen was dressed in a long traveling gown of pale blue cotton weave, without the customary fur trimmings, though the wide sleeves were trimmed with lace. As she sought to ride all light for summer, she had dispensed with the bliaud—the over-tunic—but she did wear a long velvet mantel with a rabbit trim, which she had fastened at the collar with a gold broach in the shape of a rose. She wore her hair uncovered, as was her right as queen, but it was plaited and rolled on either side of her head, I suppose to make it easier to control while riding through the woods. A small gold circlet decorated her head as a sign of her sovereignty, and she rode her own black palfrey, Venus.

What surprised and delighted me to no small degree, the nut-brown palfrey that accompanied them bore the queen's most trusted confidante: Lady Rosemounde of Orkney. She wore her hair modestly covered as befitted her married status, with linen headdress and a barbier encircling her chin. She too, wore a lighter gown, hers of bright yellow, but rather than a riding mantel she wore a forest-green linen bliaud, pleated below the bust and tight around her waist. She smirked at me, seeing the look of surprise on my face.

Remembering my manners, I welcomed them as courteously as I could, considering the fact that I was leading them into a cave. "Your Majesty, my lord Gareth, and my lady Rosemounde, this is an unexpected pleasure." I held Rosemounde's bridle, and steered her horse toward the opening of Merlin's hollowed-out home. There were a few shrubs around the cave's mouth, and I wrapped the reins around one of them and extended my hand to assist her down from her palfrey. "Welcome to the old necromancer's cave, where he was imprisoned by the nymph Nimue before I rescued him by an amazing feat of courage!"

"A feat that consisted of walking in the door, as I recall," the grumpy voice of the old mage came booming from within. "Bring them all in here and let's get this over with. I'm not really set up for entertaining!"

"Ever the paragon of courtesy," Guinevere remarked casually as Sir Gareth helped her down from her own horse. "Well, shall we step in and see this rustic hermitage of Merlin's?"

Guinevere's eyes opened wide with wonder, and Rosemounde's jaw dropped altogether, as they stepped into the dimly-lit cave. The first thing they noticed was the fireplace that lit the makeshift room about twenty feet square. Then they turned their attention to the tapestries that lined the walls, making the chamber much less like a cave and much more like a snug closet in the castle itself. Ironically, of course, there was that Holy Grail tapestry on the wall behind Merlin's bed— which, except for the two chairs around the small table with the chess set, was the only place in the room to sit.

Sir Lancelot, who had arrived some thirty minutes earlier, sat in one of those chairs as the party entered the cave, and he rose to his feet courteously. He'd had a chance to wash and shave himself since returning to Camelot the previous day, but he was still wearing the rust-stained padded gipon he had worn under his chain mail all during the quest. I could see that there was something else he was wearing next to his skin, beneath that gipon, but I did not yet know what it was.

"Your Grace," Lancelot said, bowing to the queen, "I am relieved to see you looking well. The king informed me last night that you were feeling under the weather." His blue eyes blinked at her and she looked away. She had begged off meeting with Lancelot and the king the previous evening because, of course, she could not trust herself to remain composed before her husband, having been some weeks without seeing her lover, and fretting about his welfare on this quest that seemed to claim so many lives. But I could see her eyes glisten with tears, perhaps because Lancelot felt the necessity, even here, to keep things on a formal level. He nodded to Rosemounde and to Sir Gareth, murmuring the usual greetings, and then stepped away from the chess table. "Please," he motioned to the chair. "Be seated. I prefer to stand through all of this."

The queen and Rosemounde stepped to Merlin's bed and sat there. Merlin himself took the chair Lancelot had vacated, grumbling about being treated like a guest in his own cave. I insisted that my master sit in the other chair, which left me to stand along with the Great Knight. I let him have the floor and retreated to the fireplace, leaning against the stones and folding my arms. Lancelot, having taken charge of the situation, began his tale with a flourish.

"I apologize, first, to Your Grace and to the rest of you, for my reluctance to discuss these things in Camelot. Many of the things I have to say are of such a sensitive nature that I could not conceive of discussing them freely in an atmosphere where anyone could be listening at any time, and where talebearers may lie in wait to destroy the reputations of virtuous ladies and good knights." He pushed forward his square jaw as if defying anyone present to challenge his characterization of the relationship between himself and his queen. But in his blue eyes was a kind of resignation, as if he was aware, even as he said it, of how hollow that characterization truly was. "But let me start at the beginning. As I left Camelot with all the other knights on that ill-conceived quest, I rode alone and slowly, letting my horse choose the way, for I had conceived no direction or plan as to how to search for this relic. It occurred to me while riding that such a quest as I was on required a different kind of approach. My son might achieve this quest because of his purity, but if I were to have any chance at success, I must be made pure again. I must unburden myself of my own sins, and start anew. The second day of my journey, sometime around vespers, when the shadows of the trees were growing long, I came—be it by adventure or by providence I do not know—upon a hermit's cell."

At that Sir Gareth broke in impetuously. "That must be Brother Bertrand's cell—the one Sir Gawain used to confess to."

Lancelot shrugged. "I cannot say for sure, I had never been there before. I knew though that Gawain had a confessor somewhere in those woods, and as you say, I believe the hermit was indeed called Bertrand. He welcomed me and invited me to sit with him in his cell, and while resting there he prodded me gently, asking whether I felt any desire to make my confession. At first I demurred, but after some time I did in fact work up the courage to make a full confession. It was a significant decision, I need to tell you. It had in fact been twenty-four years since my last confession."

"And you confessed all?" The queen asked bluntly, her face drawn and her lips pursed.

"All," he answered. "All," and as he continued he ran his left hand through his wavy brown hair, looking away from the queen. "I told him that I had loved a highborn lady out of measure, and for long years, and that all my deeds of arms were not done for the glory of my king or my God but solely for the worship of that great lady."

"God's flaming eardrums, and there you have the reason this tale could not have been spoken at Camelot." Everyone had been thinking the same thing, but no one made any response to Merlin.

"The hermit's reaction was swift and just: He told me that I was harder than stone, more bitter than wood, and barer than the leaf of a fig tree—which I took to mean that my heart had been hardened against God's mercy, my life had lost its sweetness and was now bitter with sin, and my soul was laid bare before God like a fig leaf. I asked what penance I could do, and the hermit told me to avoid that lady's company to the extent that I possibly could, and that as a perpetual reminder of the sin my flesh had caused me, I should wear this hair shirt next to my flesh until I felt I had atoned for my sins." At that the Great Knight pulled his gipon up enough for the rest of us to see the rough shirt of goat hair worn next to his skin, chafing it raw in places I could see even in that brief moment he displayed it.

"And so I have worn it, night and day, these weeks since the quest began. The Grail, the hermit told me, might be accessible to me if I purged that guilt, and I was bent on doing so at the time." The queen's face had flushed redder and redder as he continued, and when Lancelot paused, not a breath stirred in that cave. Never in twenty-four years had these things been openly discussed in this way, and no one, not even Merlin himself, could say where this could go from here.

"At that, I was done at the hermitage. Brother Bertrand told me to wait a few moments and he would prepare a Mass to be sung, and I could partake of the bread and wine myself, now that I had made good confession." At that word Merlin and I looked at each other with some alarm. If Bertrand gave Sir Lancelot wine, what might he have added to the mix? Could Lancelot too have been subjected to the powers of the black henbane that had undone his cousin and Gareth's brother? But we soon let out a sigh of relief when Lancelot added, "I declined, though. At that point I wanted to get away, be by myself in those dark woods to pray as best I might, and to think where to journey next on that quest."

"So, and where did you end up next?" Gareth prompted him. Guinevere had apparently lost interest, looking impatiently down at her shoes and beginning to fidget. The lady Rosemounde clearly sensed her mistress's agitation, but knew as well that Sir Lancelot must have a great deal more to relate, and her eyes moved back and forth between the two as she frowned, unsure what her role should be.

"Still I had no plan, but wandered aimlessly for many days. I fasted, and wearing the hair shirt chafed me so that I was constantly in pain because of it. Weak from hunger and from the physical strain of the chafing as well and the long riding, I believe that for some days I suffered from fever, and began to imagine things. Or who knows? Perhaps they were visions from God to help guide me in that holy quest. But in my mind, at least, I came upon a field beside a fair castle, and there were many pavilions around that field and two great parties of knights—whether at war or tournament I could not say. But the party of knights defending the castle were all dressed in black armor, while the attacking knights all wore white. And it was clear that the knights in black were having the worst of it, so I rode in and smote down several of the white party, and when my lance had broken I drew my sword and dispatched many more of them, but at long last, I was overcome and captured by the party of the white, and bound and led away into the woods. It was the first time in my life I have ever been shamed that way in battle."

"But it wasn't in battle," I couldn't help chiming in. "You just said it was in your mind."

"And in my mind it was real," Lancelot persisted. "Where else can we know what is true? To me, it was the same as if I had failed in actual battle, and I ached to know why I had failed. I found a recluse shortly after that—an anchoress who seemed wise and told me what she thought of the vision: 'You were the greatest of all knights in the earthly realm,' she told me. 'But now you have embarked on heavenly adventures, you must see the world according to different categories. In the tournament at the castle,' she continued, 'black tokened sin and white virtue—that should have been clear even to a mind as little used to abstract thinking as your own. The black were the damned and the white were the saved, and you allied yourself with the damned. The vision is a warning to you: You will win more lasting worship fighting on the side of virtue. And the choice is yours.'"

"Tell me, my lord," the queen had stopped her fidgeting and now addressed Lancelot directly and with purpose. "Did you say all of this to the king in your private audience?"

Lancelot bowed again, but his voice was much colder than Guinevere had anticipated, if I read her rightly. "Not in so much detail, madam. Yes, I emphasized how much at a disadvantage I felt as a sinful man, and insisted on my resolution to confess and atone. Specific sins were…irrelevant, to my mind, as far as the king was concerned. Sin is that which separates one from God. I was resolved to end that separation, and so to achieve the Grail."

"Well, how very fortunate that it worked out so well for you," the queen replied, not without a fairly strong dose of sarcasm. "Providential, one might even say."

"As you say, my lady," Lancelot continued, resisting taking up the bait. "I felt I had been warned, and I continued my search with new vigor, though I still had not eaten in many days."

"But tell us, Sir Lancelot," Merlin coaxed the great knight. "We have been told—your brother Sir Ector was convinced—that you did in fact find the Grail. That you encountered it in the castle of Corbenic. If that's true, it seems you must have overcome this barrier of sin and you actually found the relic, and even beat your son, the Pure Knight, to the goal. Was Ector misled in thinking this? Or is there some truth in it?"

Lancelot's eyes focused on something a long way off and he bowed his head to ponder his response. After a pause of some moments, he began a circuitous answer to Merlin's question. "The quest that the knights undertook," he began slowly, "or at least the quest that *I* agreed to take part in, was not a quest *for* the Grail, it was the quest *of* the Grail." At that my brow wrinkled in confusion, and I glanced over at Sir Gareth, who looked no more enlightened than I was. "By which I mean," the Great Knight continued, "that what was needed—what the *Table* needed—was not the physical presence of the Grail, found and brought back to Camelot to be placed in a reliquary in the castle chapel, or some such thing. What we needed was what the physical symbol of the Grail embodies."

"And what is that?" Gareth asked, curious to find out exactly what he'd been on the quest for.

"Honor. Worship. Not earthly, but heavenly fame. All of this is the Grail. To be worthy of the Grail is to have achieved these things. Deeds that are righteous, deeds that are pure, deeds that further the kingdom of God and not the kingdoms of this world, these are what the quest must consist of if one is to achieve the Grail. That is what my son taught me."

"Your son?" I asked. "You found him on the quest? No one else seems to have seen him since he took the red cross shield from King Bagdemagus at the abbey that first week."

"I spent some quality time with him…on a boat," Lancelot said, and smiled at our puzzled faces. "Let me explain the strange circumstances of that meeting. I had come in my wandering to a deep valley, where flowed a river that tumbled down from a tall cliff above. As I learned later, the place is called the Water of Mortaise. There I saw near the shore a good-sized boat, floating downstream without anyone at the helm. I thought, perhaps, it was a sign of some kind, as I had become used to expecting such things on this quest. I took off my chain mail, and lay it across the back of my horse, and started into the river dressed in my hose, gipon and hair shirt. I waded as far as I could and then had to swim the last few yards until I was finally able to catch on to the boat, and pull myself aboard. As it had appeared from the shore, the boat was deserted.

"I couldn't understand why a boat so well-made as that one should be cast adrift by someone, to float down the river and be lost. But then I saw her, lying on a fair bed, made up of green silken sheets, her long blonde hair arranged neatly across her shoulders as she lay on her back in a long gown of white samite. Her hands, folded in front of her, held a crushed fragment of vellum as she lay there perfectly arranged, motionless, and quite, quite dead."

"Who was she?" Guinevere asked, her anger at her knight overcome somewhat by the wonder of his story.

"Your Grace, she was a young gentlewoman who, according to the writing on the vellum she held, was daughter of King Pelinore," at that he glanced toward Sir Gareth, but if my master had any thought of bringing up the feud between his house and Pelinore's, he suppressed it, merely nodding as if to encourage the great knight to continue. "She was, I say, Sir Perceval's sister, and apparently my son's beloved. Oh, no, I don't mean they were lovers," he quickly corrected himself as he saw several of us blanch at the suggestion that the Pure Knight could have fallen so far so fast. "She was his inspiration, his guiding spirit and his chaste love. And her name was Dandrane. Or so I learned from the parchment which, as I discovered later, was in Sir Galahad's own hand. In his missive, he told her story: how she had met him on the quest, how she had encouraged him in his pursuit of perfection, how she had woven a belt for him of her own hair to hold his sword, how she had traveled with him and with her brother Perceval on the quest of the Grail, and finally—most strange to say—how she had sacrificed herself to save another: Galahad, Perceval, and this maiden came in their travels to a castle, where they were beset by a company of knights demanding that she perform the custom of the castle. When Perceval demanded what this custom was, the knights said that their mistress had lain for many years in great pain, with a sickness that threatened to devour her body, like a leprosy. She had been advised by an old seer, who told her that she could only be cured of her malady by washing in the blood of a pure young virgin who was also the daughter of a king."

At that all eyes turned toward Merlin, who shrugged. "You can't believe everything these old seers say," he said.

"If the beauteous Dandrane was all of these things, the knights continued, then they would take a bowl of her blood, by force if necessary. Now Perceval and Galahad were doughty knights themselves, it is no doubt, and Knights of the Round Table at that, so they would probably have made short work of these eight or ten guardians of that castle, but Dandrane would not allow a battle to take place if she had the means to prevent it. 'No blood will be spilt this day but my own,' she said. 'I agree to submit to this custom—barbarous though it is.' It was her way, you see, of keeping the peace but at the same time shaming those knights for their wicked demands.

"Sir Galahad's letter continued, to say that the blood of the lady Dandrane did in fact generate a miraculous cure in the lady of that castle. But the loss of her blood weakened Dandrane so much that she died the following day. Through chaste tears with her dying breath she made her grieving brother and her beloved knight promise to set her adrift in a boat, and thereby let God himself decide where she should make her final resting place. And so the missive ended, with a request that wherever the boat came to shore, those who found her corpse should give that mundane house of her sainted soul a Christian burial."

With that the Great Knight sighed, and a pall of silence fell over his audience. My lady Rosemounde's eyes glistened with tears. But Sir Gareth broke the silence at last by prompting Sir Lancelot to continue: "And Galahad? You said you saw him on the boat?"

"Yes," Lancelot continued, as if he had forgotten there was more to the story. "I was suffering a kind of inner turmoil, you see, after reading poor Dandane's story. Her self-sacrifice, I mean. My own feats of arms have in their own way saved the lives of many—women and children as well as my fellow knights. But all was as nothing to me in that moment, you see, because I was never truly at risk. God gifted me with strength and skill, and my own obsession with martial prowess drove me to train with such precision that, at least until that time when age robs me of my physical abilities, I have reached the pinnacle of chivalry. As far as worldly achievement goes, I am perfection."

Now if anybody else had said this, I would have scoffed or written him off as a blowhard. But in Lancelot's case, he was merely stating the objective truth. Everyone in that room knew it.

"And so there is no sacrifice in any of my deeds," he continued. "I have not risked myself in the way that this poor maid had. And her motives were selfless. It was only for the sake of the purest charity that she gave of herself. All of my deeds, *all* of them, were done for the sake of worldly fame, of worship—and for the sake of pleasing and glorifying the worldly queen on whom all my carnal love was focused. But never, as in this maid's case, for the sake of a heavenly love, or the glory that abounds eternally. And so I grieved at that moment that all I had done was ultimately worthless. I had wasted my life."

I felt the queen's piercing eyes without having to look in her direction. Something like a low growl emerged from her throat, and when I looked toward her a kind of fury had crimsoned her face. She would not in this setting let that fury out, but I knew it would come, somewhere, sometime. And Lancelot knew it too, and so avoided the queen's eyes as he continued his tale.

"And so it was almost in despair that I lifted my head and saw, standing on the bank holding my horse's reins as well as his own, a knight in white armor and carrying a shield with the red sign of a cross. I knew that it was Galahad. He called to me, 'Sir Lancelot!' Not 'father,' you understand, but 'Sir Lancelot.' I hailed him as well, and used the boat's rudder to try to guide it close to the shore where he waited. There was no sail, of course, since the boat had simply been allowed to drift, according to the young lady's wishes. Within minutes I had steered her close enough to the shore that Galahad was able to wade to the boat, the water coming only about to his knees— no deeper than what he had waded through when he pulled his sword from that stone. And he clambered aboard. I was so overjoyed to see him—I had been in despair and suddenly, like the answer to a prayer, he had appeared. I embraced him—at that moment he seemed even more than a son to me. He was like…like…new buds on the branches of spring.

"Sir Galahad had with him some bread, some cheese, some dried fish. He even had a skin of wine, all of which he carried in a pouch he had waded with to the boat, and we immediately sat on the deck and fell to. As the boat continued to drift slowly downstream with the current, our horses kept pace, following us along the shore. He stayed with me for two days, telling me of his love for the woman whose body lay here with us, and of how he understood this quest he had embarked on."

"And just what was that understanding?" Sir Gareth pushed him. "You told us the quest was *of* the Grail, not *for* the Grail. I don't know what that means. How can you search for something that is not the physical thing?"

Sir Lancelot closed his eyes, as if trying to concentrate on what he was saying. "The Grail," he began, "is at Corbenic Castle. It has always been there—well, since Joseph of Arimathea brought it here to Logres, anyway. Galahad certainly knew it was there—he remembered seeing it as a small boy, before he was fostered at the abbey. And others who have visited Corbenic know it is there— King Pelles does not display it, but he makes no secret of it, and he does bring it out for special occasions. It is said to have remarkable healing properties. What matters about a relic—and the Grail is the greatest of all relics—is not the physical presence of the object or even any miraculous event that might be associated with it, though miraculous healing is sometimes ascribed to it. No, what Galahad told me, and I think I understand it, is that a relic, especially one as closely associated with Christ himself as this Grail, is a locus of power, a manifest place where what is holy and spiritual interacts with the natural, physical world. A place where we can mystically be united with the Holy, where we can experience in this world the reality of the next."

At this latter comment Merlin coughed. He seemed irritated. I knew that he was skeptical about all things supernatural (though he didn't seem to mind that people attributed supernatural powers to himself), and that he put his faith only in things that he could explain.

"I don't know how to explain it any better, I'm afraid," the Great Knight continued, "but I'm saying that *finding* the Grail is not the issue here. *Experiencing* the Grail is what is required. And I think that is why most of the knights are failing in this quest: They aren't prepared to experience the Grail on its own terms. It takes someone like Galahad—someone like my son—who has been focused from childhood on the contemplation of the Divine, or perhaps someone like Sir Perceval, whose innocence makes him less tied to the natural world, to complete this quest. Others will fail. They will not even know where to start."

The queen was trying hard to look as if she was indifferent to the whole story. Rosemounde, on the other hand, seemed rapt with interest. Merlin remained skeptical, and Sir Gareth pursed his lips as if trying to understand but finding the explanation hard to follow. But I was fascinated. It was the way I idealized the religious life myself. Perhaps a life in emulation of Sir Galahad's was not out of reach for me—with Rosemounde bound to another, my love for her might be as chaste and pure as Galahad's for Perceval's sister, might it not? Well, in practice at any rate, if not in my imagination. Lancelot's imagination, however, was moving in a different direction.

"On the third day, Galahad bade me farewell, assuring me that he must continue his quest until he had reached his goal—which was, as I understood his philosophy, nothing less than the union of his soul with God, even in this mundane world. He called me 'father,' and I called him 'son,' and we embraced again, for what I fear will be the last time in this world. And he left the boat after we had steered it toward the bank once more. Our horses had kept pace with the boat for two days, ambling along the shore and keeping us within sight. He waded ashore and mounted up, waving to me and calling 'God be with you, my honored lord.' And then he was gone.

"I nearly despaired again after he had left, and by then I was out of food as well. I curled up in the bow of the boat—Dandane still lay undisturbed in the stern—and, fasting, I fell into a fitful sleep. The girl, the vellum note, the quest, Galahad's musings, all roiled together in my mind as I slept. In my dream, the bowl into which Perceval's sister had bled was the Grail itself, and her blood was poured out as communion, miraculously healing the sick wherever it was dispensed. And then I saw her crucified, and Galahad at the foot of the cross weeping. And I blinked, and they were reversed—and Galahad was crucified and Dandane stood weeping. And I blinked again and I saw both of them lying dead, side by side.

"When I awoke the next morning, I saw things far more clearly. Dandane, before anyone else, had apparently achieved the quest of the Grail: She had literally become one with Christ, and therefore with God. She died for the sake of the unworthy. She sacrificed herself for the sin of others. She did this in the spirit of love, not for an earthly lover but for humankind as a reflection of the divine. At that point I understood that she had, in fact, become the Grail herself: Her body was the relic of a saint, and brought me closer to God even there in that boat. To achieve the Grail, Galahad must emulate her, and that is what he was off to do. I wasn't sure I could do the same, but I knew that if I continued the quest, I would have to.

"It wasn't until I had been awake for some minutes that I realized the boat had stopped moving. I sat up to see that it had run aground. The girl had gotten her wish: God had steered the unpiloted boat to the spot where He apparently wanted her body to spend eternity. Looking up and running my gaze along the shore, I realized I recognized the place. As it turned out, God apparently wanted Dandane buried on the grounds of Corbenic castle."

"Then she was there?" I asked. "Perceval's sister? And they buried her there? And Sir Ector was right, you *were* in the castle when he came and was turned away?"

"I was there," Lancelot nodded. "When I stepped down from the boat, I was a bit dizzy from fasting, and felt dazed by the strength of my own emotions and inner struggle. When my feet touched the bank I looked up and saw the castle looming, and meant to head straight for it, but suddenly, as if from nowhere, a great lion blocked my path."

"Lion?" Merlin exclaimed. "Lions don't run free in Logres. Where on earth had it come from?"

"I can't say. It was simply a part of the excruciating weirdness of the whole experience of Corbenic. The lion stood in my way, and I moved to go slowly around him to my right, and he cocked his head as if he understood what I was doing, all the while looking at me for all the world as if he recognized me."

"Ywain's lion," Gareth asserted. "It can be no other. How overjoyed he will be to know that the lion is still loose and unharmed! He suffered such anguish at the thought of what those brigands might have done with him once they had netted him."

"Of course, that's who he must have been. Well, one mystery solved!" Lancelot smiled. "But more were to come. I made my way to the gate of the castle, and the drawbridge was down." As it had been when Merlin and I visited, I thought to myself. "I called to the guard that I had a woman in the boat who needed Christian burial. And I asked to be housed for the night. Minuit, my horse, skittish of the lion, had galloped up the hill on one side and now had made his way down and stood behind me, ready to enter the safety of the castle himself. Well, a small group of squires came out to attend us. One took my horse to be fed and watered, two others made their way down to the boat, and the chief squire led me in and gave me breakfast at a board set up in the great hall.

"The remainder of that day flew by. A linen shroud was stitched together quickly for the lady Dandrane, for she had been on that boat for a good week by now and despite her rarified sanctity, her physical remains deteriorated in the manner of all flesh. The castle's chaplain, Father Benedict, performed a funeral Mass for the poor girl in the chapel. King Pelles was courteous enough to attend along with me, carried into the chapel by four of his squires. Lady Elaine did not honor us with her presence. Indeed, I did not see her all day, and could only assume she was avoiding my sight. I can't blame her, of course, for after we had shared a bed together I had never contacted her or had aught to do with her." At that I heard a subdued snort from the direction of the queen.

"Two other squires bore the shrouded corpse into the castle churchyard, where a sexton had been digging a grave since that morning, and I followed the body and the priest to the grave, where I prayed along with Father Benedict while the squires covered the lady's body with that final swathe of earth. Finally the sexton marked the new grave with a simple wooden cross. I determined to purchase a more elaborate monument for her on my return to Camelot, though I have since decided against that notion. I don't think the girl would have liked it. Her fame and glory is heavenly, and that is what she lived for. She would not care about—might even resent—a worldly monument that tried to keep her tied to this earth.

"I stood at that grave for some time, loath to leave that silent companion I had spent so many days with aboard that boat. But then I remembered that I had not given the chaplain any token for singing the Mass and burying the girl, and so I wanted to find him and pay him something before I left that place in the morning to continue my quest. My immediate thought was that he must be back in the chapel, a room in the castle with a door that opens directly into the great hall. There was no one in the hall when I entered, and no one guarding the door to the chapel, but when I opened it, I realized that I was interrupting a private, perhaps even a secret, ritual."

I knew the room of which he spoke—it had been the room into which the procession bearing the golden cup, the spear and the silver salver had entered that evening Merlin and I spent with King Pelles and the lady Elaine. Something secret had been going on there that night as well, something about which my curiosity had never been settled. "What was going on?" I asked Lancelot.

"I did not know at first," the great knight continued. "But I was certain that it was some ritual involving the Grail. I dared not enter the room, but said a quick prayer under my breath that God might reveal something to me of what I was seeking. I stood in the doorway, glancing at the rich tapestries that lined the walls, and saw, in the midst of the chapel, a silver table on which stood the gold cup, the Grail itself, covered in a cloth of red samite. Seated in the chapel were the king, the lady Elaine, and all the retainers of their household, in rapt attention. The table was surrounded by several of the castle's squires, robed in white garments so that they looked like angels, all of them holding a brightly lit candelabra—except for one holding a bloodied spear and another a silver platter. Before the Grail stood father Benedict, dressed in his finest ceremonial garments and singing the Mass.

"I'm really not sure what happened after that. Some effect of the light perhaps. Some effect of my extreme emotions that morning. Or of my fasting perhaps. I don't know what it was, but I seemed to see things that were not there. The priest reached for the Grail, and as he took it in his hands it suddenly appeared to me that he was holding three grown men, and tottering under the weight of them. He looked to me as if he was about to collapse, and that he might take the Grail with him, perhaps damaging it in the fall. Well, not thinking, I rushed forward spontaneously, hoping to prevent injury to the priest and to the relic as well, but before I was able to touch either him or the cup, I seemed to see a great puff of smoke and feel a burning gust of air—perhaps something coming from all those candles, I thought—but then I lost all consciousness, swooned to the floor and lay there, dead to the world and, as I understand it, seeming dead to all who saw me.

"Now you must understand that I knew nothing, and was only told later what had happened. But they set up a pallet for me there in the chapel, and I lay dead to the world for twenty-four days, sustained only by a little water they were able to get me to swallow every day along with a Mass wafer, or so they told me. I could only feel that it was no accident that I was twenty-four days mending: It was one day of penance for each year I had been involved in my sinful love of the queen. There could be no other explanation."

Now, I could imagine several other explanations, not the least of which was coincidence. But I didn't venture to say so, since I did not want to throw off Lancelot's narrative just now as he was reaching its end, and besides, I could see again how uncomfortable the queen was—so much so that she had risen from the bed and was pacing toward the door impatiently, as if she did not want to hear any more of this nonsense.

"When I finally awoke, in fact, Sir Ector was outside the gates, calling to be let in. And there was the Grail—they brought it into the chapel each day apparently hoping that its healing properties might ultimately bring me to my senses. Whether that is what did it or whether it was the sound of my brother's voice, or whether I had just finally cast off my paralysis, I do not know. I only know that when I awoke, that chief squire of Pelles', that Golagros, was standing over me, looking into my eyes to see whether or not I was back among the living."

The entire story struck a chord with me, and I realized that I need no longer wonder about our meeting with King Pelles and who was being served with that gold cup, which was in fact the Grail. It was Lancelot who was served—he had been there the entire time Merlin and I sat with King Pelles, and the king had certainly wanted us to ask about him. Why he did not simply tell us Lancelot was in the next room I could not say, but I looked to Merlin for affirmation and the old mage winked at me. But another of the audience, my lady Rosemounde, had a different reaction. She started visibly when Lancelot mentioned the name of Golagros. It had triggered something in her brain, and she looked at me too, not with a wink but with the wide eyes of surprise and concern. After a look like that, I realized I would need to speak with her privately after Lancelot's monologue.

The great knight was poised to finish his story. "Father Benedict was in the chapel, as well, when I awoke, and so, for the first time, was the lady Elaine. She was curt and detached with me, but she had at least deigned to see me through the sickness so that I might not die—at least, not in *her* castle."

The words of Merlin's vision came back to me again. Surely Elaine must be the mother of darkness it had prophesied. She wanted no one dying in her castle, it was surely true, but seemed to be fine with scads of killings taking place elsewhere. I was still puzzled by the second part of the prophecy, though. The widow triumphs? Who was this widow? But I couldn't concern myself with that now. The question of the moment was, what had affected Rosemounde so?

"But I knew one thing when I awoke that I had not known before I had collapsed," Lancelot continued. "I would never achieve the Grail, not in the sense my son would have it. I had presumed to hold out hands to the cup, thinking to save it, but I had not been deemed worthy of doing so. And this was not man's decision, but God's. Why else would I have collapsed as I did?"

Again, I could think of a number of explanations…but let that go.

"And the twenty-four days were a confirmation of what I felt in my heart as I lay there: My soul was far too earthbound, too caught up in the love of my queen, for whom I hungered then far more than for the nourishment of the meats they had brought me. That bond was too strong to break so long as she was in the world and condescended to accept my service as her knight. Union with God was well and good for those who desired perfection, and perfection meant transcending the things of this world. But if my sovereign lady is *in* this world, I cannot transcend it. I must live in it, and serve her."

Guinevere no longer fidgeted impatiently. Nor was her flushed face any longer the site of anger or dismay. It had turned pale now, white as any swan, and she stared down modestly with, was it embarrassment? Fear? Coyness? I couldn't tell. And I knew her as well as anyone.

But Lancelot's tale was done. We had learned whatever there was to learn from it. I can't say I had gleaned much that would help us in our investigation, though it was certainly enlightening to have found who was served with the Grail. Even to learn that I had actually seen the Grail—and hadn't recognized it. I guess my own attachments to the things of this world were enough to deny me any chance at achieving the quest. And speaking of my attachment to this world, what was it that had startled Rosemounde so during Lancelot's monologue? As the others all rose, Merlin took it as his prerogative as host to dismiss them:

"My lords and ladies, forgive my rudeness, but I do worry that your several absences from Camelot will be remarked if you stay much longer. I appreciate Sir Lancelot's being willing to meet beyond the castle walls to tell his story to this select group, and I daresay he has been more candid with us here than he could possibly have been in the king's throne room."

"Indeed," the Great Knight concurred. "I have told all here. Much of this the king could not hear."

"What Arthur doesn't know, won't hurt him…" Gareth murmured with no small hint of irony.

"But as his most trusted courtiers, you all may be able to do more with this information than he could," Lancelot concluded.

"God's bodykins, man, you've given us a lot of meat to chew on. But go now, go, before any suspicious minds begin to work."

"Ride with us, Sir Lancelot," Gareth offered. "We'll accompany the queen and her matron." I cringed at that, but had resigned myself to it. As a married woman, Rosemounde could no longer be categorized a maid. Gareth looked to me quizzically and asked, "You're coming, Gildas?"

"Not just yet, my lord," I bowed him out of the cave. "There are a few things I think I need to discuss with my lord Merlin first, if I may have your leave."

Guinevere at the same time called for Rosemounde, and was quite taken aback when her lady also begged leave to stay. "Your majesty, I have remembered something that it is imperative I speak with Merlin about. I'm sure that he or perhaps Gildas will make sure I can find my way back to Camelot. With your leave, Your Grace," she added the last almost as an afterthought.

The queen raised an eyebrow at me as she walked out, but said nothing as she passed me, only bidding the three of us good day as she swept out with Gareth and Lancelot. When we had heard them ride off, Merlin turned to Rosemounde and me and said, "All right, children, what is it we are playing at now?"

But Rosemounde was in no mood for banter. "That name!" She cried out to us. "I know that name, that squire Golagros. There is something dire he's involved in, I know it! Because he has been in touch with Mordred!"

CHAPTER SEVENTEEN
THE TALE OF SIR MORDRED

"God's whiskers, girl, what are you saying? In touch with… how do you mean in touch with Sir Mordred?" The old man was visibly quivering with excitement. I couldn't help smiling a bit, though I was feeling the same kind of thrill myself: This was the first real clue we had come across, it seemed to me, and it had been there in front of us the whole time, if we'd only known to ask.

"I mean this Golagros came to Orkney some, I don't know, six months ago I think. He said he came as an emissary from his master, King Pelles, and had important matters to discuss with the last scion of the House of Orkney—I believe that's how he put it." Rosemounde's eyes were flashing and her voice was lowered in a conspiratorial tone. She seemed just as animated by her news as we were, until this minute having had no idea that this information might be important.

"So do you know what they talked about?" I urged her. "This could be the key to the whole unwieldy investigation." Merlin scowled in my direction at the suggestion that anything he was involved in might be construed as unwieldy.

She sagged a bit at that point. "My husband has never been one to confide in me, I'm afraid," she confessed. "He didn't even want me, as lady of the castle, to prepare a banquet for the squire as our guest, even though I argued that it would only demonstrate proper respect for the king his master if we showed this Golagros our generosity and hospitality. Mordred, well, he made it clear he did not want my opinions. 'Backtalk' he called it."

"Bastard!" I couldn't help interjecting. I must admit, I was excited for reasons that went beyond the solving of this complex investigation: If Mordred was involved somehow, I reasoned, he would have to come before the king's bench, and though Arthur was a merciful king, he could hardly brook treason in his own house. In my fondest imagination I envisioned the elimination of my lady's husband—and I knew that a widow, even a widow with the social status of my lady Rosemounde, had a good deal more freedom regarding her marital status than the unmarried daughter of a duke.

"And so Sir Mordred met privately with the squire, is that what you're saying?" Merlin pressed.

"Privately, you might even say secretly," Rosemounde replied. "I don't know if that was Golagros's idea or Mordred's, but they met in a small closet without any attendants. It is possible that no one but me, and the guard who had conducted Golagros to Mordred, even knew he was in the castle."

"How long did they meet?" Merlin wanted to know.

"Perhaps two hours. And it was only the one time—he stayed the night. I think my husband ordered a cold slice of beef and a trencher to be brought to that same closet, where Golagros slept. He was gone in the morning."

"It's certainly curious," I mused. "We've considered the possibility that Mordred is behind these events, and now *this*—it seems to put him right in the middle of it!"

"Don't get overanxious, boy!" Merlin chastised me. "You may have your personal notions about Sir Mordred, but we don't know what he had to do with King Pelles or this squire. And if anything, it seems that they came to him, not the other way around."

"They came to him twice," Rosemounde said quietly. Merlin and I looked at her with wide eyes as she went on: "It happened since we've been in Camelot. Just after this quest began, it was. As you know full well, I have preferred to lodge in the queen's quarters, but I had been summoned to my husband's closet for some service, I forget what. But while I was there a squire brought him a parchment with the seal of King Pelles on it. Mordred broke it open and read what had been written—hastily scrawled, it seemed to me, and, forgetting I suppose that I was even present, grumbled something about 'that damned squire Golagros'—so that I assumed the note must be from him once more."

"God's nails, I wish we could have seen that note," Merlin snapped. Then looking thoughtful, he asked Rosemounde, "Do you know where your husband is now? I feel this matter is coming to a head: More and more threads of this conspiracy are coming undone, and the body count seems to be getting pretty high. If he can tell us—if he *will* tell us—why these people approached him in the first place, it may be that we can finally bring this series of disasters to a halt."

Lady Rosemounde's eyes fell, and she reddened slightly, saying with a hint of irony, "My husband does not provide me with his daily itinerary. I take it he is somewhere in the castle, for I am likely to have heard it if he had gone elsewhere. But where he is specifically or what he does there, he would remind me if he ever saw me, are his own business."

While I was perfectly happy to learn how little time she was actually spending in her husband's company there in the palace, and it particularly gladdened me that he had no opportunity to continue his brutal beating of her as long as they stayed in Camelot, my heart sank with the knowledge that this ignoring of Rosemounde might be as harmful to her feelings as the abuse itself. What would she say? That at least when he beat her, she had his attention? My God, I hated Mordred and everything he did to my beloved. Yet here was Merlin, cautioning me against convicting him of conspiracy against his king and father before we had proof. Well I needed no more proof of his guilt—if not of this crime then of a hundred others—than the memory of my Rosemounde's scarred back.

"We must find him!" Merlin cried. "And we must do it now. My lady Rosemounde," he bowed with a show of courtesy that I knew was rare for him. "I assume you will want to return to the castle—the queen and others will be expecting you, and I don't want to arouse any suspicions. I will ask this imbecile squire here to escort you, if he can remember the way. Gildas," he turned to me, "find your master Sir Gareth and obtain his help to search for Sir Mordred. We should not make a huge show of this search, for if our quarry realizes we are seeking him he may very well bolt. Meanwhile I will stay here and prepare a few things, and follow you within the hour."

"But what are you…" I began.

"Enough! Go, go go!"

***

Rosemounde and I left Merlin's cave together. I admit it felt a little awkward for me. I could count on one hand the number of times I had ever actually been alone with the love of my life. And even then, I realized as we plunged into the privacy of the woods, it had been only briefly, in a corner of the castle where someone was bound to come upon us at any moment. As I took her palfrey by the bridle to lead it through the woods, the better to walk in her close proximity, I hung my head, trying to think of something to say.

But my lady anticipated me, as I should have expected, and began, half teasing as we passed out of earshot of the cave. "So, Gildas of Cornwall, you seemed a bit surprised at my accompanying the queen today. I'm so sorry if my presence was displeasing to you…"

I could hear the smirk in her voice but I didn't look up at her. If I watched her face it would only make me tongue-tied. I looked straight ahead, holding the bridle in my right hand. I knew she was just fishing for a compliment, but I figured, all right, why not bite? "My lady," I answered her. "Nothing could have given my heart greater delight than seeing you there today. Unless, perhaps, it would be the opportunity to see you home to Camelot and have a few private moments with you here…"

"Yes," she said quietly. "Here. Alone. In the woods."

Surprised at her tone, I looked up at her, astride the saddle in her yellow dress, her hair now blowing in the light summer breeze—she had taken off her headdress and barbier in the few moments she had been riding, and let her hair flow free. "Oh Gildas, it's so good to feel free, if only for an hour."

Not sure where this was heading, I steered the conversation back to the matter at hand. "My lady, I suppose it must be difficult for you to reveal to us your husband's private conversations. Do you expect any repercussions if Mordred discovers you were the one who told us of his contact with this squire of King Pelles?"

She scoffed at that. "I expect repercussions for looking at him cross-eyed," she told me openly. "But there is good cause to believe that Mordred would betray King Arthur—would destroy him if he could. He has…he has powerful motives."

My ears pricked up. Until now, I had thought that the secret of Mordred's parentage, and of the king's blundered attempt to kill him as a newborn, was not common knowledge outside of the Orkney clan and a few of Arthur's oldest advisors, Merlin among them. It appeared now that Mordred had seen fit to inform his wife of that deep grievance. "So," I said, looking forward into the woods again and stopping the horse. "How much has he told you of his relationship with his uncle the king?"

"Enough to teach me not to call him 'uncle,'" she returned.

"He told you of his mother's seduction of the young king?"

Rosemounde snorted. "Mordred refers to it as the rape of his mother. And claims it reenacted the rape of his grandmother by King Uther, which resulted in Arthur's own birth. And he claims that the king tried to kill him, along with all other noble sons born around the time of his birth, by casting them adrift in a pilotless boat with the intention that it should dash against the rocks and drown all aboard. He believes that, because of his birth and because of his suffering, he is entitled to be Arthur's heir, and he intends to succeed his father by any means necessary. That much he told me. He flung the story at me in contempt one day, when I expressed my devotion to the queen and my admiration for her husband. He wanted to hurt me by portraying Arthur as a brutal tyrant. I didn't know whether to believe him or not. Until now. Your question confirms his accusations."

Still without turning around, I stared ahead and admitted, "Most of what he says is true, my lady. But there was certainly no rape of Margause. She was an experienced woman enticing an impressionable fifteen-year old king to her bed. But Arthur did try to have Mordred killed. It's no excuse, but remember his youth and remember that his closest advisors—including, if you will forgive me for saying so, your own father Duke Hoel—convinced him he needed to eliminate the threat Mordred posed to his throne."

"Yes," Rosemounde sighed. "Don't think Mordred was slow in throwing my father's part in the affair up to me either. But you can see by this that Mordred will stop at nothing to discredit or destroy the king. He may well have contrived all of this to destroy Arthur's table and bring down his reign. Oh things are bad in Camelot and in Caerleon—you have been away on your own quest for the conspirators much of late, and may not know. Why, Bess of Caerleon, you may not have heard, has been petitioning the queen constantly in the past weeks, begging for justice in the case of her poor, dear Colgrevaunce. Nothing will satisfy her but the death of Sir Lionel."

I sighed, having resigned myself to the loss of my friend. "One knight's death will not bring back the other. And besides, Merlin and I found the drug that was used to incite Lionel, and Gawain too, to violence."

"Yes, yes," Rosemounde flung her hair back and scowled. I looked ahead again, nervous about gazing too long on the unencumbered beauty of her hair. She continued: "But more bad news has reached the court." She paused for a moment, as if uncertain whether to tell me. But now, of course, I *had* to know.

"What? What is it?" I said, forgetting my courtesy for a moment.

"Sir Dinadan!" She blurted out.

I froze. Sir Dinadan—my traveling companion, my confidante and ally in the investigation of Sir Tristram's murder. The sarcastic jokester who enlivened every room he entered. Was she about to tell me he had returned with more bad news? Or something worse?

"The latest group of knights to straggle in from this accursed quest," Rosemounde went on. "Sir Kay and Sir Bedevere arrived this morning. Defeated and disgruntled, but alive. But they had grim news. They brought with them Dinadan's shield—they said they had found it on a tree in the forest not far from Corbenic castle. There was a parchment nailed to the shield, with a message scrawled on it that read, 'The court jester will jibe no more, but in the courts of hell.' They said that they found no body, but there were two bloody arrows at the site, and scattered bits of bloody armor in the neighborhood of the tree. They thought that Dinadan must have been slain by arrows, and that perhaps some wild beast had mauled the body and carried it off. But they had no hope for Sir Dinadan. They were adamant that he was certainly dead."

"Oh Dinadan," I sighed. "You were a good companion and a loyal friend—to Sir Tristram and to me as well. I'll miss your sharp wits and sharper tongue. And Colgrevaunce—my awkward friend and kind fellow. We will have to do without your good heart as well. And Sir Safer, Palomides' valiant and courteous brother. Sir Uwain. Sir Ironside. How many more will be victims of these killers? If Mordred is a part of this he must be brought to justice. If he gets away to Orkney, I fear for you, my lady, having led us to him."

"I am safe from his bullying as long as we remain at Camelot. But I would definitely fear his mood once we've returned to the north."

I felt a burning in the pit of my stomach and at the back of my neck, and I stared forward again, afraid to look at her in my impassioned state. "The thought of that animal molesting you tears at my heart," I said. "I have been training—Sir Gareth deems me nearly ready for knighthood. I will challenge your bastard husband to the utterance if there is any chance of his brutalizing you again. I..."

"Not yet, my Gildas, not yet," her voice whispered in my ear. I spun around to find she had come down from the horse and stood close to my shoulder, her hot breath blowing on my cheek, hard and erratic, her lips nearly touching my ear. "He is still a formidable warrior, and if you challenge him it must be with the intent—and the power—to bring his tyranny of me to an end. For Gildas my love," and with that she placed her hands on my arms and gazed pleadingly into my eyes, "you *are* my only hope."

And with that, seamlessly, she embraced me and kissed me firmly and purposefully full on the mouth, tasting, I imagined, like a fine wine seasoned with honey. I swayed for half a moment, my eyes dazed and my head dizzy as if with drink, then I embraced her with eager hands and returned her kiss with all the pent-up passion of my years of adoration.

What thoughts I had been entertaining about life in the cloister vanished like the morning mist. I would be taking no monkish vows *that* season.

***

"So," Mordred sneered, his upper lip twisting in a particularly obnoxious manner. "You've been talking to my silly little wife, I suppose?"

I blanched, since of course it was the last thing I wanted him to suspect, knowing the regimen of beatings he had put her through. I was certain no one had seen us arrive at the castle together, aside from Robin Kempe of the king's guard, and he was not likely to have said anything. And Merlin had not been far behind us, as it turned out, it having taken us longer than anticipated to make our way back to the castle.

"Why would you assume that?" I countered, though I could see by Merlin's eyes that he would rather I kept my mouth shut in this interview.

"What is this, Brother?" Mordred asked peevishly, turning toward Sir Gareth. "It's bad enough I'm forced to listen to this vile old son of a whore in my own chambers," he gestured toward Merlin, "but I have to listen to the rantings of this lowborn Cornish squire of yours as well?" He scoffed and put his nose up, intimating that he felt contaminated just to be in the same room with churls like ourselves. But Gareth was having none of it.

"Listen, you spawn of incest and adultery, you're going to answer their questions, and mine, or I'm going to pick you up by the scruff of your neck and throw you in the moat, like I should have done when you first appeared like a beggar on our doorstep. Be a man for once and not a sniveling brat, or I'll do it now, I swear."

"I know it was that sow of a wife," he said resignedly, talking to Gareth and not to me, "because nobody else knows that I had words with this squire Golagros. Nobody but Golagros himself, and King Pelles his master, I suppose. But these sleuthhounds haven't had a chance to speak with either of those gentlemen, not since they returned to the castle, and they couldn't have known anything about me when they returned, or they would have sought me out immediately. So. Do I win the prize and can I go now?"

"You can go when we say you can go, boy," Merlin, having had enough of Mordred's braggadocio, was breaking out his authoritative voice. "You will answer my questions now, or I shall turn you in to the king who, blood or no blood, will set those upon you who can compel an answer."

Mordred rankled but said nothing. He did not doubt—nor should he—that Merlin would turn him over, or that the king would approve of the rack in a case like this, where at least five knights of the Table had lost their lives, along with many others killed and injured.

Resigned, Mordred spat out, "Ask what you will, you old walrus. But I've never responded well to bullying."

"You sure like to dish it out though, don't you?" Gareth shot back. "What about this meeting, when this squire came to see you. What was it all about? Come, give us the story. And don't leave anything out."

Mordred sighed mightily and rolled his dark eyes as he slouched forward, almost doubling over on himself. "This Golagros comes to see me. Says he's from King Pelles of Corbenic Castle. 'Why should I be impressed,' I say to him. He's a king in name only, just a vassal to my dear old Dad. A nobody. But he insists on seeing me alone."

"As a vassal of your *uncle* Arthur yourself, you were bound by the dictates of courtesy to give King Pelles' messenger a fair welcome," Merlin insisted.

"Which I did!" Mordred shot back, in a voice that sounded almost defensive. "We went into my private quarters, and I double-checked to see that my bitch of a wife wasn't listening in at the keyhole." He turned mocking eyes on me at that point, and snarled, "So you couldn't get *that* part out of her, could you sirrah?"

"Well you've come to the point now, haven't you, little brother? So what did you and this messenger from Pelles talk about?"

"Oh, this and that," Mordred answered Gareth coyly, glancing about to make sure he was irritating Merlin and me equally. "I'll tell you this: King Pelles, as you call him, is no lover of Arthur."

"And why is that?" Gareth fell into his brother's tone. "Enlighten us, why don't you?"

"Ever hear of a chap name of Balin? Knight of Arthur's Round Table, sent to Pelles to collect a debt. Killed Pelles' brother, from what this squire told me. Wounded King Pelles through the thighs. And by the way, you know I'm saying 'thighs' euphemistically, right?"

"But this is old news," Merlin quibbled. "Pelles and Arthur hashed this out long ago, signed a treaty; Pelles is Arthur's loyal vassal."

"Shows what you know, dotty old codger," Mordred answered. "You think a man's going to forgive that kind of wound? Balin was dead, but Arthur needed to pay, as far as Pelles was concerned. He's done nothing but brood about it ever since. So much so that his kingdom's turned to ruin, pretty much. You've seen it, right? Fields unplowed. Monasteries, nunneries abandoned. It's a wasteland. Impotent king begets infertile kingdom. Not much irony there, eh?"

"You're still not telling us what they wanted of you. God's warts, man, get on with it."

"I'm getting to it, Methuselah. So Pelles is obsessed with this whole phony ancestry he's concocted, right, where he claims to be descended from Joseph of Arimathea himself. And there's this prophecy, you see—I don't know where he got it, maybe he made it up himself, he's batty enough. Prophecy says that if his daughter, a woman of Joseph's line, has a child with the greatest knight in the world, then that child will achieve the greatest of all knightly miracles, achieve the Grail, and be Christ's representative on earth, or some such tommyrot, I forget exactly how it went."

"None of that's got anything to do with you," Gareth pointed out. "So what'd they come looking for you for, then?"

Mordred shrugged, his face taking on a mask of innocence. "Pelles seemed to believe I might be interested in joining their little conspiracy. He and the two monks, Nascien and what's the other one? Grunamund, that was it. They had cooked up this elaborate scheme. Been working on it for years. All revolved around this little bastard, sired by the renowned Sir Lancelot upon the bitch Elaine of Corbenic, this Galahad, last of the line of Joseph of Arimathea he would be. Raise him up in the monastery under this Brother Nascien, now *Prior* Nascien. Fill his head with all kinds of poppycock about the Holy Grail, and set him loose in Camelot. You get all the knights of the Table spread out and tramping about the forests of Logres, and Nascien and Grunamund, the two ex-knights, pick them off one by one. With luck maybe they even pick off Lancelot himself, or that rock of Arthur's throne, the great blockheaded brother of mine, Sir Gawain. That's when they swoop in, topple Arthur from his throne, and replace him with the new hero, Galahad, King of Logres and puppet in the hands of his grandfather Pelles, and his foster-father and confessor, Nascien himself. Quite a scheme, that. Kind of wish I had thought of such a thing."

"I get why Pelles might have been stewing for years about his treatment by Balin, and why he might have blamed it on King Arthur," I said, too caught up in the story to worry about how Mordred was going to insult me this time. "But I can't understand why Nascien and Grunamund would join forces with him. After all, Sir Nascien was close friends with Sir Balin and with Sir Brumand, who died in the Siege Perilous—and Grunamund was Brumand's squire. Wouldn't they be natural enemies of Pelles, who hated Balin so much?"

"The enemy of my enemy is my friend," Merlin mused, anticipating whatever sarcastic answer Mordred was preparing. "Brumand and Balin both detested Sir Lancelot, and Nascien and Grunamund inherited that hatred after the other two died. Arthur and his kingdom were just collateral damage to them: it was Lancelot they wanted to bring down. And so they came to you with a proposal that you help them, from the inside as it were, now that you were a knight of the Table. What did they want you to do? Ride on the quest and murder your brothers one by one, all to get back at your king uncle for not loving you enough?"

Mordred's dark eyes blazed as Merlin's remarks struck home, and he even lost his composure momentarily. "My *father* never loved me at all. Tried his best to kill me, didn't he? And you, his chief advisor, did nothing to stop it then, did you, old mountebank? Sure they wanted me to join with them. Maybe I should have done it. I don't owe this king—or this *family*" (he threw the remark in

Gareth's direction), "a damn thing. Now bugger off and let me alone. I've told you everything I'm going to."

"But not everything you know," Gareth surmised. "I don't think we're done with you yet. What about this Brother Bertrand? What did he have to do with any of this?"

Mordred rolled his eyes, as if the question were unimportant. "That silly bugger was just a tool. Nascien and Grunamund used him to keep tabs on Gawain. The blockhead told him everything. Then Lancelot visited him too, and they thought they'd died and gone to heaven. So Gawain they were able to neutralize, since they got Bertrand to slip him the herb that would make him mad and attack his fellow knights. Tried it on Lancelot too, but the big man wouldn't take it, just their luck. But old Bertrand was cut with his own knife, wasn't he, when he slipped the drug to old Lionel. Now *that* was poetic justice, let me tell you."

"But why was Bertrand helping them?" Merlin wondered. "He'd had nothing to do with Arthur, or Balin, or Lancelot, or any of them. Why should he join that group of avengers, if that's what they thought of themselves?"

"Nascien and Grunamund wanted Bertrand because he had a relationship with my dear brother, from back when Gawain was his confessor at the Green Knight's castle. And when they were all little monks together there at the Beaulieu monastery, Bertrand confessed to his prior, Nascien, why he'd left the Green Knight's employ: Seems he and Lady Bertilak had been playing a little game of 'look what I've got under my cassock' every time she went to confess in his private little confessional there in the castle. Bit of a fit of conscience, and a whole lot of fear of Bertilak's big axe, spurred Bertrand to get out of there and into a cloister. But once he'd told Nascien, then he was done for. Even when he tried to get out from under and live in a hermitage, Nascien tracked him down and threatened to give Bertrand away to the Green Knight if he didn't do everything Nascien told him to. So that's where he came in."

"And they wanted your help. So what did you tell them, brother dear?" Gareth had caught some sarcasm from Mordred.

"I told them no, damn it! Why would I be talking to you otherwise?"

"Because the three of us burst into your quarters here, and I had my sword drawn. So how do we know you declined their generous offer? We have only your word on it, and that's worth…what? The sweepings of my horse's stable?"

Mordred glared at Gareth with undisguised hatred. "Believe me or not, what do I care? It's none of my affair."

"So you talked about all these things when the squire came to visit you in Orkney? And when exactly was this?" Merlin asked, trying to steer things back to the topic.

"Some of it I surmised, but most of it Pelles' squire told me. That was shortly before I came to Camelot for the Pentecost feast, at the bidding of my king. I learned a few more details later, from a parchment Golagros sent me after this quest began."

"Things like what?" Gareth pressed.

"That was when he wrote that Brother Bertrand was in on the plot, and had concocted some potion that turned Lionel and dear brother Gawain into killing machines. When I learned that bloody Ironside and that oaf Colgrevaunce had been snuffed out. Golagros seemed to think it was a promising beginning. Thought I might be more interested in joining their little club."

The mention of Colgrevaunce in this flippant manner turned my stomach, so that any constraints I had been feeling fell away and I reached out to grab Mordred by his collar and shake him like a schoolboy. "You bastard! Colgrevaunce was twice the knight you'll ever be, you bloody, bloody bastard…" by then Merlin had reached out to hold me back, and Sir Gareth stood before his brother, his upheld hand keeping Mordred at bay, while the bastard sneered, "You're lucky I haven't got my sword, boy, or you'd be groping the ground right now, looking for your head!"

"Peace, now," Gareth warned.

"Oh, this is not the time," Mordred said. "But I'll have my sword next time we meet, you pathetic little squire, and I'll teach you what it means to touch a knight of the Round Table!"

"Seems to mean nothing at all to you, judging from your way of mourning Sir Colegrevaunce!" I snapped back.

"I mean it! Peace!" Now Gareth did have his own sword out, and brandished it to make sure we settled down, but then pointed it at Mordred and demanded. "But you did not join this conspiracy, you claim?"

"I'm done talking to you. Get yourselves out of my closet, I have nothing more to say."

"You'll tell us everything we want to know or the king will learn you've been in communication with his enemies," Gareth threatened him. "If you didn't join them why not? And why would you keep these things to yourself when you knew they were treason?"

"Why don't you go help your boyfriend Lancelot tup your uncle's queen, sweet brother of mine? Always way too pure for the rest of the family...." Mordred snarled the last bit. "I've said what I'm going to say. What do you plan to do about it?"

Before Gareth could react to Mordred's churlish outburst there was a huge flash of red and yellow sparks, accompanied by a thunderous explosion that threw Morded and Gareth backwards, looking dazed. Suddenly I knew exactly why Merlin had held back in his cave before coming to Camelot, and had let me see Rosemounde home by myself. He'd been preparing one of his fireworks displays, in the hope of cowing Mordred into telling the truth. I can tell you, if I didn't know better, it certainly would have scared me into speaking.

Merlin was in his Full Wizard Mode, straight and tall with a booming voice that overawed Mordred as his voice thundered, "Answer the question or the next fireball will splatter your worthless carcass from one end of this castle to the other!" It was all I could do to rein in the smile I felt breaking out on my face. I knew what a colossal bluff it was—Merlin never carried more than enough powder for one dazzling fireball. No one had ever called his bluff, and so his reputation as a great necromancer was still intact. But he was taking quite a risk with the recalcitrant Mordred.

But I hadn't taken into account Mordred's fundamental cravenness. Like most bullies, he was a coward at heart, and Merlin's explosion would have subdued even a brave man. Mordred wilted, lost his bravado and turned sulky, but gave in. "All right keep your blasts in check, old man. Yes, this squire Golagros was trying to recruit me. Told me Pelles was going to bring down the table and said I'd be a welcome ally. Thought I'd be glad to help them topple dear old Dad. But they misjudged me. Why on earth should I stick my neck out to put that little pipsqueak Galahad on the throne? To help that old cripple Pelles' dream come true? What would have been in it for me? Pelles thought revenge would be enough. It's not. I want the kingdom. And some day Arthur is going to give it to me."

Gareth looked at him and then glanced over at Merlin and me. Then he glared back at Mordred. "You have some plot of your own, then, that you're hatching to bring that about?"

In mock surprise Mordred answered his brother. "Heavens, the very idea!" He exclaimed sarcastically, then answered my master more soberly, "If I did, you think I'd be fool enough to just tell you? Even your pet magician isn't going to blast that out of me. Now get the hell out of here."

"One more thing," the pet magician interjected. "If you wanted nothing to do with their scheme, why didn't you report it to the king? Or to me, or to anyone?"

The smirk was back on the bastard's face. "They were targeting Sir Lancelot and my dear brother Gawain too," he said. "Getting those two lummoxes out of the way certainly falls in line with my own agenda, don't you think?"

"You disgust me," his brother spat back. "And don't think Arthur will not hear of your traitorous failure to report this conspiracy. You think that's going to forward your 'agenda'?"

"Oh Gareth," Mordred laughed as we rose to leave. "You'd be surprised what I can twist to my own advantage!"

Gareth was done. He turned his back and pushed out the door, accompanied by a deeply frowning Merlin. As I put my head down to follow Merlin, Sir Mordred stepped in front of me and forced his leering face into mine. "Don't think you've heard the last of this, boy!" He shouted in my face. "We'll meet in the lists one day, count on it!" And then, resting his hand on my chest to stop me from moving on, he put his mouth to my right ear and whispered, "You want her, eh? My sow of a wife. You'd like to hear the squeals she makes when I poke her, wouldn't you? Well you'll never have her, boy!" The whisper turned into a growl. "I'll slit her throat first, before you'll ever touch her. Believe it!"

Merlin had stopped, reached back and pulled me from the room, before I could recover from the shock of Mordred's curse. I was too astounded to give him an answer.

CHAPTER EIGHTEEN
CORBENIC

Sir Gareth rode before me, mounted on his great destrier Ajax, moving purposefully along the path leading north toward the Castle Corbenic. He bore his own sword at his side, and was clad in his best chain mail, which I had been keeping in good repair. Around his shoulders he carried his shield, blazoned with a silver unicorn on a field of gold.

But as for his helmet and his lance, I was carrying those, as best I could while riding close behind, mounted high on Ajax's foal Achilles. I wore some borrowed chain mail myself, and a sword was on my thigh. Behind me, Merlin was riding a brown palfrey borrowed from the stables. He had spent most of the trip so far grumbling to himself.

"If you're going to ride back there grousing, at least grouse loud enough to entertain the rest of us," Sir Gareth called over his shoulder. I stifled a laugh and glanced back myself, only to see the old necromancer's dark brows lowered like threatening thunderclouds over his blazing eyes.

"God's eyelids, Beaumains," Merlin answered, reverting to Gareth's old nickname from his time in the kitchens of Camelot. "What do you think I'm going to do? What would any sane person do in this situation? You're riding forward to attack an entire castle single-handedly? You're off your bloody nut. How is this a good idea?"

"We've been through all this before…"

"And I didn't like it then either!" Merlin snapped. "What am I here for if people aren't going to listen to me?"

"Look old man," Gareth explained again, with exaggerated patience. "You told me yourself that the castle is essentially undefended. Just the old king, the daughter, and a few squires."

"When *we* were there. But we don't know yet what has happened to Sir Grunamund. Is he off somewhere killing Round Table knights in his white armor? Or might he be back at the castle to protect Pelles and the Princess Elaine?"

"I can take care of Sir Grunamund," Gareth said with confidence. "If we went to my uncle with what we think, he'd deliberate, he'd get input from Lancelot and from Gawain, then he'd pull an army together and take four days to march to Corbenic. What's King Pelles going to be doing all that time? Getting as many reinforcements as he can, and preparing the castle for a siege."

"Whereas now…" Merlin began.

"Whereas now, we have surprise on our side. Pelles is not going to fight us. The squires aren't trained, except, I suppose, for this Golagros perhaps. But if I can't dispatch him, I don't deserve to be a knight of the Table. Besides…" he pulled Ajax to a halt and looked seriously back at Merlin. "The knights of the Round Table are hurting. Many of them have still not returned from the quest. Those that have are wounded or devastated. One knight can do this, and I'm the halest knight in Camelot right now."

Merlin had an answer to that. "Lancelot?"

Gareth rolled his head about in annoyance. "Yes," he conceded. "Lancelot is back and he's healthy. And no, I am not Lancelot. Nobody is Lancelot. But Merlin, you heard Mordred: This entire plot revolves around vengeance toward Sir Lancelot. We don't know what Lancelot may be riding into if he heads to Corbenic again by himself."

"If he's in danger at Corbenic, then why didn't they destroy him when they had the chance, while he lay unconscious with the Grail?" Merlin pushed.

"I don't know," Gareth admitted. "But I have a feeling it had a lot to do with the fact that you two were in the castle at the same time.

Then Ector arrived as well. No, it was too much of a chance to take. But now! Now there's nothing to stop them. Now he might just be riding into a trap!"

"Which means," Merlin said with a note of satisfaction in his voice, "that we may very well be riding into a trap as well! Doesn't it?"

Gareth gave a little half smile and turned to face forward again, nodding his head. "Maybe," he admitted as he rode forward. "Maybe, but I won't let my lord Lancelot ride into anything. Besides, I've got you two—my faithful squire and the wisest man in the realm. Nothing's going to happen to *me*."

I hoped he was right. I hoped we weren't walking into a bloody ambush. But my mind was not focused on Sir Gareth's determined quest to cleanse Corbenic Castle of this scourge. Ever since our informative but depressing meeting with the bastard Mordred, I'd been unable to concentrate on anything but that sickeningly taunting voice that bored like a dagger into my brain—'You'll never have her, boy! I'll slit her throat first, before you'll ever touch her!' Thinking of him with her made my head feel light, and I broke out in a cold sweat as we traveled, though we rode in the warmth of a summer day in the green wood.

"Mark my words," Merlin said in lower tones intended only for me. "We will live to regret this folly. There is danger at that castle, I can smell it. And the lady Elaine will not soon be taken by surprise."

This jostled me a little, and I looked back at Merlin, swaying a bit with the shift in weight as I tried to balance armor, lance, and helmet on my sturdy horse's back. "Lady Elaine? Surely you mean King Pelles—isn't he the one to be giving commands at the castle?"

Merlin snorted. "Pelles is nothing more than a pawn in the hands of his daughter. Could you not see when we were with them that she was the one in charge?"

Thinking back to the unorthodox dinner we had had with the king and his daughter, I shrugged. "It was such an odd experience, I really couldn't tell who was orchestrating the bedlam."

"Trust me," Merlin said. "She was the one. Oh, the original idea was surely the king's: He's the one who sacrificed his daughter's youth, chastity, and, I suppose, any future she might have had with a normal husband, acting as bawd in her tryst with Lancelot, for the sole purpose of producing the heir that would sweep all before him, or so Pelles thought—the one who would displace Arthur and reign as God's holy viceroy in his earthly empire. But that spun out of control, didn't it? Galahad was not someone to be persuaded to focus on earthly power. He sought the praise of heaven, and wanted only to be worthy of the Grail. Elaine kept the dream alive, though. She wanted Galahad at Arthur's court. But she wanted more. She wanted revenge on Lancelot. Pelles couldn't have cared less about that—he wanted Arthur off his throne. It was Elaine who wanted to punish Lancelot. It was she who partnered with Nascien and Grunamund, Lancelot's bitterest enemies, to entice him to Corbenic. Pelles is merely a puppet in this current scheme. For look: We know she was instrumental in enticing Sir Gawain to kill Sir Ironside, and, later, in the scheme that ended with Lionel's attack on Bors. No one forced her into those schemes. She's not just someone's accomplice. She's at the head of this. Nascien is dead. Grunamund is missing. Pelles is old and weak. It's her. Isn't that what my so-called 'vision' said? The mother of light is the mother of darkness? Well that can refer to no one but her. She is Galahad's mother, and so the mother of light. But she has given birth to this whole disastrous quest, and so can claim to be the mother of darkness as well."

"But…so, you think the lady Elaine enlisted Nascien to lure Lancelot into the field to kill him? But why? He's her child's father…"

"And her one lover. The lover she had for one night and who then abandoned her—made her feel she was desirable only when he thought she was somebody else, but in her own person was less than nothing. She wanted Lancelot punished."

"Then why not kill him when she had him at Corbenic? Gareth said it was because we were there, and Sir Ector, but Lancelot lay unconscious, by his own report, for twenty-four days. She had ample time to kill him then, did she not?"

"I would say that there were too many witnesses—this Father Benedict, for instance, and all the young squires and pages Lancelot spoke of. But I don't think that has anything to do with it," Merlin said. "I believe the lady Elaine is beyond caring who knows what she does or what they will say about it. No, there is a conflicted desire in her, I believe. There's a feeling there for Lancelot that underlies her hatred."

"You mean she's in love with him?" I asked, not completely surprised.

"I don't know that we can call it that," Merlin said, musing. "But she would give anything to have him want her for herself. She was nursing him in his time of need in the hope that he would awaken and see that she was his guardian angel. But that didn't happen."

"No," I said, thinking over his words. "It didn't. But what about the other part of that prophecy? The part about the widow triumphing? How does that fit? Does she think of herself as Lancelot's 'widow'? And if she triumphs, that doesn't bode well for us."

Merlin waved that comment away. "We have no way of knowing," he said, brushing the idea aside. "These things never completely make sense until everything is over." And we left it at that, and rode on.

The sunlight through the birch trees threw shreds of shadows across our path, and the "chip-chip-chip" of the chaffinches' trills could be heard in the branches all around us, along with the occasional tap-tap of spotted woodpeckers. Now and then grey squirrels would run across our horses' paths, dodging from tree to tree, the oaks and the rowans now and then more numerous than the silver birches. It was a peaceful ride through the warmth of that fine summer day, and it gave us—gave me, at any rate—a calming respite amid the turmoil and the passion of recent days. I thought of Rosemounde and our short tryst under the forest branches near Lady Lake, and put farther back in my mind the snarling threats of that vicious lout the law said was her husband, and thought only of her, her bright face sustaining me as we rode forward to who knew what end.

***

On the second evening we arrived at Saint Sebastian's Abbey just as the bells were chiming vespers. Sir Gareth and a skeptical Merlin entered the church to hear the office sung, and as I stabled and fed the horses, I could hear the monks chanting from the abbey church:

> *Deus, in adiutorium meum intende. Domine, ad adiuvandum me festina. Gloria Patri, et Filio, et Spiritui Sancto. Sicut erat in principio, et nunc et semper, et in saecula saeculorum. Amen. Alleluia.*
>
> (O God, come to my assistance. O Lord, make haste to help me. Glory to the Father, and to the Son, and to the Holy Spirit. As it was in the beginning, is now, and will be forever. Amen. Alelujah.)

When the service had concluded, I joined Gareth and Merlin in the refectory, where Abbot Lawrence had directed his staff to bring us a mild evening repast. We munched on brown bread and cheese, with some pease from the abbey's garden, and drank glasses of small beer. After a few minutes, we rose to greet the abbot himself as he entered the room.

"Sit, sit," he said, motioning us to be seated as he took a chair himself at the table and looked from one to another, his stony expression never changing. "You have returned, my friends," he began. "And I fear it is not on a pleasant mission."

"No, my lord Abbot, I'm afraid it is not," Merlin sighed. "I hate to use the word sir, but there is a profound evil stemming from Corbenic Castle, and Sir Gareth here believes he can snuff it out with a single blow." Leave it to Merlin to try to get the authority figure of the place on his side right away.

Brother Lawrence nodded, his lips straightened in a thin frown. "It's as you feared, is it not? King Pelles? The Princess Elaine? Responsible, do you think, for the death of Brother Nascien?"

"And so much more," Merlin nodded. "We have every reason to believe that this Nascien and the king, probably with the strong support, even the leadership, of the lady Elaine, are behind a broad conspiracy to bring down King Arthur and Sir Lancelot in particular."

The abbot shook his head in sorrow and disbelief. "I grieve that one of our own could have been involved in such a plot. There is no doubt, then?"

"None whatsoever," Gareth interjected. "Brother Nascien may have been justly slain as a result of his own machinations. Sir Colgrevaunce, Brother Bertrand, Sir Ironside, Sir Safer, Sir Uwayne, Sir Dinadan—all of these murders, my lord Abbot, and perhaps more as well, we must lay at the feet of this conspiracy. But we cannot yet say for certain who it was killed Nascien."

"But can't we make a pretty reasonable guess?" I interjected. "This Brother Grunamund, Nascien's compatriot and fellow-conspirator. Where has he been? He wasn't at Corbenic after Nascien died. And Nascien was murdered by someone who got close enough to him to kill him without a struggle. Who could have done that but his own friend? I don't know what the motive could have been…some falling out over the conduct of their plot, I suppose, but…"

Brother Lawrence had stopped listening, and his head hung low, his chin down to his chest. I glanced up at Merlin, who looked at me askance with one eyebrow raised high. There was something the abbot was not telling us.

"My lord?" Merlin ventured. "You know something we need to know?"

With a sigh, and a hint of relief that he hadn't had to bring it up himself, Brother Lawrence looked up and nodded almost imperceptively. "Brother Grunamund…"

When the abbot paused, Merlin nodded with understanding. I was at a loss myself until Merlin said, "When did you find the body?"

The bad news now made public, Brother Lawrence became less reticent.

"We found him in the woods, perhaps halfway between here and the hermit's cell. He was a good twenty yards off the path—I suspect he took off through the woods because he was being pursued. There was an arrow in his back, though our infirmarian thought that the arrow did not kill him immediately, but he died from loss of blood after perhaps dragging himself over a good stretch of terrain. The body was much deteriorated, the face very nearly unrecognizable. But his habit, his hair coloring, his size, all made it fairly clear. It had to be Brother Grunamund."

"Much deteriorated, you say," Merlin mused. "Enough that he may have been killed about the same time as Nascien himself?"

The abbot pursed his lips "It's certainly possible…" he said.

"Most likely, then, I'd say," Merlin responded. "Almost certainly struck down by the same hand. He fled, perhaps, when Nascien was murdered right before his eyes—likely he was unarmed. I suppose the killer had some skill with the bow, and wounded him as he ran, but somehow lost his wounded prey in the woods. And Grunamund, knowing help might be within reach, was trying to drag himself here…but finally found it too much, alas."

"Alas indeed," the abbot sighed.

"Oh, stifle your 'alases'," Gareth cut in. "Do I need to remind you we're talking about a monk, sworn to devote himself to a holy life of peace and godliness, cut down by fellow conspirators while trying to overthrow his king and destroy good knights of the Round Table?"

"Perhaps," Merlin conceded. "But my conjecture is that both he and Brother Nascien were killed because they were backing out of this devil's contract they had made with the conspirators of Corbenic. If so, his death came not as punishment for his sins, but as retaliation for his renunciation of that sin. Where is the justice in that?"

"It is never profitable to second guess divine justice," the abbot mused. "We may know something about the actions of these men on earth, but we know nothing of the state of their souls, now or prior to their deaths. But they are beyond our judgment now."

"Well *somebody* isn't," I burst in, redirecting the conversation. "And whoever it is, he's terribly good with a bow. Remember Sir Dinadan was killed by arrows as well."

"And who are we left with, then?" Sir Gareth prodded. "That squire, that Golagros. But he seems unlikely to be behind all of this…"

"Nothing but a pawn," Merlin said, "whose king is maimed and whose queen is controlling the board."

"Well if that pawn has become a white knight, then that's who I'm fighting tomorrow. But fighting I am. The leaders of Corbenic will surrender to me and be brought in bondage back to Camelot, or they will learn what a true sword of Arthur can do." And with that, Sir

Gareth rose from the table, and went to spread out his blanket and pallet to get some sleep. The rest of us, on cue, decided he was right, and it was time for us to catch some sleep, if we were to be up and on our way to the castle in the morning.

As Merlin and I spread out our own sleep gear, the abbot rose and made his way to the door. "Blessings on you tonight," he said, "and tomorrow as well, if you choose to be on your way before breakfast."

Merlin nodded his head in the abbot's direction and told him, "I apologize, my lord, that we will not be attending compline. But it is important for us to be moving toward our goal as early as possible. We need to keep the element of surprise," he said this with some irony, glancing over toward Sir Gareth, who seemed oblivious.

But he did stand up and call to Brother Lawrence, "My lord? Could I have a private word with you before you prepare for compline?"

"Of course, my son," the abbot answered, nodding in assent. "Come with me now, if you will."

As the two of them left and Merlin and I blew out the candles in the refectory, settling in to sleep as best we could, I looked at Merlin and asked his now shadowy figure, "What do you suppose that's about?"

Merlin rolled over and said without much interest, "Confession, of course."

It seemed odd to me, and I lay awake, anticipating Sir Gareth's return. When he did come back into the room and let himself down onto his pallet with a deep sigh, I whispered, "Taking a page from your brother Gawain's book, are you, my lord?"

Gareth gave a soft snicker and replied, "Always hedge your bets, Gildas my lad." And then, in a more serious vein, he went on. "Gawain is as sinful a knight as there is among the retinue of the Round Table. But he is among the most faithful. Whenever there is a danger he may not come back from a quest or a challenge, he confesses his sins. He has always come back from those encounters, but one day he may not. I go tomorrow into I know not what danger—as your Merlin has already harped upon enough."

"Not half enough if you're still determined to do it," came a grumbling from the other side of the room.

"You heard the abbot say that we can never understand God's

justice, and who knows but whether He may see fit to end my time tomorrow, even though I carry right on my side. If that should happen, I want to go off with a clean slate. That much, at least, I can say I have learned from my brother."

I nodded. Which, of course, he couldn't see in the dark. But I said no more, and laid my head down, as Gareth settled in for the night himself. A few more seconds passed, until we heard another grumble from Merlin's side of the room: "Poppycock" was his last word on the subject.

***

The land had become barren, with overgrown fields gone fallow and a paucity of trees. I recognized the deserted abbey, crumbling and overgrown with weeds and wild flowers, buried in last season's dead and rotting leaves. We pushed on in silence as we approached the sluggish river, empty now of any sign of the maimed fisher king. We got off our horses and led them up the craggy tor, sparing them the ordeal of dragging themselves up the steep slopes while carrying Gareth and me in our heavy chain mail.

From the top of the tor we looked down upon the square, dark fortress of Corbenic, an island surrounded by the watery moat fed by the murky water of the stream, in the midst of a brown infertile sea. We led the horses down, mounting them again at the base of the tor. Readying himself for whatever was about to follow, Sir Gareth put on his helmet and took hold of his battle lance, carrying his sword across his shoulders, and the three of us approached the castle gate. This time there was no open drawbridge welcoming us. In fact, there was no sign of life anywhere we looked in the castle at all. It appeared to be as deserted as the ramshackle monastery we had passed on the way. I began to despair of our success here: Had word of Sir Gareth's coming reached King Pelles and his daughter? Had they abandoned the castle and fled north, perhaps to join Arthur's enemies elsewhere—say, in Orkney, at Mordred's castle?

We stood speechless, directly across the moat from the gate into Corbenic, and waited in silence for perhaps a furlong way or two. But by then Merlin was having none of it. He called up to the barbican over the drawbridge in his loudest wizard voice: "Ahoy in the castle Corbenic! Let King Pelles and the Princess Elaine know that they can no longer rest undetected in their crimes. Let it be known that the king's champion, Sir Gareth, has arrived to dole out the king's justice. Surrender and we will do you no harm, but take you prisoners to Camelot, there to answer for your crimes before the king's bench."

There were a few more moments of silence as we scanned the battlements on the crenelated walls of the castle, and I could see the look of frustration on the mage's face, when suddenly a low, deep feminine voice broke the silence, booming out from the barbican:

"My father is dead," the lady Elaine called. "He finally succumbed to those wounds that have plagued him since the agent of your King Arthur maimed him those many years ago. This castle is in mourning. Be gone, you marauders at my gate, and know that when my son returns to claim his kingdom you will be among the first on whom his vengeance will fall! He will deal with you immediately after he slays his father, that recreant, faithless Lancelot du Lac."

I looked at Merlin with raised eyebrows, and Sir Gareth raised his visor, his own brow knitted in puzzlement, and whispered to us, "She's balmy, that's what she is!"

Merlin pondered for a brief moment over how to respond to this irrational self-deception, before he called out again to the barbican, "Your son's kingdom is not of this world. He has reconciled with Lancelot his father, and has gone to seek a higher mode of loving. You are alone, my lady. Surrender to us, and we will return with you and any of your retinue that remain to Camelot. The king will certainly be merciful."

There was another pause, but this time no words followed. Within the barbican across the moat I could see a quick movement, a flash of blonde hair, and then, before my eye had a chance to register the danger, a long bow appeared and the shaft of an arrow hurtled toward us like a thunderbolt, then buried itself in Sir Gareth's upper chest, piercing his chain mail. At the attack, Ajax reared up and whinnied. Stunned, Gareth lost his balance and tumbled backwards off his horse. If he hadn't been wearing his helmet, he would have crushed his head like a melon. As it was, he was knocked unconscious. And another arrow flew in, missing him by inches and burying itself in the ground a hair's breadth from his prone body.

Merlin was kneeling down to search Gareth's wounds, and I jumped down from Achilles and tried to lead him and Ajax to form a screen in front of Sir Gareth, but that lasted only a few seconds, as the next arrow pierced Ajax's rear flank and caused him to rear and buck wildly before galloping off out of range. I grabbed Sir Gareth's shield and knelt at his side, holding the shield up for protection as another arrow whizzed down that I was just able to deflect. Merlin let out an angry growl as he rose to his feet and, running toward the moat until he was as close to the barbican as he could get, reared his arm back and hurled it forward, with a shout of "Incendia!" A fireball arced through the air and struck directly at the face of the barbican, bursting before the arrow slit from which Elaine had been firing. We heard a commotion and the arrows stopped, so that it seemed clear she had fled from that particular nest.

I turned around to look at Gareth, who to my great relief was stirring into consciousness. "My lord!" I exclaimed happily, raising his head slightly as I knelt in the dust. Merlin had rushed back by then, and cautioned me, "Don't move him until I have a chance to search his wound!" The old necromancer knelt as well and gingerly fingered the arrow that had embedded itself in Gareth's chest, just below the right shoulder. "It should not be mortal," he murmured, "and he should recover from this. But we should get him back to Saint Sebastian's Abbey as quickly as we may."

"Well, *he* can hear you, you know," Gareth spoke groggily. "And *he* says we can't abandon this task until we've taken that lunatic woman prisoner."

As if in answer, we heard the creaking of the drawbridge lowering, and as it came down it revealed, to our horror, a knight in full armor astride a pure white horse. The armor was like polished alabaster, and the shield blank and white as well.

From where his dazed head rested in the crook of Merlin's left arm, Sir Gareth's eyes opened weakly and in a voice stern though faint he commanded, "Arm yourself, Gildas of Cornwall. Your time has come."

So it was indeed up to me. And if I failed, Gareth and Merlin too would be defenseless against this phantom avenger who had already killed or wounded at least half a dozen of Arthur's best knights. I picked up Gareth's helmet from the ground and was slipping it on when, over my shoulder, I caught a glimpse of the white knight kicking his horse into a gallop, lowering his lance, and coming toward us. It was a villainous act, without regard to even the crudest sense of chivalry, but that was no surprise—this was the knight, after all, who had slain the unarmed Sir Safer without warning. I did the first thing I could think of: I grabbed Sir Gareth's shield and held it up at the last second when the knight bore down with his lance. It forced him to deal a glancing blow to the shield, but, more importantly, the unexpected block to his thrust threw the knight off balance completely, and as his horse galloped past, he began swaying and jerking in his saddle as he strove to stay upright while his destrier continued to gallop toward the river.

It gave me the precious time I needed to mount Achilles—as quickly as I could with the helmet, shield, and fifty pounds of chain mail on my back—and turn to meet the white knight head on. Merlin handed me Sir Gareth's sharp leaf-pointed battle lance. "I wish I had another fireball to help you with this time, but I spent all I had on that princess archer. Give it your all, my boy, for Arthur, for Logres, and for your bloody Cornwall as well!"

I grasped the twelve-foot weapon by the hand-grip and lodged the skirted part into my right armpit, proffering the solid oaken lance while covering my left side as well as I could with my master's golden shield, emblazoned with its silver unicorn rampant, holding it by its riveted grip and resting it on Achilles' neck. I found myself wishing that I had brought my jousting saddle, with its protecting pommelto in front and its raised cantle behind to help keep me in the saddle. I would have to joust in my riding saddle, and hope to keep my balance, whatever the strength of the white knight's blow.

By now he had righted himself, turned his horse, and begun to bear down on me, his own lance proffered and urging his horse into a gallop. I leaned forward at the optimal thirty-degree angle, and inclined the lance slightly to the left, to pass the white knight on that side. I squeezed Achilles with my thighs, urging him into a trot and then a canter, hoping to reach full gallop just as the white knight met us. My feet pushed hard into my stirrups and I tried to aim for the rivets at the center of the white knight's blank shield. I tensed my arm just as he struck my shield solidly with his lance, and I was able to ward off the blow, but I knew that my lance thrust was poorly done. I'd had too little time to focus on the offense since he had come upon me so fast, and the blow glanced weakly off his shield to the left.

I stopped Achilles' gallop with a touch of my spurs, and turned to ready myself for the next joust. Focus on the four rivets, I remembered Sir Gareth telling me. "Your left hand will help prevent you from losing, but your right hand is the only thing that will help you win." Remember that, I kept telling myself, as my heart began to hammer so that I thought I could actually see my hauberk vibrating with the beat. Focus, Gildas, I told myself. This is the knight who killed Sir Safer, who wounded Sir Ywain and Sir Gawain. This is the person responsible for Sir Dinadan's death. And for dear Colgrevaunce. He cannot be victorious here, or it will be Gareth and Merlin added to that list.

My mind was focused, and now all of my hate was focused as well. I felt like a berserker, giving Achilles his head and galloping full tilt at the White Knight. He seemed to sense my rage and determination, and I thought I even saw him hesitate for an instant. But my mind was on those four rivets at the center of his shield, and I was gripping my own shield with all the strength of my left arm, while added to the force of my right was the speed and power of Achilles' formidable charge. I felt a strong jolt in my shield arm, and an even stronger one in my right side, almost simultaneously. But I felt the pressure on my shield arm disappear as quickly as it had come, and felt my lance push forward through whatever it had encountered. When I spurred Achilles to a stop and spun him around to survey the field, I saw first the splintered remains of what had been the white knight's lance, and then saw the knight himself, lying on his back on the ground where my blow had knocked him.

I rode quickly up to him and dismounted. Though he seemed stunned, he was trying to pull his sword from his scabbard and to get up, but I had my sword out faster and held the point under his chin, within striking distance of his carotid artery. "Make another move toward that sword and I'll slice your treacherous throat and think no more of it than killing swine."

"A lovely image, that," Merlin said as he came up behind me. "Perhaps you should work on your taunts, young Gildas. But as for your fighting prowess, God's biceps, you have given us a surprise, dispatching this fellow so quickly. You may be a dunce, but you're a formidable one. Now let me relieve him of that sword, and we can talk reason to him. Listen!" he addressed the overcome knight now kneeling weaponless in the dust with my sword still at his throat. "You are going to the court of King Arthur, there to stand trial for your crimes against the king and his knights. If you answer our questions truthfully, things will go much easier for you!"

"I'm not sure how reasonable I feel like being, old man," I answered, flicking my sword into his neck enough to draw a drop of blood. "How many of our friends is he responsible for killing or hurting? How reasonable was he when he cut down Sir Safer without warning?"

"Vat wuven nee!" came a muffled voice from inside the great white helmet. I looked at him, puzzled, and then said, "Why don't you take off your helmet, fellow, so we can understand what on earth you're saying." I took off my own helmet to listen, but did so gingerly, careful not to lower my sword from his gullet.

When the White Knight removed his own helmet, to no one's surprise he revealed the close-cropped brown hair and freckled nose of the young squire Golagros. "I said," Golagros asserted, breathing heavily, "that it wasn't me that killed your Sir Safer. That was Brother Grunamund. And it was Nascien who wounded Sir Gawain and Sir Ywain, and brought down King Bagdemagus. I...I admit it was I who killed Sir Gliglois, but it was a fair fight."

"Except for the fact that you attacked him without provocation, I'm pretty sure," I responded.

"So you're saying that the White Knight was never a single knight, but only one of you three dressed in white armor," Merlin began. "I suspected as much, since this White Knight appeared everywhere in the forests of Logres. He'd need to have had supernatural powers to have been in so many places almost at once."

"That was Nascien's idea," the squire told us. "He figured if the White Knight was popping up anywhere and everywhere, then Arthur's knights would think he was something supernatural and be confused, edgy, maybe easier to overcome. And it worked, pretty much."

"What about the potions mixed by Brother Bertrand?" I wanted to know. "Was that Nascien's idea too? To set the knights against one another?"

"Not the potions. Nascien knew Bertrand from the monastery, and he more or less blackmailed him into hearing Gawain's confessions, but what he really wanted was to trap Lancelot. That was the main target for Nascien and Grunamund—they wanted Lancelot dead, if they could manage it. But the potions—that was *her* idea."

"The Princess Elaine," Merlin said, with a note of triumph. "So essentially this whole conspiracy was her scheme, is that what you're saying? Ha! The mother of light and dark, or of good and evil, or whatever in blazes it was. My 'vision' proves true again." As the old man pumped out his chest, I felt a convulsion in my own, and coughed a bit. There was some sort of mist drifting around us there.

I looked over to where Sir Gareth had raised himself up on one elbow and was watching us barely within earshot. He coughed a bit as well, though perhaps it was to get our attention. "Say," he called in a fairly weak voice. "Can we finish up the small talk and get me to a surgeon before, I don't know, before I bleed to death perhaps?"

"God's wounds, Gareth, you're right. Let's finish the questioning later…"

But Golagros was already pouring out information. It was as if his defeat had allowed him to release all the pressure of the secrets he had been bearing for the past several months—or perhaps several years. "Lady Elaine was essentially in control from early on," he admitted. "It was the king's idea to mate her with Lancelot, as I understand it, but once she had taken that step, she went on to plan the course of action afterward. She wanted Galahad to take the kingdom and to be the power behind the throne. She was the one that recruited Nascien and Grunamund to help with the conspiracy. The Grail quest was Nascien's idea, but she used it to her advantage. She wanted Lancelot dead as much as Grunamund or Nascien did, but she wanted Arthur dethroned as well. And she was willing to do anything to accomplish it. So Bertrand's potions. She was closely involved in both Sir Gawain's trap—allowing herself to be molested by Sir Ironside—and in the tricking of Lionel, setting herself up as the damsel in distress to lure Bors from his brother's rescue. She is the one who killed Sir Dinadan after I had captured him as the White Knight—he had made some rude joke about her being the cast off sheath of Lancelot's sword, and she put an arrow through his eye."

I coughed again. By now the smoke was too obvious to ignore, and I began looking around to see what the source might be. Merlin was focused, though, on questioning the squire. "And what about King Pelles?" he asked. "Was she telling the truth? Is he really dead?"

Now Golagros looked pained, and his freckled nose wrinkled as his brown eyes pooled with unwonted tears. "She's really quite mad by now, you know. The king died three days ago. She has him there in the chapel—she hasn't let anyone, even the chaplain, in to see him. Claims that the Grail will have the power to bring him back to life. Everyone else has deserted her. The men who helped with the earlier trickery of Bors and Lionel and the others—they had gone before you two visited the first time. And after Brother Bertrand had been killed, cut with his own knife, as you might say, when Nascien and Grunamund wanted to pull out and even talked of confessing to the king, she met them at the hermit's hovel, lulled them into a false security, and then dispatched them. After that, everyone was wary of her. But now, with her father…they've all left. The squires, the servants, all the retainers, even Father Benedict."

"But not you," Merlin pushed. "And why haven't you…what is that smoke?" Merlin broke off and began coughing as a cloud of black smoke was now drifting over us.

Once again a weak voice came to us from where Gareth lay immobile on the field. "The castle! It's coming from the castle!"

We all looked with horror toward that fortress, and saw where the smoke billowed from the residential side of the castle grounds. "The chapel!" Golagros shouted, and sprang up before I could threaten him any more with my sword. He ran toward the drawbridge, with me close at his heels and Merlin keeping up as best he could.

We raced across the bailey to the doors of the great hall, from which we could have made our way into the chapel. By now we could see flames crackling from the windows of the chapel, and Golagros pulled and banged upon the door to the hall, but it was bolted from the inside. I even took a few whacks at the steel handle with my sword, but to no avail.

"I think I may be able to climb through one of the windows into the hall," the squire called to me, and tried to leap up to grab hold of the window ledge, but it was far too high for him. And after two tries we saw that the smoke had begun to pour from the hall windows as well, and then we saw the ceiling, lined as it was with those magnificent wooden panels, burst into flames itself.

"It's no use," Merlin said quietly behind us. "If the king's retainers were still in attendance, and the squires, we might have formed a kind of bucket brigade, pouring water on the fire from the well, but that could never be done with only three of us, and besides," he looked up at the flames rocketing skyward from the hall's wooden ceiling, "the fire has already spread too far. There's nothing we can do."

"There has to be!" Golagros cried, frustrated and weeping unabashedly. "She cannot perish like this…she cannot be left to…" he trailed off, and swung his hands and limbs, writhing without direction in his grief and frustration. "I was her page…" he said, as if that explained it all.

And to me it did. I could only imagine myself, and the feelings I would have if Queen Guinevere were in similar straits. Oh, I could understand this squire's motivation from the beginning. Even as he saw the moral weakness of the Princess Elaine's conspiracy, even as he saw the madness of her final days, his loyalty would never waver. He was hers until death. And, it seemed, perhaps beyond. I was looking into a distorted mirror at what I would myself have become, had I been page to Elaine and not to Guinevere.

But Corbenic was dead, and there was no saving it. The rich tapestries, the finely crafted wooden ceilings and trim, doors and furniture. The rich vestments, even the Grail itself were now perishing in the refiner's purifying fire, and with them would burn the body of the king who had set all this grief in motion, and the daughter who had kept it going to this ignoble end. When we heard the agonized, low-voiced wail of the lady Elaine's death throes, we knew that the quest was over. And we took the slumping, shattered Golagros into custody. We had a long ride in front of us, needing to get Sir Gareth, and Ajax, to the infirmary at Saint Sebastian's Abbey, and the squire Golagros to his trial in Camelot.

CHAPTER NINETEEN

THE TALE OF SIR BORS

Merlin and I dropped Sir Gareth off at Saint Sebastian's Abbey, where Abbot Lawrence and the other monks were saddened and astonished to learn what had happened at Corbenic. But they took Sir Gareth in, and weak as he was, Brother Luke still assured us he would recover—as would Ajax, whose wounded flank proved to be less serious than we had at first feared.

Getting Golagros to Camelot and before the king then became our only priority, and when Merlin and I left the abbey, we pushed our horses hard to arrive before noon on the second day. On the way I grilled the squire fairly closely in hope of finding something that would implicate Sir Mordred in the conspiracy as well, but nothing Golagros told us conflicted with Mordred's own story, and Merlin finally told me to drop it, I was beating a dead horse. In Camelot, Merlin presented the case before the king in the great hall, with the rest of the court looking on. Golagros was interviewed and freely admitted to his part in the conspiracy, implicating King Pelles, Brother Nascien, Brother Grunamund, the hermit Bertrand, but especially the lady Elaine, who now more than ever emerged as the chief architect of the conspiracy. And all those principals were now dead, as it happened. I admit that I was hoping for leniency for the poor squire, who had after all only followed the lead of his superiors and was young enough to learn from his mistakes, and to become a valuable knight in his own right.

And the king, it turned out, was of like mind. He found Golagros's loyalty to his mistress a mitigating factor in the one serious crime he could be convicted of himself—the death of Sir Gliglois—particularly since Golagros's own confession was the only evidence against him, and according to his story that death had resulted from a fair joust. The squire's only sentence was not to leave Camelot, at least until the king had decided what to do with him.

And so the case of the great Grail conspiracy was over. We had solved it, but it had been a frustrating process. So many knights had died, as had all the conspirators. And so much had sprung from the mistakes or the unanswered wrongs of the distant past. Sir Galahad himself had been conceived years ago chiefly as a means of paying back Arthur's realm for the sins of the reckless Sir Balin, and the monks had become involved to avenge the perceived slights of their friend Sir Brumand, and his death in the Siege Perilous, all so very long ago. The story is never complete, it seems.

But Camelot was a drearier place for long months after the arrest of the squire Golagros. Eventually all the surviving knights made their way back to Camelot, many of them disgruntled and bitter at having spent the better part of a year on what they had come to regard as an impossible quest and a colossal waste of time. Sir Colgrevaunce was dead, and Sir Dinadan. I missed them more than I could have anticipated. The absence of Sir Safer had sunk Sir Palomides into a deep melancholy. Sir Ironside, Sir Uwain, Sir Grummor Grummorson, Sir Gliglois, all were dead as well. Gawain, Ywain, Gareth, and King Bagdemagus had all recovered from their wounds, but Bagdemagus had retired, of course, and the others still dragged about in a deep gloom. For this they had ample cause: Three other knights—Sir Bors, Sir Perceval, and Sir Galahad himself—had not returned from the quest, and were feared dead. Lancelot, who upon his return had nothing but confidence in his son's destiny, was quiet now, and moped about the castle without purpose.

So you can imagine the relief when, on Ash Wednesday of all days, a cry came from Robin Kempe in the barbican over the gate into Camelot, calling out that a lone knight was approaching.

Was it one of ours? Everyone in the bailey was frozen in anticipation. Robin, who was just as eager as the rest of us to see if it might be one of our missing knights returned at last—from where? From prison? From some foreign land? From a long convalescence after a serious battle wound?—Robin called out again: "It's a great brown destrier he's riding. I can make out some color on the shield— it's a red background…"

Quickly I did a mental checklist. Sir Galahad would have a red cross on his shield…but his horse would have been white. Unless he'd lost his original mount and was returning on a borrowed destrier, or one won in battle. As for the others…

Robin called again, this time with full certainty: "The coat of arms is an Ox argent rampant on a field Gules!"

A huge cheer went up among the knights and squires in the bailey. For the silver ox, rearing up, on a bright red field was the coat of arms of Sir Bors de Ganis. And the horse? "It's Pegasus!" Robin cried in excitement. Bors still rode his great brown horse, the one he would let no one else care for—no stable hand, no squire had ever brushed or fed the great Pegasus, but Sir Bors cared for that horse as if it had been his own child.

I looked around the yard, and could see that the gloom that had loured over Camelot since the end of the quest had lifted, at least for the moment, in the realization that in fact, the quest had not ended—not, at least, until now. Sir Lancelot was of all men the most buoyed by the news. As Robin ordered the drawbridge opened, Sir Bors appeared. He was gaunt, dusty, worn out and sagging in the saddle from long and weary riding, and he hesitated a moment before entering, seeing the great crowd that had gathered to greet him. Cautiously he dismounted and led his horse across the bridge to the cheers of the assembly. By now the news had swept through the halls, the kitchen, the solars, the battlements, and the barracks in the keep, and there were hundreds now cheering the returned hero. Bors scanned the crowd until he saw Lancelot pushing his way to the front, and you could read in Bors' face the relief he felt—as if he could now let go the great burden he had been carrying for the better part of the year. He embraced Lancelot and they whispered greetings to one another, and I could see the tears welling up in Bors' dark eyes as once again he scanned the gathered throng.

But he could not find his brother. I had glimpsed Sir Lionel when Robin had first identified Pegasus: He had been hanging back on the outskirts of the great crowd. Now he had disappeared again. Ashamed, as well he might be, to face his brother again, and in front of all that mob. Perhaps he would never have the courage to speak to Bors again. Perhaps the fact that Bors was alive had been enough to satisfy him.

***

The king was savvy enough to know that far from being the greatest court in Christendom, Camelot had been floundering the past few months, its self-confidence weakened in the wake of the disastrous quest, and he recognized that the time had come to change the discourse. Having met privately with Bors de Ganis, Arthur had opted to bring all the court together in the great hall and give Bors a chance to tell the story of how the Grail was achieved. It was Arthur saying, "Do you see? We did not fail in the quest after all. Knights of the Table Round had been successful—indeed, only Knights of the Table Round could have possibly attained such a goal." Arthur's knights must be made to realize that they should be proud of their efforts, and especially of the efforts of those who saw the quest to its conclusion.

And so Merlin and I were packed with a few hundred other courtiers into the great hall, the squires Thomas and Lovell close by. Sir Gareth and his brother Sir Gawain stood on the dais against the wall of the room, one on each side of Arthur, who sat on his throne wearing his heavy crown of state. A royal blue cloak with ermine trim rested on his broad shoulders, and he actually held a golden scepter of power—quite an unusual gesture for him, but he was determined to make this afternoon one that was filled with glory. On the other side of the hall, seated high on a dais of her own, Guinevere sat, a coronet of gold encircling her wavy golden hair, which was swept up, again uncharacteristically, on the top of her head. She wore a gown of royal blue samite fringed with ermine, a perfectly coordinated match for her husband. They were leaving nothing to chance in this display of royal pomp and power. Seated on either side of her were the queen's ladies-in-waiting—the ladies Anna and Vivien at Guinevere's left, and my lady Rosemounde in privileged position on her right. It had been a great relief to me that Mordred had not bolted back to Orkney when he had the chance. Or it may not have been his choice: The king was an astute politician, and must have recognized that keeping Mordred close was much safer than giving him a wide scope to hatch his plots. Not that Rosemounde's presence at the castle enabled me to see her even clandestinely: Mordred's threats were a significant deterrent to my ardor, and I would do nothing to put my lady Rosemounde in harm's way.

The buzz in the hall was raucous, and the king pursed his lips in annoyance. He handed his scepter to Sir Gawain, who lifted it and pounded it several times on the dais, until all voices had ceased and all eyes were on the king. "Know," he began, "that I have called you here for a court entertainment, to cheer you after what has been a long summer and an even longer winter. Sir Bors de Ganis has agreed to regale us with his account of the successful end of the Quest of the Holy Grail, an end for which only Sir Perceval, Sir Galahad, and Sir Bors himself were present. Sir Bors," he called into the crowd. "If you would, please come to the dais so that everyone can see you, and hear you. Give him your attention, Lordings, and you'll find his account entertaining and informative!"

I had some serious doubts about that, as did the other squires around me. "Pull the other one!" Thomas said, snickering quietly. Sir Bors was as doughty a knight as any in Camelot. He was broad and thickly muscled, not quite as tall as his close kinsman Sir Lancelot, but wider and bulkier. He had cleaned up from the disheveled drifter who had arrived at the castle two short days prior. His brown hair was close-cropped, and he had shaved so that his face bore only his customary tiny pointed beard on the end of his chin. He was a paragon of courtesy, and respected by every man and woman in the court. But, as many of the knights liked to joke, his name could not have been more appropriate: "Bors is a bore," was something of a watchword, especially among the younger knights. Don't get me wrong, Bors was as courteous and kind as any knight in Camelot. He was just not very exciting: He was a man who lived mainly in his head, and not his heart. His decisions were rational and well thought out—and never, never emotional.

And so I didn't expect to be swept away by Bors' passionate tale—as I sometimes was by Sir Gareth's stories. But if *what* he had to say—the completion of the quest—was interesting enough, the *way* he said it should matter little. Bors mounted the dais, hung his head, gathering his thoughts, and finally raised his face to the assembled court and began his tale.

"You are all no doubt aware," Bors began, "of how I passed the early part of this quest—of the regrettable deaths of Sir Colgrevaunce and the hermit, Brother Bertrand." I looked around the crowd in the hall, searching for Sir Lionel, but if he was there I couldn't find him. I did see, in the far corner, Bess of Caerleon, Colgrevaunce's grieving widow, who at mention of his murder broke down in tears, to be comforted by a few of the women who stood round her.

"When I rode off from there, I hoped not to encounter Lionel again on the quest. There could be no happy reunion until the wounds of that encounter were healed, both within and without. In taking my adventure through the forest, I met another Cistercian monk coming the other way. I recognized him as Brother Grunamund, and, disturbed about the battle with Lionel, I felt the need for spiritual guidance, to try to understand what had happened.

"But I had asked the wrong monk.

"Grunamund told me I was to blame for choosing to help the woman over my own brother. Sir Lionel, he told me, relied upon me and so was my responsibility. His life was in danger to boot, Grunamund told me, and what was the woman likely to lose? Her virginity? If she was deflowered in a rape, she would still be a virgin in God's eyes. Therefore my choice had truly been a sinful one, and displayed my lack of trust in God's mercy.

"I could not credit his reasoning, but out of respect for his tonsure I did not dispute him, and he went on to give me a penance: I was to ride to a castle over the next hill, where a Lady was in need of my services. I took Pegasus over the hill and found a pleasant castle where I was received by a large assembly of ladies, six of whom brought me to the top of the tall tower of the castle keep, where the lady of the castle stood, bedecked in a long sheer gown of white samite that left little to the imagination. She was petitely built, with golden hair and a deep, soulful voice."

I looked at Merlin and he raised his bushy brows at me. So Bors had encountered the lady Elaine one on one. Clearly she had been unsuccessful in whatever trap she had laid for him. But how?

"And she told me she had loved me from afar for many years, and she would have no other lover but me—and she demanded that I become her lover there and then. Now the proposal was so inappropriate and so suspicious to me that it would have been absurd for me to have accepted. But she increased the pressure, threatening, insanely, to throw herself to her death off that tower if I did not become her lover. To make matters worse, all of the other ladies began to weep, and begged me to save their lady's life. I admit I had a few qualms, but with all the unexplained deceptions that had been revealed since the beginning of this quest, I could scarcely credit this threat. I admit to being somewhat surprised when the lady turned her back to me, stepped to the edge of the tower, and threw herself down. Taken aback, I stepped to the edge and saw a body swathed in white lying at the foot of the tower."

A collective gasp filled the hall. I heard voices whispering words like "heartless" and "callous prig." I admit I would have felt the same, if I didn't already know that the lady Elaine quite obviously had not died. And Sir Bors surely had figured that out himself.

"I admit that one reason I was sure the whole thing was a trick was that I had, after some thought, recognized the lady as the same one I had earlier rescued from what I now realized was a staged 'rape.' Which meant that, though she had *apparently* fallen to her death, that had to be a trick as well. And further, Brother Grunamund was not to be trusted, but must be behind many of these bizarre events—including my brother's unwarranted attack on me and Sir Colgrevaunce."

"Hmmph," Merlin said in my ear. "We should have had him with us! We would have solved this case a lot sooner." I nodded, and at the mention of Colgrevaunce's name, looked around to see whether

Bess was still where she had been standing earlier. But I had lost her in the crowd.

"Well," Bors continued, "at that point I nearly despaired that the quest was all for naught. If this Grunamund and his crew had tricked us all into searching for a phantom in the woods, they could certainly have no good motive, and I should probably forsake the quest and return to Camelot, where it may be I was needed more. But somehow I couldn't give up on the notion that above the machinations of these people, the idea of the Grail was inspiring and spiritually valuable— and I had only the look on Sir Galahad's face when he saw it above the Round Table to go on. Something inside of me—call it my soul— longed for whatever Galahad had seen. And so I rode on, believing. And that belief was confirmed when serendipity brought me to a wide river, and a boat manned by Sir Galahad himself and Sir Perceval."

"Ah," Sir Lancelot cried from the first row of listeners. "I know that boat! The boat on which I found the lady Dandrane!"

Bors looked up in some surprise. "The very same. I heard her story from Sir Perceval—her purity, her sacrifice, her acting as Galahad's inspiration. But she was dead and buried before I joined them on that boat." He had addressed this last mainly to Lancelot, but now raised his head and his voice to address the rest of the crowd. "I learned of their adventures from Perceval and Galahad themselves, and feel honor-bound to relate them here because…" He paused and looked around, as if gauging who he was likely to hurt by his revelations. "Because I regret to tell you all that they will not be returning to this court. One at least, is now a member of the Heavenly court. The other has joined a holy order in the east, to live out his days in pure contemplation of the divine spark.

"But surely I'm getting ahead of myself. Perceval, it seems, had left Camelot in high spirits, thinking to catch up to Galahad and even engage in a kind of competition with him to see who could be the first to find the Grail. But the Grail quest was never a competition. Before long Perceval was beset by twenty knights, one in white armor, and brought down, but was saved when Galahad himself rode in among his attackers, scattering them and saving Perceval, who longed then to join with Galahad to seek the Grail together. But Galahad told him he must achieve the Grail on his own, and rode off through the woods. Disgruntled, Perceval rode until he came to a hermit's cell—that same hermit that had sheltered my brother and…was later killed. He confessed to the hermit, and accepted a small repast there, drinking a cup of wine the hermit had supplied."

Merlin scowled and looked down at me. "Accepting a drink from that hermit is never a good idea."

"When Sir Perceval left the hermit's cell, he says, he felt as if he had entered a world of faerie, where nothing was what it seemed. His horse grew lame, and a lady dressed in black appeared and loaned him a powerful black destrier, but as soon as he mounted the horse it began to gallop at a blinding speed, covering four days' journey in but an hour until, climbing to the edge of a high cliff, it threatened to leap into the sea with Perceval on its back. He says that at that moment he crossed himself out of habit—and the horse quite suddenly shook him off and plunged in flames to its death in the sea."

There was a deal of scoffing among the assembled nobles (I think I even heard one mutter "pull the other one"). But Bors merely shrugged. "I only report what Perceval reported to me. In his mind, he was convinced that these were real events. Cast upon the desert shore, Perceval witnessed a great, proud lion step out of the forest."

"My lion!" cried Sir Ywain. "Alive and well?"

Sir Bors looked at him with sympathy. "Very likely yours, yes," he answered. "I mean, as far as I know, he is the only lion in Logres. But what Perceval said is that the lion was immediately attacked by a great dragon, spewing vile poison and attacking the noble beast's flank. Without thinking, Perceval drew his sword and charged the serpent on foot, plunging his sword into the belly of the creature and slitting it lengthwise. The dragon fell dead, and the lion, in gratitude, fell at Perceval's feet, bowing its head into the sand."

"That's my boy!" Ywain cried, his eyes glistening with tears. "Only he would do that—I've seen him do it." A number of us felt uplifted by the news that Sir Perceval had seen the noble beast, though we had no way of knowing exactly how long ago this was— and for that matter, we had no way of knowing how accurate that tale was, since the story of the horse seemed wildly fantastical. But not so much as what was coming.

"Now Perceval claimed that after his ordeal with the horse, and his struggle with the serpent, he was worn out, and fell asleep on the beach. When he awoke, the lion had moved on, but a small black ship was just beaching itself. Its crew brought out a grand pavilion and set it up on the shore, and from the boat a beautiful woman came, richly dressed in sable furs and rich black satin. She beckoned to Perceval to come into the pavilion with her where they could talk.

"Now here's what she told him. Or what he says she told him: she was angry with him for having killed the serpent, which was, it seems, her personal pet. That in itself should have been off-putting, I should think, but as she spoke with him she had her servants bringing in fancy dressed meats and strong wine, plenty of wine. And all this time she was plying him with words and licentious glances, and telling him that she is a noblewoman who has been dispossessed by her ruthless half-sister, and she needs a champion to restore her to her former state of glory. Perceval by then was losing his wits, and when they had finished the banquet put before them, she had another bottle of wine brought and sent all her servants away. As soon as they were out, she slipped out of her luxurious garb and lay naked before him, saying he could have her if he became her man there and then.

"Well Perceval, of course, the lusty young man that he is, or was, was more than willing to jump on that offer as soon as he could doff his armor, which he began pulling off eagerly. But just as he readied himself to consummate this act, Perceval, as he tells it, purely by chance—or perhaps by providence—caught sight of his sword where he had cast it to the ground, and the cross made by its hilt put him in mind of the nature of this holy quest he had embarked upon. Without a thought, on impulse, the lad crossed himself.

"And that was all it took. As soon as he had crossed himself, the beautiful pavilion turned upside down and vanished in a cloud of black smoke, and he saw the gentlewoman and all her retinue board the ship, and he lay on the sand panting with shock and exhaustion, and suddenly realizing he had been rescued from the brink of hell cried out to his God, "Lord, protect me, for I have almost forfeited your grace." And as he said it the black-clad noblewoman cursed him from the ship as it pushed off, yelling out that he had betrayed her. The water burned as the ship passed over it. So said Sir Perceval."

I looked at Merlin and raised my right eyebrow. He looked at me and pursed his lips. "Well," he said sotto voce after a moment's pause. "Perceval was always an imaginative lad."

"Imaginative?" I answered. "Off his nut, I'd say."

"Remember he had drunk with Brother Bertrand," Merlin reminded me. "That same drug that pushed Gawain and Lionel to murder might well have caused these kinds of hallucinations in Perceval. Or perhaps it was a different drug altogether. But how are we to know what is delirium and what is tangible truth in Perceval's account?"

"Well," I said, looking down toward the front of the crowd at Sir Ywain. "I hope the part about the lion is true, for Ywain's sake."

"Undoubtedly it is," Merlin replied. "For it seems unlikely that Perceval would have hallucinated the beast's idiosyncrasies so accurately. But that dragon? That seems far-fetched."

"What about the woman who tempted him? By the description it could well have been the lady Elaine herself."

"That is almost certain," Merlin nodded. "Some of the rest—the cloud of smoke, that disappearing flying horse…"

"Pure fantasy," I shrugged. "But real, I suppose, in Perceval's mind."

"When the gentlewoman's boat disappeared, Sir Perceval was feeling disgust with himself for acting worse than a beast himself, for losing his dignity, his courtesy, and perhaps even his soul. In disgust and self-loathing, he drew his sword from his scabbard and rove himself cruelly through the thigh."

Amid the shocked gasps that followed that revelation, I turned to Merlin with deep concern: "We're not talking euphemistically here again, are we?" I asked him.

"God's bodykins, I pray not!"

"You, pray?"

"Figure of speech," Merlin answered me. But Sir Bors went on.

"Perceval fainted from the pain and loss of blood, and lay face down in the sand. It is certain he would have bled to death in that wilderness, had not the boat bearing the lone Sir Galahad—by chance or by design, you may choose for yourself—not grounded itself in the sand at that very moment. Sir Galahad found Perceval, nearly unconscious, and quickly (and skillfully, from what I saw) bound up the wound and staunched the bleeding."

"Then probably the actual thigh…" Merlin whispered to me.

Sir Bors went on now to relate the adventures of Sir Galahad himself that had brought him to that place, and essentially this was the story we had heard earlier from Sir Lancelot, with Bors extolling the virtues of the angel-like Lady Dandrane and her piteous death. Galahad had serendipitously found the funereal boat once again after Sir Lancelot had abandoned it, and cast himself upon the waters to see where God would let him drift, and it had landed him there, on that shore with the bloody Sir Perceval. It was there that Bors finally came upon them by wildest chance or fortune, and the three of them determined to see the quest through to its conclusion together, relying on the boat and God's will to take them where they needed to go.

As it turned out, God must have had a strange plan for them, because when their small boat floated out into the narrow sea between Logres and Gaul, they were almost immediately picked up by a swift sailing Viking warship, bound to the great inland sea toward the Holy Land.

"Sir Perceval was too weak from his wounds to attempt any fight, and Galahad was delighted to be moving in that direction, so I let them disarm me and put my faith in the overall purity and innocence of Galahad, trusting that there was in fact something in him that God would protect," Bors told us. En route, Sir Galahad had prayed fervently for the right to choose the time and place of his own death, and firmly believed—and convinced Bors and Perceval—that God had granted him that right. When they had reached Sarras in the Holy Land, Bors continued, with surprising speed, so sleek and fast was that warship, the three of them were immediately sold as slaves to a Saracen lord of that land. For the first few days, the three of them performed their tasks efficiently and contentedly, taking the lead from Galahad, who saw it all as part of God's plan, though they refused at all times to take part in any Muslim rituals or prayers, and prayed daily among themselves, which their Saracen master was perfectly willing to allow. But on the third day, Galahad, in the midst of a task he was performing, passed a crippled beggar in a public square, whose legs were twisted and deformed from a childhood accident. Galahad, looking to the heavens, called on the power of Christ to heal the lame man, and to the astonishment of all in that place, the cripple got up and walked. You can imagine the furor this caused. The commonfolk were dumbfounded but ecstatic and praised God for the blessing. But the Saracen authorities, and our new master in particular, were highly suspicious, and quickly came to believe that these three foreigners in their midst were demon possessed, for they thought only the power of Satan could heal that illness when their daily prayers to Allah had not done the trick.

"And so Perceval, Galahad, and I were all thrown into prison. We lay in the same chamber, our arms and legs in chains, for days, and given only filthy water to drink. We were brought no food—perhaps they intended to starve us. Perceval and I began to lose all hope, but Galahad reminded us in a strong voice that man does not live by bread alone, but by every word that comes from the Father. And I know you will scarcely credit it, but it was there and then, in that dank prison, in our darkest hour, that this quest of the Grail was achieved.

"For it was there in that cell that the Grail appeared before us. Sir Galahad, of course was the first to see it. His eyes grew wide and glowed with an otherworldly light, and he spoke to it: 'Sacred vessel! Bright relic! You come to fill us with God's word in lieu of food, God's grace instead of wine. These things will sustain us, here and forever, wherever we are, in this world or the next.'

"I saw nothing but the air, but Sir Perceval opened his weak eyes and squinted in the direction of Galahad's speech, then relaxed his dry, cracked lips into the grimace of a smile. 'I see it!' he says. 'Feed me!' he calls out to the Grail. 'Feed me with spiritual food, and I shall not be afraid.' Then he goes off into the twenty-third Psalm, and begins to pray 'Yea though I walk through the valley of the shadow of death, I shall fear no evil, for thou art with me…'

"But still I saw nothing. I think perhaps that I, unlike those two dear souls, am too much of this earth and not sufficiently spiritual to have had sight of that instrument of grace. But I closed my eyes and listened to Perceval intoning the Psalm, and my heart felt strangely filled, in a way I had not felt before. I don't know how to say it but that my mind transcended that time, that place, that prison, and felt itself free and at one with all of God's creation. I felt an overpowering love for God and for all of God's creatures and for all of my fellow sufferers in this wide world, not only my cell-mates there but those who had imprisoned us. For that moment I felt that I knew what it was like to be in heaven."

As a public speaker, Bors was never likely to attract a huge audience, or make his living as a preacher, but in those few moments he did soar beyond the limits of his solid earthly form, and had that great hall mesmerized.

"But we must return to earth or die," he finally continued. "And that is what happened to the three of us in that cage. Shortly after our vision of the Grail, our Saracen guards came to us and told us that, since we were apparently warriors in our own country, the Saracen king had agreed to let us go if we would fight for him in a coming battle against his traditional foes, the 'Shiites' (for the people of Sarras were what are called 'Sunni'). We agreed, and were freed and fed enough to strengthen us. As asked, we donned our armor and fought in the subsequent battle. Perceval and I acquitted ourselves well, I must report, but Sir Galahad was invincible. He defeated anyone in his path, and swept all before him—but, just as in his encounters on the quest here in Logres, he never slew a single enemy, he simply overpowered them and put them out of the battle.

"To make a long story short—and believe me, that is what I am trying to do—the Saracen king of that place was killed in the battle, but his victorious troops were unanimous in making Galahad the new king of Sarras. He accepted with humility, and with Perceval and me as his chief lieutenants, made laws and governed for some two months, establishing a legal system in which the Saracens and Christians of Sarras, the Sunnis and the Shiites as well, could live in peace and mutual respect. Through his works Galahad was, you might say, sharing the grace and peace that the Grail had brought to him with all the people of that land.

"But now, you will recall that I mentioned how Sir Galahad was convinced that the Lord had granted him his wish to die at the time and place of his own request. Well, this past Christmas season was upon us there in Sarras, and Galahad, looking down from the royal palace at the garden of peace he had created, and recalling the joy that had filled his soul with his vision of the Grail, looked up then into the heavens—and he told us that he was seeing a vision of Christ among the angels, and he could not bear absenting himself from that bliss any longer. That was when he asked God to let him die. I am sorry to report to this assembly that, not half an hour later, he seemed suddenly taken with an illness, and slipped gently from this world. When he died, Perceval insisted that he saw the soul of Galahad borne to heaven. You may say," he warned the skeptics among us, looking directly into Merlin's face, "that Galahad likely took poison of some kind, and that Sir Perceval, as he was wont to be, was overcome by his own imagination. And I cannot say that I saw anything of Galahad's soul. But neither did I see him help his passing along by any drink or drug. So think what you like. I know what I think.

"But that is how the quest of the Holy Grail ends. Sir Perceval had been too much in the realms of the spirit to have any desire to return to his former life, and when I left, had determined to join an order of eastern monks there in Sarras. So he will not be returning either. For myself, I am too bound to my connections in this world to leave them before my time:" He nodded to Sir Lancelot. "And so I have returned. And the quest has ended."

There was a burst of spontaneous cheering from the assembled crowd, and knights clapped their hands, smiled at one another, patting one another on the shoulders in a show of rough camaraderie. Arthur's gambit had paid off, it seemed. The quest had not been a failure after all. These three knights, these glorious three, had preserved the honor of the Table Round by seeing the long and arduous quest to its very end. And though two had been lost, this one had returned—this one rare pearl among the ranks of lesser but striving humanity.

The king now rose to speak himself. "Sir Bors, you have acquitted yourself well, and if I may say so, have redeemed the honor of this Order of Chivalry. Welcome home to Camelot, and may you serve here as one of our chief knights for as long as you desire. For now, let us think upon some ample reward to grant you at another time, at least to partly reward you for your great courtesy."

Sir Bors dropped to one knee and bowed his head to his sovereign lord, who placed a hand on his head. As Bors rose, he reiterated what he seemed to want to underscore as the great theme of his tale: "The meaning of the Grail is grace and peace—and the achieving of the Grail is the having of those things in our own hearts. In that spirit I call upon my brother, Sir Lionel, to come forward to me, so that I may make peace with him and embrace him in love."

At that word the crowd parted, and from the back of the hall stepped forward the slow, bent figure of Sir Lionel, his black beard unkempt and his garb disheveled, as his conscience had been eating away at him the more violently since his brother's return. Sir Bors descended and awaited Lionel's approach at the foot of the dais, and when the two met, they fell into one another's arms in a loving embrace.

"Forgive me, brother," Sir Lionel pleaded, choking back tears.

"I do, with all my heart, I do!" Sir Bors answered with equal emotion.

"*But I do not!*" screeched a harsh female voice, coming from a figure that sprang suddenly and without warning from the edge of the crowd. Her hair was flying wildly and from out of the tangle of those locks and her brown smock an arm appeared, arcing quickly and powerfully over her head toward Sir Lionel's unarmed back. It plunged a large cross-hilt dagger some eight inches into Lionel's flesh. Before anyone could move, she had raised her arm again and made a slash at the knight's unprotected throat, so that a burst of blood stained the white sleeves of her blouse before two knights finally restrained her, wrestled the knife from her, and wrenched her arms behind her back. As Sir Bors knelt agonized next to his brother's body, facedown now in a pool of his own blood, Bess of Caerleon stood panting as from an ordeal, shouting, "That is for Colgrevaunce! That is for my poor noble boy!"

Like the rest of the audience, plunged from the apex of good feeling to the depths of anguish in the space of mere seconds, Merlin and I stood mouths agape, staring at the bloody mess that Arthur's hall had become.

"The widow triumphs," I said, as the significance suddenly came to me. "It's your prophesy, Merlin! Bess, the widow triumphs. How could we have known?"

"Yes," Merlin said, his voice dull with horror. "I was right. I predicted it, after all." After a pause, he added, "It would be so much better to be wrong sometimes."

SAINT DUNSTAN'S ABBEY

The mouths of the young monks and novices were hanging open when Brother Gildas finished his tale. It was a twist they hadn't expected, not when it seemed that everything in the sprawling story of the Grail was being wrapped up so neatly. The old monk looked at them with a half-smile, knowing that none of them had anticipated that particular ending. For several moments, no one made a sound. A soft breeze stirred the leaves in the courtyard enclosed by the cloister, where the abbey's oldest monk enjoyed entertaining the youngsters with tales of King Arthur and his knights, a figure who had thrived a generation before any of them was born, and had by now become the stuff of myth and legend.

Brother Gildas, forty years a Benedictine monk of Saint Dunstan's Abbey in Hereford, near the Welsh border, had been telling his tales so long that the abbot and the prior, both of whom had grown into their positions under Brother Gildas's eye, and had spent a good part of their early years listening to him weave the tapestry of Camelot, turned a blind eye to this harmless breech of protocol. Brother Gildas's tales were as much an institution as Saint Dunstan's itself.

"But…but…what happened? Sir Lionel was…did he…" Notker, the dark-eyed young monk with the stammer, began to ask.

"I'm sorry to say that Sir Lionel died of his wounds within the hour. There was no saving him. Mistress Bess had done her work well."

"And what happened to her? Was she punished for her crime?"

queried the thin-lipped, thin-nosed Brother Nennius, who always liked to dig for the details, and seemed to be trying to memorize Brother Gildas's stories.

"Her crime?" Brother Gildas echoed thoughtfully. "She called it justice. Was it her crime? Was it Lionel's? Was it Brother Bertrand's—or Brother Nascien's? Or was the ultimate crime Sir Balin's? The story really is never complete—it goes on and on. But Bess was found to be mad by Arthur's court. She was locked up in the convent of Saint Mary Magdalene near Caerleon—to be watched over by the prioress and the sisters. And she seems to have been content there. It took her from the court, which was a mercy since that place had become nothing but pain for her now that Colgrevaunce was gone. She did the laundry and worked in the gardens at the convent, and was, I think, content with her life."

"Um, wh...what about th...the squire, Golag..g..g..gros?" Brother Notker asked. "What d...did Arthur d..do with him?"

"He stayed, as I said, in Camelot," Brother Gildas replied. "And after some time, showing himself to be a clever lad and penitent for his part in the great conspiracy, he was ultimately made squire to my good friend Sir Palomides. Palomides' old squire, you might remember, had earlier been killed in mortal combat with Sir Colgrevanuce, for his part in the plot against Sir Tristram. And he proved a fine and faithful squire. Palomides always seemed pleased with him."

"And Sir Bors? Did he fit in as well, back in the court?" It was the red-haired young monk, oldest of Brother Gildas's audience, who asked. "I would think, after an experience like the one he had, it would confound him to live a secular life again."

Gildas smiled, recognizing that the red-haired youth was thinking more of himself than of Sir Bors, and answered sympathetically: "I think there were times that the worldliness of Arthur's court offended him. But he was always a most courteous knight, and more popular with the other knights after the Grail than he had been before. They respected him as the one living Grail knight. And of course, he was always Sir Lancelot's biggest supporter. Nothing could break that friendship."

"And did Arthur ever reward him, as he promised to do?" the red-head wanted to know.

"Indeed!" Brother Gildas asserted. "With both King Pelles and the Princess Elaine dead in the last days of the quest, and with Corbenic in ruins, there was no one to inherit the kingdom that had become known as the Waste Land. And so, in recognition of his triumph in the matter of the Grail, Arthur gave it to Bors in fief. Bors, of course, was the son of King Bors de Ganis, and so had inherited vast lands in Gaul. But as lord of the Waste Land, Bors directed his overseers to treat the farmers well who came back to the lands, and taxed them lightly, and the land became prosperous again under his lordship. And it became known once again by its old name of Listeneise."

"And how did Arthur fill all the empty places at the Round Table? Was he able to? There would have been many, were there not?" Brother Nennius wanted to know. Again, he was keeping a list in his head, Gildas thought, with all these remembered details.

"There were many," Brother Gildas agreed. "King Bagdemagus, Sir Ironside, Sir Safer, Sir Colgrevaunce, Sir Uwain, Sir Grummer, Sir Gliglois, Sir Dinadan, Sir Lionel, Sir Perceval, Sir Galahad…" he recited the long list as if it were a litany. "The following Pentecost saw the largest induction of knights since the beginning of the Table. And it was, of course, my big chance. Yes, that was when I achieved my goal. I became a knight of the Round Table—too late of course, for it to matter in the lady Rosemounde's marriage negotiations."

A small cheer went up from four of the assembled monks, who then looked at one another with embarrassed grins and settled down. They had known that at some point Brother Gildas would get to the story of his own knighting, and were ecstatic that the time had finally arrived.

"But that is another story, I'm afraid," Brother Gildas finished, "And will have to wait for a different day. The shadows are lengthening in the cloister, and compline will be upon us soon."

There was an audible groan, but then the young blue-eyed monk with the tonsured blond curls asked, just as Gildas had known he would, about the lady. "And what about Lady Rosemounde? Was she safe from Sir Mordred's bullying?"

Brother Gildas allowed himself a small half-smile. Young brother Abelard was what Merlin had liked to call a Romantic: He was always very interested in the fate of the ladies. But then, so was Gildas himself, so he had a soft spot in his heart for the blond-curled youth. "As long as they remained at Camelot and did not return to Orkney, Rosemounde was safe—Mordred dared not touch her when the queen was Rosemounde's close confidante. And King Arthur would not allow Mordred to leave the court, because he simply did not trust him off scheming by himself. The elaborate plot that Pelles and Elaine had constructed to try to dethrone him did cut Arthur to the quick, and made him far more wary of those who might be deemed his enemies. By imperial 'invitation,' Mordred remained for the time at Camelot. And my lady Rosemounde was safe for a time." Until she wasn't, Brother Gildas thought to himself. But that, as he always told his young listeners, was another story, and must be saved for another day. Which was fine as far as he was concerned: The story of the Grail was long and arduous and, for him—revisiting the deaths of his friends Sir Colgrevaunce and Sir Dinadan, not to mention Sir Safer, brother of his friend Palomides—almost more than he could bear at one time.

Finally the young monk with the large, protruding ears, made more marked by his short tonsure, spoke up. "The lion?" He asked.

Of course, thought Brother Gildas. I should have known somebody would ask about the lion.

"Sir Ywain's lion?" Gildas began. "Yes, he was still alive. Sir Lancelot had seen him. And Sir Perceval, if his story was indeed based in reality. But let me tell you this: On a bright morning in June, not long after Pentecost of the year following the Grail quest, Robin of Kempe could be heard in a voice booming from the barbican across the bailey at Camelot, shouting, 'A great beast! There is a great beast approaching…and it appears to be a lion!' Sir Ywain, who was in Camelot at the time, having come, of course, for the Whitsunday induction of the new knights of the Table, climbed the battlements to look out, and saw, bounding toward him out of the woods and across the plain, angling along the river that passed by the castle's front gate, his own noble beast and friend. When the lion reached the moat, he sat back on his haunches and roared. It was a sound that frightened most of the women and many of the men in Camelot, but several of us recognized the fellow's voice. Robin cranked down the drawbridge and Sir Ywain rushed out, embracing the lion, who gamboled and played with him like a huge dog. Ywain rolled about with him for hours, and when the King forbade the lion's entrance into the castle, Ywain determined to sleep outside with the animal. His cousins, Gawain and Gareth, brought out a pavilion, and shared the tent with Ywain, the lion sleeping beside the pavilion's door. The next morning, Gawain brought Ywain's destrier and his arms out to him, and Ywain rode off happily, expecting to have a few adventures on the way to his Lady Alundine's castle, where he and his lion would stay.

"And *that*, my young friends, is how the last of all the Grail adventurers returned to Camelot. Ah, what marvels that lion might have told us of, if he had deigned to sully himself with human speech. But listen…"

The abbey's bells had begun to chime, calling the brothers to the office of compline. They all began to stand up, and Brother Gildas's hand moved automatically to bless them as they rose. As they began to move off, Brother Nennius sidled up to him on the right, and whispered into his ear, so that the others could not hear, "Pull the other one!"

Brother Gildas laughed aloud—the first time he had done so in many days, and answered Brother Nennius in good humor. "Oh, you doubt the bit about the lion, eh? Well, let's see what you say about my next story." And when Nennius raised a hand to ask, Gildas cut him off, saying, "Tomorrow, brother, tomorrow. You'll just have to wait."

And he continued to smile all the way to the chapel. He wasn't making the lion up. He could see Ywain playing with him even now, in his mind's eye. He could see them all: Colgrevaunce. Bess. Dinadan. Guinevere. Rosemounde. A lifetime ago. A story that was never complete.

CAST OF CHARACTERS

Accolon: Sir Accolon of Gaul was a young knight in the early days of the Round Table who became the lover of Morgan le Fay. Through a scheme of Morgan's, he nearly killed Arthur with his own sword.

Agravain of Orkney: Sir Agravain is a nephew of King Arthur, one of the brothers of Gawain and Gareth.

Ambrose: Father Ambrose is priest of King Arthur's chapel at Camelot.

Arthur: King of Logres, holding sovereignty as well over Ireland, Scandinavia, Scotland, Wales, and Cornwall, Brittany, Normandy, and all of Gaul. And he is claimant to the emperor's throne in Rome. He is the son of Uther Pendragon and Ygraine, former Countess of Cornwall.

Bagdemagus: King Bagdemagus is a petty king of the land of Gorre, one of Arthur's faithful vassals and a knight of the Round Table. The elderly king is retiring from his service at the Table, but decides to stay a bit longer to join the adventure of the Grail.

Balan: Brother to Sir Balin. The two ultimately kill each other unwittingly.

Balin: Sir Balin le Savage, known as the Knight with Two Swords, was an impetuous knight in Arthur's service early in his reign. He came into possession of a charmed sword by slaying the lady Lily of Avalon, and eventually used the sword to maim King Pelles. Ultimately, he used the same sword to unwittingly kill his own brother.

Bertilak: Lord of the castle in which Gawain takes refuge on his way to meet the Green Knight.

Benedict: Father Benedict is the priest at Corbenic castle.

Bertrand: Brother Bertrand is a hermit living in a cell in the woods two days' ride from Camelot. He is Sir Gawain's confessor, and was formerly chaplain in Lord Bertilak's chapel, as well as a monk in Brother Nascien's Beaulieu Abbey.

Bess of Caerleon: Born a commoner, daughter of a carpenter, she is happily married to Sir Colgrevaunce, and devoted to him for avenging her rape (see *The Knight's Riddle*, book two of the Merlin Mysteries series).

Bors: Sir Bors is Sir Lancelot's cousin and his closest companion. He is brother to the powerful knight Sir Lionel. He is steady, logical, and true. He is also pious, and is one of the three chief Grail knights.

Brandiles: Sir Brandiles is a relatively obscure knight but one closely devoted to Sir Lancelot. He was Colgrevaunce's master and sponsors him for knighthood.

Brumand: An early knight of the Round Table, whose renown went into decline when Sir Lancelot joined Arthur's knights. To prove he was the greater knight, Sir Brumand sat in the Siege Perilous. This did not go well for him.

Colgrevaunce: Close friend of Gildas and originally squire to Sir Brandiles, he becomes a knight of the Round Table but does not survive the quest of the Grail.

Dandrane: Beautiful and chaste sister of Sir Perceval, and hence daughter of King Pelinore. She is Galahad's chaste love and inspiration.

Dinadan: Sir Dinadan was the late Sir Tristram's closest companion. He is a skilled knight but better known for his sharp tongue than his prowess. He is most reluctant to join the Grail quest.

Ector de Maris: Sir Ector is the brother of Sir Lancelot and the second son of King Ban of Benwick. He goes in search of the Grail but ultimately, like most of his fellows, gives up the quest. Like Sir Bors, he is fiercely loyal to Sir Lancelot and his interests.

Elaine of Corbenic: Daughter of King Pelles, the Maimed King of Corbenic, the Grail Castle. Lancelot, tricked into believing Elaine was in fact Guinevere, sired Galahad upon her during a one-night stand.

Florent of Orkney: Eldest son of Sir Gawain, saved from execution by the testimony of the nymph Nimue, who married him and took him to live in the palace of the Lady of the Lake.

Gaheris of Orkney: Sir Gaheris is son of King Lot of Orkney and Queen Margause—whom he is known to have beheaded when he found her in bed with Sir Lamorak. Gaheris resembles his younger brother Sir Gareth in coloring, but not in temperament.

Galahad: Son of Sir Lancelot and the lady Elaine of Corbenic Castle, daughter of the maimed King Pelles. He is the chief Grail knight, and was raised in a monastery at the insistence of his mother and grandfather, where he was trained and molded for the role he was born to assume as the purest of knights.

Gareth of Orkney: Knight of the Round Table and younger brother to Sir Gawain, Sir Gaheris, and Sir Agravain, and half-brother to Mordred. He is son of King Lot of Orkney and Margause, the daughter of Ygraine and Duke Gorlois of Cornwall and so Arthur's half-sister, which makes him King Arthur's nephew. Gildas is squire to Sir Gareth.

Garlon: Sir Garlon the Red was brother to King Pelles and governed in his name. His death at the hands of Sir Balin provokes the battle that results in Pelles' maiming.

Gawain of Orkney: Sir Gawain is Arthur's nephew and heir apparent. He is son of King Lot of Orkney and Arthur's half-sister Margause, and the older brother of Sir Gareth, Sir Gaheris, Sir Agravain, and Mordred, and father of Sir Florent and Lovell, his new squire.

Gildas of Cornwall: Son of a Cornish armor-maker, squire to Sir Gareth, former page to Queen Guinevere. Gildas narrates the story and is Merlin's assistant in his investigations. He is eighteen years old at the time of the Grail quest, and remains in love with Lady Rosemounde, lady-in-waiting to the queen.

Gliglois: Sir Gliglois is a knight of the Round Table killed by the White Knight on the Grail quest.

Golagros: Squire to King Pelles at Corbenic Castle.

Grummor Grummorson: Sir Grummor Grummorson is a knight of the Round Table drowned during the Grail quest.

Grunamund: Squire to Sir Brumand and later monk at Beaulieu Abbey under Brother Nascien, Grunamund is an avowed enemy of Sir Lancelot for Sir Brumand's sake.

Guinevere: Queen of Logres, and married to King Arthur. Gildas was formerly a page in her household. She is the daughter of Leodegrance, king of Cameliard, an early ally of Arthur's. Her long-standing affair with Sir Lancelot, Arthur's chief knight, is a perilous secret in the court. She is fiercely protective of her lady-in-waiting, Rosemounde of Brittany.

Hectimere: Sir Gaheris's squire.

Hoel: Duke of Brittany, and Arthur's vassal and close ally from the beginning of his reign. He is the father of Lady Rosemounde.

Ironside: Sir Ironside, known as the Red Knight of the Red Lands, was a longtime knight of the Round Table, but a boorish one without courtesy. He becomes the victim of Sir Gawain's anger on the Grail quest.

Isolde: La Belle Isolde was the daughter of the king and queen of Ireland, and was queen of Cornwall, married to King Mark. A famous healer and herbalist, she once saved the life of Sir Tristram with her potions. She was also Tristram's secret lover, and died upon seeing his dead body.

Kay: Sir Kay is King Arthur's seneschal, which means he is in charge of the king's household. He was Arthur's foster-brother when they were boys, and Arthur promised Kay's father Sir Ector that there would always be a place for Kay in his court. He tends to be something of a braggart and a bully.

Lady Lily of Avalon: Imperious noblewoman responsible for the death of Balin's father and the confiscation of his lands. She brings to Arthur's court the fateful sword that will deal to Sir Pelles the dolorous stroke that maims him.

Lady of the Lake: Queen of Faerie, a being of great mystical power. She is responsible for giving the sword Excalibur to King Arthur. She lives in an enchanted palace north of Camelot on a lake named for her.

Lamorak de Galis: Sir Lamorak was the son of King Pelinore, who killed King Lot and thus began a feud with the house of Orkney. Sir Gaheris caught Sir Lamorak in bed with his mother Margause and let him escape, but Gawain, Gaheris, Mordred and Agravain killed Sir Lamorak later in ambush.

Lancelot: Sir Lancelot is the greatest knight of Arthur's table, and is the secret lover of Queen Guinevere. He is the father of Sir Galahad, and also the son of King Ban of Benwick, and his close kinsmen—Sir Bors, Sir Ector, and Sir Lionel—form a powerful bloc of Round Table knights. He also was the one who knighted Sir Perceval, and he is therefore closely allied with all three Grail knights. His romantic relationship with the queen hampers his own serious quest of the Grail.

Lawrence: Brother Lawrence is abbot of the small Cistercian monastery of Saint Sebastian, which houses the shield of the Grail knight.

Lionel: Sir Lionel de Ganis is brother to Sir Bors, and thus cousin to Sir Lancelot and Sir Ector. A large and powerful knight, he suffers serious difficulties during the Grail quest.

Lot: King Lot of Orkney was an enemy of Arthur's who would not accept the fifteen-year-old boy as king of Logres. With an alliance of other kings, he made war on Arthur to get him off the throne, but was ultimately defeated and killed. He was married to Arthur's half-sister Margause, and was the father of Gawain, Gaheris, Agravain, and Gareth.

Lovell of Orkney: Sir Gawain's second son, and his squire.

Luke: Brother Luke is an aged Cistercian monk, infirmarian at the abbey of Saint Sebastian.

Margause: Mother of Gawain and his brothers, Margause was the wife of King Lot of Orkney and was one of Arthur's half-sisters, daughter of his mother Ygraine and Duke Gorlois of Cornwall. Not known for her high moral standards, Margause was killed by her own son Sir Gaheris when he caught her in bed with Sir Lamorak.

Meliagaunt: The son and heir of King Bagdemagus, Meliagaunt has been his father's squire for a long time. He deals with his father's rashness and absent-mindedness with a kind of stoicism, but there is definitely some frustration below the surface.

Merlin: Arthur's chief adviser in his early days, Merlin helped Arthur solidify his realm, win the war against King Lot and his allies and the war with Ireland. Rumored to have magical powers and to be able to see the future, Merlin is essentially just a more logical and scientific thinker than most of his contemporaries. He is often called upon to solve the mysteries of Camelot.

Mordred: Sir Mordred is the youngest brother of Sir Gawain and Sir Gareth, the youngest child of Arthur's half-sister Margause. He is married to Gildas's beloved Rosemounde. He is also, secretly, the king's own bastard son.

Morgan le Fay: Queen of Gorre, wife of King Uriens and mother of Sir Ywain, Morgan is King Arthur's half-sister, the daughter of his mother Ygraine and Gorlois, Duke of Cornwall.

Nascien: Brother Nascien is prior of the Cistercian monastery at Beaulieu and was one of the brothers responsible for the raising of Sir Galahad. He is a former knight himself (under Arthur's father Uther Pendragon) and has some reason to resent King Arthur and certain members of his court, for the sake of his cousin, Sir Brumand.

Nimue: Lady-in-waiting to the Lady of the Lake, Nimue lives in the Lady's mystical palace and never ages. Her beauty enchanted

Merlin, who remains in love with her though she has definitively rejected him.

Palomides: Sir Palomides is a Moorish knight who has joined the Round Table and, like his brother Sir Safer, become a Christian. He was Sir Tristram's great rival for the love of Isolde, and is known as a composer of love poems. He is a close friend of Sir Gareth and, by extension, Gildas.

Pelinore: King Pelinore was an early ally of King Arthur and killed King Lot in battle, thus kicking off the feud between his house and Lot's. His children include Sir Lamorak, Sir Perceval, and the lady Dandrane.

Perceval de Galis: Sir Perceval is the young and innocent brother of Sir Lamorak, and so the son of King Pelinore, who killed King Lot and thus began a feud with the house of Orkney. Perceval has renounced any such feuds, and, championed by Sir Lancelot, is devoted to chivalry. He is one of the three chief Grail knights.

Peter: Peter is Queen Guinevere's young page.

Robin Kempe: Captain of the King's Guard and of the Royal Archers, Robin spends a good deal of time on guard in the barbican of Camelot, when he isn't training his archers. One of Robin's favorite pastimes is goading Gildas of Cornwall, for whom he has a good deal of affection.

Roger: Roger is the chief cook of Camelot.

Rosemounde of Brittany: Lady Rosemounde, former lady-in-waiting to Queen Guinevere who is the object of Gildas's deepest affections. She was married to Sir Mordred in Gildas's absence so that her father could make a valuable political alliance with King Arthur.

Safer: Sir Safer is a Moorish knight, though now a Christian convert. He is brother to Sir Palomides and his closest companion and confidante.

Thomas: Young sandy-haired squire to Sir Ywain, Thomas is one of Gildas of Cornwall's closer friends.

Tristram: Sir Tristram was nephew to King Mark of Cornwall, and in love with his uncle's queen, La Belle Isolde. He was married to Isolde of the White Hands, half-sister to Rosemounde of Brittany. Merlin and Gildas investigated his death (in *The Bleak and Empty Sea*, the previous book in the Merlin Mysteries series) to clear the name of Rosemounde's sister.

Uwain: Sir Uwain les Avoutres was the natural son of Ywain's father, King Uriens of Gorre. Uwain has ill luck on the Grail quest.

Vivien: Lady Vivien is one of Queen Guinevere's ladies-in-waiting. She is French by birth, has green eyes, and enjoys romances, poetry, and gossip.

William of Glastonbury: Bishop of the great cathedral of Saint David in Caerleon.

Ywain: Sir Ywain, known as the "Knight of the Lion" because he often goes on adventures with his pet lion, is another nephew of King Arthur, the son of King Uriens and Morgan le Fay, Arthur's half-sister through his mother Ygraine. Sir Ywain is devoted to his cousins Sir Gawain and Sir Gareth. His grief at the loss of his lion during the quest, however, suggests that that relationship is his most significant.

ABOUT THE AUTHOR

Jay Ruud is a retired professor of medieval literature at the University of Central Arkansas. In addition to *Fatal Feast*, *The Knight's Riddle*, and *The Bleak and Empty Sea*—the first three books in his Merlin mystery series—he is the author of *"Many a Song and Many a Leccherous Lay": Tradition and Individuality in Chaucer's Lyric Poetry* (1992), the *Encyclopedia of Medieval Literature* (2006), *A Critical Companion to Dante* (2008), and *A Critical Companion to Tolkien* (2011). He taught at UCA for fourteen years, prior to which he was dean of the College of Arts and Sciences at Northern State University in South Dakota. He has a Ph.D. in Medieval Literature from the University of Wisconsin-Milwaukee.